Praise for the Seaside Knitters Mysteries

"Comforting. . . . Goldenbaum has created an idyllic world in which good friends, good works, and discussing the passing of time and changes in the community are as important as solving crimes." —*Publishers Weekly*

"*Murder Wears Mittens* is not another crime mystery like any other mystery. Sally Goldenbaum's characters feel for one another. It is a brilliantly written crime mystery, full of suspense and human warmth. Sally Goldenbaum knows how to monopolize your attention with her characters and writing style." —*The Washington Book Review*

"Good friends, good food, and a murder combine in a delightful holiday cozy." —*Kirkus Reviews*

"An intriguing murder . . . Izzy and her fellow Seaside Knitters feel an obligation to find the truth. . . . Happily, a sock pattern is appended." —*Booklist*

"The Seaside Knitters are a wonderful group of friends who care about each other, and readers will care about them, too." —Nancy Pickard, *New York Times* bestselling author

"A quirky and colorful yarn." —*Women's World Magazine* (Book Club Pick of the Week)

"Another spectacular book from Sally Goldenbaum. . . . A mystery filled with cozy characters in a charming small town that will have you a little sad when it ends and anxious for your next visit." —*Escape with Dollycas*

"One of the best in the series and I can't wait to see where we go next in this d
—*L

Books by Sally Goldenbaum

The Seaside Knitters mysteries

Murder Wears Mittens
How to Knit a Murder
A Murderous Tangle
A Crime of a Different Stripe
A Dark and Snowy Night
A Twisted Skein
The Herringbone Harbor Mystery

The Queen Bees Quilt Shop mysteries

A Patchwork of Clues
A Thread of Darkness
A Bias for Murder

A Twisted Skein

Sally Goldenbaum

Kensington Publishing Corp.
www.kensingtonbooks.com

KENSINGTON BOOKS are published by

Kensington Publishing Corp.
900 Third Avenue
New York, NY 10022

ISBN: 978-1-4967-2045-3 (ebook)

ISBN: 978-1-4967-2944-6

First Kensington Hardcover Printing: December 2023
First Kensington Trade Paperback Printing: November 2024

10 9 8 7 6 5 4 3 2 1

Printed in the United States of America

For my family

Cast for *A Twisted Skein*

The Seaside Knitters

Birdie Favazza (Bernadette): Sea Harbor's wealthy and wise octogenarian, widow of Sonny Favazza

Cass Halloran Brandley (Catherine Mary Theresa): Co-owner of the Halloran Lobster Company; married to Danny Brandley; baby son, Joey

Izzy Perry (Isabel Chambers Perry): Owner of the Sea Harbor Yarn Studio; married to Sam, an award-winning photographer; young daughter, Abigail (Abby)

Nell Endicott: Retired nonprofit director; Izzy Perry's aunt; married to Ben Endicott, a retired lawyer and family business owner

Friends and Townsfolk

Amelia Barlow Elliott: Wife of Peter Elliott, mother of Josh Elliott

Archie and Harriet Brandley: Owners of Sea Harbor bookstore, Danny's parents

Betty Warner: Checker at grocery store

Cliff Anderson: Dentist, father of Rose and Jillian

Ella and Harold Sampson: Birdie Favazza's housekeeper and groundskeeper

Elizabeth Anderson: Married to Cliff, mother of Jillian and Rose

Father Lawrence Northcutt: Pastor at Our Lady of Safe Seas Church

Harper Mancini: Married to Leon, a real estate company executive

Harry and Margaret Garozzo: Owners of Garozzo's deli

Hazel Wallis: Auto mechanics teacher at Sea Harbor High
Henry Staab: Cemetery caretaker
Jake Risso: Owner of the Gull Tavern
Jillian Anderson: Rose's twin sister
Josh Barlow Elliott: High school teacher in Sea Harbor
Judith Garvey: Sea Harbor High School principal
Leon Mancini: Company executive, married to Harper
Liz Santos: Manager of the Sea Harbor Yacht Club
Lucky Bianchi (Luigi): Birdie's godson, owner of Lucky's Place
Mae Anderson: Shop manager at the Sea Harbor Yarn Studio
Mary Halloran: Cass and Pete's mother, church secretary
Mary Pisano: Newspaper columnist, owner of Ravenswood-by-the-Sea B and B
Merry Jackson: Owner of the Artist's Palate Bar & Grill
Natalie Simpson: Teacher at Sea Harbor High School
Pete Halloran: Cass's brother, co-owner of the Halloran Lobster Company
Peter Elliott: CEO of real estate company, Josh's father
Polly Farrell: Tea shop owner, leader of bird-watching group
Richard Brooks: Mechanic at Pickard's Auto Repair Shop, bird-watcher
Rose Anderson: Jillian's twin sister
Shannon Platt: Waitress, school receptionist
Tommy Porter: Police detective
Willow Adams: Fiber artist and owner of the Fishtail Gallery

Chapter 1

Rose Anderson sat at a picnic table on Merry Jackson's restaurant deck, the smell of fall in the air. A light shower of leaves fell from the old oak tree that grew up through a round hole that covered the wooden slats of the floor.

The Artist's Palate Bar & Grill, a popular hangout in the center of the Canary Cove Art Colony, was the perfect place to have it out with her sister. Not a formal setting, noisy enough to keep conversations private, and with the additional privacy of the table hidden partially behind the tree.

Another bonus was that both she and her sister, Jillian, had always loved the bar and grill. Between waitressing at the Artist's Palate and working at Izzy Perry's yarn shop, the twins had snared the choicest part-time jobs during their long-ago teen years.

But as the sky darkened and the young waiter stopped asking her if she'd like another glass of water, Rose knew in her bones what she'd probably known all along: Jillian wasn't going to show.

Finally, sensing the waiter was now wondering what her intentions were and was starting to come on to her, she decided to call it a failed effort and head back to the small cottage behind Willow Adams's Fishtail Gallery, where she was staying.

She pulled out a couple bills to reward the waiter's attentiveness, then slipped her purse over her shoulder and started to stand. Before she was upright, a hand pressed lightly on her shoulder, and Rose sat back down. For a second, she thought she had misjudged her sister. Jillian had shown up, after all.

But it wasn't Jillian. Instead, Rose looked up into the smiling face of Merry Jackson, the owner of the bar and grill. Merry leaned over and hugged Rose warmly.

"I've seen you a zillion times around town since you've been back," she said, "but it seems one or both of us were always in a rush. Finally, I get to give you a belated welcome hug."

Rose smiled broadly, delighted to see the woman who had been a role model for her when she was in high school. In addition to managing her bar, Merry, with her incredible Stevie Nicks voice, had turned the high school singing group into a top-notch choir.

"Are you waiting for someone?" Merry asked. "You look pensive."

"No, nothing. Jillian was going to meet me here. I guess something came up. Anyway, it's great to see you, Merry. Can you sit for a minute?"

"Absolutely." Merry scanned the deck with an eye practiced in picking up staff needs, customers' displeasures, and spilled beer. Then she gave a quick nod to the vigilant waiter standing by, who almost instantly reappeared with a bottle of wine and glasses.

"You looked more like a wine person tonight than beer," Merry said, looping a leg over the bench opposite Rose. She poured them each a glass. "This is perfect timing. The lull before the storm that comes when galleries and studios lock up and night life begins. I was so happy to see you sitting over here."

Merry put her elbows on the table, her face open and welcoming. Her clear brown eyes met Rose's. "You and Jillian were always two of my favorite teenyboppers." She laughed at herself. "Does anyone still use that term? Anyway, it's so good to see you, Rosie. Now fill me in on the last half dozen or so years of your life in ten minutes, before someone breaks something behind the bar."

Rose laughed. "Gads. Has it been that long?"

"Well, whenever it was, we were sad when you moved out of our slice of paradise. But here's to your return, for however long it might be." Merry held up her glass.

Rose looked at her wineglass. She rarely drank. A lime seltzer was much more to her liking. But rather than ruin the moment, she picked it up and tapped it to Merry's, then took a sip. The warm feeling as it slid down her throat surprised and pleased her at once. Maybe it was her mood, but for whatever reason, being with Merry Jackson was warming her evening. She took a few more sips, listening as Merry filled her in on art colony talk.

"Willow Adams is thrilled you'll be helping in her gallery and learning the ropes. Be careful, though. Willow knows talent when she sees it, and she may never let you go."

Rose blushed, pleased with the compliments. "She's great." The tension in her shoulders began to ease.

She found herself answering Merry's questions about her life at NYU and living in New York. The sadness over both her parents dying during her and her twin's college years. She was talking more than usual, answering Merry's questions, embellishing here and there. Her cheeks felt warm, and the conversation flowed like the wine as her body slipped into a warm and comfortable place. It felt good to share, even the difficult events of the past few years.

But coming back to Sea Harbor for a while, she told Merry, had been one of the better decisions she'd made.

"Of course it was. This will always be your home," Merry said.

Rose nodded. "And a far better place to sort out the next step in our lives."

The wine had definitely loosened her tongue, enough that this might be the perfect time to talk with Merry about Jillian. And the burden Elizabeth Anderson had laid on her daughter with deathbed wishes and secrets.

But before any words got out, a server beckoned to the restaurant's owner that she was needed. The deck crowd was multiplying, a bartender hadn't shown up, and the DJ was having trouble with the mic. Merry sighed as she jumped up, apologizing. She left Rose with a quick hug and a promise to have a long talk with her soon.

Rose watched her walk away, feeling unusually comfortable and good about herself. The wine had calmed that anxious part of her. She stared at the wine bottle, then filled her glass with the remainder and sipped it slowly, smiling and moving her shoulders to a Billie Eilish tune floating across the deck.

A crowd of artists and townspeople hugged greetings to one another as they mingled in the evening air, as if their presence outdoors on the deck would last forever, forestalling the colder days ahead. She lifted her head to catch the breeze and cool the flush on her cheeks. Reacquainting with Merry Jackson had somehow buoyed her resolve. She felt good. Strong. The Rose that knew her own mind.

Minutes later, she slipped some bills under the napkin holder, caught her balance as she stood too quickly, then made her way across the deck and down the steps, holding on to the railing tightly. She hesitated at the bottom, smiled at some strangers, and then began walking down Canary Cove Road, heading toward downtown Sea Harbor.

You surprise me, Rose Anderson, she whispered to herself. *Let's go find our Jilly. Have a sister-to-sister talk. You and me.*

A few blocks away, before the road curved south toward Harbor Road's town center, a familiar street wound off to the right. Rose stopped beneath a lamppost, leaned against it, and looked down the narrow street. A dead-end street that stopped not far from the water's edge. What had started out as modest cottages years before had been renovated into family homes lining both sides of the road. Halfway down the block, a street-light illuminated a blue and white WELCOME sign above NUMBER FIVE COTTAGE ROAD. Rose squinted to be sure it was *her* sign, the one she'd painted when she was nine. It marked the house she and Jillian had grown up in.

A foggy wave of melancholy carried her thoughts. In spite of everything, she had had a happy childhood, good times. A mother, a father, a sister. And lots of love circling the girls always.

She leaned for a moment against the streetlight; her thoughts were murky and muddled, but the unfamiliar feeling running through her wasn't unpleasant. Whether it was from the memories or from the wine, she wasn't sure, and she didn't really care. A couple walked by, smiling at her, and then they turned and ambled down the old, narrow street toward the sea. Rose watched as they passed the Anderson home, and then she turned away. *Enough with the memories*, she thought, heading toward Harbor Road, only vaguely aware now of her plan.

In a few blocks the sidewalks widened, and Sea Harbor's shopping and dining center lay just ahead. The road itself had been a surprise to Jillian and Rose when they returned to town this year. It had been turned into a one-way street during the Covid pandemic and then kept that way. A few more trees had been planted to shade the benches that the town had put in, some with memorial plaques. Vintage streetlights cast shadows across the familiar sidewalks, the shops and eateries and salons. Enormous cement planters held mums, flowering kale, and ornamental cabbage, happily announcing a new season.

Rose paused briefly in front of the window of Izzy's yarn shop. She glimpsed light coming from the back of the store and could picture exactly what was going on in the knitting room: Four of her favorite people on earth were sitting near the fireplace, the fire lit, no matter the weather. Eating, drinking wine, and knitting amazing creations. A Thursday night ritual that had turned into a feast of friendship for the four women. Izzy, Nell, Birdie, and Cass. Women who had each made a positive difference in Rose's life.

She walked on, past the Brandleys' bookstore and a wine and cheese shop that had been a toy store during her growing-up years. The years away had changed some things, but Sea Harbor would always be home. It was where she was born, where she'd had her first crush. Her first heartbreak, her first nearly everything. The place her whole family loved.

But coming back this time, the family had shrunk. It was just her and Jillian.

She tried to pull her thoughts together, to focus. *Why were there tears in her eyes?*

Standing beneath a store awning, she fumbled while trying to pull her phone out of her back pocket, her thoughts ricocheting back and forth.

Jillian. That was who she was looking for. *Her twin sister, Jillian.* She clumsily typed a message into her cell phone.

Hey, you. Where are you! I'm here.

But for a brief minute, she wasn't quite sure where "here" was.

And where was her younger sister? Although she was only fourteen minutes older than Jillian according to their birth certificates, she had been a pound bigger and had been born healthy, while Jillian had been sickly at birth and had spent weeks in the hospital. From then on, Rose's role in life had been one of Jillian's protector more than her fraternal twin. No matter that Jillian's weak start in life had ended early on and she'd grown healthy and strong, taller than Rose and a champion swimmer. But their mother had never let go of her worry about Jillian's health in body and soul. *You're the strong one, Rosie. Our rock*, she'd say. *Watch out for our Jilly.*

High school graduation had taken the Anderson twins away from Sea Harbor to NYU; freedom was how both Rose and Jillian had viewed that time, as they'd stretched their wings and thrown themselves into challenging university programs. No motherly reminders of what to do, what not to do. They'd returned only for holidays—and for the two darkest days of Rose's life.

"A sailing accident," her mother had told them over the phone as the twins' New York aunts rallied to get the weeping girls home to bury their father.

Rose only vaguely remembered the funeral.

What she remembered more was her mother calling a Realtor to sell the little house on Cottage Road and then leaving Sea Harbor herself. And seeming to do so with great relief.

She tried to shake off the memory, discomfort filling her woozy head. She looked down the street toward Jake's Gull Tavern, then took a deep breath and walked in that direction, trying to step out of her memories and clear her cluttered mind. She frowned, collecting scattered thoughts. *Jillian. Focus on Jillian.*

Jake's bar was crowded, with groups of people standing outside, waiting for space inside. Loud music poured onto the street each time the door opened.

Rose walked across the street and looked through the windows. On the other side, a tall countertop with stools ran the length of the window. She felt suddenly ashamed and wobbly, not sure at all why she was standing alone outside a bar, staring at a group of strangers on the other side of the window, with them staring back at her. She felt exposed, as if she were naked. She started to turn away, almost tripping on her own foot. But just then several of the group vacated their window stools, offering Rose a view farther into the bar. She placed a hand on the window, steadying herself, and spotted her sister sitting on a stool at the crowded bar. She was smiling at a woman next to her. Or maybe at old Jake, who was telling a joke as he pushed the handle of the bar coupler.

She tried to see who Jillian was with, squinting to see faces. A man a few barstools down stood and seemed to elbow his way over to where Jillian sat. A baseball hat was pulled low on his head. The figure blurred as the man placed a hand on Jillian's shoulder, then whispered something in her ear.

Rose watched her sister look up, a full smile on her face, and slide off the stool.

Yes, Rose thought, her heart beating fast, as she stared at the figure, who turned sinister in her woozy mind.

That man, she thought, trying without success to pull his features into view.

One more wine, she thought, and perhaps she'd make her mother's request come true.

Chapter 2

"I believe they call me a 'dude,'" Birdie said, wiping a dollop of cream from the corner of her mouth. "Have I told you that?"

"A what?" Cass hooted, splashing a drop of white wine into her own bowl of soup.

"Not that kind, Cass." Birdie flapped away the image with her veined hand as she laughed along with her friends. "We birders have our own language, and while a few are called twitchers, I am considered a dude. I would prefer amateur or ornithophile, or simply a bird lover, but such words are not a part of my esteemed group's birder parlance. *Dude*, apparently, means I am not quite as serious about bird-watching. I don't write down every beautiful bird I see or even photograph it. Nor do I travel far and wide to spot a certain bird. But some of our small group are quite competitive and are known to have done that."

The octogenarian set aside the empty bowl of Nell's sweet corn ravioli. She sat back in the well-worn leather chair that was always reserved for her on knitting night in Izzy's shop.

The shop's calico cat, Purl, was curled up beside her, sleeping soundly.

"Competitive?" Nell asked. "You hadn't mentioned that when you first joined."

"Well, you learn things as you go."

"But that's crazy, right?" Cass said. "My Halloran Lobster Co. crew sees billions of birds. My brother Pete's boat has a pet gull that perches on the bow every day."

Birdie laughed. "But the Halloran crew are looking for lobsters, not watching birds. There's the difference."

"The bird-watchers take notes on what they see?" Nell asked.

"Some do. And sometimes I wonder if the twitchers miss some of the astonishing beauty around them by pulling out cameras and notepads. But, no matter, each to her own."

"So you like them?" Nell asked.

"They are all lovely folks, and they allow me great freedom, not thinking twice if I decide to wander off in the woods to look for a sweet singing bird on my own. I am loving it. The intoxicating scent of the pines, the colors and pounding of the sea, and sometimes seeing the miracle of a magnificent skein of geese flying in formation above me. Don't you just wonder how they know where to go? Or where they should stop for lunch? It's a miracle that makes me pause and puts me in my place. We humans aren't quite as smart as we think we are sometimes."

The group was quiet for a few minutes, taken with Birdie's words and enjoying her obvious love for her recent hobby.

And trying to figure out how the birds actually did know where to stop for lunch.

Izzy refilled wineglasses. "So tell us about these bird-watching folks that you're spending so much time with."

"Well, you all know Polly Farrell, our trusty leader. I was having tea in her Canary Cove tea shop last summer, and she showed me some photos of where the group had gone. Polly is such a robust, wonderful soul, and she keeps the more serious in the group from killing one another. It's an eclectic group. Some members come and go, depending on the day, the weather, the place. Even the kinds of birds we might see. All sorts of things. Richard Brooks always comes—he works at Picard's Auto Repair Shop. And there are one or two whose names I can never remember, but when they hug me like an old friend, I hug them right back and tell them it's great to see them, too. Although often I have no recollection of when we last met. Or even if."

"Face it, Birdie," Cass said. "You've met everyone in Sea Harbor."

Birdie smiled.

"One of my customers recently joined your group," Izzy said. "Harper Mancini. Do you know her? Young, pretty—"

Birdie laughed again. "Harper Mancini? Yes, I certainly do. She is a charming young woman, although I don't think Harper would call herself a birder. Nor would anyone else call her that. She comes with her much older husband, Leon. I think she's still living in that honeymoon stage and wants to be with him wherever he is, doing whatever he does."

"She talks about the group when she's in the here. She loves all of you. She said the group is funded somehow," Izzy said. "Is that true?"

"Apparently, although that isn't anything I'm interested in. But Polly says there's a grant she applied for that covers bird-watching trips to other places. They use it for individuals . . . sort of a merit thing. You have to earn it somehow. One woman used the money to travel to some remote place to record a rare bird. She seems very wary of the other, more serious birders, especially Josh Elliott. She may be afraid she won't win the next trip." Birdie shook her head at what she thought was the silliness of it.

"Josh is a super guy," Cass said. "He's a friend of Lucky's.

Quiet, which makes him the perfect friend for Lucky, who never stops talking."

"Yes, he's quiet. Josh has an incredible knowledge of our feathered friends. Some of the more serious bird-watchers consider him competition, though I don't think he has a bone of competition in his body. Oh, and there's another fellow, an old friend of mine, who showed up one day, and I nearly fell over in surprise. Henry Staab, who's even older than I, which he wears as a badge of honor."

"Henry Staab?" Izzy asked.

"You know Henry, Izzy. We all do. He lives in that little stone house out at the cemetery that he's managed for a thousand years. He's a dutiful caretaker for his 'family,' as he calls those buried there."

"Oh, of course," Izzy said.

"I love that guy," Cass said. "My lobster guys call him the Hermit."

"That he is," Nell said, smiling as if at something the others couldn't see. She passed around a basket of sourdough rolls and looked at Birdie, the smile still in place. "Don't I remember a rumor that Henry once proposed to you, Birdie?"

Birdie's laugh was so contagious that Izzy and Cass joined in, not sure of what was so funny.

"Yes, indeedy, he did," Birdie said, finally catching her breath. "He proposed right after I got engaged to my Sonny. He didn't want me to make a mistake marrying the love of my life. Crazy old man. He's always been old, I think. And always a little crazy."

"Is he one of the serious birders?" Nell asked.

"Absolutely not. I think he likes the company. Henry marches to his own drummer—he comes and goes. I'm thinking of buying him a good, strong walking stick, though. He's been known to fall once or twice."

"Maybe he's falling for you," Cass said. "Do you suppose he thinks he might have a second chance . . . ?"

Birdie nearly choked on a bite of a warm roll. She took a quick drink of water. "What a thought," she managed to say, subduing her laugh. "Actually, I think he fell for pretty Harper. One day he was lumbering along to catch up with her on a birder hike through Ravenswood Park when he tripped and sprained his ankle. Harper is one strong woman and picked him right up, helping him out of the woods. It wreaked a little havoc with his ankle. But, anyway, he's a 'dude' like me. But he seems to have his ears tuned to all sorts of things and keeps tabs on the tenor of the group. Henry can be quite an interesting gossip. He says I wouldn't believe the things he knows from his cemetery residents."

"Well, it's great you're doing this, Birdie. You're a trouper," Izzy said.

"No, dear. That would be 'dude.'"

"Dude Birdie," Nell said. "It has a certain panache to it." She leaned forward and refilled the wineglasses with Birdie's pinot gris.

The wine was part of the Seaside Knitters' Thursday night ritual: wine from Birdie, a fire laid by Izzy, no matter the time of year, a dessert bought or made by Cass's nanny, and an amazing soup or salad or casserole brought by Nell. It was a sacrosanct night, a time for friend therapy or simply a time to be together to toast, to eat, and to knit with "friends like no other," as Cass often described the group.

Izzy took a sip of her wine and then, as if having a sudden thought, got up and disappeared up the steps to the store's main room. A minute later she returned, carrying a beautiful hand-knit dove. "I think she should be yours, Birdie."

"She's lovely, Izzy," Birdie said. "The symbol of peace."

Nell reached over, took the bird, and touched the soft, fine stitches. "This is beautiful. Where did you get it?"

"The editor of *Knitting in Style* magazine gave it to me. She must have known this event she talked me into hosting would disrupt my life and my well-being in one fell swoop. Which, by the way, it is succeeding in doing in spades. I must have been crazy to agree to it." She began clearing the plates from the table, far more noisily than required.

Birdie reached over and touched the soft knit feathers, then looked over at Izzy. "And you could never be crazy, my dear, fashion show or not."

Izzy harrumphed and continued cleaning, pausing once to look around the table. "You're supposed to be my friends. Why didn't one, just *one*, of you stop me?" She swept one arm out, taking in the knitting room. "Just look at this holy mess."

The room had been left in shambles from another day of customers designing and knitting, tinking and frogging and speculating on whose creation would be featured in the *Knitting in Style*–sponsored fashion show.

"Every day is like this," Izzy added.

Cass leaned forward and refilled Izzy's wineglass to the very top. "As a matter of fact, I *did* try to stop you, Iz," she said.

"You didn't try hard enough," Izzy snapped.

Birdie pulled another piece of stray yarn off Izzy's sweatshirt. "This will be a good thing. Mark my words. The fashion event has added a positive spirit to our autumn days. Even people who don't care about knitting are looking forward to it. And don't forget, my dear godson Lucky is going to build you a beautiful runway."

At the mention of her friend, Cass looked up. "That's great. If nothing else, Lucky Bianchi's charm will inspire the entire town to support the event. That guy could make a blobfish smile."

"I agree with Birdie. It's a good idea, Iz," Nell added. "These past few years have been difficult for the whole world. Celebrations and events like this are food for the spirit and help bring our little corner of the universe back together again."

"And," Birdie added, as if they had planned the little talk to buoy up Izzy's sudden bad spirits, "it's a tribute to you that the editors picked your shop, Izzy. There are plenty of fiber and knitting places up and down the North Shore, but *Knitting in Style* picked yours. It will all be quite wonderful."

"Maybe so," Izzy murmured half-heartedly. "The magazine sponsors are being hands off, for the most part, which is a good thing. And you're right, Birdie. Lucky is a great asset. He's already coerced a few others into building what we need—something suitable, down to earth, but innovative. The publishers made it clear that their goal is a seaside fashion show . . . with homegrown knit fashions. Not like those held in Paris and New York, but special in their own homegrown way. They want knitters themselves to walk the runway so the photographers and editors can get their photos and videos and story." She stopped for a moment, frowned again, then added with a touch of defiance, "And then go away."

Cass laughed. "That's the spirit, Iz."

"It will work out," Nell said. "A messy yarn room for a few weeks is manageable."

"And just imagine the masterpieces that will come out of it all. That's often the way of art." Birdie pointed her knitting needle at the beginnings of a garment hanging on a hanger on the far side of the room. "Like that one." She took off her reading glasses and squinted. "Even unfinished, it's quite amazing."

Izzy looked over at the shimmering beginnings of what might be a long, elegant dress or a sweater or shawl, though it was still difficult to tell. Even though it was still in pieces, it promised to be unique. Tiny knots had been formed into the edges of the cuff on the one arm that was finished. And there were several unique stitches that Izzy herself couldn't identify.

"I think one of Mae's nieces is working on that. It will be one of a kind, just like the twins. Jillian and Rose are a multi-talented duo."

The beginnings of the knit creation seemed finally to mellow Izzy's mood.

"If it's a sweater, it will be a magnificent one," Birdie said.

Izzy nodded. "Remember when Rose and Jillian were teens and decorated the shop windows? Their designs were always off the grid—fanciful, surprising. Both the Anderson twins have imaginations running out the wazoo."

Nell reached into the bag at her side and pulled out the beginnings of a vest for Ben. She fiddled with a tangled strand of yarn, then looked up. "Mae said she doesn't see as much of Jillian and Rose as she thought she would, especially with one of them living in her rental cottage out back."

"Pete's seen Jillian around town the past couple months," Cass said. "Occasionally with some of the teachers from the high school, where she's doing that innovative teaching practicum. But more often with Josh Elliott, who's probably mentoring her. Anyway, she seems very happy being back, Pete says."

"Their mother's illness and death must have been difficult. Maybe being back in their hometown for a while will help them prepare for whatever is next in their lives," Birdie said.

Izzy agreed. "I hope Rose is able to enjoy life, too. She's great. So smart."

"Mae seems to be concerned about both of them," Nell said. "It's probably hard to let them grow up. She feels responsible now that both their parents are gone."

"But they're adults. Aren't they both going to end up PhDs? Doctors, just like their dentist dad," Izzy said. "They are grown-ups, not kids."

"I had an aunt like that who wouldn't let me grow up," Cass said. "I was forever and ever seven years old to her. Pete always told me it was because she didn't like me much after I turned eight. But, for whatever reason, Aunt Pru was still giving me pink hair bows for my birthday when I was in high school."

A drizzle of wine escaped along with Izzy's laugh. She wiped it off, then sobered and said, "I'm like that, too. Not the hair bow thing, but I have trouble admitting Jillian and Rose are adults. I think it's because I loved having them around when then they were teens . . . the laughter and silliness. I miss those days. I wasn't too much older than they are now."

Cass raised one eyebrow.

Izzy waved her off. "Anyway, I loved the energy they brought in. Tall, limber Jillian, with her flyaway, curly hair highlighted in different colors every other week. She'd make a great runway model."

"And dear serious Rose," Birdie said. "Quiet and smart and watching out for everyone. Yes, they'd both make beautiful runway models, although Rose doesn't much like being in the limelight."

Izzy picked up her cell phone and marked the change in mood by turning on her "happy" Pandora channel. Soon the voice of Cyndi Lauper, explaining melodiously that "girls just want to have fun," filled the room. The conversation moved easily away from stressful days to the vest Nell was knitting, Izzy's new collection of vibrant hand-dyed yarns, and the wild balaclava that Cass was knitting for her husband, Danny, in space-dyed yarn. They all knew Danny was the more accomplished knitter of the couple, but Cass never gave up the chase.

Town news and gossip slipped in as the hours melted away, with attention always drifting back to yarn and stitches, the feel of magnificently soft yarn and the soothing rhythm of needles knitting and purling, and Purl keeping the tempo going with her soft purr.

Eventually, after a yawn or two had slipped in between stitches, Birdie pushed her small body out of the large chair and announced that it was time for her to help Izzy straighten up the messy room and for Nell to drive her home for a good night's sleep. Rising early to check out her birds was putting some limits on her bedtime.

"Let me," she said, taking a rag from Izzy to wipe off the table.

"Oh, out with the two of you, then," Izzy said, tugging the cloth away from Birdie. "Aunt Nell, you look tired, too. Cass will stay and help me. She owes me one."

"For what?" Cass shot back, already straightening chairs and wiping off the coffee table.

Izzy handed Nell her empty casserole dish, then waved both her aunt and Birdie up the three steps and out the front door.

Chapter 3

Nell and Birdie stood outside the shop's blue door, breathing in the cool evening air and looking up at a perfect sky.

Finally, Nell turned to Birdie and said with a grin and tip of her head, "Do you suppose they think we're old?"

Birdie raised her silvery eyebrows and smiled. "Well, we won't ever tell, will we?"

The fact that Nell, in her sixties, was some twenty years younger than Birdie held little significance to them or to the two younger Seaside Knitters. Although sometimes Cass and Izzy—and Nell, too—gave special attention to Birdie, an attention she always graciously waved off and appreciated, both at once. The four women's friendship, which had been established early on and had grown deeper with the years, had nothing to do with their age span. Although they all knew and loved that it had been invisibly enriched by it.

Birdie slipped one arm through Nell's as they began walking down the one-way street toward Nell's car.

Traffic was light at the yarn shop end of usually busy Harbor Road, with late-night strollers examining the books in the

Brandleys' bookstore windows and the many assorted items in McGlucken's Hardware Store. Bike riders with neon stripes on their warm jackets pedaled along the side lane.

The two friends walked through the new parklike setting, which had once been the other traffic lane on the downtown street, waving to an occasional neighbor along the way.

At the far end of the street, a green park area bordered the harbor, and across the street from it, music and the sounds of happy revelers filled the air and rolled down the gaslit sidewalks whenever the door of Jake Risso's Gull Tavern opened.

"It sounds like Jake has a full house tonight," Birdie said, looking down the street. "Ella tells me weekends now begin on Thursday nights. Even wedding celebrations."

"Jake always has a crowd. Although I hear Lucky's Place over near the old fish pier pulls in a crowd, too."

Birdie smiled at the thought of her godson owning a bar, knowing that the only reason he did was that his wealthy father, Anthony, Birdie's dear lifelong friend, had willed it to him when he died, probably hoping it would give Lucky a focus.

"My Luigi is definitely lucky. Things he touches seem somehow blessed, if one can call a bar blessed."

"Hopefully, his magic will bode well for this runway event that has Izzy so upset."

As they neared Harry Garozzo's deli, their attention was drawn to a commotion in the one-way street. Several horns honked, and a few loud voices disturbed the evening air.

Nell squinted and made out a vintage black car stopped in the middle of the street, blocking the cars coming out of Jake's parking lot. Now that the street was one way, the drivers were held captive by the stalled car.

"An accident?" Birdie said aloud as they quickened their pace.

Harry Garozzo, his hands crossed over his baker's apron, stood with a small group of bystanders outside his deli, trying to figure out what was going on. He spotted Birdie and Nell and, with a sweep of his large arms, waved them over, then cleared a space beside him. "Trouble in River City," he whispered to his two friends as he pointed to the stalled car in the street. Behind it, several angry drivers provided an eardrum-offending cacophony of sound.

"Those old cars are a mess. Can you imagine the cost of filling the tank? I think some old fool is out there blocking the whole mess just for kicks or excitement," Harry said. Then he chuckled. "Looks a little like one of Anthony Bianchi's old cars." He moved out of the way so Birdie and Nell had a better look.

"Who is in it?" Birdie asked, looking at the black car and trying to place it.

But Harry had already lost interest and was shuffling back into his deli, shaking his head at an unwanted disturbance. He had the next day's baked goods to attend to.

Nell looked again at the stalled car. The windows were rolled down, and the occupants in both the front seat and backseat were leaning out.

Nell took a step closer, her eyes widening, and motioned for Birdie to follow her look.

"Oh, my," Birdie said, bringing one hand to her mouth.

Standing in the center of the street, blocking the car from moving forward, stood mild, gentle Rose Anderson.

Chapter 4

Rose's palms were planted flat and firm on the car's hood, and her face was flushed. The four surprised occupants in the car were leaning out, their elbows balanced on the window frames. It seemed to be a passenger in the backseat that had Rose's sole attention. Her eyes were glued to Jillian Anderson, her twin.

The few people left at the curb were quiet, as if watching a movie.

Rose's words carried through the night air like wobbly arrows, slightly slurred, and her hands on the car appeared to be holding her up.

"You didn't show up, Jilly. I waited and waited. You're acting . . . you're acting crazy."

"Me? I'm acting crazy, Rosie?" Jillian said, leaning out the window. But her words were more compassionate than accusatory.

Birdie and Nell moved closer, hoping to hear a possible explanation for Rose holding up traffic.

"Please, Jilly, this isn't good for you. I promised Mom—" Rose's eyes remained fixed on her sister as her voice rose and fell, then wobbled, with words running together. "Just come with me. We can go get a burger."

The last sentence seemed incongruous, and bystanders watching from the curb chuckled, deciding it must be just a silly squabble, and moved on.

To Birdie and Nell, Rose's voice held a mixture of pleading and fear—all slurred, as if Rose had had a few drinks, something they knew wasn't typical of her. Her words fluctuated up and down and then seemed to tumble together.

Impatience set in, and horns began to blare again as drivers lost interest in the drama and seemed more intent on getting out of the jam and on to their homes.

Instinctively, Nell took a step off the curb, then stopped short as Rose's voice began to fade, her hands no longer on the car and her body weaving slightly.

Jillian's face matched the color of Rose's, but her words were gentle and clear as she opened the car door and started to get out.

"You'll get hurt, Rosie," Nell heard her say. "Come. Get in the car with us. Please. I'm so sorry for forgetting about meeting you. I love you."

Birdie turned to Nell, her brows pulled together in concern, as drivers of the trapped cars began hurling a few threats at the car.

Rose looked toward the sounds, and her slender body seemed to deflate right in front of them. She wiped her now-damp face with one arm, standing back from the car and looking at her sister, as if surprised to see her there. She murmured something that sounded vaguely like an apology. The words seemed to take every last bit of breath in her. She turned away, one palm pushed out toward Jillian, as if urging her back into the car. Then she moved clumsily off the street and into the shadows.

As Rose disappeared, someone in the backseat pulled Jillian back in the car so it could move on, and the line of cars began to move down Harbor Road.

As soon as the street was clear, Birdie and Nell hurried across it.

"Rose?" Nell called, expecting her to step out of the shadows of the narrow alley next to an ice cream store. She called again, then looked up and down the street.

Birdie checked the alley.

But Rose Anderson seemed to have disappeared into the night.

Chapter 5

Nell collected her lattes at Coffee's and walked out onto Harbor Road, nearly running into a small man several inches shorter than herself. She quickly checked that her drinks were still intact.

"I'm so sorry," she murmured, then looked into the weather-beaten face staring at her.

The face immediately broke into a grin. "Nell Endicott, what're you doing drinking all that caffeine? Don't you know it'll kill you?"

"Henry Staab," Nell said, laughing. "Good grief, you're the last person I'd expected to see here this early in the day." She looked down at his foot. "So how's the ankle?"

"Ha. You tell that Bernadette that what happens bird-watching stays at bird-watching."

"I'll do that. What brings you to our end of town?"

"I'm on an errand of mercy." He waved a Red Sox hat at her. "A fair lady left this up at my place, and as long as I was coming in for supplies, I thought I'd return it."

Nell tilted her head to one side, a curious look on her face. "Your place?"

"My buddy Rosie Anderson. The parents are buried up there with me, you know. She comes up to the cemetery like clockwork, chugging her way up the hill on that old bike of hers. Making up for lost time, I guess, now that she and the sister are back in town. Good girls, both of them."

"Yes, they—" Nell began, but Henry went on.

"Sometimes Rose and I have tea after she talks or argues or whatever with her mom. Well, she has tea. I have a small libation."

"She talks to her mom?"

"Oh, that she does. They have a go at it, those two. Long heated conversations. Sometimes I can see that Rosie doesn't like what she's hearing from her mom." He chuckled, thinking about it.

"Does Jillian come with her?"

"Nope, not with her. But she comes up hiking with one of my birder buddies and stops in to visit her folks' graves. Good hikers, those two. Nice as the day is long. I've shown them my special trails into the woods up there. People don't realize those woods are shortcuts to great areas, like even the old quarry area and some other places birders go. I showed Rose some of my trails a day or so ago, too. The two of us hiked in and sat at my special lookout place. That's when she left this behind." He lifted the hat up.

"The hat." Nell nodded, still frowning at the image of Rose arguing with her mother. "I'm headed to Izzy's yarn shop, and I could see that she gets it, if you'd like. Rose is in there often . . ."

"Well, sure. Good of you, Nell." He rested the hat on the cardboard carrier of lattes. "If it's got coffee stains on it next time I see her, I'll know where they came from."

And with that and a chuckle, Henry shuffled off toward his old pickup truck.

Nell watched him drive off, chuckling as the image of Henry Staab proposing to her dearest friend popped into her head.

Realizing the drinks were getting cold, she collected herself and walked quickly toward the yarn shop, knowing both Mae and Izzy would welcome the caffeine on a busy Friday morning. The runway show had created a true knitting frenzy.

She walked in and spotted Mae Anderson, already surrounded by morning shoppers, and handed over her coffee. Mae accepted it gratefully, but there was little time to talk as three customers vied for the shop manager's attention simultaneously. Nell tried to read her face and detected no worry. Simply a very busy Mae managing the shop with care and fastidiousness.

Somehow, Nell had thought, without any logic to it, that chatting with a cheerful Mae would help dispel the uncomfortable feeling she had carried home after seeing Mae's twin nieces in such an odd situation. But when she had described the incident to Ben, the whole thing had sounded more like a *Saturday Night Live* skit than a crisis, which Ben had been quick to note. The Anderson twins weren't teenagers anymore. They were smart and accomplished adults. And some of the bystanders had probably found humor in the accident-free incident.

Yet Nell had still carried a nagging feeling to bed with her. Maybe the feeling was something else entirely and had nothing to do with the Anderson girls. She had mentally thumbed through the possible causes of her discomfort: Birdie hiking through the woods alone; Izzy frustrated with a runway; Ben's annual checkup, which was coming up.

Or maybe simply the weather or world news. But, gratefully, whatever the cause, it hadn't been enough to keep her awake last night. After a few minutes of gentle, slow breathing, she had fallen asleep.

And today was a new day. She turned away from Mae and walked across the crowded shop to the small fiber room near the back, its white walls filled with framed photographs of sheep and alpaca and goats. "Our magnificent benefactors,"

Izzy called the subjects of the photographic art. She had added a bookshelf filled with books about the well-loved animals and their beautiful contribution to the world of knitting. There was also a small couch and a pair of rocking chairs to lure customers into resting awhile in the quiet space—or, as the police dispatcher often did, into napping.

The storeroom door off to the left was open a crack, and Nell spotted a light coming from the small room. She walked on in.

Izzy looked up from sorting through a basket of baby alpaca yarn. "You're a lifesaver, Aunt Nell," she said, reaching for the latte. She nodded to one of the two chairs in the small space. "Can you sit for a few?" she asked, a smear of cream already gracing her upper lip. "What's up? You have that look on your face."

Nell laughed and dropped the latte tray into a waste basket. She closed the door and sat down. "Okay, which look is that?"

"The one that says your mind is on other things—none of them being here in my storeroom."

"And none of them worth talking about. Mostly errands today. But seeing Mae out front reminded me of something Birdie and I saw on the way to my car last night. Ben convinced me later that Birdie and I have imaginations that often run on overdrive. But when it's someone you know that you're imagining about, somehow you don't let go easily."

"So?" Izzy asked, not sure at all what Nell was talking about.

Briefly, Nell replayed the scene.

"That's weird," Izzy said. "It doesn't sound like Rose at all. She's so calm and composed. And she doesn't even like the taste of alcohol. Are you sure it was our Rose?"

"Yes. It was difficult to see all the passengers in the car, but Jillian was definitely one of them. She was trying to get Rose to move—at least that's what it looked like. Anyway, the whole episode didn't last long. I suppose it just seemed so odd because we knew the people involved."

"Probably just a sisterly spat."

"Most likely," Nell said.

"I can imagine me doing something like that at a certain age, especially after a glass or two of wine. I could be emotional sometimes. It was probably a good thing I had brothers instead of a sister."

Nell laughed. "Anyway, seeing Mae reminded me of it."

"Oh, Mae's a rock. She hasn't said anything, although she's been quieter than usual these days. She's happy about the twins coming back to Sea Harbor for a while. She's secretly hoping they'll stay forever, I think. Lots of grieving in her life recently. Her own husband, then the twins' dad. She was close to her brother. And now the girls are really the only family she has."

Izzy pulled a skein of cashmere yarn out of the basket and instinctively cuddled its softness with her fingers. Then she looked back at her aunt. "I love those twins. Jillian's so personable. There were always boys around. Now it's men, I guess. Sometimes a guy would show up here in the shop when Jillian and Rose were helping us out in the store. Jillian would insist that the guy help in the Magic Room with the little kids and also pay attention to Purl. She used to tell me it was a test. If a guy wasn't nice to little kids and animals, he needed to scoot."

Nell chuckled. "It's hard to think of anyone being angry with Jillian, but a sibling relationship can hold all sorts of emotions and secrets others aren't privy to. That was certainly the case with your mother and me."

"Oh?" Izzy raised her brows.

Nell laughed. "But then sisters grow up and love each other dearly. And that's exactly what we did."

A sudden pounding on the storeroom door startled both women. It was followed by a loud, commanding voice. "Hey, ladies, come out of your cave. Your lifeboat is here."

Izzy pulled the door open, trying to put on her irritated face. Instead, she dissolved in laughter. "Stop it, tough guy. You just made me spill coffee on my jeans."

Lucky Bianchi stood with his feet spread apart and a grin on his face. He forked one hand through messy blond hair, his long body nearly filling the open space. In one hand he held a hammer. "So, boss lady, let's get this show on the road."

"The show needs a *runway*, Lucky. Not a road." She motioned for him to back up so she and Nell could get out of the room. "Let's talk where there's more air."

"Sure. And just so you know, I have an artist coming to supplement my carpentry skills," Lucky said, giving Nell a quick hug. "She'll be here shortly."

"We need all the help we can get," Izzy said. "Who did you charm into helping you?"

"My good buddy Willow Adams. She's resistant to charm, though. Truth is, she thinks what I'm building might be too 'ordinary.' Can you believe it? Ordinary? Anyway, she's bringing another person so that the two of them can make sure the runway, as she put it, has a great 'aesthetic,' whatever the 'h' that means."

Nell and Izzy laughed.

"Willow says her pal knows a lot about knitting, although we'll have to see how that translates into using a hammer, right? Her name is Lily something . . . no, maybe Magnolia? No. Iris, I think?"

"How about Rose?" Izzy said.

"That's it." Lucky snapped his fingers. "Rose. Of course. 'What's in a name? A rose by any other name—'"

Izzy shushed him from quoting more Shakespeare. "That's great. She'll make sure it happens. Rose is wonderful."

"Willow says she's talented and serious. A nice kid."

"She's not a kid, Lucky. She's an adult. Getting a doctorate,

I think. She's nice and smart—a super-talented adult. As for serious, well, hmm. Compared to you . . . ?"

"Okay, got it." Lucky grinned again, a lopsided grin that seemed to be a semipermanent facial fixture. "Hey, wait a minute. Is she *the* Rose? Jillian Anderson's sister?"

"Yes," Izzy said. "And multitalented, just like Jillian."

Lucky scratched his chin, as if processing something in his head. Finally he smiled again.

"So you've met her?" Izzy asked.

Lucky nodded, looking amused. "In a manner of speaking," he said, then changed the subject to details about the platform he had committed to build.

"Before you get too involved in important decisions, I'm leaving," Nell said. She smiled and slipped her bag over her shoulder and started toward the door, then stopped and turned around.

"I almost forgot this." She pulled the baseball hat out of her bag.

"Nell," Lucky said, grinning. "You're finally joining our wild Sox games at the bar. I knew you'd come around."

Nell laughed and handed the hat to Izzy. "This is Rose's. She forgot it up at Henry Staab's."

"What?"

Nell explained and commented on how much Henry loved seeing both girls up at the wooded cemetery spot. "It'd be great if you could pass it along. And now I really am off. I have things of my own to take care of."

"Things of your own? Sounds mysterious," Lucky said.

Nell chuckled. "The only mystery is what will be fresh at the market today and how many people will show up for dinner."

Lucky slapped his head. "Ah, I get it now. Ben's famous Friday night grill fest. My pop used to talk about how he'd show up sometimes with his old buddies. It drove my mamma crazy because he'd manage to disappear without her knowing where he'd gone."

Nell laughed. "I remember those days. They didn't come often, but when they did, you'd know they were here. All the neighbors would know, too. The musketeers, they called themselves, always with a nod to Birdie, their honorary member. Your dad would bring his own Scotch and amaretto cocktail mixings and turn our deck into a Frank Sinatra songfest."

"You should come sometime, Lucky," Izzy said. "Continue the tradition."

Lucky laughed. "Maybe I will. I bet even Ben can't make a Godfather cocktail like old Anthony taught his son to make."

Nell smiled at the memories, then waved goodbye.

Izzy hugged her aunt, then watched her hurrying through the main room of the shop.

"You have a cool aunt," Lucky said, watching her. "We're pretty fortunate to have these wise women in our lives."

"Wise woman? Did I hear my name?" Willow Adams walked into the room, her small energetic body managing to make a big entrance.

She hugged Izzy and grinned at Lucky. "It's about time you appreciated me, carpenter man."

Lucky gave Willow a giant, lift-off-the-floor hug. "Hey, will-o'-the-wisp, you're alone. Where's our flower girl?"

"Rose," Willow said, finding her feet. "Her name is Rose, Lucky."

"Rose," Lucky repeated.

"Rose isn't here," Willow said. "And neither am I. We have a show at my gallery coming up, and things aren't as ready as they should be, so I need to get over there. And Rose is a little under the weather today. I think she had a late night last night."

Lucky grinned, as if he was somehow privy to Rose's late night.

Willow went on. "So, anyway, we're meeting tomorrow at your place, Lucky."

"My place?"

"What?" Izzy interrupted. "You're going to plan my runway stage in a bar?"

"I checked with Mae, and there's a class here," Willow said. "My gallery isn't going to work. There's traffic on Saturdays. Lucky's Place has plenty of room. We'll be there only an hour or two. Just to get our arms around whatever it is we're doing. And in the afternoon it'll probably be nearly empty."

"I take offense at that," Lucky said, attempting a frown. "My place is never empty. And you're saying my place is third choice?"

"Yes," Willow said. "Actually fourth. We considered my studio, but it's a mess."

"Well, okay, then. Actually, it's a good choice. There's lots of inspiration circling around that fine establishment."

Willow gave him a satisfied grin.

And Izzy winced. Then smoothed her forehead quickly. She loved these two people. All would be well. The models would be walking on more than air. Surely.

She hoped.

Chapter 6

A sudden shift in the wind blew away the day's Indian summer in one wild breath and left Sea Harbor with a chilly evening and the knowledge that autumn had definitely set in, with winter on its coattails. It also shrunk the Endicotts' Friday night dinner to a smaller than usual group.

"Sometimes it's nice to just have the regulars," Izzy said, leaning forward on the porch lounger to dip a giant strawberry into a pot of rich liquor-laced melted chocolate. The wind had finally settled down, leaving behind the drop in temperature. She huddled back against her husband Sam's chest, humming along to Fleetwood Mac's "Dreams."

"Regulars," Jane Brewster repeated with a smile. "We surely are that." The artist looked at Ben and Nell, then over at her husband. "How many years have we come to the Endicotts' deck for incredible meals and friendship, Ham?"

Ham stroked his thick beard, his deep brown eyes smiling. "Too many to count—or too old to count. Or a combo, maybe?" He raised his brandy snifter and looked around at each of them and then paused at Ben, Nell. And his wife, Jane. "Here's to old friends," he said, a catch in his voice.

"Hear! Hear!" the others chimed in.

As the Endicotts' oldest friends, the Brewsters had been family from the day they had stopped by Sea Harbor on their way back to California from vacationing in Maine. A brief stopover that had convinced the artists that Sea Harbor needed an art colony. So they had created one, bringing to birth the Canary Cove Art Colony. And they had never left.

Birdie raised her hand. "I do believe I, too, was at that initial soiree," she said. "Peppery grilled swordfish steaks and a corn salad is what I remember."

Laughter filled the dark night, and Nell quickly acknowledged that the beloved Birdie Favazza was probably the glue that had turned that night so long ago into a beloved tradition that was now embedded into their lives.

At Cass's shivering request, Ben passed around Hudson's Bay blankets in case the firepit and portable heating he'd recently installed needed a boost. "These heating panels could extend my Friday night grilling well into the chilly months," he explained proudly.

"So you think we'll have Christmas Eve out here?" Danny Brandley joked.

"I hope so," Ham chimed in. "New Year's Eve, too." He took a drink of his brandy.

"Maybe we could have the fashion show out here," Sam suggested. "Get Lucky off the hook for having to build a runway for that fancy magazine show. And Ben could grill."

"Speaking of runways," Jane said, "I stopped in at the Fishtail Gallery today. Rose Anderson was helping Willow plan a gallery exhibit and doing an amazing job. She's a wonderful fiber artist and seems to pick up on the whole gallery business quickly, too. Between her and Willow, there is a bucketload of talent there, and I'm happy they both love Canary Cove. It bodes well for when Ham and I decide to sail off into the sunset."

Ham chuckled. "I'm with Jane on this one."

Izzy smiled, as if she were somehow responsible for it all.

"My fervent hope is that Rose and Willow will keep Lucky in line so the runway gets built in time for the show," Izzy said.

Jane laughed. "At least they'll have a good time. But explain it to me. I get the runway part—a wooden platform by another name. So Lucky is taking that on?"

"Right. And the women will make it far more than a plain old wooden stage like they have in the Paris runway shows. They will make it amazing. And I have no idea how."

"Well, at least the stage won't collapse," Cass said. "Bianchi is pretty much good at anything he tries."

"It's your influence, Birdie," Nell said. "Lucky claims his godmother has given him special powers."

"He's right, of course. He's thinking about going bird-watching with me, although I'm not sure he'd be able to keep quiet. On the other hand, he'd love learning the ins and outs of bird-watching."

"Learning to watch birds?" Danny asked. "Don't you just look?"

"Hey, that's my line," Cass said, nudging him in the side.

Birdie took a sip of the Irish coffee Ben had handed to her. "Believe it or not, some of the group are quite competitive. Polly Farrell told me that there was a regional competition once before they had formed the group. Josh Elliott won, and the next morning he found a pile of dead gulls on his doorstep."

"Geesh," Izzy said, her face wrinkling into an "ugh" expression.

"I remember that," Cass said. "Mary Pisano wrote about it in her About Town column. The headline was something like A FOWL DEED."

"Well, let's hope the poor gulls died a natural death and not as a result of someone's jealousy," Jane said.

"When's your next outing, Birdie?" Ben asked.

"Sunday, depending on the weather. Although some of our more dedicated members don't really care if it's raining or freezing cold or sizzling hot. Nor do the birds, I suppose. We're going to the old quarry area."

"And what's your feeling about the weather?" Ben asked.

"Well, that's a question, isn't it?" Birdie paused, as if thinking about the planned outing. And then she said with some conviction, "I'll go as long as it's safe. Even the birds won't be putting on a show if there's lightning around. But otherwise, I'll go. I'm looking forward to it. I used to hike over in that area a long, long time ago." She picked up her hot toddy and sat back in the chair, wrapping her blanket around her.

"The Josh you mentioned is Amelia Elliott's son, right?" Jane asked. "His mother and the whole Barlow family have always been generous to the art association."

Birdie nodded. "Amelia was generous to everyone. And then died way too young. A sudden heart attack, I think. Just a few years ago."

"I met her husband, Peter, a few times," Ben said. "He was CEO of his wife's family's commercial real estate company. A shrewd businessman."

"Shrewd?" Nell said. "I know from experience you don't interpret that word to mean *clever*."

Ben chuckled. "Well, even though it was the Barlows' company, Elliott was the one who ran it after he and Amelia married. I met with Amelia once, too. A business thing."

"I remember that," Nell said. "It was after Peter Elliott died."

"Right," Ben said. "Father Northcutt asked me to help answer some questions Amelia had about her family's business and their trust. It was similar to my family's, so I was able to clarify some things for her."

"Well, for all the trauma Josh has gone through, he's a kind man," Birdie said. "He's a little 'off the grid,' as the kids say. But he gives that expression a very nice name."

"The teens who come in the shop gossip about teachers all the time, and they like 'Mr. Elliott' a lot," Izzy said.

Jane nodded. "Apparently, Josh doesn't play by the rules—and he somehow gets away with it. Merry Jackson teaches choir over there. She says he's brilliant. But does his own thing. That probably makes the kids like him even more—a maverick teacher. What could be better?"

A sudden gust of wind blew through the small group and scattered a pile of napkins across the outdoor table. Nell reached over and gathered them up, then looked up at the sky. "What does that sky tell us?" she asked. "The blackness looks green. Ominous."

"Ominous . . ." Birdie said softly, her face more serious than Nell's. "Yes."

The others looked over at her.

Birdie was wrapping a blanket around her small shoulders and standing up, as if to get a better look at the sky. "There's something about all this talk that has me feeling slightly jittery. Ominous. That kind of feeling."

"Perhaps we're just getting tired. I, for one, am about to call it a night." Jane stood and looked over at Ham, who was trying unsuccessfully to suppress a yawn. He pushed his ample body out of the chaise.

Cass got up, too. "We need to go. Danny and I are off to the city tomorrow. He's having a book reading at the Boston Public Library. My wonderful, important mystery writer husband will sign autographs while I watch with adoring eyes." She leaned over and pulled Danny out of his chair.

"Give me a call or text when you're back," Izzy said. She collected a few empty plates and headed for the deck door.

Birdie looked around as others moved and stretched, then followed one another inside and toward the front door.

"We're just like the birds," she said. "Flocking together." She followed Ham and Jane to their car, then paused, one hand on the open door. She looked up at the sky again.

"Do you still have that feeling, Birdie?" Jane asked. "As if something's wrong?"

Birdie hooked her arm through Jane's. "No, not wrong. Just a little off-kilter, that's all."

Jane looked into Birdie's eyes. "I see a touch of worry."

"Just a prickling, Jane dear. A feeling that all's not right with the world. But it could be because I've forgotten an appointment, or the weather might be changing, or maybe, quite possibly, it's nothing at all." She smiled and slid into the backseat of the car, her brows pulled together, not satisfied with her own description of how she felt.

They drove in silence through downtown Sea Harbor, then up the hilly road toward Birdie's home. Shortly before reaching the drive, Ham suddenly veered to the left, and the uncomfortable feeling came back to Birdie with an uncomfortable force.

"Sorry, ladies," Ham said, bringing the car back into alignment. "I didn't want to hit whatever poor creature was lying in the road. Apparently, another driver didn't veer fast enough."

Birdie turned and stared out the car window, looking back at the motionless dark lump that Ham had expertly managed to miss.

A dead seagull lay in the middle of Ravenswood Road.

Chapter 7

"Hey, Rose," Jillian called out, walking into the Fishtail Gallery and closing the door behind her.

"Over here," Rose said, sticking an arm into the air without looking up. She was staring at a table covered with small plein air paintings. Each one featuring a different spot on Cape Ann. Some in vibrant greens and yellows and blues, depicting the energy of the sea. Others soft and mellow in more muted shades, showing the sea, sailboats, and sunsets.

"I tried to find you yesterday to apologize," Jillian said. She stood just inside the front door, as if she wasn't quite sure it was safe to approach her sister. "I called Willow, and she thought you might be sleeping in. She said you were a little under the weather." Jillian took a few steps across the small gallery.

Rose finally turned and looked over. "Yes, sorry," she said.

Jillian wasn't sure what the "sorry" was for, but took that as a good sign. She talked as she walked across the room. "Here's the thing. I'm really sorry about the other night. I honestly forgot that we were meeting at the Artist's Palate. Honest. I had to meet with some high school students after school. They were very talky. And then a couple teachers asked me to join them at Jake's. One beer, they said, and they'd give me a ride to Merry Jackson's place. Well, anyway, they were gossipy. Talking about school policies. Asking me questions, as if I'd know anything? So when a guy I know offered me a ride, I took him up on it. I guess it all threw me off enough that I totally forgot. Call me a featherhead."

"Who?" Rose asked, her voice sharp.

"Who what?" Jillian said, but then she went on, as if wanting to get her complete apology out while she had a chance. "It's not an excuse, Rosie. It's simply the truth. You deserve better. I texted you a zillion times yesterday."

Rose was still.

Jillian looked at her strangely, wondering if she'd heard a single word of her apology.

Finally, Rose said, "I'm sorry I didn't answer your texts. And Willow was right—I wasn't feeling great." She managed a smile. "And, hey, I'm sorry, too. I acted a little, well, crazy. Actually, *very* crazy. I'm ashamed. Blame it on Merry Jackson."

Jillian was relieved. There was actual remorse in her sister's tone. And the smile was almost warm. "Yeah. I saw Merry. She told me you disappeared from her deck before she could suggest some caffeine or water. Or a cool breeze. You never did like wine much—even the expensive kind, which Merry was probably pouring for you."

"Right. I never did. And after the way I felt yesterday, I probably never will. It's poison."

Jillian pulled out a chair and sat down. "But wine aside, Rosie, that was still kind of over the top for you, standing out in the street like that. Why? It was the kind of thing I'd do, but not my careful sister. It was clear that something wasn't right—"

Rose lifted her palm to stop Jillian from talking. "It wasn't really about you forgetting to meet me. I just thought we needed to talk."

Jillian took a quick breath. "I know that, Rosie. And I know what you're concerned about. It's because I've been spending time with—"

"Spending *days* with. I don't see you anymore. Even Aunt Mae mentioned it. It's . . ."

"I know. He's older. That bothers both of you."

"I don't care how old he is," Rose said.

"Then what?"

"It's just that it's a bad idea for you, Jilly."

"Bad idea? For me to spend time with a man? To be friends with him? Hey, Rose. I like him very much. You liked him, too, once. Remember that environmental ed class in high school?"

"That was you, Jillian. I never took that class."

"Oh. I forgot. But you knew who he was. Everyone did. He was a new teacher and lit up the school, even though he made us work like crazy. But we all learned so much. And now . . . Well, there's a whole other side to him that you don't see when you're a student."

Rose seemed to push away Jillian's words. "He just isn't—" Rose stopped as a group of women walked into the gallery. She welcomed them with a smile and then turned back to her sister. "And I promised Mom—"

"I won't go there again, Rose," Jillian snapped. "Don't do the 'Mom thing' with me. Please don't. We're adults. We make our own decisions."

The fact that her same-age sister had taken on the role of protector wasn't something Jillian would ever swallow easily. In fact, she hated it. But for the moment she pushed it aside. "Hey, let's go out together some night. Just the three of us. You'll see for yourself that he's a great guy. He's serious and nice, loves all things nature. He reads a lot. Hates big parties. He's not like the guys I knew in college or high school."

She tried to answer in a way her sister would understand, but was sad that she had to be explaining anything at all. She was an adult. Rose was an adult. And justifying relationships of any kind was childish.

She swallowed her emotion in one gulp and said, "Rose, he's the best friend I've ever had. He's like a . . . like a gift. A gift I wasn't looking for or expecting. I think maybe that's how the best gifts come to us."

Jillian could see Rose was making an effort to listen. Maybe. So she went on.

"And there's no 'good or bad *for me*.' It's not a 'for me.' He and I don't own each other. That's not what our relationship is about."

Rose took a deep breath, suddenly exhausted.

Jillian turned around at a noise behind her, relieved at the distraction.

Willow Adams walked into the main gallery from her studio in the back. "Hi, Jillian. If I'd known you were here, I'd have come out sooner." She gave her a quick hug. "But right now I need to steal your sister away. We have a date over at Lucky's Place. With Lucky, no less."

Jillian looked at her watch. "Lucky's bar this early? A date? Hmm."

Willow laughed. "We're going to brainstorm runway ideas. This way there's food available. His truffle fries are great."

"So is he," Jillian said. "He helped me out the other night. Gave me a ride—"

"A ride? Where?" Rose asked.

Before she could answer, Willow stepped in. "I keep telling Rose she's in for a treat. She hasn't met Lucky yet."

Jillian chuckled. "Sure you have, Rose."

"I have?"

"He was driving me home when we ran into you—almost literally—the other night."

"What?" Rose's mouth dropped open. An immediate flush traveled from her neck to her cheeks. "But I thought it was . . ."

"Things aren't always what they seem, Rose," Jillian said, her tone too sweet.

Rose wiped a hand across her forehead. "Oh, good grief. The man must think I'm daffy."

"Lucky never met a daffy person he didn't like," Willow assured her. "No fears."

Rose stood and pulled her sweatshirt over her head and looked at Willow. "Well, it is what it is. Let's go see if this Lucky is as nice as you all seem to think he is. Or if he works well with deranged people. Either way, let's do this."

Willow's presence had lightened the mood. Rose even looked semi-happy. And that made Jillian happy, too. "Izzy told me that your runway will be something special," she said. "She's psyched that you'll give it some pizzazz—not to mention impressing the magazine folks. Between the two of you, it'll outshine the models themselves."

"Well, we'll try, right, Rose? If only we can keep Lucky in line." Willow grasped a tumble of thick dark hair and slipped an elastic band around it. "By the way, how's your own knitting project for the show coming along, Jillian? Izzy says it's a mystery."

Jillian chuckled. "Mystery lady, that's me. Nope. I'm just improvising as I go. I'm luring some of the high school kids into my knitting net. And once they found out that you can make up your own rules once you learn the basics, they were in. It's 'dope,' or whatever it is they say when they like something. Everyone should know how to knit, right?"

"Absolutely. In the meantime, if you're just hanging around this afternoon, you're welcome to come help us for a while."

"Thanks, but no thanks. I know my limits. All I can do with yarn is knit and purl, while you two will somehow turn plywood into a work of fiber art. Besides, I've got places to go and things to do."

"And people to meet?" Willow added.

Rose looked at her sister, her face questioning. But then, instead of pursuing it, she took a step toward Jillian and hugged her close. "I do love you, Jilly," she whispered into her ear. "Whatever happens, don't forget that."

Rose and Willow then flew out the door, leaving a confused Jillian watching them hurry away.

Lucky's Place was an old bar made new. But not that old, and not that new. The location was prime, situated at the beginning of a long pier and right next door to Gracie Santos's Lazy Lobster and Soup Café.

But it wasn't the name or location of the place that made |it new.

When Lucky and the previous owner had inherited the bar and restaurant, his co-owner had named it the Harbor Club—a name some thought a bit pretentious for a sports bar, even a recently spiffed-up one. Lucky chose to be a silent partner back then and didn't care much for the details about the bar he'd inherited, leaving the particulars up to his co-owner. A man he neither trusted nor liked.

But when the partner died unexpectedly and the establishment became mostly Lucky's responsibility, the place became just that—Lucky's Place, simple, comfortable, and welcoming. The place still had plush booths, two fireplaces, and an amazing deck that hung over a small beach and the ocean. But, as most customers agreed, the vibe—the spirit—was different. Lucky's Place had become Sea Harbor's very own Cheers, definitely a place where everyone knew your name. Even Jake Risso, owner of the Gull Tavern across the harbor, didn't resent the competition, agreeing there was plenty of room in Sea Harbor for two great places in which to watch a game and have a beer.

On this Saturday afternoon, Lucky's had its usual mix of customers—four women playing mah-jongg at a wide booth in the back, popcorn bowls nearly empty; a noisy group of men sitting around the long, curved bar, watching a game on one of the large TVs, beer and sandwiches lined up in front of them. And outside, in the small alley between the bar and a lobster shack, a group of diehards played on Lucky's new pickleball court.

A group of loud fishermen came in, needing a beer before heading home. The carried the smells of the haddock and cod and striped bass that they'd had weighed and sent off to the middlemen.

On the opposite side of the bar, a comfortably padded banquette stretched the distance of the wall, with room enough for a group of bowlers celebrating a win or strangers who didn't mind bumping elbows with the couple next to them. It was there, nearly empty at this sunset hour, that Willow introduced Rose Anderson to Lucky Bianchi.

Lucky was still for a minute, as if inspecting Rose. Then he grinned. "Hey, it's a pleasure, Rose. Though I believe maybe we've met—"

Lucky immediately saw Rose's look of embarrassment and eased her out of it instantly. "I guess I met you online. I googled you, Rose Anderson. You're an NYU award-winning artist, just like my buddy Willow here. I'm clearly out of my element with you two, but hey, looks like the gods are being good to me. I'm going to enjoy every minute of it."

Rose smiled, knowing exactly what Lucky Bianchi had just done to ease her awkwardness. And the real reason why she had looked familiar.

And with that, she and Willow sat down together on one side, with Lucky on the other, and spread out papers and pictures they'd collected, sketches of simple, narrow stage platforms. Some of the sketches were already scribbled on with markers and notes. And quick designs of yarn art with a watery look that would make Neptune himself proud were drawn in the margins.

Lucky sat opposite them, cans of seltzer and a basket of truffle fries within easy reach.

The three were an odd sight, their hair mussed, jeans and sweatshirts soon covered with black and red spots of marker. And in spite of Lucky's promise that it would be a quiet, inspiring place to work, Willow and Rose had their hands full shooing away a steady flow of Lucky's friends who came by to say hi.

Lucky laughed when they complained. "Sorry, you two. Just doing my customer relations bit." He pulled out another drawing he'd done of a possible platform for Willow and Rose to look at.

"Hmm," Willow said, looking at the drawing. "It's a little, well, basic?"

"It looks like the delivery ramp at a grocery store," Rose added.

"Hey, Rose, you're hurting my soul," Lucky said with great drama, pressing his hands against his heart. He glanced down at the sketch, then nodded. "Delivery ramp. Hmm. Well, maybe. But I see potential there for a grand delivery ramp, not your vegetable crate sort."

Another large group walked into the bar then, spotted Lucky, and headed their way.

Rose and Willow saw them coming and moaned.

"You're like flypaper," Rose said, scribbling again on the paper in front of her.

"Flypaper." Lucky laughed. "But, hey, Miss Rose, we're making progress here, you and me. You're speaking to me directly. Almost eye to eye. It's all good, even with that nice frown of yours. I mean, after trying to get me to crash my gorgeous old car the other night, then not looking me in the eye earlier, I was beginning to think I bothered you. Or, maybe, that you just plain didn't like me. It's been known to happen."

Rose tilted her head to one side, swallowing the touch of embarrassment that rose up again. Then she pretended to give Lucky's comment consideration.

Finally, she shook her head in a hopeless way, then looked down at the sketches, letting a thick strand of brown hair fall over her face to hide a smile. Lucky Bianchi definitely had a certain flair.

Chapter 8

Later that day, as the sky began to darken into an eerie color that portended rain, the customers in Lucky's Place changed over to a more energetic group, with the music rising a few decibels and developing a livelier beat. Willow and Rose, immersed in their designs, never noticed the change or that Lucky had excused himself and was now busy checking on kitchen and staff rotations and welcoming friends who had come for dinner or drinks or sometimes just the music or to sit in front of the large fireplace.

As Lucky circled the room, Izzy and Sam Perry walked in and claimed two empty seats at the bar. Lucky waved their way and walked over.

"Good to see you two." He grabbed a large basket of peanuts and planted it in front of them. "Where's my favorite curly-haired blonde?"

Sam laughed. "Abby's entertaining her favorite grandaunt and uncle. You'd think it was Christmas. Being read to by Uncle Ben is a real treat. Did you know he used to do community theater?"

Lucky laughed. "Sir Ben Olivier. Abby is a lucky princess. But bring her around soon for lunch. I told her I was naming a hot dog special after her. So what are you two up to?"

"A wild and crazy night. We're heading to a movie that starts in an hour. But no movie's complete without Lucky's truffle fries."

"You got that right." Lucky turned to the bar server and added burgers to their order.

As Sam and Lucky began debating the weather and the possibility of getting in a late-season sail, Izzy spun the stool around and checked out the room. She waved to a group of friends near the fireplace who were moving their bodies as Toby Keith belted out "I Love This Bar." Feeling relaxed for the first time all week, she moved her shoulders to the beat, letting it all go—the worry about business and staff and a runway show coming up.

When she turned back to the bar, Lucky had disappeared, but Sam was pointing to a long table on the far wall. "Have you checked out who's here?" he asked.

Izzy looked over and laughed. "That's dedication for you. It's my runway crew for the fashion show. Working in the bar. I'm impressed—and a tad guilty. It's Saturday."

"Don't be guilty. You're the boss lady, Iz. You assign. They design."

"You're right. I think Rose is in her element creating something beautiful. How can they possibly make a runway beautiful? But Willow assured me they can. 'Beautiful knit creations deserve a lovely stage,' she said. And they seem to get along great. I'm sure Lucky doesn't mind hanging out with both of them."

"Lucky man, that Lucky," Sam said.

Once the hamburgers appeared, Izzy dug in while Sam stood up, having noticed a familiar face walking into the bar. He waved him over.

"It's Josh," Sam said to Izzy as the man headed their way. "Ben and I ran into him over at the marina yesterday and got to talking about sailing together."

"You'll have the whole town on that boat at this rate." Izzy spun her stool around and waved.

"What luck," Sam said, shaking Josh's hand, when he approached. "Seeing you twice in one week."

Josh laughed. "Hi, Izzy. Haven't seen you for a while, but I get reports on your store from my students who hang out there."

"And I know all about you because you're the teacher my teen customers spend lots of time discussing."

"Hah, teens. They're a strange species. But tolerable. Interesting too. Sometimes. Some of them seem psyched about some event you're having."

"It's fun to watch them. You're right. Gen Zers are their own breed."

Sam pulled out an empty stool. "Hey, can you sit a minute? Let's pinpoint this sail before the icebergs arrive. Still interested?"

Izzy sipped her beer and watched Josh as the two men talked, fitting him into the image of the epic man that the teenagers talked about. And the genius birder that Birdie knew. The son of a wealthy family who lived like a beach bum. No wonder he was so likable, she thought.

He fit the beach bum image tonight, wearing an old hiking jacket and torn jeans, his thick black hair curling up in the front as if protesting being brushed. A small knot of it was pulled back, with a band holding it at the back of his head. It didn't look intentional, but more like the hair bothered him and he didn't have time to cut it off. The glasses looked sort of professorial, she thought, but not much else about Josh Elliott did—not the strong, angular face, the five o'clock shadow of a beard on a square chin. None of the components equaled a conventionally handsome look, but somehow, when the parts were all pulled together, there was definitely something intriguing about the unassuming teacher.

She blinked when Josh and Sam both finished talking and looked at her. She banished her thoughts. "So," she said quickly, "I didn't know you were a sailor, Josh."

"Sailor? So far, I know enough not to get hit by the boom. That's about it. Maybe someday."

"Josh wants to see the birds out on Thacher island," Sam explained. "Ben suggested we give him a lift on the boat."

"That's right. You're a birder. I knew that."

"Right. And Thacher is part of the Atlantic flyway," Josh said.

His voice had changed slightly, turning deeper. A great voice for a teacher, Izzy thought. Great eyes, too. She'd not noticed that before.

"It's a perfect spot to view birds in migratory flight," Josh went on. He touched the stem of his glass as he talked. His voice was serious but with a bit of drama in it, which made Izzy want to hear more. She had the not unpleasant sensation of sitting in a classroom, with a blackboard behind the teacher, wondering if she should take notes. And hoping she wouldn't be called on. She was beginning to get what the kids were talking about in her shop.

A shadow fell across the three, and Josh stopped talking. Lucky Bianchi stood behind Josh, one hand on his friend's shoulder.

"My lucky night," he said. "Three of Gloucester's finest right here in my humble establishment. So, Josh, I don't see you in here much, bud. What's up? You lost?"

Josh laughed. "Some seem to think so. But no, I'm just passing through, playing postman. No offense, Lucky, but I'm not staying." He pulled an envelope from his pocket and handed it to the bar owner.

"Feels like a summons," Lucky joked, lifting one eyebrow. "What am I being served with?"

"The dates and contact info for the lecture you promised me. Let me know if these dates work."

"Lecture?" Izzy asked. "You?"

"Lucky talks to my classes each semester," Josh said. "Keeps the kids up to date on environmental issues around Sea Harbor. The things fishermen—and the fish—have to deal with."

"Lucky, you amaze me at every turn," Izzy said. "Birdie says you have superpowers. I think I believe it."

"Who'd have thought, right?" Lucky said. "You can call me Professor Bianchi if you want. But only you, Iz." He gave her a quick bow, then suggested Josh have a burger and truffle fries on the house.

"No thanks, buddy. I'm out of here. Got things to do."

"Big date?"

"Yep. Hopefully, with a skein of geese flying south. It's migration time."

"Oh, sure. I almost forgot. Be sure you watch out for my most amazing godmother."

"Birdie, of course. She's a great lady. She and Polly keep the not-so-interested people in line so the rest of us can do our thing."

"That's my godmother."

"Birdie and my mom knew each other way back when," Josh said. "My mom wanted to get involved in volunteering around town, and Birdie took her under her wing. And she had a pretty great wing. Mom was an introvert, and Birdie helped her a lot. She told me a couple of nice stories about their friendship, one that defied the age difference. I think Birdie was kind of her godmother, too."

"Birdie said she'll be there tomorrow," Izzy added. "Early, she said."

Josh nodded. "Yep. Best time of day. Sometimes, if the place we're going is good for camping, I grab my gear and go out the night before. It puts me in the right frame of mind. Lets me get my head on straight. Tomorrow we're going to a spot near the old quarry. It's one of my favorite spots."

Izzy shivered. Camping on a perfect summer night, preferably on an air mattress and not too far from bathroom facilities, was great. But not on a chilly night, with rain in the forecast.

"You must be one of the dedicated ones," she said. "Birdie explained to us that she's considered a 'dude' by the group. So what are you called? A twitcher or birder or—?"

Josh gave a short laugh and brushed off the question. Izzy guessed from his expression that Josh wasn't into labels. Maybe labels were trivial to the more serious in the group. Or Josh simply didn't care about what he was called.

Josh took a drink of the beer Sam had put in front of him, then set it down and looked around at the three of them. "So," he said. "It was good running into you guys. Have a good time, but I'm off—"

Lucky laid a hand on his arm. "Not so fast." He pointed to the opposite side of the bar, toward the two women sitting near the long table. "Before you leave, come meet my committee. Talented women. You need to be up on things, Elliott. Who knows, maybe they could lecture for you, too, and you'd never have to teach." Without waiting for an answer, Lucky started off, leaving Josh frowning but with little choice other than to follow him.

"Just two minutes," Lucky said without looking back.

Izzy slipped off the stool. "I'm coming, too," she said to their backs, following the reluctant Josh around the bar and across the room.

Willow looked up as the threesome approached. Rose didn't move, oblivious to the newcomers and seeming to be completely lost in something she and her pencil were designing.

"Josh, meet Willow and Rose, amazing artists," Lucky said. "They're turning plywood into art."

"Hi, Josh," Willow said, waving off the introduction. "We know each other, Lucky." She looked up at Josh and smiled. "How's it going turning our youth into tomorrow's finest?"

"Working on it, Willow."

Rose was deep in thought, her face down and one hand scribbling on a piece of graph paper, ignoring the activity around her.

Josh glanced politely at the back of Rose's head, then over to the sketches on the other side of the table as Lucky explained what they were doing.

As the others talked, Izzy stood behind Rose, looking over her shoulder at the sketches coming to life on graph paper. "Wow. Amazing, Rose. Whoever thought a runway could be art?"

Rose stopped and twisted her neck, looking up at Izzy. She pushed a handful of loose hair behind one ear and smiled. "Where'd you come from? You're being polite, by the way, but that's okay. I appreciate it, anyway. You can't make much out of these scribbles, but the runway will be nice when finished. And interesting and beautiful. Trust us."

"So how's Lucky to work with?"

"Hmm," Rose said. "I think he'll do. Sorry about my being preoccupied, but if I don't get this idea down, it'll sail out to the universe and leave me behind." She turned back to her papers and continued turning swirling pencil lines into something Izzy couldn't quite identify.

"Yes, it will be fantastic," Izzy murmured, not at all sure what "it" was, but knowing what she said was true. Rose was a true artist. Izzy liked seeing her like this, in her element. It was the Rose she remembered as a teenager: studious and kind and talented, and finding joy in her art, whatever it was—painting or fiber art or designing amazing knitting patterns.

Izzy looked over at Lucky and Josh. "Making art out of a runway is quite an amazing task," she said. "Who would have thought?"

Josh nodded in agreement, clearly unsure as to what he was

agreeing to. Then, subtly, he nodded toward the wide entrance door and looked at Lucky. "That's where I'm headed, buddy. This time for real." He thanked Lucky again, gave Izzy a good-bye wave, and headed toward the exit.

Izzy watched him walk away, remembering things she'd overheard in her shop, things from his students, who clearly loved him. But there was some controversy, too—although on the surface, Josh Elliott seemed to be one of the least contro-versial people imaginable. She frowned now, trying to remem-ber details.

Lucky followed her look. "Josh is a good guy. Life hasn't al-ways been easy for him, but he makes it work. He's a great teacher and good friend."

Rose looked up for the first time since she had spoken with Izzy to see who they were talking about. "Hey, sorry. When an idea comes to me, I have to grab it before it disappears. Who's amazing?"

Willow laughed. "Rosie's come out of her den."

Rose laughed, too. "I guess I do get in my own world some-times. But what did I miss? Who were you talking to? Who's a terrific teacher?" She stood, her pencil still in hand, and craned her neck to see whom they were looking at. But it wasn't her sister.

It was a man with curly black hair, striding across the room in a purposeful way. He turned to the side a few times to greet people briefly, his face becoming more visible as he turned.

Suddenly Rose's eyes widened, and her face seemed to change color. "Teacher?" she said with a gasp.

Izzy glanced at her.

Before she could ask her if she was okay, Rose had dropped her pencil and moved away from the table. In the next minute she was hurrying through the crowd, following Josh Elliott as he made his way to the door.

"That's strange. What do you think that's about?" Izzy asked, puzzled.

Willow shook her head. "Maybe he taught her in high school, and she just recognized him?"

Lucky frowned. "If so, I hope he gave her good grades. Rose doesn't look happy."

"I'll see if she's okay," Izzy said and headed toward the door.

She was still a few yards away when she saw Rose tap Josh Elliott on the shoulder. No, not a tap. It was more of a thump.

Josh turned around. He saw Rose and then stepped aside to get out of the way of a couple coming in. He looked at her with a confused expression on his face, then touched the corner of his glasses, as if straightening them to see her better. His polite look dissolved into a frown as Rose glared at him.

"Hey, what's up? Is something wrong—" he began, but Rose's voice cut him off.

"I'm sorry. But it's you that's wrong. Your family. That's what's wrong. I'm so sorry. I don't want to be rude. I barely know you. But please . . . please leave my sister alone. You . . . Our lives just don't mix."

Izzy could hear most of the words, spoken with a tone that she didn't recognize as Rose's voice. Slightly pleading, slightly angry.

"Hey, I'm sorry, ma'am, but I don't know . . ." And then he stopped, his brows pulling together. He looked at Rose more closely. "Oh sure. You're Rose. Jillian's sister. I remember you now—"

Rose ignored his words and continued talking, stumbling on her own words but afraid of stopping. "It's Jillian, you see—"

From her spot a few yards away, partially hidden by a huge wooden mermaid from Willow's gallery, Izzy could see the confused look on Josh Elliott's face, but Rose seemed to be on a mission.

"I'm not sure what—" Josh was trying to say, but the expression on Rose's face stopped him.

Her face was only partially visible to Izzy, but she could

hear Rose's words. Controlled now and strong, but not sounding like Rose at all.

"I'm sorry, but whatever it is with you and Jillian, it can't be." Her voice lifted with each word, causing several people walking into the bar to look her way. "Please, for everyone's sake."

"Hey, I don't know what you're talking about. It's Rose, right? But I can see you're upset. Why don't we go outsi—"

Izzy could see Josh's face clearly now. His expression was kind but confused. As if he wanted to help Rose, like he would if she were a student in distress. But Rose didn't seem to see the kindness in his face, or maybe she didn't care.

The decibel level of a crazy Pete Seeger version of "Old Time Rock and Roll" rose dramatically at that moment, the sound rolling across the barroom, and for a minute Izzy couldn't hear anything. She moved closer, feeling an illogical need to protect Rose, even though Rose seemed to be the one in charge. The one hurling threats, if that was what they were.

Josh reached out as if to touch her arm. "Let's figure this out together . . ."

Rose stopped talking then and took a step away from him, as if his calm, kind words were upsetting her, throwing her off balance. She looked at him briefly, shaking her head, as if trying to put her thoughts in order.

Then, without another word, she turned away from Josh Elliott and hurried out into the damp early evening air.

Chapter 9

Birdie Favazza woke up Sunday morning with a head full of fuzz. She'd awakened briefly shortly before dawn, when a sudden storm pounded against her windows. But almost as quickly as the storm had come, it went away, leaving Birdie with a restless dream about hundreds of gulls filling puddles in the Sea Harbor streets.

But a shower and mug of Ella's strong coffee helped considerably. She'd been wanting to do a little exploring in this area for a long time, and when Polly Farrell had announced that it was this weekend's destination, Birdie had immediately signed on.

"It'll be muddy, Birdie," Ella scolded as she hustled around the kitchen, her jerking movements saying more than her words.

Birdie felt somehow chastised, as if she herself had personally caused the brief but torrential downpour.

"No one in their right mind goes off to look at birds on a day like this," Ella continued, her voice rising. "You'll slip and break your neck. Harold should stay with you."

"You are a dear friend, Ella," Birdie answered. "But I will do no such thing. And although our Harold is a lovely man and knows everything there is to know about gardens and repairs and changing the oil on my Lincoln, he doesn't know a sparrow from an owl. He would be very bored following us birders around. And quite possibly a distraction."

Seeing a speck of sunlight through her kitchen window, Ella finally held her silence. And in the time it took for her husband to bring the Lincoln Town Car around, Birdie had collected her binoculars and backpack, a warm vest and floppy hat, and bright yellow waterproof boots, and was ready to go.

Birdie looked out the window of her ancient Lincoln Town Car, leaving Harold in his own world of catching the news, with an occasional reproof to her that it was a bad idea to go watching the birds after that crazy storm. And his wife was right: he should stay there with her today. Or they should both just go home. The latter being his personal preference.

Birdie chuckled, assuring Harold she'd come back alive. In spite of the soggy ground, the sun was gaining space in the cloudy sky and the crisp air was invigorating.

What Harold didn't know was that this excursion entailed more than the joy of seeing the beautiful birds heading south. She'd been looking forward to this bird outing for days, ever since Polly had told her about it. The chance to return to a place that she had visited nearly a half century before. Leaving things unfinished had always unsettled Birdie. Apologies left unattended. Letters half finished. Texts not answered. Somehow her journey down memory lane in the old granite woods was like that. She had wanted to go back for a while now. And somehow this seemed to be the perfect time.

Several cars and a bike were already in the parking area when Harold drove into the out-of-the-way area called the old granite woods. A misnomer, Birdie's husband, Sonny, had once observed. It was the quarry that was granite, not the woods. And they'd both laughed, knowing that Sonny himself, having provided the funds for the town's main pier, had named it Pelican Pier, although pelican sightings in Massachusetts were rare.

Sonny's words came back to her as she climbed out of the car, her yellow rain boots landing in a small puddle. She waved Harold off and walked to the edge of the road, watching him maneuver the car around and making sure that he actually left.

She gripped the walking stick that Harold had carved for her out of a beautiful piece of hickory and followed the sounds coming from the quarry area. Smiling, she remembered Harold's insistence that she never go "out in the wilds" without his stick. She also remembered his surprise when she had agreed wholeheartedly with him that it was a wonderful gift and she would definitely use it. It was the one piece of birding equipment she had neglected to buy, but the rocky and rutted trails called for exactly that. "You may," she'd told him, "be saving my life," something her dear friend and groundsman was enormously happy to do.

Ahead, Birdie spotted the small quarry, its sculpted granite ledges the perfect illegal jumping-off spot for the town's teenagers. The still water of the quarry reflected the cloudy sky, stray sprinkles of light dropping on the water like starlight. Small plants, living in the cracks of the quarry walls, seemed to lift their heads to the morning sky.

Polly Farrell's voice drew Birdie's attention away from the quarry and to the other side of the clearing.

"Welcome, Birdie," Polly called out over the heads of the gathering group. She waved a sheet of paper in the air, welcoming her.

Birdie waved back, then watched from a short distance as Polly checked out others in the group. Several members stood off to the side, fiddling with camera lenses and binoculars and studying lists. *Serious birders*, Birdie thought.

Betty Warner, who rarely spoke to anyone, waved at Birdie,

too, but with a frown on her face. Betty was very serious about her hobby, Birdie knew.

"I know her from somewhere," Birdie murmured to herself, but she still couldn't quite fit her into a slot.

She sensed tension in the group today, not the pleasant camaraderie she usually felt. She looked around for Josh Elliott, definitely a regular, no matter the location or the weather or the time of year.

Thank heavens she didn't see Henry Staab in the group. If he had come, she'd somehow have had to call Harold to come get him and take him and his already injured ankle home.

In the distance, the green sea pounded against the steep rocky hill. The group was starting to move around, zipping backpacks and jackets.

Nearby Betty Warner seemed to be glaring at Richard Brooks with a deeper frown than the one she had afforded Birdie. No, Birdie thought, she was *sneering* at the nice auto repair mechanic.

Leon and Harper Mancini, the only husband and wife couple in the group, saw the sneer, too, and Birdie noticed that it caused Harper to frown in disapproval. Her older husband, a serious bird-watcher, just looked away.

"Bad karma?" Birdie asked Polly, who had walked up beside her and was watching the same exchange.

Polly chuckled. "It's no surprise. That small group is always trying to best one another. They send their lists and photos in to different associations that have monetary awards. I think Betty needs the money. But usually Josh Elliott wins. And he doesn't give a hoot about winning. He just sends his list in to have a record of his birds."

Birdie looked over at Betty again. She was probably in her fifties but had a worn look about her, as if life had not always been kind to her. And perhaps that explained the look she'd given Richard.

"But look at our sweet Harper," Polly said, pointing toward the young woman. "She loves all of us, bless her. And she expects everyone else to feel the same way, including that much older husband of hers."

Birdie smiled at the contrast. Harper was young, outgoing, and attractive, nothing like Leon Mancini. But she seemed devoted, always at her husband's side on birding days, even though it became clear early on that she didn't know a crane from a sparrow. Leon, in contrast, was serious about his hobby and seemed to think those in the group were a bit beneath him.

Harper walked up to Polly and Birdie, a worried look on her face. "Where's Henry? And that nice new guy from Rockport? And Josh?" Harper looked around the group. "But I'm so glad you're here, Birdie. You bring magic to our group. Right, Polly?"

Polly chuckled. "That she does, Harper. And you bring a bit of it yourself, keeping that husband of yours in line."

Harper grinned, then hurried back to Leon's side as he began packing up things, ready to walk toward the ocean site.

Polly followed, directing the birders to the bank of boulders.

Birdie again spotted Betty, who was also heading down the path to the sea, manipulating her body around a formation of granite boulders.

Richard watched her walk away, too, a strange expression on his face. He seemed leery of Betty Warner, perhaps because of her string of impressive bird sightings. Or maybe the sneer had gotten to him. Birdie shook her head at her own wonderings, then brushed them away.

Most in the group were now moving toward the path, a short walk to the boulder hill that sloped down to the water's edge. Bird-watching bleachers created by nature herself.

Betty Warner was in the lead, but she suddenly stopped and turned around, as if she'd forgotten something. She skirted the others on the slippery path and headed toward Birdie, the frown still on her round face.

"Ms. Favazza, the boulders down there are wet from the storm last night. You'll kill yourself if you try to walk on them." Her voice was loud enough to be heard over the pounding of the sea.

Loud enough to be heard in Newfoundland, Birdie thought.

Betty continued, one hand now on a hip. "Do not go down there." She wriggled a finger at Birdie, her head also moving. Strands of brown hair fell out from her frayed bucket hat.

Birdie listened and nodded politely, unsure of her role in the conversation.

Then Betty looked beyond Birdie, toward the woods in the distance. Her finger wriggled again, this time pointing toward a barely visible trail that led into the woods. Her voice was louder this time.

"And don't you go into those woods, either. They're dangerous. It's no place for you. You'd be best to go on home. Right now." Then, without waiting for an answer, she turned away and headed back to the path.

Birdie started to call out a thank-you, if that was what was required—she wasn't quite sure if the woman had given her advice or an order or a reprimand. But it was well intentioned, she felt sure.

Then Birdie lifted her chin and laughed. Of course. It was the grocery store. Once the woman's voice had registered with her, she had recognized her immediately: the checkout lady from Market Basket, the one who always reminded her to hold her bag on the bottom. The same lady who followed her out of the store one rainy day, holding an umbrella over Birdie's head. That was how she knew Betty Warner. Birdie chuckled again.

Just like the birds, she thought, she knew Betty Warner by her voice.

Betty's broad shoulders disappeared down the path as Birdie watched, shaking her head and thinking about the interesting group the birds had somehow brought together. Perhaps there'd be more surprises on her bird-watching outings.

She took a few steps away from the path to the ocean, lest Betty Warner was watching to be sure she didn't follow the group. A noise from the thick woods opposite the quarry caught her attention, and she turned, then stood perfectly still as she met the eyes of a red fox standing near a thicket of sumac bushes. At first, she marveled at the beautiful animal's stealth as he stood there for a long moment, looking at her. When his look didn't falter, Birdie shifted her stance, feeling some discomfort, as if the animal was connecting with her in some way.

Finally, the fox turned and walked slowly back into the dark woods.

Birdie watched until he had completely disappeared. His look stayed with her long after he had disappeared.

Chapter 10

Birdie stood quietly, watching through her binoculars as the bird-watchers settled on the boulders, their heads turned toward the sky and binocs held tight. The clouds were thick, but that certainly wouldn't stop the birds' migration. However, Betty Warner was right: the slippery rocks might well stop Birdie. She had intended to explore the woods after watching the migration, but maybe this was the time to do it.

There were plenty of birds to see in the woods. Perhaps a red fox to follow. And most hopefully, there'd be memories to revisit, ones that still filtered in and out of her dreams nearly half a century after they had been born.

She and Sonny had found these woods on an early morning hike fifty-some years before. And in the woods, just a short hike in, they had come across a special spot: a small area with a lookout bench, a huge granite boulder and, just steps behind it, a hidden camping site.

Heaven was what Sonny had called it. And heaven it was, Birdie thought now.

Would it still match her memory all these years later? Or

would the area be overgrown and inaccessible with invasive bittersweet vines and thick, unmanageable weeds?

She looked over to the woods, then gave herself a satisfied nod and walked over to the path Betty Warner had warned her away from.

It pleased her that the once hidden path still appeared less trafficked than the others in the woods. She headed in, her walking stick leading the way. Overgrown roots crisscrossed the path like a giant's arthritic fingers. The uneven terrain made Birdie cautious but also invigorated and nostalgic, as she remembered the times she'd had Sonny's ready arm to steady her.

Raindrops from the canopy of trees above her fell onto her floppy hat, but she barely noticed as she continued on, breathing in the damp air. Her rain boots made gentle sucking sounds as she stepped through the rain pools along the path, sending tiny critters skittering away from their quick drink.

A short distance farther, she stopped to look up into the pine trees and to listen to the morning sounds.

"Bird-watching is half listening," Josh Elliott had told her. And for Birdie, who did her listening through hearing aids, being alone to listen was a necessity.

First, she discerned the witchety-witchety-witchety song of a yellowthroat, high up in a tree. Then, with her face lifted high, she heard the lovely clean whistle of a northern cardinal. Josh had called the sounds the "chorus of dawn," and Birdie placed a palm on her smile, restraining herself from joining the choir.

If her memory was correct, she was already close to the lookout area. She wondered briefly if the whole thing could have been a mirage. Or a memory created out of a dream.

But it was neither. Around a curve in the path, the trees seemed to disappear, and Birdie stepped into a small clearing. The giant granite boulder was there, filling half the space, and in front of it, a smooth stone bench invited hikers to rest. The woods hugged the area on three sides, but on the other, a majestic panorama of the Atlantic Ocean opened up. She soaked in the view, then finally turned away and walked around the boulder, then back into the woods, her heart beating faster.

So far, her memories were intact. But she hadn't yet reached Sonny's heaven.

Birdie tested the wet path gingerly, prodding it with the tip of her walking stick. Then she continued slowly on a dark path, tangled branches blocking out the dim morning light, and for the first time, Birdie wondered about her decision to come alone.

But before her thoughts came together, she stopped suddenly, holding her breath.

The tall branches gave away. And just yards ahead of her, a dense haze blanketed a small, perfect circle of land.

It was still there, the special clearing that she and Sonny had once imagined a Pawtucket tribe had created. To camp. To feed themselves over a fire. To rest.

She and Sonny had done exactly that.

And today, all these many years later, it was laid out almost exactly as her memory had pictured it, seemingly untouched by time.

A circle of tall beech trees guarded the intimate space. In the center was the firepit, ready to warm campers, to heat soup and kabobs. Birdie squinted into the shadowy area, making out the outline of the campfire, imagining it ready to light. She peered through the fog, then took a few careful steps forward. The mud stuck to the bottom of her boots, forcing a wobbly gait.

A step later she nearly lost her balance on a soggy mound, hidden in the uncertain light. She jumped, startled, then leaned forward and squinted down at an old collapsed pile of canvas, its crevices holding puddles of water.

An old tent, she supposed, feeling an unexpected twinge, as if the thought of other humans in this space was somehow wrong. Then she shook away the silly thought. Sonny had called it heaven, after all. Surely others would have been welcome.

She could see the firepit more clearly now and breathed in slowly, as if she could almost smell the cedar embers.

Suddenly, her eyes opened wide. She frowned, paused, and then looked over at the rock-lined pit. The scent wasn't in her memory. It was coming from the now-sodden firepit.

Her heartbeat quickened, and she looked around sharply. Then shook her head. Even if campers had been here, they would have been run off by the storm.

She moved on, finding her way to a low wall of granite rocks that circled around the firepit. It appeared to be a long, curved bench to sit on.

The closer she got to the firepit, the more pungent the odor was, like that of a fire put out by a giant storm.

She lifted one leg over the low wall to get closer to the fire area.

In the next second, she jerked her leg back and stopped, frozen in place.

Later she would remember that in that precise moment, *everything* stopped: her thoughts, her memories, her breathing, her heart.

Then, slowly, they all came back, and she lifted herself over the low granite wall, one hand flat on its side for balance and the other gripping her walking stick.

She looked down at a figure, strewn with dirt and leaves and wet with rainwater. One arm was outstretched, and two feet were pointed toward the fire, as if being warmed on the ashes.

The body was lifeless; the eyes were unseeing—but seemed to look up at a skein of majestic Canadian geese flying to the Carolinas.

Chapter 11

Nell stood at her bedroom window, thankful for the rain, which had left a mist over their spacious backyard. It had been a dry summer, leaving the trees and bushes thirsty and somewhat shriveled. The leaves were having trouble living up to their New England reputation. The middle of the night storm would help.

Noises coming from the floor below brought a smile and sent her into the shower. Ben had let her sleep in. But he was up, and the comforting smell of coffee was winding up the back staircase. The whirring of the food processor announced the beginnings of Ben's Sunday morning blueberry scones.

By the time she had dressed, the cooking sounds were joined by others: footsteps moving across the family room floor. Deliberate movements.

At first, Nell assumed it was the Perrys. Izzy, Sam, and little Abby loved Ben's Sunday scones, and they were expert at dropping in about the time the pastries would be coming out of the oven. They also knew he'd have made plenty of extras, as was the Endicott way.

But as she headed toward the stairs, instead of the expected cheerful giggling of her grandniece, somber voices filtered through the morning air.

She hurried down the stairs and into the kitchen.

Birdie and Tommy Porter, a young Sea Harbor police detective, stood at the kitchen counter, their postures stiff.

Tommy was nearly family to Ben and Nell, having grown up just down the street. He had mowed their lawn all through high school. But his appearance today in slacks and a jacket, not his usual worn jeans, with a grim expression on his youthful face, put Nell on alert. She looked down and noticed mud on the cuffs of his slacks.

Then she looked at Birdie's pale face. And without a word, she moved across the room and wrapped her arms around her dearest friend.

Tommy nodded at Nell, as if giving affirmation that Birdie needed exactly what Nell had given to her.

"It's been a difficult morning," Tommy began. And then he added quickly, "But Birdie's fine."

Birdie nodded. "Yes, I am. But our bird outing ended earlier than planned. There was an accident—"

"What?" Nell said, urgency in her voice. "What happened? Birdie?" Her mind immediately checked all the possibilities. Harold, Birdie's driver, had been in an accident, someone had slipped on the boulder hill, or—

"I'm really fine, Nell. I'll explain. But not until I sit down and have a cup of Ben's coffee. A glass of water would also help." She managed a small smile.

Birdie had felt stiff when Nell hugged her. Her dear, calm, loving friend wasn't fine, no matter what she said.

"Sitting is good," Birdie said, planting her small body on one of the tall kitchen stools. She managed another assurance as to her well-being.

Ben had already poured steaming mugs of coffee for all of

them and passed them around the island. He brought out a small bottle of Baileys and nodded to Birdie. "You look like you might need a splash," he said.

"I love you, Ben Endicott," she said. "But no thank you."

Tommy took a huge swallow of coffee, then dove in with a brief explanation. "Birdie was out at the old granite woods area with that bird-watching group." He paused briefly, then went on. "The boulders near the sea were slippery from the rain and waves, so she wisely went off by herself, taking her own bird-watching hike in the woods. That's when she came upon an accident. A bad one. A man had fallen in the woods, near what looked like an old campsite. He was dead."

Nell's quick intake of breath was audible.

Birdie, looking more composed now, spoke up quickly. "I knew the area. It was a place Sonny and I had once enjoyed. I wanted to see if it was still there. It was. But so was someone else. The poor man may have had a heart attack or stumbled and hit his head. For a brief moment, I thought he was just sleeping. But it was muddy and cold out there, and not a very good spot in which to sleep."

"Cell phone reception isn't great out there, either," Tommy said, "but Birdie managed to find a spot and called nine-one-one. Chief Thompson asked me to ride out with him. We thought it was probably someone homeless, alone in the woods. The chief is still there with the medical examiner, covering all the bases."

"Bases?" Ben said.

"How he fell. Time of death. Protocol. Like Birdie said, it was wicked muddy out there, not a good place."

Ben pulled a tray of scones from the oven and slid them onto a plate. "Was it a homeless person like you thought? There are plenty of out-of-towners around for peeper season. And people like to camp near the quarries."

It was the question on Nell's mind, too. But from Birdie's

demeanor, she suspected it wasn't a total stranger. It was someone Birdie knew. She stopped herself from saying anything and looked over at Tommy. He looked sad, more like the young boy who had sat at that same counter, eating her chocolate chip cookies, than the policeman he'd become.

Tommy nodded. He looked at Birdie, then back at Ben. "Yeah. We know who it was. I didn't recognize him at first. He was muddy, and . . . well, he looked different. No glasses. Kind of messed up. But once I got close and the EMS guys moved in, then, well, then I knew him." He took a sharp breath, as if something was caught in his throat.

Birdie looked up. "He was in our bird-watching group. I'd noticed him missing at the beginning of the outing because I knew he'd been looking forward to being there, but I—"

"Josh Elliott," Tommy said. "He was just a little older than me. Birdie knows him. Maybe you guys do, too. He taught my little brother in high school. One of the best teachers Sea Harbor High ever had."

"Josh Elliott," Nell said slowly. Oh, my. The wonderful teacher they'd recently been talking about. Jillian Anderson's friend.

"I shot baskets with him at the Y sometimes," Tommy continued. "He never seemed sick or anything. But sometimes hearts can just give out. Josh was one of those people you don't forget, you know? A little off the grid sometimes, but in a way that was good. It was never for show. Just for following beliefs. And he's not that old . . ."

Nell looked at Birdie. How awful for her to have been alone in the woods and then to have found someone dead. Someone she knew and liked.

"His mother was quiet and lovely . . ." Birdie was saying, as if pulling things out of her memory and trying to put them together.

For a moment the room was still, absorbing the news.

Ben filled the silence with a question. "Why was Josh camping when your group was going bird-watching the next day?"

"I don't know." Birdie frowned, trying to focus back on what she'd seen. She shook her head, as if clearing it. "Actually, I do know. Or can guess. I found him in the woods, near the spot where we were meeting today. He sometimes camped out the night before an excursion, if there was a place nearby. I don't know how he found this place, but he apparently knew about it. He told me that camping out the night before helped separate his week of teaching and his time in nature. That must have been it."

"I can understand that," Ben said.

"I remember that about him," Tommy said. "He loved the outdoors. He took my brother's class on a field trip to Halibut Point once. I was home from college and went along. It was pretty fantastic. He talked about how smart birds were. Made us realize we're not the only creatures in the universe." Tommy managed a smile.

Nell was still trying to imagine the scene on which Birdie had stumbled. How frightening it must have been for her friend. And she'd been all alone.

"Where did you say this was?" she asked, trying to clear her head of too many images.

"Out near the old quarry woods," Tommy said. "We used to sneak into that quarry to swim as teenagers. We'd see bird-watching groups out there sometimes, especially during migration times. The ocean's on one side, and these great thick woods are on the other three sides. Parts of it are kind of hidden, like so many places around Cape Ann. And this one is hilly and can be deceptive. You think something is far away, but if you climb up a hill, it can be right on the other side. I guess that's why we liked that spot."

Birdie listened and seemed content to let it go with Tommy's explanation.

But Nell was watching her, and she knew her old friend through and through. She strongly suspected there was more to Birdie's experience at the quarry site—or maybe in the woods, where she'd come across a dead body—than she was saying.

"I don't know much more than that," Tommy said. "They guessed he died around midnight, maybe one. But if you're okay, Birdie, I better get over to the station. I told the chief I'd check Josh Elliott's personal information and write up a report before—"

The sentence dropped off as Tommy's cell phone vibrated in his pants pocket. He pulled it out and stepped over near the deck doors to answer it.

Ben refreshed the coffee, and Nell passed another scone to Birdie, then realized she hadn't touched the first one.

"Jillian Anderson is a friend of Josh's," Nell said to Ben. "I wonder if she knows what's happened."

Ben frowned. "It's early, but who knows—"

Tommy turned around, interrupting Ben. "Sorry to interrupt," he said, reaching for the keys he'd dropped on the kitchen island. "I have to run."

Nell frowned, disturbed by the look on the young man's face and the change in his voice. The sadness about Josh's death that they'd seen on his face earlier had been replaced by a grim, concerned, and professional look.

"It's never an easy job," he mumbled, more to himself than to the others, and then, with a half-hearted wave, he excused himself and hurried out of the house.

Chapter 12

Izzy was alone in her shop that Sunday morning, partially hidden from view behind a table as she rummaged through a new box of needle sets, when Jillian Anderson, a knitting bag slung over one shoulder and her cell phone in one hand, walked through the door.

"Hey, Iz," Jillian called out. "Aunt Mae said you'd probably be here. But I can't see you. Where are you?"

Izzy poked her head up from behind a display table. "Aunt Mae was right. Hey, good to see you, Jillian."

Jillian slipped the cell phone in her jeans pocket and walked across the room. "Any chance I can hang out here for a while and get some knitting done? I've been a little negligent about this whole fashion show project."

"Of course you can. I'm thrilled for the company. And I'm impressed with the beginnings of your creation, but I can't quite figure out where you're going with it."

Jillian laughed. "Me neither. I may raid Rose's pattern stash. Though she's kind of peeved with me right now and may nix the idea.

"She's what?" Izzy asked, but instead of answering, Jillian turned and looked toward the front door of the shop.

"But what's with the open door, Izzy? I could be an ax murderer. Don't you lock the door when you're here alone?"

"Lock doors? Come on. This is Sea Harbor, Jilly. You no longer live in a big city full of sin." She grinned. "Consider yourself safe. Now let's catch up. I haven't seen much of you the past weeks. Lots going on in the high school world?"

"The kids are great. Most of them, anyway. I like it a lot, although you're right. I haven't been around a lot. There's a guy I'm working with at the school. And, well, we've become good friends, spending time together," she said, a lightness to her voice. "Anyway, I need to spend a little time with needles and yarn today. And where else can I find incredible inspiration than here, right?"

Izzy waited for a minute, hoping Jillian would backtrack and expand on the relationship topic. When that didn't happen, she said, "Well that's great, Jilly. And you're absolutely right about the inspiration. You're like Danny. He writes in the library sometimes, figuring the millions of words on the shelves will somehow find their way into his mystery novel. And in exactly the right order."

"Exactly what I'm thinking. Surely being surrounded by these amazing piles of yarn will give me a boost." Jillian handed Izzy a bag of pastries. "And these can be lunch. I was late getting over here."

Izzy opened the bag and swooned as she smelled the buttery, crisp kouign-amanns. "My favorites," she said, leading the way across the shop to the back knitting room. "We need to have my Aunt Nell tease the recipe out of Cake Ann's bakery. And I'm starving. Breakfast was, like, hours ago. I'm due for food."

She grabbed a packet of napkins from a shelf near the stairs and headed down into the knitting room. "I have a ton of things to do down here, so I'll keep you company. We don't open on Sundays until closer to the holidays. That gives me good time with Sam and Abby. But today I'm trying to make sense of the mess this fashion show is making of my shop. And Sam and Abby are doing fun things without me. They're headed to the train museum in Wenham. Abby wants to be a conductor when she grows up. Or president. She's not sure which."

She put the napkins on the coffee table, then glanced back at Jillian, realizing she was jabbering to the air. Jillian was standing on the bottom step, intently thumbing through messages on her phone.

"Everything okay?" Izzy asked.

Jillian looked up. "Fine. I was just checking my other life. No big deal."

"Okay. Well, I've got some bad coffee down here and the remains of a fire that I made earlier. Let's sit before we work, get our fingers sticky from those pastries, and make our stomachs happy." She motioned toward the glowing remains of the fire.

Jillian walked over to the hearth and began to warm her hands. Izzy plopped down in a chair across from her. "So, now can I ask what's being created in that knitting bag of yours, and the amazing beginning of something hanging on my wall?"

Jillian glanced over at the beginnings of the garment. "I think Danny Brandley and other writers would call me a pantser. I'm knitting by the seat of my pants, or at least I sort of am. Praying for the knitting spirits to inspire me. And I'm not doing too well on that front."

"Is it for yourself? Someone else?" Izzy thought about the stories being passed around about Jillian and Josh Elliott. Although she'd followed Jillian's love life openly through the years, somehow this one seemed more private, especially since she hadn't expanded on her relationship when she'd come in. But no matter, Josh Elliott was a wonderful guy. And an amazing teacher, according to the teenagers who wandered in and out of her shop.

And although Jillian had said very little about her new relationship, there was one thing Izzy was sure of: Jillian liked Josh Elliott a heap more than her sister did.

"Rose, maybe," Jillian said, looking up from a skein of yarn she'd pulled out of the bag. "This is her color."

Izzy quickly thought back, almost forgetting her question. "Rose? Nice," she said quickly. "A surprise?"

A rattle of the door upstairs and quick footsteps stopped Izzy from getting an answer.

Jillian looked up, too, and teased, "I told you, Izzy. The axman cometh. Even in small town Sea Harbor."

Izzy laughed and moved toward the stairs. "I'm not expecting anybody, but you never know. Maybe it's for you?" she said, taking the three steps up as one. She stopped at the archway and looked across the sales room.

Rose Anderson stood in the shadows just inside the front door.

"Rose. Hi. What a surprise. Geesh, this is my lucky Sunday. Two Andersons."

"So Jillian's here?" Rose's voice was strained. "I was hoping she'd be."

But her expression was anything but hopeful. "Hey, Rose, what's the matter? You okay?"

Rose's face was drawn and her lips were quivering as she walked across the room toward Izzy.

"Jillian's fine," Izzy said. "No worries. She's down in the knitting room." She nodded toward the archway behind her, then stopped talking. Of course Rose knew where the room was. But something was definitely wrong. "Rose, something isn't right? What is it?"

Rose took a deep breath. "Oh, Izzy, it's so sad. And it's all my fault."

She walked past Izzy and down to the knitting room as if it was the last place in the world she wanted to go.

Jillian looked up. "Hey, Rosie. I thought that was your voice." She shoved her yarn and needles back into the bag. "What's up?"

Rose didn't answer. Instead, she walked over and embraced Jillian tightly. "Oh, Jilly, I'm so sorry." Her voice was strained.

Jillian moved slightly apart, took a quick breath, and then looked into Rose's sad face. "Hey, it's okay. Whatever it is you're sorry about, please forget it. You're forgiven. Consider it a blanket forgiveness." She half smiled, trying to coax one out of her sister.

Izzy stood by, feeling helpless and completely confused. She watched Rose collapse into a chair as if her legs no longer worked. "I can make myself gone if you two need privacy," she said.

"No, don't leave, Izzy. Please stay," Rose said.

It sounded to Izzy like a plea.

"Yes, stay," Jillian said, trying to lighten the mood. "Who knows? We may need a referee."

Rose leaned forward in her chair and stared at Jillian, forcing her to listen. "Jillian, it's about Josh Elliott," she managed to get out. "It's—"

But Jillian broke in, one hand up in the air, to stop Rose from going on. Her expression had turned from pleasant to serious, with a touch of anger thrown in. She stared back at her sister. "Please, Rose. Not again. I understand you have a problem with Josh, but you don't understand my relationship at all. Let's not get into this again. Not today. Not ever. Let's just pretend this never happened."

"No," Rose said sternly, shaking her head and sucking in her breath. "Listen to me, Jilly." Then she caught her breath, looking as if she'd suffocate from the news if she didn't release it in the next breath.

"Josh Elliott is dead," she said, sinking back into the faded chair, as if all the air inside her body had been released and there was nothing left in her—or of her.

"Just let go of it, Rose," Jillian said sternly.

Izzy froze. She could see from the look on Rose's face that

she wasn't talking about a sisterly misunderstanding. Or the death of a friendship or relationship or anything so metaphorical. "Jillian," Izzy said slowly, "I don't think you're hearing what Rose is telling you." Then she looked over at Rose.

Jillian froze. "Rose? What are you talking about? Why are you here?"

Rose straightened up and tried to pull herself together.

"Josh was found in the woods this morning. He . . . he died last night."

And then she seemed to lose her ability to talk as huge tears rolled down her cheeks.

Jillian stared at her sister. "Died? No, Rosie. You're absolutely wrong. I saw him last night. He's not dead."

Izzy grabbed some bottles of water and handed them over, then sat down on the hearth, her elbows on her knees. Stunned. She'd seen Josh last night, too. Alive and well and looking forward to watching birds.

"He was going . . ." Jillian pulled her phone out and stared at it again. Frantically, she tapped in a number. She waited a minute, and then she looked up, shoving the cell phone back into her pocket. "He's my closest friend," she said, looking at Izzy with hope in her eyes, as if that ensured this was all a terrible mistake. "I . . . I love him."

Izzy tried to sort through it all. Was it true? How would Rose know this? Surely Sam would have called if it had been on the news. "Rose, are you sure? How do you know this?"

Rose took a deep breath and wiped her face with her coat sleeve. "Lucky Bianchi. We were working on our design for that runway. Willow and me. And Lucky. He got a call." She rubbed her eyes. "All he knew was that Birdie Favazza found Josh. I'm so sorry, Jillian. I am so, so sorry . . ."

Chapter 13

It was almost noon when Birdie and Nell finally left the Endicotts' home and walked down to Harbor Road. The front door to Izzy's yarn shop was slightly ajar when they arrived. On a normal Sunday, they wouldn't have thought twice about the door being ajar—or at least unlocked. Izzy or Mae would have come in to straighten shelves or organize supplies for the week's classes or simply to tally receipts. Today they closed the door tightly behind them, and their surprise was tinged with concern. It wasn't a day for unlocked doors.

The two women looked around the empty room, trying to determine who was there and where. For a minute they stood in complete silence.

Their day, their world, had changed.

It was the call Ben received from Chief Thompson later that morning, once the body had been examined and removed from the woods, that had changed the day from bad to terrible. A call Jerry Thompson had made out of friendship, a call to his friend Ben with news that he needed Ben to share with Birdie Favazza, knowing the news would be passed along to her with care.

As sometimes happens in small towns, even minor events, like cats being stuck in trees, become news. And when there's *real* news, news that can easily become coated with rumors as thick as chocolate frosting, the news can become a wildfire. And the hope was to talk with those who were concerned before the rumors were lit.

"Aunt Nell," Izzy said, coming up the stairs and seeing her aunt. "I'm so glad you're both here."

And then she looked more closely at her aunt's face, and at dear Birdie standing beside her, looking even smaller than usual.

"Mae thought Jillian might be here at your shop?" Nell said.

Izzy nodded. "She is. Rose came over to tell us about Josh's accident. It's so terribly sad. Jillian is heartbroken—"

"Rose is here?" Birdie said, surprise in her voice.

Izzy nodded. "She told us you that you found Josh, Birdie. How awful for you. I'm so sorry."

Birdie responded by patting Izzy's arm. "I'll be all right. But there are so many who won't be, I'm afraid. Not for a long time."

Izzy started to turn toward the steps, then paused. "Sam and I talked to Josh at Lucky's Place last night," Izzy said. "Somehow that makes it even more surreal. He was alive and energetic. Looking forward to things in his life. And then a few hours later, to just . . . die. It's not right."

Birdie and Nell were silent.

Birdie glanced toward the knitting room. "Let's go down with Jillian and Rose."

At first, it looked to Nell like the knitting room was empty, but then they saw Rose and Jillian standing side by side over at the back window, not touching or talking as they looked out at the waves lapping up against the seawall below.

It was Jillian who turned around at the sound of their footsteps. Her face was expressionless at first, and then she saw Birdie.

Without a word, she walked over and wrapped her arms around her. Birdie responded, pulling her close.

When Jillian finally pulled away, her cheeks were damp.

"Let's sit," Birdie said softly.

They all moved to the comfortable chairs near the fire. The knitting room was a place like home—a place that would hold them safely, or at least that had always been the hope.

Jillian sat on the raised stone hearth, looking into the fire, which Izzy had revived. Purl, the shop calico cat, leapt up next to her and pressed her furry form gently against Jillian's side, as if sensing that that was the place where she was needed most.

"Rose said he fell or had a heart attack or something," Jillian said to no one in particular. She looked over at her sister. "But he was so healthy . . ."

"I guess that's what people think when something like this happens to someone who shouldn't be dead. Not suddenly like that," Rose said.

"Yes," Birdie said. "That's how it seemed . . ." Birdie stopped for a moment and took a deep breath.

Nell looked at her friend. She could read Birdie's thoughts: *Pull off the Band-Aid. One quick movement. Dragging out bad news is senseless and even more painful.*

And she could feel her young friend's pain.

Birdie leaned forward, her arms resting on her knees, her eyes on Jillian. Her face kind and caring. But her voice was calm and definite when she spoke. Not leaving room for suppositions or denials.

"The police are looking into Josh Elliott's death as a possible homicide," she said. "They suspect someone may have killed him."

The day seemed to fall apart in that minute, not in little

pieces, but in huge swatches, which would soon rain down over the whole town.

A death. A murder. The loss of a well-loved teacher. Emotions were tugged loose and scattered in the chilly ocean air, as if not sure where to land. It would be days before they would find their right place.

Chapter 14

Once back in her home, Nell found herself at loose ends. Ben had texted that he, Sam, and their grandniece Abby were headed to the boat dock. It was too chilly for a sail, but there were always things to do, and Abby loved sitting behind the wheel and playing captain. She also loved the apple cider donuts that her doting uncle Ben would pick up on the way.

Nell knew the other reason they were going to the boat. It was to stay out of the mainstream. To not be forced to respond to the news of a favorite Sea Harbor teacher's death as it snaked its way through the town. Although small, the group of birders who were gathered and questioned at the site was enough to ensure that one would leak the news—what little there might be.

The raw newness of death was difficult to absorb and put into words.

No, Nell corrected herself, it was impossible. Yet words were the only means people had to try to get their arms around it. To understand it. The incredible need to understand why and how things happened, so there was no mystery left, no uncertainty—nothing to be afraid of. So people talked, no matter how well intentioned. And the words were most often, without intent to be, meaningless. Sometimes even dangerous.

She completely understood Sam and Ben's need to avoid people, even friends. It was the need to avoid responding about a needless, unnatural, tragic death. The pat words that said nothing. She felt the same need acutely.

She rummaged around in the kitchen, then checked her email. And went through three-day-old mail. But after a couple hours, her restlessness had only grown.

She glanced at the clock, surprised that the day was almost over, the sky darkening. She looked around her kitchen and family room. It felt empty. *She* felt empty. She didn't need conversation, but she very much needed a distraction.

Maybe it was because of the normalcy of exercising or going to a place where she could be alone with her thoughts. Or maybe it was simply that her body told her what it needed at that moment. But whatever the reason, she pulled on a pair of sweats, grabbed her towel and a warm jacket, and headed to the YMCA.

As Nell had hoped, the Y was less crowded at this hour on a Sunday. It was a place where she could be alone and not be alone at once. She walked into the pool area, breathing in the pungent smell of chlorine that lay on top of the calm blue water. A woman walking in ahead of her wrinkled her nose at the familiar odor. But Nell loved it. The smell was comforting, the smell of her Kansas childhood, of wet towels and bodies and laughter at the neighborhood pool, of safety and lazy, carefree days. Calming and gentle.

Nell dropped her towel at the end of an empty corner lane, pulled on her goggles, and dove into the pool. She was only an adequate swimmer, but gliding through the still water always felt right and good and perfect. She swam without thought, her strokes moving her body smoothly as she tried to clear her mind of the morning hours. Of her dear friend coming across a body in a deserted wood.

Of murder.

After a respectable number of laps and her body feeling the welcome exertion, Nell stopped and pulled herself up on the edge of the pool, her legs left dangling in the water, and took off her goggles. She breathed deeply. In and out.

In the adjacent lane, a young woman swam silently, her movements so precise they caused barely a ripple, long arms slicing through the water silently. Nell watched the graceful movements, the arms moving in slow motion—controlled and smooth.

The woman paused at Nell's end of the pool, one hand on the edge. She glanced over at the next lane, looked away, and then looked back again. "Nell?" she said. "Is that you?"

Nell was taken aback. Somehow being in the pool meant anonymity. It was often difficult to recognize people.

But Jillian Anderson's voice overrode the disguise of swim caps and goggles and wet hair.

"Jillian, I didn't realize it was you," Nell said, surprised. She tugged off her swim cap and shook her hair loose. "I guess we both needed a swim today."

Jillian nodded and pulled herself up onto the edge of the pool. Her voice soft, she said, "Josh used to talk about the comfort of water. He told me it was because we had blue minds."

For a moment they sat still, letting the silence and Josh's words settle between them. Comfortable and comforting at once.

Finally, Jillian turned toward Nell, her fingers curled around the pool edge. "Nell, do you think Josh suffered?" she asked.

Her eyes were moist; whether from the pool or her heart, Nell couldn't be sure. Jillian's question struck her. It was one of caring. Not curiosity. Not anger over the crime, not asking for details. Nothing other than wanting her close friend not to have suffered.

Nell reached over and laid her hand on top of Jillian's. "No, Jillian. I don't think he did."

Nell's answer was a definitive one, yet one they both knew was simply what they needed to believe. It was the right answer to the question at that moment, no matter how credible.

"Rose and I gave Birdie a ride home today, after you left Izzy's shop," Jillian said. "I'm so sorry for her having to go through this. She has such an open heart. Josh told me once that his mother told him that Birdie Favazza was the soul of Sea Harbor. Wise and kind and accepting. Finding Josh like that must have been so difficult for her."

She paused for a long time, and then she said so softly Nell had to lean closer to hear the words.

With anguish in her voice, Jillian said, "Yet, somehow . . . somehow I'm comforted that it wasn't a stranger who found him. If there was any part of him that could still sense, still be aware, anything . . ." She stopped for a second, her words stuck in her throat, and then she finished. "Well, if there was any second of consciousness left, I am grateful it was Birdie who was there with him."

Jillian's eyes met Nell's for a minute, as if there was more she wanted to say, and then she looked back into the pool water. "Did you know Josh?" she asked.

"I must have met him at events over the years. He was an amazing teacher, I've heard. A good man."

Jillian nodded. "Yes." Her legs began moving in the water with her thoughts. She watched the small waves ripple out until they disappeared, and then she said softly, her eyes still on the water, "He is also a kind and honorable and amazing man. I've never met anyone like Josh. There has never been anyone like him." Jillian nodded along with her words. Affirming them.

Finally, she looked over at Nell, her voice immensely sad, "In a decent world, Josh Elliott would still be alive."

This time, when Nell saw the tears roll down her cheeks, she knew where they came from.

"Yes," Nell said softly.

Jillian went back to concentrating on the wavy movements of her legs in the water.

"You and Josh were close," Nell said, not a question, but an affirmation of what she was hearing.

"Close . . ." Jillian's brows pulled together in thought. "Very. Josh and I were friends." She paused, then corrected herself. "No that's not accurate. I have plenty of friends. Josh was different. He was my soul mate. I don't know why or how that happened, and so quickly—it was like we'd known each other in another life. Time was irrelevant. We didn't have to waste any of it getting to know one another. We understood each other in a way that was new to me. It's as if we could see inside each other, never judging, but just accepting what we found there. Good and bad."

She grabbed a towel from behind her and wrapped it around her shivering shoulders. And then she continued, as if needing someone to know and to understand.

"You get it, Nell. I know you do, because you and Birdie have that same kind of unexplainable connection. Words don't explain it well. It has nothing to do with age—I mean, he's more than ten years older than I am. Or circumstance, or even history. It just happens, and when it does, it's a gift. And you shouldn't have to explain it to anyone, no matter how others may interpret it. Josh was simply my dearest friend."

Nell listened quietly. Jillian clearly didn't want or need a response. She needed only an attentive friend. And affirmation. And yes, Nell knew exactly what she was saying.

Finally, Jillian slipped back into the water, pulled her goggles in place, and looked back at Nell.

Her movements showed Nell how weary she was.

And then she said, "And the saddest part is that my twin sister didn't get it. Not at all."

Nell showered, dressed, and left the Y a short while later, leaving Jillian alone to swim as many laps as she might need to be able to sleep tonight.

She drove home, feeling with some certainty that Jillian Anderson would be all right.

Nell wasn't at all sure about her sister Rose.

Chapter 15

Ben and Sam were sitting in the family room, in front of the fire, martinis in hand, watching Abby building a racetrack for her dolls.

Nell walked in from the garage and took in the scene, grateful at the signs of life in her home. Her heart lifted. This was the best medicine—people she loved, the cozy family room, the smell of pine logs on the grate.

At the sight of Nell, Abby was up and flying across the room, then grabbing Nell tightly around her knees. Nell gripped the back of a chair and leaned over, laughing, and cuddled her grandniece close.

Sam hurried over. "Okay, buddy," he said, grabbing his curly-haired daughter and tossing her into the air while Nell regained her balance. "Are you trying to play football with your aunt NiNi? That was quite a tackle. I think you won."

Abby giggled while Sam brought her back down to earth and released her to cling to Nell's side, explaining to Nell that his wife was still at the yarn shop but would be over soon.

Nell and Abby sank into the slipcovered love seat near the fire, Abby now clutching her bunny blanket in her small square hands. The Perrys' large dog, Red, who'd been rescued and adopted into their family at the same time Abby had been born into it, lay in front of the Endicotts' fireplace, soothing his now arthritic bones.

Ben handed Nell a martini, and for a short time, they were content to sit with Red, listening to the crackling fire and Abby's sweet voice explaining the pictures in her book.

It was so terribly deceptive, Nell thought—this peace and harmony that they had created by blocking out the outside world. While just beyond the closed doors of their home, and all the families settling in for the night, there was relentless, painstaking activity. Police working through the night, examining medical reports, transferring a body, and delving into the intimate lives of innocent people, hopefully to find one that wasn't so innocent.

Ben leaned down and stoked the fire, and they might have stayed there forever, sinking into the peace and quiet, if the front door hadn't suddenly opened, bringing in a gust of cold air.

"Santa?" Abby said, looking up with hope in her huge blue eyes.

"Too soon, pip-squeak," Sam said. "We have to deal with goblins and turkeys first."

A second later Cass walked in, the smell of the cold fall air coming with her. "Danny and I are gone for one day and the world falls apart," she said, wriggling out of her coat. Then she scooped up Abby, hugged her tight, and handed her over to Sam, who had his daughter's pajamas slung over one shoulder.

"Danny's picking up your wife from the shop," Cass said to Sam as he carried Abby toward the stairs and the bed Nell kept ready for Abby day or night. She waved a kiss off to her god-daughter.

Ben looked across the room toward the kitchen. Cass had made her way to the refrigerator and was rummaging around for a beer.

Nell saw Ben's look and gave a weary smile. She hadn't given a thought to dinner—and apparently, Ben hadn't, either—which wasn't the way either of them usually worked. The day was completely off-kilter, and thoughts of eating had gotten lost in the shift in their lives.

Cass walked back to the warmth of the fireplace, carrying her beer and a bowl of nuts. "No worries," she said, as if she'd been in on their nonverbal conversation. "Danny and Izzy are picking up pizza from that new place—stone fired and even sort of healthy, or so they say."

Nell smiled and urged Cass to take Abby's vacated seat. "It's still warm," she said as Cass sat down beside her. Nell gave her a spontaneous hug. "I'm glad you came by."

"Where else would we be? It's so weird that we were all just talking about Josh a couple days ago. And Birdie's bird-watching group. I can't get my arms around it all. Everyone likes Josh. Lucky was hit hard by all this. People like Josh Elliott don't get murdered."

Ben finished his drink and set it on the coffee table, then leaned forward in the chair, his arms resting on his knees. "The thing is, everyone has secrets. Even good guys like Josh."

"Secrets," Cass said, mulling over the word. "I suppose. But if he had a true secret, it probably died with him. So where do the police go with that?"

They sat in silence for a minute as Sam rejoined them and dug into the peanuts. "It's going to be a long night for our men in blue."

"Let's hope it's only a night," Nell said. "But I can't imagine where they even begin."

Another gust of wind, this one accompanied by the sweet odor of baked garlic and onions, and basil-rich pesto on top of burrata.

"Deliverywoman," Izzy called. "Tips accepted."

Danny Brandley was close behind, trying to balance pizza boxes and a bag of salad.

Cass rushed over to her husband to save their dinner from creating a colorful mess on the Endicotts' pinewood floor.

"Good catch." Danny leaned over and planted a kiss on Cass's forehead.

"Does anyone know what Birdie is up to?" Ben asked. "There's a big empty space here without her."

"I drove over to her place earlier to let her know we were coming over here with pizza," Danny said. "But mostly I wanted to see how she was doing. I know Birdie can handle almost anything, but it couldn't have been easy for her out in those woods and coming across a dead body."

Nell shivered at the thought. "How was she?" she asked Danny.

"She's doing what Birdie does best—helping other people deal with the day. I found her in the kitchen with Ella and Harold. Ella was slicing onions for some kind of soup. She and Harold were both spooked at what Birdie'd been through, and Birdie was comforting them. They repeated the story all over again. They were both drowning in guilt that they had let her go out that morning.""

"*Let* her go?" Izzy said. "They—and the royal mounted police—could not have stopped Birdie because of a little soggy ground," Izzy said. "She had felt safe, or she wouldn't have gone."

"That's true," Nell said. "And she *would* have been fine—if there hadn't been a murder."

The reality of the day silenced them, another sharp reminder that they had been trying to block out, locking themselves in a cozy room with a warm fire and people who loved one another. And people who were very much alive.

Ben took the quiet moment to bring plates and napkins over to the low table in front of the fire. Sam took over taking drink orders. Soon the quiet was interrupted only by the crackling of the fire, the crunch of crisp-crusted pizza, and Dionne Warwick's flawless voice singing about friends.

After a while Nell put her empty plate on the low table and concentrated on her glass of claret, feeling the air in the room grow heavy with unspoken thoughts. She took a few sips and then said, "Jillian asked me today if Josh had suffered."

Izzy's eyes filled. "This is hard for her. She and Josh were so close. I didn't realize that until recently. I could feel it in her, what they meant to each other."

Nell nodded. She had felt it, too. Her conversation with Jillian at the Y had left her feeling that there had been much more Jillian had wanted to say about Josh. About her and Josh. Or maybe more had been said, and she hadn't heard it.

"I wonder . . . ?" Nell began, but the sentence hung unfinished in the air as activity outside the front door drew all their attention back to the front of the house.

A knock, then the bell. And then the swoosh of cold autumn air.

Before Ben could get up, Willow Adams had hurried into the family room.

She quickly scanned the gathering around the fireplace. Relief washed across her face. "I'm so relieved you're all here." She looked back toward the kitchen at the other end of the large living area and then around the whole room. "Are the others here . . . ? Rose? Is she here maybe?"

"Rose?" Nell looked puzzled, as did the others in the room.

"I think she's probably with Mae. Or maybe her sister? You heard the news, Willow . . . ?"

Willow nodded, her face sad. "Lucky is pretty torn up about it—as much as one can tell from him."

"And almost a decade of students who thought Josh hung the moon," Izzy added.

Willow looked back toward the front hallway. Then explained that Lucky was with her. "He's on his phone in the car, or he'd have come in, too. He was with Rose later this after-noon. He has a way with her, helping her through some things. I was with them, too. But then Rose left suddenly. Just took off without a word. And now we're not sure where she is. She was on her bike, so I don't suppose she could be far. But Lucky says she does long-distance hikes. Anyway, we want to find her. I saw the cars here and thought maybe—"

"I'm sorry, Willow," Nell said, now worried herself. "I thought she and her sister might both be with Mae."

"No, she's not there. But I'm sure she's okay," Willow said quickly in that way that said, "I have no idea if she's okay, but it's what I hope."

"Mae came over to the gallery, looking for her, because the police had called," Willow went on. "And now Mae's worried."

"The police called about Rose?" Ben asked. "Why?"

The first thought of those gathered in the room was never said out loud. But it was as clear as if they had shouted it to the rafters. A thought filled with fear. There had been a murder in their town. A man was dead. And someone had killed him. Could he kill again? Did the police suspect Rose might be a target?

Willow's eyes widened, as if she felt their fear. "Oh, no. No. I really think Rose is okay. I think she just needed to be alone for a while. This whole thing about Josh, about him being close with her sister, and now . . . now being found dead. it's too much."

"But why are the police calling Mae?" Sam asked. "Why are they looking for Rose?"

"They just wanted to ask her about something," Willow said, sounding protective of, and slightly defensive about the young woman she'd been working with so closely.

But there was more to it than that, Nell could see. And what-ever it was, Willow looked afraid.

Willow looked at the floor for a minute, wondering what to say next. Then she looked back toward the front door, as if she was sorry she had come in. She looked at the people she knew and cared for. And she told them the rest.

"The police called Mae because they found something today that they think belongs to either Jillian or Rose, and they weren't sure where they lived. They wanted to check it out."

Everyone was looking at Willow. Confused, their worry shifting gears.

"A key ring," Willow said. "They found a key ring, and Mae's address was on it. So they called her. Mae said, 'Yes, it sounds like it belongs to Rose.' She had given one to each of the girls. It held keys they might need while here—to the cottage, her Jeep, if they needed it—along with a couple of other things—a silver dog tag with Mae's mobile number and plastic discount cards for the market, one for the Y—those kinds of things."

"How did they know it was Rose's?" Nell asked. And for an unexplainable reason, she desperately hoped it wasn't.

"Because Mae had added a small colored pendant on each, just for fun. The police had found a pendant that looked like an art palette and an *R* on it. But now no one seems to know where Rose is. Mae is worried about her."

And it was obvious to all of them in the room that Mae wasn't the only one.

Willow's voice dropped off, and she took a deep yoga-style breath and released it slowly. Then she spoke quickly, as if she didn't really want any of them to hear her.

"They found the key ring up in the old granite woods, in the muddy ground right beneath Josh Elliott's body."

Chapter 16

Ella resisted Birdie's suggestion that it would be easier to have dinner at the kitchen table along with her and Harold that night. And after that, she assured Ella, she was going to take a long, hot bath and go to bed.

But Ella said no. The bath was fine, but Birdie needed a cozy room to eat her dinner in. She needed a fire, a soft rug, and a view of the night sky, not of Ella's six-burner stove.

"Harold has laid a fire in the small room that you and Sonny loved, and that's where you'll eat," she said.

Birdie gave in easily. She was too weary to argue, and secretly she loved the small, intimate room that overlooked the harbor water. It was originally intended to be a room for a nanny, but when children didn't happen, it became their room for two—a place where she and Sonny shared meals nearly every day, morning and evening, during their too-short married life. With the table just big enough for the two of them, a small fireplace, and seascape paintings on the wall, the room became a soft, loving blanket. It was exactly what she needed tonight.

The sky was already dark when Birdie settled down at the table. A bowl of French onion soup sat in front of her, sending up a fragrant steam of wine and herbs and creamy Gruyère cheese. A basket of Ella's freshly made sourdough rolls and a pot of sweet butter sat next to the bowl. Her housekeeper had also placed an old-fashioned cocktail in front of her, insisting that it was a perfect companion tonight.

Birdie took a deep breath, then looked out the gentle curve of windows that framed the autumn sky. The days were getting shorter, and except for a pumpkin-colored Mars blazing in the east and a few lone stars, the sky was an endless black blanket. Beautiful and unreal.

She took a small sip of her drink. *And its deep beauty masking reality*, she thought.

But reality couldn't be masked for long. Reality was the death of a young man—a life lost needlessly and tragically.

And reality was what would follow as soon as the news created a wider net, capturing the town. Reality was a fact that would cause doors to be locked and suspicion to creep into ordinary lives. It was a fact that maybe someone they passed on a morning walk or chatted with in the hair salon or the deli or bar had abruptly taken someone else's life away.

A murderer.

Birdie tore her thoughts away from the image of a man on the ground in the middle of a woods and concentrated instead on the meal Ella had prepared for her.

With the help of the cozy room, Ella's soup, and the old-fashioned drink, she might be able to keep reality at bay for a short while longer.

When the doorbell rang, Birdie looked up, startled at the intrusion into the quiet. She hadn't heard a car drive up. She could hear Ella shuffling to the front door, most likely planning to send whoever it was—probably neighborhood kids selling raffle tickets—on their way. She would explain kindly but in her matter-of-fact way that it was dinnertime, and not an appropriate hour for solicitations.

Minutes later, a murmur of voices floated down the hallway. Ella appeared in the dining room doorway, but not alone. A young woman, partially hidden in the shadows, stood behind her. She was holding a bike helmet in one hand.

"I'm sorry, Birdie," Ella began hesitatingly. "I didn't want to disturb you, but I thought you'd want to . . ."

The woman behind Ella shifted into view, and Birdie stood up immediately, her drink sloshing over its rim and onto the table.

"Rose, dear," she said, "please come in." She walked over and gave Rose Anderson a hug, something she suspected Ella had wanted to do also once she saw the sad look on Rose's face.

Jillian bought a sandwich from a small café next door to the Y and climbed into her Jeep, then drove out of the parking lot and headed north.

She couldn't go back to Aunt Mae's, where there'd be someone who would love to sit with her, to give her a hug, to listen. She knew her aunt wanted to know everything about her life, especially about Josh Elliott. But she couldn't do that tonight. Not right now. She couldn't share her Josh. She just needed to hold him close.

Jillian knew how much her aunt Mae wanted to take her and Rose's parents' place as best she could. Which was the farthest thing in the world Jillian wanted or needed. She'd been smothered with her own mother's concern her whole life. She knew Rose had suffered, too, being assigned the role of protector, of making her twin sister's life "safe." A role she knew deep down Rose resented as much as she did. That kind of protection made no sense; it was purely a product of her mother's paranoia.

Somehow, she and Rose had survived. Or at least she had,

she thought now, suddenly not at all sure what damage it had done to her sister.

But in this moment, all Jillian wanted to do was call Josh. To tell him that her best friend had died. To have him come to her and sit with her, his arms wrapped tightly around her, making her safe. To look at the stars with her and help her find something there that made sense.

And to have him help her heal.

The tears began as she drove along the ocean, and then, without conscious intent, she turned onto a familiar road and began driving up a forested hill. The tears came more freely as she neared the top. She pulled into the low-lit parking area and fumbled her way out of the car. Her tears turned to sobs as she ran along the dimly lit path and turned in between the neat rows of green. Then, finally, her body collapsed onto the cold ground, her palms flat on the granite gravestone.

Her voice was hoarse and thick.

"Oh, Daddy," she sobbed. "When did our lives fall apart?"

Birdie sensed that Rose was about to break in half. She looked younger and more vulnerable than when she last saw her. And she looked so terribly sad. A sadness so thick it would be difficult to break through it.

Birdie took her coat and helmet and set them aside. "I hope this helmet goes with a bicycle and not the other vehicle," she said. "They make such a terrible racket."

Rose managed a smile and nodded, but the sadness didn't disappear.

"I'm glad you came here," Birdie said with a kind smile. She gestured toward the span of windows across the small room. "This view helps me breathe sometimes. Even when there's a nor'easter about to batter Harold's lovely gardens or the roof on the greenhouse, watching nature at work puts me in a good place. Come, share nature's tonic with me." Without waiting for an answer, she motioned for Rose to sit in the dining chair facing the windows, then pulled out a chair for herself.

Rose sank into the cushioned chair and focused on the sky and sea and the harbor lights in the distance.

Birdie watched the tension in the young woman's body lessen slightly. Her shoulders relaxed. Her jaw unclenched, and the soft, intelligent beauty she'd always seen in Rose Anderson began to reappear.

Rose looked up as Ella reappeared with another bowl of soup and a pot of tea.

From the gracious thanks Rose gave to Ella, Birdie suspected it had been a while since she'd eaten. And tea seemed an appropriate match for the look on the young woman's face.

Birdie was also slightly surprised—and amused—that Ella brought tea and not something stronger. But it took only a second to realize why. Ella was amazingly tuned in to life in Sea Harbor. She would surely know from Mae Anderson, her friend and occasional bridge partner, that Rose didn't drink. And Harold, who knew all the Harbor Road gossip, would have told his wife about the unfortunate incident on Harbor Road a few nights before, the one that involved a slightly tipsy Rose Anderson, of all people.

The good and bad of small-town living in a nutshell, Birdie thought. But the good certainly overshadowed the bad.

Most of the time.

"This is just a perfect space," Rose said, looking at a Winslow Homer painting on the wall. "How can you ever leave it?"

Birdie chuckled and buttered a piece of roll. "Sometimes it's hard. But life eventually lures me out. And I'm usually happy it has done so."

"Usually," Rose said with a nod.

"Today hasn't been an easy one," Birdie acknowledged.

Rose picked at a piece of roll, then set it down on the plate.

"I keep thinking of you coming across that man in the woods, Birdie. I can't get it out of my mind."

"You mean Josh Elliott," Birdie said. She was surprised at Rose choosing an impersonal way of addressing her sister's friend. "Well, I'm trying not to think about that. Instead, I'm thinking about the good man I knew."

"You knew him?"

"I did. Not well, but he was in my bird-watching group and a good friend of my godson, Lucky."

Rose offered a half smile at the mention of Lucky's name.

"And as you know, in a town like this, we're all connected in one way or another. Especially when you're as old as I am. Josh's mother was much younger than I am, but we knew each other. Again, a small-town benefit. Age doesn't matter much when getting to know one another."

"You knew his mother?" Rose's voice rose, as if Birdie had said something important.

"Yes." Birdie took a spoonful of soup. "Amelia died not too long ago. She was a lovely person. Generous and kind. I liked her very much." Birdie paused, thinking of the active, gracious woman who had spent so many hours helping others. As terrible as Josh's death was, the one saving grace was that Amelia Elliott didn't have to live through the anguish of it.

"How did you know her?"

"How?" Birdie paused at what she thought was an odd question. Then she wrinkled her forehead and thought back. "If my memory serves me correctly, I met her some time ago at the Bountiful Café, that soup kitchen over at Father Northcutt's church. She was very quiet. But kind and very pretty. We were friends of a sort. Amelia donated not only time but also money to keep the café in business, as it were."

Rose didn't respond. Instead, she turned her attention to twisting her knife through the baked cheese covering her soup, releasing the steamy aroma of caramelized onions and wine.

Birdie did the same, allowing the silence to settle between them as the tangy soup held center stage.

"Jillian is so sad. And I can't help her," Rose said.

"Maybe you can't help her today or tomorrow, or even next week. Sometimes people need to be alone to fully absorb a loss. But you'll be there when she needs you. And that's what's important. She's fortunate to have you."

She could see from the look on Rose's face that she didn't quite believe her—or that perhaps she thought someone as old as she was couldn't quite understand. And that was true. She didn't quite understand the dynamic between the two sisters in recent days. It wasn't because of age. Never having had a sister was what put her at a disadvantage. But there was definitely a cauldron of emotions churning in and between the twin sisters.

"I think she may have loved him," Rose said. Her forehead furrowed.

"Love comes in many ways and colors," Birdie said. Then she asked carefully, "But you didn't like Josh Elliott, Rose. Why was that?"

Rose answered quickly. "I didn't know him. Not really. I thought he was a good teacher when I was in high school. Kids in his class liked him. But as an adult, well, I didn't know him enough to dislike him."

Ella knocked lightly on the doorframe as Rose's comment hung in the air.

She walked in with two plates of warm apple crisp, a curl of whipped cream on the top, and set them in the middle of the table. "For when you are ready," she said, collecting the soup bowls. "It's the most comforting of desserts."

She disappeared before thanks could be given, leaving behind the sweet aroma of cinnamon and apples.

Rose took a deep breath and released it slowly. She turned her attention back to the windows and the sea.

Birdie took a sip of her drink and sat quietly, watching Rose's face. It was difficult to read, but there was pain there.

Finally, Rose looked back. "Thank you for letting me barge in on you like this, Birdie. I don't usually do things like this. I hadn't really planned it. But I should have at least called as I headed this way—"

Birdie chuckled and shook her head. "Good heavens. This is not a home that stands on formality, Rose. You're always welcome here. Even if it's just to have a safe haven. And that's something we all need after a weekend like this."

"Need . . ." Rose looked at the bowl of apple crisp as if the answer to needs or why she was there was somewhere in the crisp topping. "The truth is, I didn't know where else to go."

Rose looked surprised at her own admission. She smiled at Birdie and went on. "And even as a teenager, you were always willing to listen to Jilly and me in the yarn shop. You always made us feel amazing. But this has been such a tough day for you. An awful one. And here I am, adding to it . . ."

"This has been a rough day for you, too, Rose. And there will be hard days ahead for the whole town. The loss of a life— and especially in this horrible way—has ripple effects that touch all of us."

Rose didn't answer, and Birdie wasn't sure if she was even listening. But she was sure that there were thoughts of some sort struggling in her head, trying to get out. Difficult ones, from the look on her face.

Finally, Rose sat back in the chair and looked at Birdie. "Have you ever been asked to keep a secret, a promise that was tearing you up inside?"

Birdie hid her surprise at the question, which seemed to have come out of nowhere. But she gave it her full attention. "A wise man once said that if you reveal a secret to the wind, you can't blame the wind for passing it along to the trees. Is it that kind of a secret?"

"*The Prophet*, right? We read him in college. Some loved it. But I don't know. It's too romantic, I think. Or maybe too broad?"

"Yes, or maybe a wise caution?"

Rose seemed to give that some thought, her eyes moving from Birdie to the window.

"I suspect your question isn't really about me, Rose. We've all been asked to keep secrets at some time or other. Some are easy to keep, and some resolve themselves. And there are others that are difficult to keep for any number of reasons."

"But if you promise someone that you will keep the information to yourself . . . and it seems inordinately important to that person so you agree. Then . . . I don't know . . . It seems almost unethical to break that promise."

The issue seemed so heavy for Rose that she looked older as she talked about it.

"Let's think about this," Birdie said. "Maybe the answer to that question can be found by finding the answers to the unknowns. Would anyone be hurt if the secret were revealed? Or is it something that can't be kept bottled up inside, because it's simply too heavy and might injure the person holding it?"

Rose nodded. "Yes," she said softly.

Birdie was silent, not at all sure what Rose was saying yes to. Or where she was going with this. She clearly needed a safe space for her thoughts. And that was something Birdie could easily provide.

"Jillian and I had secrets when we were growing up," Rose said. "It drove my mother crazy. She was protective of us, of Jilly especially, and she needed—or thought she did—to know everything about what was happening in our lives. But then . . ."

Rose's thought fell off, unfinished. She picked up her fork, fiddled with the crumbly topping on the apple dessert, then scooped up a small forkful.

"And your father?" Birdie asked.

"My dad? Do you mean, was he protective? No. Not like my mother. He did fun things with us, but he gave Jilly and me more freedom. He didn't care about the same things my mother did—or at least not with the same attention. He wasn't a worse parent or person for that. Other things maybe, but not that."

"I knew your dad," Birdie said. She thought about the friendly dentist who'd become her friend. Cliff Anderson was quiet, a behind-the-scenes kind of man who seemed to be more comfortable in the shadows. "Cliff Anderson was always the first to volunteer when help was needed, sometimes bringing you girls. My housekeeper, who stays on top of such things and is friends with your aunt Mae, told me that Cliff often didn't bill patients he suspected were hard on their luck."

Rose smiled. "Yes, that was my dad."

"I was fond of him. Everyone was. I remember one holiday season when your dad donned a Santa Claus outfit because the usual Santa had called it quits. Your dad needed plenty of extra padding. But he smiled through it all as he came into the harbor on a lobster boat, with a handful of elves beside him and buckets of candy ready for the waiting kids. No task was beneath him."

Birdie was watching Rose as she talked about her father. At first, Rose smiled at the Santa memory, and Birdie imagined she was probably one of those elves, she and Jillian, sitting on a lobster trap and sailing in with their dad. But then, just as quickly, the smile faded, and the expression that took its place was no longer readable.

"Birdie, what happens next with all this?" she asked.

"With this?" The abrupt change of conversation had thrown her a bit.

Ella walked in then, saving Birdie from answering a question she didn't understand. She was having problems following the flow of Rose's conversation. It was as if Rose had a string of thoughts and concerns in her head and was randomly pulling one or another out into the open, not necessarily in order.

"I'm heading to bed in a bit," Ella said, "but Harold is around." She looked at Rose as she collected their plates from the table. "He's already put that bike of yours in the trunk of the car. He's taking you home, Rose. Your aunt Mae is a friend of mine, and she wouldn't want you out on the street tonight. Nor do we. So that's that, then."

Before Rose could object, Ella had turned and walked out of the room.

Birdie knew what Ella was thinking but not saying: *There may be a murderer somewhere out there.*

"That's settled, then," she said out loud. "Ella is not one to be crossed."

"I'd never argue with one of Aunt Mae's friends. The ride will be nice. I like biking, though. It's better for the earth, and it keeps me grounded. I've pretty much canvassed all of Cape Ann on my bike since we've been back. Jilly uses that old red Jeep Aunt Mae handed over to us to get her to the high school every day, so I use the bike—and I like it."

"We're kindred spirits. I still have my old bike in the garage, although I think Harold would have a heart attack if he saw me on it. I used to ride all over town on it. But as for you, tonight's not a good night for riding around dark streets."

Ella's appearance had brought welcome air into the room. And in spite of the reality of what had happened just hours before, the warmth of the fire and Ella's apple crisp had worked some magic. Rose looked more relaxed, her face more open, and there was a definite trace of a smile on her face.

Then, suddenly aware of Birdie watching her, Rose put her hands on the arms of the chair and pushed it back a few inches. "Birdie, you must be exhausted." She glanced at the old ship's clock above the fireplace and stood, looking around for her jacket and bike helmet. "It's late."

"I'm fine," Birdie began, but Rose had already slipped into her jacket and was shaking her head. "No. I do need to go. I've taken up so much of your time."

"It's all I have, dear."

"You're generous. But I left two friends rather abruptly and didn't tell them where I was going. Willow will probably be worried if she doesn't see lights on in the cottage behind the gallery. She can see them from her house on the hill. I was . . . well, I was a little emotional when I left, so she's probably on the lookout for me." She headed toward the door. Halfway across the room, she stopped and looked back. "Birdie, thank you. You have saved me . . ."

Birdie walked over and slipped her arm in Rose's. "No thanks are necessary. And I hope you're feeling better. Sometimes food helps. And sometimes releasing thoughts so they're outside yourself, where they can breathe a little and you can look at them more clearly. That can help, too."

The two walked together down the short hallway toward the front door. Birdie glanced out the window and saw that Harold was already out in the drive, headlights on, and warming up the car, as if he were somehow prescient. Or, perhaps, it was because he knew his wife well, and she had hinted that it was time for the guest to leave and everyone should go to bed.

Birdie opened the front door, then gave Rose a warm and prolonged hug. She pulled away finally, and it was then she noticed a few tears meandering down Rose's cheekbones.

"Rose—" she began.

But before she could finish, Rose had turned away and hurried down the steps. In the next minute she was safely inside the old Lincoln, and Harold was driving away.

Birdie stood at the open door, watching the car head down the long drive and around the corner onto Ravenswood Road, disappearing into the night.

Finally, feeling the chill, she closed the door and stepped back into the warmth of the foyer, rubbing her arms.

The vibration of her cell phone startled her for a moment. Sunday nights rarely brought interruptions. Normally, it was a lazy night for Birdie, a night for knitting and reading—or occasionally an Ella-cooked supper with her close knitting friends. But this Sunday wasn't a normal day or night. And Rose was right. She was very weary. She pulled her phone from her pocket, not at all sure she wanted to answer it.

The hello at the other end was strained.

"Nell, what's wrong?"

"Rose is missing." Her friend's words were finely cut, short, the way Nell spoke when the call involved a somber situation.

Birdie answered quickly. "No, Nell, she isn't missing. She's been here with me. Harold is dropping her off to Willow's cottage shortly. Why did you think she was missing?"

Birdie heard Nell's sigh of relief. "Willow and Lucky stopped by a while ago, looking for her. They were worried. And with everything going on, they . . . we . . . ."

"Of course," Birdie said. "It's a night to be worried. I understand. Which is why Harold drove her home. It isn't a good night for anyone to be wandering around." But she heard more in Nell's voice than relief. The strain remained.

"How was she?" Nell asked. It was a tentative question. As if Nell wasn't sure she wanted to hear the answer.

"She was fine, Nell. Or as fine as any of us are, I suppose. Worried about her sister. But there's something you aren't telling me. Why would you be looking for Rose?"

Nell paused for only a moment and then told Birdie what the police had found. Before Birdie could ask, she added, "And that's all we know."

"Oh, my. That poor girl," Birdie murmured.

She stood for a long time after she and Nell ended the conversation, looking out the long window beside the front door. Thinking back over her evening with Rose. It had been a confusing and digressive kind of conversation with a conflicted and sad young woman. She tried to revisit it, wondering if there was any hidden hint of the lost keys or how they had ended up where they did. When Rose stepped into the car, she had looked back once, and Birdie had seen a confusing mix of emotions playing out on her face. Birdie had interpreted what she saw to mean that Rose had much more she wanted to talk about. But maybe the time wasn't quite right.

Her own mind felt clouded, too.

It had been a weekend like no other, with images Birdie hoped to expel from her mind. But she would surely try.

A short time later, she crawled into her tall, wide bed. But sleep took a long time to come.

Images of a body, cold and motionless, in a place Sonny Favazza had once called heaven moved across her mind in slow motion.

Followed by a whisper of a prayer that a young woman could easily explain a lost key ring.

Chapter 17

The two women ran along the nearly empty beach, the crash of the incoming tide blocking out the sounds of their footsteps and the distant gulls' cries. It was a pensive early morning run with stops and starts and little talk.

Izzy was looking ahead as she ran, her streaked blond ponytail bouncing between her shoulder blades. Finally, she said, "It's a horrible nightmare, Aunt Nell."

Nell was slowing down, nodding at Izzy's back. Finally, she stopped completely and leaned forward with her hands on her knees. She took in a deep breath.

Suddenly Izzy noticed that she was running alone, speaking to the air. She stopped and backtracked to where Nell was nodding and taking in another deep breath, releasing it slowly.

"All I heard you say was 'nightmare,'" Nell said, her words coming slowly, along with her breath. "It's definitely that. Except this one doesn't go away when we wake up."

They stood quietly for a minute, catching their breath and their thoughts. In the distance a lone sailboat rocked steadily back and forth as the tide rolled in.

"I feel like that boat," Izzy said. "Rocky. Tilting. Not sure what's going to hit us next."

A frothy wave crashed on the shore as she spoke, then flattened out, the water rolling up to where they stood before sliding back into the sea.

Nell and Izzy looked down at their damp running shoes, then turned and walked up the beach toward dry sand.

"Today's paper took a short story and made it into one that was way too long," Nell said. "The reporter was trying very hard to fill in the gaps without having anything to say. There was nothing concrete for her to write about. I actually felt sorry for the reporter. What a difficult job."

"Was Birdie mentioned?"

"No. All the writer seemed sure of was that there was a bird-watching group in the vicinity. And that Josh had been a part of it. I think Chief Thompson is trying to keep Birdie's name under wraps. He knows she'll be peppered with questions if people know. And she doesn't have any answers, either. It will be news soon enough, I suppose. It's hard to keep things hidden in a small town."

"The whole thing is so messed up. It's screwed up on all sides. I think of the students who need to mourn the loss of a teacher they loved. A man who maybe changed their lives, at least according to some of his students who come in the shop. They need to have their feelings for him acknowledged. Sam read me some of the online comments from students and former students this morning. Their hearts are breaking."

Along with Jillian Anderson's, Nell thought. "But we both know that it's the murder that makes the headlines. Not necessarily that Josh was a good teacher. And you're right—the way he died robs people of that time to grieve. They somehow are forced to put it on hold for a later time. The murder clutters up the loss of a fine man whom people will miss. Unfortunately, now it becomes a search for those who *didn't* like Josh Elliott that will soon be sucking up all the air in Sea Harbor."

"Were there any details at all? Real or made up?" Izzy asked.

"You're thinking of Rose. You mean about the keys?"

Izzy nodded. "That's such a strange thing . . ."

"I don't think that's public. The paper stated only that the wooded area is still roped off and the police are questioning anyone who might have been in the area. It's still so early." But she knew, and Izzy did, too, that early is what matters when looking for a murderer.

They began moving again, at a walk this time, leaving their planned run back on the tide-soaked beach.

"Poor Rose," Izzy said. "I can't stop thinking about her. Do you know why she went to Birdie's last night?"

"Birdie wasn't sure that Rose herself knew. She seemed a little lost, Birdie said. And sad."

"Well, Birdie was a wise choice. She's the consummate listener. But Rose had us all so worried. I mean, Aunt Nell, there's a murderer out there somewhere. Maybe in our town? And Rose is out there in the dark all alone?"

Nell wanted to discourage the thought that there was a murderer in the town. It could be a stranger, someone who had claimed that spot in the woods and wanted Josh Elliott out of the way. A vagrant passing through. But she didn't really believe those thoughts herself.

"It's a chilling thought, I agree," she said. "Birdie said Rose rode her bike over, which makes it worse. Maybe Rose wasn't worried because the Andersons had lived those few years in a big city. The fact that a murderer might be close by didn't seem to be a fear of Rose's. But the thought definitely didn't escape Birdie and Ella. Harold took her and her bike back to Willow's."

"And then there's the key business. Do you think if Rose had been in that woods . . . do you think she could have seen or heard something? If so, she could be in real danger. It's all so scary."

"But why would she have been up there, in the exact place

where Josh died? Birdie was surprised when I told her about the keys. Rose hadn't said a word to her about them. In fact, Birdie suspected Rose wasn't even aware that her keys were lost, or if she was aware of it, it somehow didn't matter enough to her to even bring it up."

"It's such a coincidence . . ." Izzy was quiet for a minute, then shook her head and spoke softly, as if not wanting the wind to carry her words. "You know what Danny Brandley says, something he sticks to when he's writing one of his mysteries. *There are no real coincidences.* Once you look closely, he says, there are always connections. Or, anyway, that's the way mystery writers look at it. But then, I guess they do make up lots of things."

"Hmm," Nell said. And yet, deep down, she suspected that there was some truth in the saying. Which brought back the image of Rose's keys lying beneath a dead body. And she knew Izzy was thinking about it, too.

"Willow called me late last night to tell me Rose was finally back. When she told Rose about the keys, Rose didn't react at all. There was no attempt to explain it. It was almost as if it were a non-incident—as if the keys had been found somewhere in Canary Cove, and not where a man had been murdered."

"That's strange."

"I wonder how Mae is doing with all this."

"Ben called her last night. He offered to help Rose if she wanted someone to talk with. The police will surely need an explanation of how the keys got there, and Ben's pretty good at giving advice. He'll try to call her today."

The vibration of Izzy's cell phone paused the conversation. Izzy slipped her phone out of her pocket and read the message while Nell looked away.

With a text or call came a note of fear. The byproduct of uncertain days, Nell thought with a shiver. How quickly a normal day—drinking Ben's strong coffee in the morning, reading the paper, advising a nonprofit board later or maybe building a Lego city with little Abby—could disappear in a flash. Or at least the feeling and spirit and fun they brought into her retirement life.

It was what death could do. What murder could do.

Izzy finally stopped walking and reread the text before tapping in a quick reply. She looked over at Nell, who was watching a dog gamboling on the beach, leaping over the incoming waves as his owner observed his pet from a safe, dry spot.

"It's from Cass. She said there's going to be a memorial service for Josh Elliott. It's tomorrow."

Nell turned around quickly. "Tomorrow? How can that be? The body won't be released that soon."

"Not a funeral. But a memorial service of some kind, I guess."

"Where?"

"Our Lady of Safe Seas. Cass heard it from her mother first thing this morning. Even Mary Halloran was surprised at the timing of it. She felt a little pushed out of what was going on, Cass said. She's usually in charge of those things at the church."

"It must be true if Mary mentioned it," Nell said. "She knows everything that goes on over there. The prerogative of being the church secretary for dozens of years, I guess. Did Cass say who made that decision? Josh's mother and father aren't alive. And there's barely been time to process—" *To process what?* Nell wasn't sure where to take her own thought.

"No. She didn't say. It would probably be a relative, right?" Izzy said. "I wonder if Lucky knows who the family member would be. He and Josh were good friends."

Nell didn't have answers. The unknowns were building up, and the answer to how high the pyramid would grow before the answers were found and the town would be whole again didn't seem to be anywhere in sight.

                              *   *   *

Izzy had considered not opening the yarn shop that day, but once she arrived to put the CLOSED sign on the door and check on things, she found Mae Anderson already at work, straightening sacks, checking the POS system, and adding paper to the receipt printer.

"Mae, you don't need to be here," she said, shrugging out of her coat.

"Where else would I be? A nod to normalcy is the best thing to do today." Mae looked at Izzy over the top of her reading glasses, daring her to challenge the thought.

But Izzy could see, in spite of Mae's matter-of-fact tone, that her eyes were tired. "You haven't slept," she said, walking over to the checkout counter and reaching out as if to give Mae a hug.

But Mae shrugged it off. "None of that, missy. Let's just prepare for a shop filled with gossip that we will politely ignore, and perhaps we'll have a good sales day."

"But how are you really? How are Jillian and Rose?"

Mae sat back on a tall stool behind the counter and poured two cups of coffee from the carafe she'd brought in with her, a by-product of the fact that Izzy made horrible coffee. She took a long swallow. "I'm concerned, I guess. But I don't even know what I'm concerned about. Rose told me weeks ago that Jillian was becoming friends with an older man from the high school. And, of course, once I knew that much, I kept my ears open, and even though Jillian didn't talk to me about it, I knew who it was. Now that man is dead.

"And this whole lost key thing? I haven't heard from Rose, except for a text that said I shouldn't worry. Someone must have stolen her keys, or she lost them somewhere. The murderer maybe? Good grief. I suppose it should have been a concern for me. One of those keys was to the Jeep I loaned the girls. And my house, though it's rarely locked, anyway."

"But it's all okay now," Izzy said, slightly relieved that Mae wasn't more worried. Her shop manager was seeing things in a more positive light than she had expected. In fact, she didn't seem as concerned as Izzy herself was, nor as perplexed as Sam and the others had been last night, after Willow had come by. Maybe it was because Mae was Rose's blood relative—and somehow the cold facts that the police might be gathering were easily discarded by Mae because she knew and loved her nieces—and any vague connection they might have to a murder was to ridiculous to even think about.

At least that was what Izzy hoped she was thinking.

"Anyway, it'll all be okay," Mae said, "even though I'd hoped to see more of the girls while they are here in town." She stopped, then frowned at Izzy. "Did you hear what I called them? *Girls*? They are grown women, and here I am, thinking about them as girls. Shame on me."

"But you still feel responsible for them," Izzy said. "And seeing them sad or upset or whatever has to be difficult for you. They're your kin. Your brother's kids."

Mae managed a smile. "That's it, Izzy. Cliff adored his girls. And I adored him. He was an amazing little brother. Kind and smart. The very best. Well, you knew him. You know that."

"He gave me this smile," Izzy said, grinning and showing her white teeth.

Mae chuckled. "Well, anyway, with Cliff gone now—" She paused, and Izzy could see those words were still difficult to say.

Mae went on, "And then the girls' mother passing, too, with that awful cancer—well, I think I need to be some kind of a surrogate. And I'm doing a lousy job of it. I mean, Jilly lives in my backyard, and I never see her. I know she's busy, but . . ." She took another drink of coffee and shook her head.

"And Rose?"

"Rose checks in on me, I'd guess you'd say. That's Rose, the protector. She comes around now and then. We even play cards sometimes. And she's invited me to a couple of the gallery shows. She's always been the rock in that family. The one who took charge. Her mother counted on her—too much, in my humble opinion. Sometimes I worried she wouldn't be allowed to just be a kid. Jilly was the one Elizabeth seemed to protect, though Cliff always told me Jillian was absolutely able and capable and smart, and she needed no hovering. No coddling. We can all see that now. She's great. But who am I to say or judge, never having been a mother?"

"Were you and your sister-in-law close? She was a great knitter, I remember. She came in the shop often. She was always pleasant around here and seemed to have many friends."

Mae took her glasses off, then pushed them into her gray-streaked hair. "Yes, she was quite a knitter. Elizabeth was one of those people who, when she decided to learn something, went all the way. And became good at it. As for being close, I don't know how to answer that. She was always pleasant to me. But close? She was younger, of course, and had a whole group of friends from the kids' schools and different organizations she belonged to, PTOs and all of that. So I wasn't that kind of friend. But I adored my brother, so I worked on his wife and we enjoyed each other. We had family celebrations, lunches at the Ocean's Edge now and then, things like that. And, of course, I was always happy to babysit. But Elizabeth was private in some ways, too. Different . . ."

Mae had eased into the conversation and seemed to be relieving herself of some thoughts as she answered the question.

Izzy listened.

"Being a mother was what mattered most to her, even before she was one. It's what she wanted in life. Cliff used to say that she had the twins' lives planned for them from the day they were born. Maybe even before that. I used to think that poor Cliff was sometimes far less important to Elizabeth once she had the girls, but—"

A rattle on the front door broke into Mae's sentence.

"Oh, good grief," Mae said, looking at the wall clock and slapping the side of her head. "It's past opening time." She scurried across the room to unlock the door before Izzy had a chance to move.

As Mae opened the door, a crowd of customers poured in, teasing the beloved shop manager about trying to lock them out and hugging her at the same time. Mae absorbed their happy spirit and teased them right back.

And for one brief moment, Izzy felt like it really *was* a normal day.

Chapter 18

By Tuesday morning, the entire town of Sea Harbor and neighboring environs knew Josh Elliott had died. And it seemed to Izzy and Cass, standing against the back wall of Our Lady of Safe Seas Church, that the same entire town was packing itself into Father Northcutt's church to pay their respects to a man they knew. Or knew of. Or hardly knew at all but didn't want to be left out.

Or quite possibly they were lured in by Mary Pisano's About Town column in the daily paper, which began:

> Sea Harbor is deeply grieving the loss of one of its own, a dear and beloved teacher in our fine high school. Josh Barlow Elliott has enriched the lives of many young people in our town, exposing them to far more than what is written in textbooks. Be it the intelligence and beauty of birds or the intricacies of ocean life, of gravity and planets and vernal ponds, Josh captured the minds of our young people, preparing them for life and so very much more.

Mary went on for another three paragraphs, turning Josh Barlow Elliott into a saint and an educational trailblazer and a man of all seasons. Embellished with things no mortal man could claim.

"I love Mary Pisano, but I am guessing that the Josh Elliott I know would be mortified at such effusive praise." Izzy kept her voice low as people streamed past them, looking for empty spots in the pews.

"And so would some of his fellow teachers," Cass said. She nodded toward a small group of people sitting together in one of the back rows. "I think the woman with the blue hair and chunky fake pearls taught me algebra eons ago. I recognize the pearls."

Izzy looked over at the teachers. They were leaning in toward one another, talking quietly, their faces grim. *But not especially sad*, Izzy thought. "Did you pass?" she asked Cass.

Cass grinned. "There is no algebra in real life, Iz. Everyone knows that."

Over Cass's shoulder, Izzy saw Jillian Anderson walking in. She stopped just inside the double doors, looking around the church, as if she were suddenly lost. Then she looked over at the group of teachers.

The woman with the pearls noticed her and nudged the person next to her. Within a few seconds the group glanced back at Jillian, then quickly turned back toward the front of the church.

Izzy thought she recognized the teacher at the end of the pew, who was younger than the others. An attractive red-haired woman who came into her shop now and then. Midtwenties or so. Just then the woman turned around and spotted Jillian. But instead of avoiding eye contact as the others had done, she gave Jillian a small wave and a sad smile, then slipped out of the pew, walked over to her, and hugged her briefly. When they pulled apart, Izzy noticed that the teacher had tears in her eyes. She spoke a few words to Jillian, then returned to her pew.

At that moment Mae walked up behind Jillian, and slipped her arm through her nieces's. Together they slipped into a pew some distance away from the teachers.

"Well, at least there's one in the group that seems to have some feelings for what's going on here. The others aren't especially friendly," Izzy said.

Before Cass could offer an opinion, Nell and Birdie walked in, spotted them, and walked over.

"It looks like a full house," Nell said. "I think you two found the best place."

"An easy escape," Cass said, "not that I'd ever consider such a thing."

Nell smiled as she and Birdie found their places against the wall.

Just then the organ started playing, and a hush fell over the church as a young priest walked out and began the service.

"Where's Father Northcutt?" Izzy whispered.

"It's the new guy up there," Cass said. "Ma says they're cutting back on Father Larry's duties."

Nell looked up and watched the younger priest. She thought of their old friend Father Larry, who was involved in so many Sea Harbor lives and deaths. Even though the Endicotts didn't belong to his "official flock," as he called his church parishioners, they had bonded as friends years before. The young man behind the altar had huge shoes to fill.

She pushed her thoughts aside as the choir in the loft above them began singing. This was followed by a prayer. And in no time at all, or so it seemed to Nell and the group standing in the back of the church, the memorial was over.

"Almost before it had begun," as Birdie put it later. Prayers had been said, a reading read, and familiar hymns sung. Finally, there had been a short remembrance of the deceased, delivered by the young priest, who, it was clear from his words, had never met Josh Elliott.

Before the recessional hymn, it was announced that everyone was invited to a short reception in the church meeting hall across the parking lot, where the women's society would be providing coffee and sweets.

"Well, now, that was interesting," Birdie said as they walked out into a sunny fall day.

"You mean *interesting* as in 'weird,'" Cass said. "If you didn't know who was being memorialized before walking in, you sure wouldn't know walking out. At least you wouldn't know much. Lucky said he'd called the church and asked if he could speak at the service, explaining that Josh was a good friend. But he was told the memorial was going to be short and there wouldn't be time."

"Your mother told him that?" Izzy asked, her brows lifted. "No way she would."

"You're right. She wouldn't. And didn't. Someone who was helping with the service took the call. My mother had taken the week off. She offered to go in to help, but was told everything was taken care of."

"Well, that was an understatement," Nell said.

"I watched all those young kids coming in. Many were Josh's students, I imagine," Izzy said. "But I'm not sure they received much comfort, if that's what they had come for."

They stepped aside at the bottom of the church steps to get out of people's way as a steady stream headed across the parking lot to the meeting hall—the old grade school, which had recently been turned into offices and an activity center.

"The whole service was kind of sad, but not in the way it should have been sad. Do you know what I mean?" Izzy said.

Nell gave her niece a hug. She felt the same way, even though she couldn't put her finger on why. "We should go over to the reception for a minute or two, don't you think? If there are relatives there, it would be nice to pay our respects. Also, I told Ben I'd sign his name to a guest list."

"That's cheating," Cass said. And then she asked more seriously, "But who are we paying our respects to?"

"To the family? I'm assuming there are relatives here." Nell looked over at the wide wooden doors to the meeting hall, held open today for the crowd. She noticed a familiar figure standing there in his tan slacks, a crisp white shirt and blue jacket. "There's Tommy Porter. He'll know."

Tommy saw them looking his way and waved.

"Hey," he said when they approached. "Sad day."

Birdie patted his sleeve. "It is certainly that. Josh was a good man."

"You knew him, right?" Cass asked.

Tommy nodded. "We weren't that far apart in age, and you know how it is around here. Once you pass thirty, you're all the same age. Josh and I sometimes played pickup basketball at the Y. I'm not sure why, but the guy left an impression on my life. On lots of others, too, from the groups of kids I've seen walking in."

A group of teenagers passed by them as they talked. Several openly crying and others hugging and consoling one another.

"Teenagers are immortal in their own minds," Nell said softly. "Death has no meaning. Especially such a tragic one."

"Tommy, do you know Josh's relatives?" Birdie asked. "We'd like to pay our respects."

Tommy started to answer, but just then, he spotted the police chief. Jerry Thompson was walking away from the church and heading toward his car. "There's my boss," he said. "I need to talk to him. I'm actually on duty today."

"On duty? What do you mean?" Nell asked as he started to walk away. But before the words were out, she immediately realized what he meant.

Tommy stopped and turned back. He nodded. "There's a good chance there's information floating around here that could help us out. Or . . ." He paused.

"Or more than information?" Cass asked.

"Well, yeah. You probably know from Danny's mysteries that the guy we're looking for might be in plain sight of all of us. We just need to keep our eyes open. And ears."

And hearts, Nell thought. *Sometimes that's where the answers can be found.* She glanced at Tommy's jacket and shuddered, knowing that it probably hid "protection," should it be needed.

"You all know me well. So you know I'm not an alarmist, but you're my friends. Heck, you babysat me." He looked at Cass with a half smile. "I want you safe. Not that anything'll happen in there, but just in general. I mean, there's a bad guy out there somewhere. Josh Elliott should be with us right now. Not in a morgue." His voice had moved from professional to personal in a split second: it was tinged with anger and frustration and sadness.

Nell watched him, thinking how difficult it would be for a policeman to keep revenge out of his head when he had feelings for the victim. Tommy Porter was human. But he was also tough, smart, and professional. Plenty of traits that would help him handle the human.

With a quick "Be careful," he was gone, hurrying across the pavement to talk to his boss.

But his words hung there in the air, a black cloud blocking out the sunlight.

"That makes one pause," Birdie said. "Tommy's a good man with a difficult job."

They moved on then, climbing the steps into the church meeting hall, taking Tommy Porter's words with them.

But the words dimmed as they entered the meeting hall. A safe and peaceful place where bad things didn't happen to good people. A place filled with people they knew, with students and families and friends. Not with murderers.

They stood for a minute inside the wide doorway, adjusting to the change in lighting, then walked over to a quiet corner spot to look over the crowd.

"It still smells like it did when I went to grade school here," Cass said, checking out the space that had once held classrooms and school offices. But today it held a crowd of people—many already lining up at the long tables on one side of the room. Paper plates and napkins were stacked at one end, and lining the narrow tables from one end to the industrial-sized coffeepots at the other were platters of muffins and donuts, slices of cake and homemade chocolate chip cookies. Behind the sweets-laden table, several aproned women from the church scurried around, fussing over napkins and checking on sweetener and coffee creamers.

Bookcases lined the other side of the room, with groupings of chairs creating comfortable zones. But most of the crowd stood in small groups, some talking about the death of a fine teacher, their voices low, as if they were still in church. Others trying to make sense of what had happened in their town, to somehow make the fear go away. And, as it happened, theories and rumors also traveled around the crowd, propelled by a need to explain away an unexplainable act.

Sea Harbor mourned its own and held them close, no matter the everyday things that sometimes pulled people apart. There was always a new day that pulled them back together again.

Birdie looked around the room, hoping to a find a relative of Josh's to meet and talk with. Although, of course, she had no idea what that relative would look like.

But instead of recognizing someone she had never seen before, she spotted people she did recognize standing in a group near a side door. At first, Birdie was surprised. Huddled together like a flock of penguins were some of the members of her Feathered Friends birding group.

And then she remembered the group text Polly Farrell had sent out the night before, which included the place and time of a memorial service for one of their own.

And of course they'd come. At least some of them. *The regulars*, she thought. They had all known Josh and maybe were among the last people to see him alive. Surely, they were among the first to see him dead.

She stood as tall as her nearly five feet allowed, looking for Polly. At that moment, their eyes met. Polly's face lifted in what looked to Birdie like relief. She smiled and motioned with both hands in the air, waving for Birdie to come over.

Birdie slipped away from her own friends and made her way around and through the crowd, unexplainably happy to see her birding group. The last time they'd been together had been that awful morning, which now seemed like several lifetimes ago.

Polly wrapped her arms around Birdie, nearly burying the small woman in her embrace.

Finally, Birdie pulled away and looked up into Polly's tearful face. Before she could say anything, Polly took Birdie's hands in her own.

"I'm so sorry, Birdie. How dreadful all this has been for you. I can't believe any of it is real. We were all right there, so close. I've replayed the whole thing so many times in my mind. All the what-ifs." She shook her head.

Birdie looked at the others and noticed they had moved closer, listening to Polly.

Betty Warner had a somber look on her face. Birdie noticed her name tag from the grocery store clipped to her purse and her green store jacket sticking out from beneath her coat. She must have come right from work. Richard from the car repair place was there, looking uncomfortable and sad. Harper Mancini, dressed in black, with a stylish hat, stood next to her husband, his expensive suit and silk tie making him stand out in the group. But rather than looking sad, he seemed perturbed to be there, a scowl filling his otherwise handsome face. There were several other people, too, standing in the back.

And all of them, except Polly and Harper Mancini, looked like they wondered when it would be appropriate for them to leave.

Birdie looked more closely at Leon, surprised at his body language. Of all of them, Leon had the closest association with the Elliott family, and as a longtime employee of Josh's father, he must have known Josh for many years. As Peter Elliott's second in command, he had taken over the family company when Peter died, something the Elliotts' son, Josh, apparently, had had no interest in doing. But now that Birdie was seeing his disinterest—anger?—in the family up close, she realized she'd never seen any communication between him and Josh on bird-watching trips, either. *Odd*, she thought.

Birdie watched as Harper moved closer to her husband, her eyes on his face and her finger moving slightly in a scolding movement. Birdie couldn't make out what was said, except that it brought an even deeper scowl to Leon Mancini's face. He didn't seem to be the sort of man who took kindly to a reprimand. And perhaps coming from a young wife, it was even more difficult. Yet he had married Harper, who, as young as she was, didn't seem to hesitate to speak her mind when she thought somebody was being remiss in his expected behavior.

Polly went on talking, still clasping one of Birdie's hands. "Josh is really why we have this birding group. Did you know that?" She looked over at the others. "Did any of you know that? I guess that would make him our founder. He came into the tea shop one day for one of those healthy drinks I finally included on my menu. I remember the day. He looked like a ragamuffin. Torn jeans, a crack in one of his boots, and a broken stem on his glasses. But what stood out were the magnificent binoculars hanging around his neck. I recognized them—Swarovski EL. The best. I've always loved birds, too, and that very day, over some crazy protein drink, Josh and I became fast friends. We bared our souls as we shared our favorite birding experiences, and decided that we'd go out together the next weekend. It was one of those unexpected meetings that's meant to be. Serendipity at its very best."

"And that was the beginning of Feathered Friends?" Harper asked. The excitement in Polly's voice was contagious. Even the others seemed taken in by it.

"It was. And slowly others came along. We even got a grant or two from avian societies and bird conservatories to help us pursue our hobby. Life is good."

Then Polly's own words seemed to stop as she slipped out of her birding world and became acutely aware of the church meeting hall, the somber mood, and the reason they were there. The demise of a dear friend. An accomplished bird-watcher. Her face fell. "Until it isn't so good anymore."

Birdie had finally retrieved her hand. "But I love hearing that story, Polly. It would have been a nice one to tell at the church memorial service if there'd been an opportunity. Maybe there will be another time."

Betty Warner spoke up unexpectedly. "I was the first person to join the group. And Josh Elliott taught me some things. He was a good teacher." It was said in a blunt way, but with surprising meaning.

"He was a decent guy," Richard concurred. "Didn't know much about cars, but I taught him a thing or two now and again."

Leon Mancini muttered something that was inaudible.

His wife, Harper, took a few steps away from him, as if not wanting to be associated with whatever he had said.

"Do you know if Josh's relatives are here?" Richard asked.

"Josh never spoke about other family to me," Polly said, "except for his dear mother. And his dad, but he said little about him. I know the grandparents on the Elliott side died some time ago. So I don't know. But wouldn't relatives have participated in the memorial at the church?"

"It's usually done that way," Betty said. It was an almost scolding comment, addressed to the unseen or unrecognized relatives.

"Well, no matter," Polly said, "I think it's good that all of us came. Somehow, I think Josh would have liked that, and I hope—"

But her sentence was cut off by a sudden movement. Brushing his way past Betty Warner, Leon headed toward a nearby exit door, pushed it open, and let it bang shut behind him.

The group stiffened in silence.

"I'm so sorry about that," Harper said with forced lightness, her face red with embarrassment. "That's what happens when he doesn't eat breakfast."

Then they all began talking again, easing the awkward position in which Leon Mancini had left his pleasant wife.

Birdie took that moment to say a hasty good-bye to them all and to give Polly a hug, promising to stop by the tea shop soon. She worked her way back through the crowd, trying to avoid eye contact with neighbors and friends as word spread that Birdie had been part of the "tragedy in the woods," as some were referring to Josh's murder, having read Mary Pisano's latest column.

She made her way back to Izzy, Cass, and Nell, relieved they were in the same spot.

"We wondered where you'd disappeared to," Izzy said. "Then I spotted Polly Farrell and figured that was your Feathered Friends group."

"It was. I'm pleased they came. It's strange how something tragic like this can make you feel closer to people. Except for one of them—but I'll tell you about that later."

"Did they mention talking to Josh's relatives? We've been looking, but we're not at all sure what we're looking for," Cass said. "People who look like strangers, I guess. Maybe dressed in more traditional church clothes."

Birdie repeated Polly's thoughts about relatives. "But surely someone planned this," she added.

"Look over there," Nell said, pointing to a familiar figure standing near a bookcase. Father Northcutt, the longtime pastor of the church, was talking with a tall, broad-shouldered woman in a severe black suit that looked slightly tight and uncomfortable. Their faces were somber, and as the women watched, Father Larry patted the woman's arm lightly. A consoling kind of pat.

Birdie squinted. "Hmm. I don't think I know her. Maybe a relative?"

"She's definitely dressed for a funeral," Cass said. "But she looks slightly familiar. I think I know her from somewhere around here."

"I think I've seen her, too," Nell said. "Gloucester or Manchester, maybe?" Nell took a few steps closer to see the woman more clearly, but instead, Mae Anderson filled her view, giving Nell a hug. "Here you all are," she said.

Jillian was a few steps behind her aunt, her face pale and tired.

"I'm heading back to the shop, Izzy," Mae said. "We can't let things fall apart. Would one of you give Jilly a ride when you leave?" She gave her niece a quick hug, then quickly disappeared, anxious to get out of the crowded hall.

"Aunt Mae isn't comfortable in places like this," Jillian said. "I told her I wanted to help at the shop for a while after this. I need something to do. At least I think I do . . ."

Izzy nodded. "I'm going there, too."

Cass tried to lighten the moment. "Mae told me once that funerals and cocktail parties both gave her hives. Give her a room filled with knitters dropping stitches and she'd be a happy camper."

Jillian managed a small smile. "Right." She waved to a small group of students who had waved to her with sad faces. "Those poor kids. They don't know what to make of this, how to handle it. They loved Josh."

"No, and being here probably isn't what they need," Birdie said. "But they will figure out what that is. And you will, too, Jillian."

"Yes. I will. And it won't be in a church hall or at any memorials or by trying to forget. Josh always said watching the sun rise was what he needed to figure out the things that mattered to him. And he could always count on there being one. I shall look for sunrises." She took a deep breath, then released it slowly while looking around the room.

Nell followed her gaze. She seemed to have settled on the small group of teachers that they had noticed in the church. They were eating donuts and chatting in a way that didn't speak of memorials. Or funerals. Or a favorite teacher, now dead. It looked to be more about the luxury of an unexpected free day or what was on sale at the mall. But then she quickly dismissed her thoughts. They were unfair and most likely incorrect. People grieved in different ways. Perhaps the smiles were over sharing happy memories of Josh Elliott.

Jillian watched the teachers for a minute. Then she turned away and said softly, "Josh was the best gift that Sea Harbor High School ever had. And a few of them didn't get it. Not at all."

A few tears began to roll down her cheeks, and she moved deeper into the circle of women, shielding her emotions from the room.

A movement directly behind Jillian caused Nell to look up, directly into Father Larry Northcutt's gentle Irish eyes.

The priest stood directly behind Jillian, taking in the group with one warm glance. "This is what I needed to see—my favorite women in all the world, all in one spot." He then moved slightly and placed a hand on Jillian's shoulder, seeing not much more of her than the side of her head. "You must be Jillian. I've heard nice things about you."

Jillian half turned, wiping her eyes on the sleeve of her jacket. "Oh, hi," she said, looking slightly uncomfortable.

"Jillian, this is Father Northcutt," Nell said, noticing her confusion. "He's the pastor here. And a very dear friend."

"That I am, Jillian, although I'm actually enjoying being put out to pasture for a bit these days. I'm finding it's good for the soul. But the last part of Nell's intro is still intact. We are dear friends."

Jillian recovered and managed to say, "Of course, I know who you are now, Father. I grew up here." She managed a smile. "Everyone knows you. My father spoke of you often."

"Well, now, sure they do. One of the nice things about being a pastor here in Sea Harbor for as long as I have is that one gets to know everyone in town and beyond, no matter where or if they go to this church or that one or the mosque or synagogue, or maybe no church at all. So of course I knew your family, Jillian. Cliff Anderson happened to be not only the best dentist on Cape Ann but also a fine man and a good friend."

The tension began to fall away from Jillian's face at the mention of her father. She moved over slightly as the circle widened and Father Larry became a part of it as he related, with many embellishments, a story about sharing an Irish whiskey at the town fishing pier with her father—and even catching a few croakers in between swigs.

"You dad was truly a good man. And he loved his girls more than you can ever imagine." Father Larry repeated the last part of his final sentence twice, as if sending a message to a daughter from her father's grave.

Jillian listened, drinking in the priest's words. For a moment she was silent. Then she said, "I know Josh didn't go to church, but his mother came to your place, I think. I suppose that's why the service was here. But . . . did you know him? I think he mentioned going over to talk with you once."

The others were silent and uncomfortable, feeling like shadows on the wall, unintentionally listening in on a private conversation but with nowhere to go.

"Did I know Josh?" Father Northcutt massaged his white beard with one beefy hand, his still bushy brows pulling together. Then, instead of answering, he asked, "You cared deeply about the young man, didn't you?"

Jillian was quiet, as if giving careful thought to the question. "Yes," she finally said.

Nell was watching Father Northcutt's expression. He was nodding, as if his question to Jillian had really been a rhetorical one. And as if he also knew—as did the women surrounding her—that her simple yes wasn't simple at all, but was pregnant with meaning.

He continued. "But in answer to your question, yes, I did know Josh. From the time he was a little squirt. But primarily, I got to know him more intimately through his mother, the way we sometimes get to know someone from someone else who loved them. We get to know them through that love, I think. And his mother certainly loved her son, Josh. Fiercely."

Jillian's face was still. She seemed completely wrapped up in what Father Northcutt was saying. "You knew Josh's mother, too," she repeated.

"Yes, I did. Amelia Elliott and I became close friends over the years. Her life wasn't always easy, but she spent much of it doing things for others, and we were fortunate at the parish to benefit from her generosity. But we weren't the only ones. Amelia was a hidden gem in Sea Harbor, and the town is better because of her, even though it's one of those best kept secrets that all towns have."

He looked at Birdie, then back to Jillian. "Our friend Birdie here and Amelia used to dish up food in our soup 'bistro,' as we called it, entertaining our diners in grand style. Your father even showed up now and then and donned an apron."

Father Northcutt smiled at the memory. Then went on, "Amelia was an introverted person normally, but she loved the diners, and they loved her. They even got her to sing for them one time. Josh was there that day, if I remember, playing his guitar. And proud as he could be of his mother."

They were all listening now, enjoying the sweet story.

"Did you know Amelia before her husband died?" Jillian asked.

"Well, yes, I did. I met Amelia early on, several years before that horrible crash that killed Peter, her husband. She was in the car that day, too, you know, and her rehabilitation was a painful one. Josh was a teenager, but he had to grow up fast those days. And he did. He made sure that everything was done for his mother while she recuperated. I visited her often. Being a listening ear as she talked through the loss of a husband. I think she recovered so fully because she wasn't ready to leave her beloved son."

"I wish I had known her," Jillian said softly.

"I don't know you well, young lady, but I know one thing for sure. Anyone Josh Elliott cared for like he did for you, with his whole heart and soul—and I know that to be true—his mother would have loved in equal measure. I am sorry she didn't have that opportunity."

Jillian took in a breath, almost as if breathing in the priest's words.

"Amelia and I had great conversations," he went on. "She had entrusted me with a copy of her end-of-life wishes, things like that, which initiated lots of good talks. She wasn't much for chitchat or for glitz and glamour and expensive toys, as her husband was. She was, as you might expect from knowing Josh, down to earth, kind, and even a little reclusive. We had a great time figuring out the thorny things in life. She'd had some difficult times, but her most recent years were days of pure joy. She was sublimely happy. I can say that for a fact. The stars had somehow aligned. It made Josh happy, too. It was one of those times in life when you have to weigh things carefully, and find your own truth in the decisions you make, no matter what others might think is the proper way of doing things."

Father Northcutt paused, as if pondering how much to say to the young woman who was hanging on his every word.

The others were listening and wondering what he meant.

He smiled and continued, but with a lighter tone. "I've kept in touch with Josh since she died. He was a good son. A good man who marched to his own drummer. And who sometimes was honest to a fault."

Father Northcutt looked around the makeshift circle, pausing at each of the women in turn, all longtime friends of his. Then he looked at Jillian and cupped one of her hands in his as he smiled at her as if she were the only other person in the room. His eyes were warm and comforting.

"See these women surrounding you?" he asked. "You are in good hands and hearts right here in this circle's embrace, my dear," he said. "The finest of fine women. Don't ever forget you are loved."

Then he turned away and walked toward the donuts and muffins, his cheeks rosy, his jowls moving, and his aging eyes bright as he greeted people along the way.

It was only later, as Nell and Birdie were driving the winding road toward the Sea Harbor Yacht Club for lunch, that they realized they'd left the memorial service without seeking out Josh's relatives.

"Or if," Birdie wondered out loud, "there were any relatives there at all."

Chapter 19

Izzy's yarn shop was crowded by the time she and Jillian walked in from the service. Mae was struggling to keep up with customers at the checkout counter.

"Oh, Mae. I'm sorry. You need more help."

"Well, I do have help, though I use that word loosely," Mae said. "Luna Risso has taken over the knitting room. I'm not sure if she's decided to be a help or hindrance today. I hope it's not bedlam down there."

Izzy walked over and stood at the archway, looking down the few steps into the cozy back room. The curmudgeonly helper was guiding and scolding and encouraging would-be fashionistas who were attempting cable and lace stitches for possible runway garments.

Izzy waved at the older woman, a neighbor of Cass's, who had mellowed slightly in the past year, though not completely. It had been almost a year since she had walked into Izzy's shop on a particularly busy day, scolded Mae and Izzy for not managing the situation better, then taken off her coat and announced herself hired. But on her schedule. And only if there wasn't something more interesting to do that day. Like a political rally or a council meeting she could interrupt. Or if Cass's nanny needed her to watch toddler Joey for a while.

Luna seemed to be in a patient mood today, which was essential when dealing with new knitters. And for all her strident remarks, those she helped seemed to love her—criticisms, commands, and reluctant praise included.

Izzy surveyed the group and smiled.

It was what she loved most about her shop—the intimacy it encouraged. The young moms sitting on floor cushions near the fireplace, strangers one day, friends the next. Esther, the police dispatcher, sat near the fireplace, a pile of yarn on her lap, giving Mayor Beatrice Scaglia ideas on how the town should be run. The old library table was surrounded by regular customers and some that were new to Izzy. From the corner speaker a medley of indie hits had some singing along or moving their shoulders as their knitting needles clicked to the rhythm. Knitting was a common bond. And a calming one, too.

Her shop had become a refuge. That was what she had wanted to create when leaving her Boston law career and opening up this little shop those years ago. It was what she herself had been looking for. A safe, warm haven. And even on a busy day, that's what it was.

Jillian came up beside her and looked into the room.

"Would you rather escape to the quiet fiber room with the rocking chairs?" Izzy asked.

Jillian shook head. "No. This is fine. I'll help Luna if I can—for a while, anyway."

Izzy looked at her pale, sad face. But it was clear Jillian didn't want to talk about feelings today. She just wanted to get through it. Luna would be a perfect distraction.

Jillian grabbed a bottle of water from the small refrigerator off the stairway and walked down into the gathering. Luna immediately looked up, then walked over to Jillian and gave her a brief hug, something Izzy had never seen Luna do to anyone except Cass's little boy, Joey. The woman was as unpredictable as Sea Harbor weather.

Izzy smiled and walked back to the checkout counter.

"How's Jilly doing?" Mae asked quietly, packaging up a set of bamboo needles for a customer. "She never really talked to me about Josh Elliott—not that I'd been seeing that much of her. But once I knew his name, I could make a few connections. His parents were patients of Cliff's. His mom . . . well, I knew her, too. Sort of."

"Sort of?"

"It's another complicated story. But as for Jilly and Josh, one day Rose stopped by with this bug in her bonnet that Jillian had a boyfriend who was totally wrong for her. It wasn't like Rose. She's always so calm and levelheaded. Commenting on her sister's relationship didn't seem to be something she'd do, and she spoke about it in such declarative terms. It wasn't an opinion the way she presented it. It was fact."

"She did seem determined about that," Izzy acknowledged. "Was Rose even at the funeral? I didn't see her."

"Yes. She was there. She came with Willow and Lucky. I was actually happy to see she was with friends. Willow says she keeps Lucky in line. They've all become friends in a very short time, working on this silly runway together."

"It's not silly," Izzy said, trying to tease a smile from Mae.

"Course it isn't. But everything seems insignificant right now. Except the things that aren't. I was surprised Jillian hadn't contacted Rose. I thought they'd want to be together today."

Izzy had had that same thought. The twins were close. Or at least they always had been. But somehow Josh Elliott, for whatever reason, had come between them.

At that moment a long string of customers began lining up to have their purchases checked out, and Mae turned away from Izzy, caught up in her job. Her smile back in place.

Izzy walked away, greeting people, straightening displays, and answering questions as she made her way toward her small office. On the other side of the shop, she spotted Laura Danvers, a good friend and an active member of the Sea Harbor community. She and her banker husband were well respected for supporting and contributing to nearly every good cause in town, with education being one of them. But what Izzy remembered when she saw her today was that Laura was PTO president at the high school, a position her friend had accepted this year, when her oldest daughter, Daisy, became a freshman in the school.

She made her way across the room and gave Laura a warm hug.

"Are you doing okay, Iz?" Laura asked, standing back and looking into Izzy's face. "It's a pretty tough time, isn't it? I spotted Jillian Anderson heading down to the knitting room, and I could almost feel her grief. What a terrible day for her. Well, for all of us. Josh was a remarkable teacher. One of the best. The school will have a difficult time dealing with his loss."

"So you know that Jillian and Josh were close?" Izzy asked, surprised. Jillian had seemed so protective of her relationship with Josh.

"Well, I don't know much. But I'm up at the high school a lot. I ran into her a few times when I was there for meetings this fall. Remember back when she babysit for us? Daisy loved her. Anyway, she asked about the kids, so we had lunch and caught up. She was doing great with the high school kids, by the way. No surprise there. She didn't say much about Josh. Just that they were good friends. But you know how it is, Izzy. Sometimes you can just tell. Besides, every workplace has busybodies."

"So other people at the school know? Teachers?"

"Well, Josh wasn't a big socializer. I mean, he was a great guy, but I don't think he went out of his way to be friends with the staff. But where there's a faculty lounge or a watercooler . . ." Laura shrugged.

Izzy nodded. "I saw some teachers at the service. They didn't seem particularly welcoming to Jillian. I hope that wasn't the reason. They also didn't seem especially sad."

"Oh, that group. I saw them, too." She waved a hand in the air, as if dismissing them. "There's a small group of teachers that have been at the school so long they think they have squatters' rights. Anyone 'new'—which means less than a dozen years—is kind of a threat. Although that's a guess. I haven't quite figured out the dynamics at the school yet, but my impression is that Josh just did his own thing. And from what I saw, he was doing a great job. He knew kids well. He refused to let them fail."

"So what was the problem, then?" Izzy asked.

They walked through the fiber room and made their way into Izzy's small office.

"Well, Josh didn't always play by the rules," Laura said, sitting down near Izzy's desk. "He did what he thought was best for learning. In fact, he probably didn't even know what the rules were."

"Not a bad thing for a teacher to do."

"Right." Laura laughed. "Though, from what I observed, it wasn't always a part of the normal way of doing things. Spontaneous field trips, missing important school assemblies, not holding regular parent-teacher meetings. One day when I was there, his class missed an all-school pep rally because there was a bird migration that he wanted them to see."

Izzy started to smile, imagining she'd have loved to be in that class. "I suppose it could be awkward," she said.

Laura shrugged. "I don't know. The principal seems to be a decent person and was not too bothered by it, although I know some of the teachers complained to her. Especially about the parent-teacher meetings. Apparently, Josh's attitude was that he's always there if they have a problem he thinks needs a conversation. Here's the way I see the guy—Josh taught from a passionate worldview that kept both himself and his classroom engaged. He taught a freshman class, too, and my Daisy absolutely loved him. I admire the principal for somehow allowing it to work without a revolt on her hands. Do you know her? Judith Garvey?"

"I've heard the name," Izzy said. "But I don't think we've met."

Laura laughed. "That's right. I forget. Unlike me, you were a late starter on the childbearing front. Little Abby has a few years to go before she enters the big time. That's when you get to know the principals. Hopefully, not too often. I miss Abby's age."

Izzy laughed. "Abby loves you. Any time you need a pre-school fix, come our way. But back to the principal. Did she and Josh get along?"

"They seemed to respect one another. Judith seems nice. I hear she loves the outdoors, climbing mountains, hiking, all that. So maybe they were able to connect on some level like that. Josh loved getting his students out in the fresh air."

"Was she a teacher before going into administration?"

"I'm not sure. Most principals are. I know she cares about how the teachers connect with their academic subjects and with the kids. She told me about a technique of Josh's that she'd seen one day and thought was stellar. She was walking down the hall near his classroom, and the room was so silent that she stood by the door to see what was going on. She thought maybe they were taking a test, but it turns out Josh had thrown out a question to the class, and when no one answered, he simply waited in silence, leaning against his desk. Like for fifteen minutes or so, forcing the kids to adjust to the silence and then *think*. And finally, they did."

"I love that. Birdie does that with people. But doing it with a roomful of hormonal teenagers is another story. Do you think the teachers were jealous of Josh?"

"Maybe. Certainly not all. But a few, maybe. But in spite of the fact that he didn't always play by the rules—or maybe because of it—he seemed to be voted teacher of the year frequently."

"They do that in high school?" Izzy frowned, wondering about the wisdom in that sort of thing.

Laura smiled at Izzy's obvious disapproval. "Apparently, Josh agreed with you. He told his students not to vote for him."

"So what did the winner get? A crown?" Izzy asked.

Laura chuckled. "No, my skeptical friend. It was a real award. Seems a wealthy man from Boston established an award in memory of his wife, who used to teach at Sea Harbor High. A nice thing to do, right? It's a pretty significant award—last year it included a summer seminar in England, along with a monetary allowance. Nothing to sniff at."

"And Josh won?"

"Every year he's been there."

"I guess that could cause a bit of jealousy," Izzy said.

"What isn't widely known is that Josh never accepted the award benefits."

Izzy didn't ask her good friend how she knew. Laura Danvers and her husband were involved in so many Sea Harbor community efforts and on committees that they were often privy to things. And both Danvers were always discreet and trusted.

Laura checked the large watch on her wrist and stood up quickly, then gave Izzy a hug. "I'm off to a board meeting at the library."

"Of course you are. You're just like Aunt Nell."

Laura laughed and gave Izzy another hug. "Thank you," she said. "That's high praise. I'd love to be Nell Endicott when I grow up."

Chapter 20

"She's here," Birdie said, coming back to the dining table at the Sea Harbor Yacht Club after a quick trip to the coatroom. She piled their coats on an empty chair.

She and Nell had been seated at the end of a table, long enough to seat the ten people attending the Essex County Foundation meeting, which they'd committed to attending several weeks before.

"A luncheon meeting, of all things," Birdie had said, not entirely comfortable with going from a funeral to a partly social meeting at a yacht club, as nice as it might be.

"Who's here?" Nell asked.

"The woman in black," Birdie said, keeping her voice low and sitting down beside Nell.

Nell was confused. "Who?"

"The woman who was speaking with Father Northcutt at the reception. The one we thought might be one of Josh's relatives."

Other members of the foundation board were talking among themselves, pulling on coats and getting ready to leave, not paying attention to the private conversation at the end of the table. Nell leaned in close to hear Birdie.

"Yes. At least I think it was the same person. I didn't get a good look at her at the reception, but I remember the severe black suit. The poor woman looked uncomfortable."

Nell remembered that, too. "It didn't fit quite right. A size too small maybe. The way my dress-up outfits fit after the holidays. Where did you see her?"

"Coming out of the powder room as I grabbed our coats. It looked like she was going into the meeting room off that hallway."

"Maybe Josh's out of town relatives were meeting here," Nell said. "That makes sense, since they don't live in Sea Harbor."

"If, in fact, that's who she is. The thing is, I think I've seen her before," Birdie said.

"Liz would know," Nell said, looking around the room.

Liz Santos, the club manager, was standing at the far side of the room, being her competent, gracious self, greeting guests and managing staff at the same time. Liz knew nearly everyone who walked into the club, and she treated each person as if they were dear friends.

Nell caught Liz's eye and waved to her, and in the next minute, the club manager had excused herself from a couple getting seated and had walked over to them. "I didn't see you two coming in." She gave each of them a hug. "You are bright lights in my life on a sad day, that's who you are."

Birdie nodded. "We saw you at the funeral, but you were on the other side of the church."

Liz nodded. "It was a big crowd. I almost didn't go. Something about the suddenness of the memorial, when Josh's body was still . . ." She stopped and took a breath. "And it wasn't really a funeral, was it? It all seemed so fast. I can't get my arms around what happened. I guess none of us have."

"It's difficult for everyone," Birdie agreed.

"And so frightening. And then the memorial was so quick. It's all so unfair. Too much tragedy for one family to bear."

Birdie patted Liz's hand.

"Having the service so quickly surprised us, too," Nell said. "But maybe the relatives felt they needed to have something soon if they were from out of town. It's hard to know how people handle grief. We're all so different."

"But there wasn't any family there, Nell. At least I don't think there was. I've known Josh since forever, and I know he didn't have family here in Sea Harbor except for his mother and father. And truly . . ." Liz crouched down between the two women, her limber yoga body and model's shape belying the three children to whom she'd given birth. Her voice was hushed. "I didn't feel Josh's spirit at that memorial at all. It was like whoever planned it forgot to invite him. There wasn't an intimate feeling. Nothing that spoke of Josh. I felt cheated somehow."

"Did you know him well?" Nell asked.

"Not as in 'a good friend.' He was younger. But you know how it is in small towns. I knew him and liked him. He hung out with Lucky Bianchi. One summer he bussed tables at my mom's Sweet Petunia Restaurant when I was hostessing there. He was quiet, but a nice guy always, even as a teen. He worked hard, was supersmart. I am sure he was an amazing teacher." She stood back up and placed a hand on the back of Birdie's chair, checking out the dining room to make sure things were running smoothly. Then she turned her attention back to Nell and Birdie.

"I once went to a talk Josh gave at the library about birds be-cause my oldest, Maria . . . She's nine now. Can you believe that? She was obsessed with birds for a while, drawing them, doing reports on them, sitting in a tree and conversing and mimicking their songs. So Alphonso and I took her to hear Josh speak—it was for a benefit Josh's mother, Elizabeth, was involved in. That evening he taught us, well, us and the whole crowd of people who were there, that we might not be the only intelligent creatures on this earth. Maria found out that crows' IQs are about equal to a seven-year-old's, and for that whole year, she would not let her six-year-old brother forget that he wasn't as smart as a crow."

Birdie laughed. "That seems to have been a theme with Josh—and maybe your little Maria, too. Putting us all in our place." Birdie smiled at the memory of her first bird-watching trip with the group, when Polly Farrell had cajoled a very reluctant Josh into explaining to the group—experts and amateurs alike—why a skein of geese flew in a V formation. What she'd noticed at the time were the severe looks of distaste on a couple of the birders' faces. They were clearly affronted by a "youngster" trying to explain such basic bird facts. And worse, being forced to listen. She had figured they'd soon quit the group and move on to do their own thing. But she'd been wrong. Ding and Dong, as Polly Farrell called them in private, had come back. "It was because of the free trips," was Polly's take on it.

"So, how was your meeting?" Liz asked, regaining her professional composure and changing the subject.

"It went well," Birdie said. "It's a wonderful group, doing good things. But that brings something else to mind. Is there another meeting going on here today? I thought I heard voices from the front meeting room earlier."

Liz looked out toward the lobby, now filling with people leaving and others coming in. "Yes, there is. It's probably winding up about now."

"What group was it?"

"An educational organization. A very nice group. Principals and school district officials. They meet in different towns around the county throughout the year. This fall a local principal was in charge and arranged to have it here. I thought they might cancel today because of the service, but they decided not to since people had come from around the North Shore."

Liz brushed off her tailored silk pants, then looked up at a woman walking toward them. "As a matter of fact, here's one of them."

Birdie and Nell followed her gaze and watched as a woman in a black suit approached. She smiled at the three of them and then reached out to shake Liz's hand. "I didn't want to leave without thanking you."

"How did everything go?" Liz asked.

"Perfectly. A feather in Sea Harbor's educational hat. The meeting accommodations were wonderful," she said. "And it was truly a pleasure working with you."

Liz smiled and turned toward Birdie and Nell. "Have you met our Sea Harbor High School principal? Judith Garvey, meet my dear friends."

Liz finished the introductions as Birdie and Nell pushed their chairs back and stood, greeting the now identified woman in black.

Judith Garvey stood eye level with Nell, equally tall but bigger boned, with thick brown hair pulled back and fastened at the nape of her neck with a clasp. Nell suspected that her snug suit and hairstyle made her look older than she probably was. She was guessing midfifties. Nell also suspected that the principal didn't particularly like wearing the black suit—and hadn't worn it often.

"We've certainly heard your name," Nell said. "And we've attended some of the musicals and hockey games at the high school over the years. You've done an amazing job expanding the programs and facilities at SHHS."

Judith Garvey warmed at the praise. "It's wonderful, isn't it? I've heard your names, too," she said.

"These are certainly difficult days at the high school," Birdie said. "Please accept our condolences. The school community is a family, and I know you have tough days ahead."

"It's difficult for all of us. Josh was a beloved teacher. Yes, we're a close family at the school, and we'll all get through it together. There's a generosity in our school, in the whole town. People help one another."

"I'm sure you have a lot to do with that. Are you from Sea Harbor originally, Judith?" Nell asked.

"Not originally. But moving here some years ago was the best decision I've ever made. I truly love my job. It's been a lifesaver for me."

"You're clearly devoted to the school and the kids," Liz said. "That will help everyone get through this tragedy."

Judith took a deep breath. "I hope so. It's the kind of tragedy I never thought could happen in this peaceful, loving community. You can't prepare for something like this, because it isn't supposed to happen. Josh Elliott was a fine teacher and a good person." Her voice cracked slightly, and she stopped for a moment. Then said with a sad smile, "The students are grieving. The staff. Parents. It's a difficult time for the whole town."

Judith then graciously thanked Liz again, explaining that she needed to get back to the school to meet with the grief counselors she was bringing in for the students and staff. She smiled at Nell and Birdie and had started to turn away when Birdie reached out and touched her arm.

"I won't keep you, Judith, but I have a question you might be able to answer. Although we all knew Josh—and his parents, too—we weren't able to meet any of his extended family at the service. We don't know them and wondered if you know where they're staying. We'd like to offer our help."

"His family?" Judith asked.

"The relatives who arranged the memorial with the church."

Judith looked down at her hands, then took a deep breath.

Birdie immediately regretted the question. It seemed to have caused the high school principal confusion, although Birdie wasn't sure why.

"I'm sorry, Judith," she said quickly.

Judith shook her head and worked to regain her composure.

"No, I'm the one who should be sorry. And I understand your asking about that. When I talked to Detective Porter, he explained that the police were unable to locate any extended family. They went through my records, which didn't show any family emergency numbers or the like—except for Josh's mother, of course.

"I believe it was the older priest who confirmed that there were no relatives. It seems that Josh was an only child, as were his father and his mother." She paused for a minute, seemingly saddened that Josh Elliott was an only child. "Anyway, the police explained to us that once the body was released, the parish would arrange for the funeral Mass and an appropriate burial. Josh's mother was closely connected to the church.

"But when I sent that message out to the staff, they were upset. Because of the students, they said. They thought it would be better for the students if there was a memorial for Josh as soon as possible, one they could attend, which would help everyone with their emotions. Students and teachers both. It would help the kids concentrate on the teacher they respected and liked, and not on the awfulness of his death. And then slowly move on."

"So they thought a quick, short memorial would help the students heal?" Nell asked. She tried to hide her surprise.

"Yes. And maybe their parents, too. And the community—all of us, really. Waiting until a murderer is found before we could pay our respects and honor Josh's memory could be a long and painful and emotional wait."

"So the staff arranged the memorial service?" Birdie asked.

"Yes, all of Josh's coworkers. With the young priest's help, of course, arranging the appropriate prayers and such. It was important to the staff." The principal went on, as if she felt the need to explain the teachers' wishes. "We were all a little blindsided by the whole thing, just wanting to do what would be best for the students. The teachers, especially, wanted what would be helpful to them."

Judith checked her watch. She looked up and apologized, but she had to leave. "The teachers know their students best. I hope you understand."

Nell and Birdie stood there and watched Judith Garvey make her way toward the yacht club lobby. And one thing was clear as they watched the principal disappear. No. They didn't really understand.

Chapter 21

Tommy Porter walked out of the Fishtail Gallery just as Izzy was reaching for the door handle to go in.

"Hi, Tommy. Are you collecting fine art now?"

Tommy slipped a small notebook into his pocket and put on his sunglasses. "Don't I wish. The wood carvings in there are fantastic." He put his hand on the head of a five-foot-tall wooden dolphin that sat just outside the door to the gallery. "Like this guy here. He'd be good company."

"But my guess is you're not on a buying spree today."

"Nope. Rose and I finally connected, so I came over to see about the keys she lost."

"To see about the keys . . ." Izzy repeated. The ones she had lost in the woods . . . which had sunk into the mud . . . where a murdered dead man lay.

Tommy was a good friend. But somehow when he took off his jeans and tee and put on those khaki detective pants, a crisp white shirt, and a suit jacket, the friendship seemed less secure, more cautious. Certainly less fun.

It was especially true when he was visiting people close to her, like today. And not because he wanted to see the gallery or the wooden statues and the other wonderful art inside. And not because he had nothing better to do than drive across town to see about someone's keys. And what did that mean, to *see* about the keys? Tommy Porter was there because a man had been murdered. And he wanted to find out how Rose Anderson's keys had ended up beneath him.

"Hey, Iz. Good to see you," Tommy said. "Hope to see you around. Janie says hi."

But the casual good-bye didn't ring true to either of them. Although she was half a dozen years older than Tommy Porter, she suddenly felt smaller, younger. Less in control. And she didn't like it.

"Sure, Tommy," she said in an unnatural, cheery tone. "I've got to go, too." She opened the door and hurried inside.

Willow's cottage, a small wooden cabin with large windows and a bright red door, was nestled in the trees just a few yards from the gallery's back door.

The front door was still ajar from Tommy's departure when Izzy walked in. She closed the door behind her.

Rose was standing at a small counter in the cottage's kitchen and sitting room combination.

"Did you see Tommy Porter?" Rose asked.

"I did. He was admiring the art in the gallery."

Rose forced a laugh. She offered Izzy a cup of strong black coffee and motioned toward a stool on the other side of a small island.

Izzy sat, sipping the coffee. She soon set it down, grimacing. "This coffee is worse than mine, Rose."

"I know. I worked hard at it."

"So Tommy was visiting you?"

"Well, yes. It's about time, right?"

"He's talking to everyone. It's kind of a tangled mess right now."

"And it seems I'm tangled up with the best of them."

"The key ring," Izzy said.

"I guess. The truth is, I didn't know I'd lost those keys until I heard the police had found them. I figured they'd give them back eventually. I rarely use them. And then I forgot about them. I truly did, Izzy," she said. "It didn't seem important, somehow. I was way more concerned about Jillian, about her sadness. Her anger at me, which had been growing over the days before Josh died."

She took a drink of the bad coffee. "And sure, finding the keys where they found them—that was a bad coincidence. But it was so preposterous that I didn't even worry about it. I didn't. I wasn't there that night that he was murdered. I didn't do anything. You know that. That's the truth. And now Tommy Porter knows it, too. And what he does with it, whether he believes me or not? Well . . ." She shrugged. "It is what it is."

"But you can see how . . ."

"How they would think I murdered Josh Elliott? No, I can't, Izzy. How would I do that? Why would I do that? Because I didn't like him and my sister being close to one another? That's crazy." Her face was flushed.

Although her words were strong and defiant, Izzy saw a flicker of fear in her eyes. Rose Anderson was intelligent. She knew what it looked like to others. And she knew others could even come up with a reason why she'd do it.

But in that moment, without Rose saying another word, Izzy knew that she was absolutely telling the truth about not killing Josh Elliott or anyone else.

The anxiety she'd walked in with had disappeared, and Izzy wanted to reach over and hug Rose, but she realized that was the last thing that Rose wanted or needed at that moment. She didn't want to break down. She wanted to be strong. And most of all, in spite of her bravado, she wanted to be believed.

"So you explained it all to Tommy, right?"

Rose took another drink of her own cup of bad coffee, then

got up and got them each a glass of water. "Here. This will take the bad coffee taste away." She sat down on the other stool and looked at the water as if she wanted it to take away more than the taste of coffee.

"Yes, I told him. Do you know that the spot where Josh died, while it seems far away from the road, is just a short hike through the woods from the cemetery?"

Izzy wasn't sure what Rose was saying, but Rose continued on, as if surely Izzy understood.

"Well," she continued, "it is. I've spent a lot of time at that cemetery, visiting my mother's grave, and I've gotten to know the area. I discovered the woods, and I love to hike. Sometimes it takes the edge off. I mean after visiting my mother's grave. My friend Henry Staab told me about a nice lookout place a short distance through the woods and said it would be good for me to sit there sometimes."

"You know Henry Staab?"

"Yes. From spending time up there. He's a nice person. One day I was there late, but it was still light enough to see. So Henry and I hiked up and around that area. All the way to the firepit. We talked for a while, and I must have lost my keys. Like I said, I rarely used them, so I didn't miss them. And that's what happened, Izzy. Every single word of what I said is true."

Izzy nodded, watching Rose's face carefully and weighing the conviction she had heard in her voice. But there was something else there.

Or not there.

Izzy's short time in the courtroom, defending people—some who lied and others who told the truth—had helped her hone the skill of reading faces and bodies. A skill that helped her detect not only the truth but also complicated truths—ones that sometimes disguised more than they revealed.

And those were often the most difficult ones to deal with.

Chapter 22

Izzy's shop looked like a hurricane had hit it.

And in a way, it had. It had hit the whole town. The murder of Josh Elliott was a storm surge sweeping up morale and people and tossing them back down on the shore. With a wallop.

But no matter what was going on in the world, Thursday night knitting was sacrosanct for the four friends. Tonight would be no exception.

Izzy busied herself clearing away needles and yarn to make room on the library table for Nell's white chicken chili. The savory aroma of lime and cumin and garlic filled the room as Nell put the casserole dish on a warming plate.

"Do we know who the police have talked to?" Izzy threw the question out to anyone who might answer.

"The week is winding down," Cass said. "Surely they've narrowed this down."

"Apparently the police are doubling back and interviewing people again," Nell said. She leaned over and lined up small cups of olives, sour cream, and shredded cheese to garnish the chili. "But the chief told Ben the investigation still has hit lots

of brick walls. And there is an enormous amount of circumstantial evidence that could fall apart too easily."

Goose bumps appeared on Izzy's arms, and she rubbed them
briskly, then grabbed a sweatshirt from the back of a chair and
pulled it on.

She and Sam had been holding their daughter, Abby, close,
even hesitating to let her go to her safe, wonderful preschool.
As town talk had billowed, the stance of denying the idea that
the murderer could be someone they might know, a neighbor
or even a friend, had worn thin and become frightening. Izzy
had found herself looking at people who came into her shop
differently. And she hated that, and the awful feeling that followed it. The act of narrowing down the pool of suspects made
matters worse. It was as if the murderer was getting closer to
them.

Cass sat down near the fire Izzy had started in the corner of
the knitting room. The weather had turned again, as if matching the town's mood: gray skies and high tides. And the fire
was welcome. She leaned toward it and rubbed her hands.
"Lucky said lots of people saw Josh the night he was killed,
probably because he'd been in the bar earlier that day. They're
trying to track them all down."

"That included Sam and me," Izzy said. "Some policeman—not
Tommy—came by the house and asked Sam and me about it."

"And?" Cass asked.

"We told him what we knew, which wasn't much. That Josh
hadn't stayed long, and he didn't say where he was going. But
we'd talked about the bird-watching trip planned for the next
morning. He had been in a good mood and was looking forward to it. He'd been more talkative than he sometimes was.
Sam and I assumed—and the police did, too—that he'd decided
to go out to the woods that evening, spend the night at the
campsite, and get an early start."

"I remember seeing a tent there," Birdie said.

"The police asked Sam and me if we knew who else Josh had talked to in the bar."

Nell paused from filling bowls with chili. "How would you know that?"

"Right. It was a Saturday night, even though it was early. Josh had come in only to give Lucky something, so he probably didn't talk to many others. But, anyway, we told him just what we knew—he talked to us, to Lucky and Willow. And on his way out, he talked with Rose." Izzy carried a tray of soup bowls over to the low coffee table near the fireplace and sat down.

Birdie looked up from her chair next to the hearth. "Rose and Josh talked that night?"

"Yes. I didn't really want to get into that with the police, but others had heard the two arguing, so I thought I should mention it. I wasn't in a place where I could hear clearly—and the policeman didn't ask. They'll want to talk with Rose again, I'm sure. She can tell them herself what was said."

"Was it the same argument we'd heard before?" Nell asked.

"Pretty much, as best I could hear. Something about Josh and her sister. It was definitely not what you'd expect someone like Rose to argue about in a crowded bar."

"So similar to the Harbor Road incident last week," Nell said.

"Not that dramatic. And this time she hadn't had anything to drink." Izzy thought back to the pieces of conversation she'd overheard. "There was one thing that seemed odd," she said. "Rose mentioned her family, not just Jillian, but their mother. Something about Josh hurting her mother? I must have heard that wrong, though, since Elizabeth Anderson isn't alive. Josh looked perplexed."

Izzy stopped talking. It seemed the more they talked, the more guilty Rose Anderson looked. And Izzy knew she wasn't guilty.

Cass leaned in and filled four wineglasses. Once spoons and napkins and all four bowls of chili were on the table, everyone settled in and picked up their glasses, toasting their evening of knitting and the gift of their friendship, just as they had done each week, each month, each year.

Soon the uncomfortable talk was stilled while Portuguese sweet rolls and the creamy chicken chili, took over. In the background, the relaxing vibe of Norah Jones's café piano music provided comfort.

For a while they savored the soup in the kind of easy silence that longtime friendship nurtures.

Eventually Birdie wiped the corners of her mouth with her napkin and sat back, her small body sinking back into the large well-worn leather chair. She took another sip of wine, and then she brought all of them, herself included, back to the real world.

"All right now. Let's talk about this. About Rose. And admit out loud what we know to be true. Rose Anderson is a definite suspect in Josh's murder." She spoke calmly, as if stating a simple fact.

Everyone came to attention, but Cass managed to shush Birdie for two minutes while she refilled her soup bowl, then hurried back to her chair.

Birdie went on as Cass sat back down. "It's hard for us to face that fact because we care about her. She's sweet and kind and generous, and she has also suffered enough, losing both her father and mother within a short span of time. She doesn't need this."

Cass was closest to the wine bottle, and Izzy held out her glass for a refill.

"Birdie's right," Nell said. "Chief Thompson is perplexed, according to Ben. They've ruled out drifters and a couple of homeless people who sometimes wander that area. And the usual autumn leafpeepers traveling through. From what they've discovered from tips and people they've interviewed, they are eighty percent sure that Josh's murderer is local, probably someone from Sea Harbor or one of the towns within an arm's reach. But their guess is someone from right here. So their search has narrowed."

"Considering all that," Birdie said, "we need to acknowledge what the police are looking at—Rose's Harbor Road incident and heated argument with Josh Elliott, all witnessed by people, and then the key ring . . ."

Birdie paused, and Izzy quickly spoke up.

"I agree with what you've said, Birdie. And that we need to do what we can to help. It's all too close to home to ignore. The fact that Josh was a schoolteacher makes it especially hard. It's frightening, especially for the kids and their parents. If one teacher could be killed, could others? Was there something, someone, lurking in Sea Harbor High? All sorts of grim fears. So yes, we should start by looking at what the police are looking at. But we also need to keep in mind one thing. Rose didn't do it." Izzy was moving her spoon in the air as she talked. She put it down and continued.

"Rose didn't kill Josh." Her voice was confident and calm and coated with conviction, as if somehow she had an ironclad alibi for this young woman. Or the real murderer had been caught and had confessed.

"Phew. Glad we got that out of the way," Cass said. Then she immediately grew serious. "Iz, that's what we all want to bel—"

"No, this is different, Cass." Izzy's voice had switched to the attorney's voice she had once used when in a Boston courtroom, arguing before a jury. The years when she'd pressed for facts over opinions, for proof before judgment. At least whenever she could. But although the voice was the same, this was not that.

"I can't quite describe how I know," Izzy said. "It's not an emotional thing, I don't think. It's something else."

"Deep down, we all believe Rose is innocent," Nell said,

waiting for her niece to explain her definitive statement. "You're speaking as if you *know* that, Izzy. How?"

They all listened carefully, wondering what Izzy knew that they didn't. Of all of them, Izzy was the fact person.

"I know it up here." She pointed to her head. Before they could poke holes in what she had indicated as certain proof, Izzy continued, starting with Rose's hiking explanation for the lost keys.

Nell listened carefully, remembering her conversation with Henry Staab just before Josh was killed. "Henry told me about it the other day. He'd become friends with the girls when they visited their parents' graves. Especially with Rose, Henry said. Sometimes he and Rose hiked together on paths he'd trampled down himself. One trail led to that same place where Josh was found. It's a shorter way to get to the lookout and campsite than the trail that starts up at the old quarry woods. Henry is probably the only person who knows it's there."

"Except for people he became friends with, like Rose and Jillian," Cass said.

Birdie smiled. "Henry is a good soul. And I'm sure he loves having someone to talk to."

"Mae mentioned that Rose spends a fair amount of time at the cemetery, visiting her mother's grave," Izzy said, her spirits lifting as Rose's story gained ground. "The key chain could have been lost anytime, not necessarily the night Josh was killed."

"What about the rest of what the police are looking at? Rose's arguments with Josh? Rose's open dislike of him?" Cass asked. "It sounds like it was excessive."

"That's true," Izzy said. "And I have to admit that I don't quite get it. I don't think Jillian does, either. But there was something in Rose's voice yesterday, when we talked, something that told me she was absolutely telling the truth when she said she didn't murder Josh Elliott."

Izzy stopped for a minute to get a grip on what she was saying. Then she went on. "Of course, feelings don't stand up in court. I know that, and I respect it. But it's more than a feeling that I'm talking about. I knew from her voice, from her face, and even from the way she stood. I knew from all of her that she was telling me the truth."

Izzy let that settle for a minute on the three skeptical faces.

"Okay, but there is something else," she said.

"Something else," Cass repeated.

"Yes. There's more to that truth than what Rose was willing to share with me. That's the thing that bothers me. It's true she didn't murder Josh, but it's a complicated truth. She didn't kill anyone. But there is more to the story than her innocence. And whatever that something is, it might be important to find out. It might help lead us to whoever did kill Josh Elliott."

"I'm not sure what you mean," Nell said.

"It's hard to explain. She's innocent, like she said. But her feelings about Josh Elliott are more complicated than her simply not wanting him in her sister's life. That simply doesn't add up."

"I'm wondering if Tommy felt that way after talking with her. Did she say anything about her talk with him?" Birdie asked. "Perhaps she's explained it all."

Izzy thought back to her talk with Rose over the awful cup of coffee. Rose really hadn't said much. It was almost as if the "I didn't kill Josh" sentence had been enough. Or should have been.

"I don't know what Tommy walked away with. Rose didn't know whether he believed her or not. But I doubt he was as sure of her innocence as I am. This is tough for him—he wants to be all things to all people. And then he's confronted with in-terviewing friends and neighbors. People who just may have been involved in a murder. When I saw him outside Rose's place, I resented him a little. I wanted to tell him to leave Rose alone. To go away. Finally, I came back to what I knew all along—that the poor guy was only doing his job, and a very hard one. I mean, what would I do if I were in his place? So this morning I hit an early power yoga class, and I think I've let go of it. At least for now."

Cass stacked the empty soup bowls and took them to the small sink near the stairs. She washed her hands and headed back. "I get that, Iz. I've felt that way, too. We know Rose. Tommy may, too. I don't know. And he probably knows half the people he's had to interview this week. The police academy must teach them how to turn off the personal and just follow procedures, ask the hard questions, no matter who they're talking to."

Cass pulled out her knitting bag from beneath the chair and retrieved a ball of space-dyed yarn for the hat she was making. She stared at it. And then she lightened the mood by holding it up. "This thing will cover up Danny's whole face, as if he were robbing a bank or something. And then maybe Tommy will have to interview him."

Birdie did the same, pulling out the squishy, soft merino yarn she was using to make a wild slouchy hat for Abby.

And along with the yarn, the conversation veered slightly.

"Beautiful colors," Nell said, reaching over and touching the fine colorful yarn Birdie would miraculously turn into an unusual winter hat.

"The color is called chrysanthemum—from the flowers that bloom in a dozen different colors," Birdie said. "And I think every single mum color is in this single skein. It will be perfect for my colorful granddaughter."

With the table cleared, Nell brought back a carafe of coffee and mugs and knitting began in earnest.

Izzy smoothed out her half-finished vest, feeling the need to move her fingers. She began untangling a loose clump of yarn, her thoughts moving back to Rose Anderson. And a murder. And suddenly it all seemed as tangled as her yarn.

"So," she said, picking up the mess of yarn in her lap and plopping it on the coffee table. "We need a next step."

"Well, it's all right here in front of us," Nell said, fingering a piece of the tangled yarn. "We need to find out why Rose didn't like Josh, and get that out of the way. Then we need to target people other than Rose who could have killed Josh. And we need to do it soon. We can't leave Rose under that painful cloud of suspicion. Rumors will leak."

"So we need to think beyond Rose. And I think one place to look is the high school," Birdie said. "There's something going on at that school. Something with the staff. I don't think they were as fond of Josh as the principal wanted us to believe. She's a motherly type, and I think she wants to protect her flock. But the fact that the teachers arranged a memorial that lacked Josh's spirit—in fact, that lacked Josh—makes me wonder."

"What about the students' parents? Did they like Josh as much as the kids did?" Izzy asked. "Lucky was joking the other day about the drama of teachers giving failing grades. It was a joke, but it reminded me of a girl in my high school class who failed an important math test that would likely affect her college applications. Her dad was so mad when the teacher wouldn't change it that he threatened the woman with bodily harm. And I think he actually did some nasty things to her, like writing on her car. He didn't kill her. But he made it clear he'd like to. A grown man. Weird."

"Jeez. A lesson for us, Iz. When our perfect children are in high school, let's definitely not be crazy parents."

They laughed, but the thought lingered, and the foursome resolved to check into Josh's relationship with the parents as well as the teachers at SHHS.

"What about the bird-watching group?" Nell looked at Birdie.

Birdie thought for a moment, finishing her cast-on row and concentrating on joining the knitting in the round. Without looking up, she said, "Yes. That's a good idea. I will do a little information gathering. A couple in the group had issues with Josh, but normal issues. Not ones that end in murder."

"But people kill for little things," Cass reminded her. "Ordinary people. Like that dad Izzy told us about. Anger. Jealousy. Something simple, personal. And to the person doing the killing, it might not seem like a small thing at all."

The reminder sobered the group.

"I was in the tea shop today," Birdie said. "Polly Farrell told me that all of our group have been interviewed at least once or twice, so maybe the police have come up with something suspicious. The birders are decent people who love birds. But there's some competition there. Winning contests is definitely not on my 'big thing' list. But I don't know about others."

"I heard a checker in the market today talking about tips on the police hotline. She mentioned the bird-watching group and that there was some friction in the group," Nell said. "Most people didn't know we had a bird-watching group here in Sea Harbor. Suddenly, it's common news."

Birdie frowned, wondering who the checker in the market had been. Surely, Betty Warner wouldn't bring attention to a group she was a part of. "Friction?" she said. "I suppose not everyone loves each other, but that's normal. When you look for things like that, you'll find them, and then suddenly they're blown out of proportion. I don't see things like that. But I saw Harper today, and she mentioned that Tommy Porter had been to her home a couple of times. She and Leon were talked to together and separately. She informed Tommy that the birders are fine people and whoever said such a thing must have talked to the wrong people. Or didn't understand birds. Or wasn't very nice."

They all laughed, imagining Tommy dealing with Harper Mancini. She probably gave him a little talk about loving the people in his jail before he left.

"I can't quite picture Harper looking at birds," Izzy said. "She comes in here in the trendiest workout clothes, looking amazing. But Harper in birding gear?"

Birdie chuckled. "Oh, no, Izzy. No birding gear for Harper. She frowns on our dour attire and has suggested she take us shopping. She dresses in skinny jeans and puffy jackets and fancy knee-high boots. But, then, she also doesn't look at too many birds."

Izzy laughed. "Well, she's entertaining. There's a place for everyone. People enjoy her, and she's a decent knitter, too. She's knitting her husband a bright orange necktie with a bird image. He's the guy Uncle Ben mentioned who took over the Barlow family's commercial real estate company when Josh's father died."

"Why didn't Josh take it over?" Cass asked. "That's what good kids are supposed to do."

They laughed, knowing Cass loved her father's lobster company as much as Patrick Halloran had. She had grown up knowing which lobsters to throw back, which to keep. The best areas, the worst for tangled lines. And she had never considered—or wanted—any other profession.

"I suspect Josh liked the idea of running a commercial real estate company about as much as I would," Birdie said.

"Well, Harper is glad he didn't take it over," Izzy said. " 'Her man', which is how she often refers to Leon, loves running a company. She's savvy enough not to talk about the healthy amount of money he makes running it, but it's clear she enjoys spending it."

"I don't think about Leon as an executive," Birdie said. "My birders don't talk about what they do in real life. And it's difficult picking out executives in birding attire."

"The offices are in Beverly," Nell said. "But no matter, it's a coincidence that Leon is connected to the Elliott family."

Birdie agreed. "I wouldn't have guessed that Josh and Leon even knew each other. There was never much chitchat between them. Harper talked with Josh, but she talked to everyone. She's a very friendly soul."

"Do people mind her being there?" Cass asked.

"Sometimes. She's a bit of a flirt—and then there's the talking, as Izzy has discovered. Sometimes Polly has to ask her to be quiet. Birders like to listen, but to birds, not to someone talking about parties and clothes and knitting. She does love to knit."

"Who does she flirt with?" Cass asked.

"Well, everyone. Even me." Birdie laughed. "At least she likes to talk to me. And Josh. Although she got little response from him. And others, too. She even charms Henry Staab when he's around. Which, of course, he loves."

"What does Leon Mancini think about the flirting?" Nell asked.

"I'm not sure, now that you ask. He may be so interested in the birds that he doesn't even notice. Well, except for something that happened a few weeks ago. Harper was wearing boots with rather high heels and took a nasty fall. Leon was busy photographing a migratory skein and ignored her calls to help her. Finally, Josh walked over and picked Harper up. Without a word, he took her out to his car and drove her off to urgent care."

"Geesh. Leon Mancini might not be the gallant knight that Harper talks about," Izzy said.

"Or maybe his passion for birds got the better of him," Nell said. "Was he okay with Josh being the hero?"

"He didn't exactly see it that way. The two gentlemen had words later on," Birdie said.

"I don't think Josh is the kind to have words with someone, except maybe for a student who refused to succeed," Cass said.

"Apparently, Leon was angry with Josh because he had 'run off' with his wife, as he put it, in front of the whole birding group. Polly keeps things so pleasant that it was a surprise for everyone. Josh didn't say much, except that he was miffed he'd had to miss spotting a bald eagle that day. And then he added that Leon was a jerk—or maybe he used a stronger word—for disrespecting his wife. Of course, that last comment had Leon threatening Josh that he'd be dead if he ever touched his wife again. Or something foolish like that."

"What did Josh do?" Cass asked.

"He walked away and began cleaning his binoculars. But it was an unusual bit of drama between the young and the not so young men. Especially because Josh Elliott never seemed to get upset about things. Not being civil to a woman seems to be something that could cause harsh words."

"As it should," Nell added. "Or to anyone."

"And Harper? Was she embarrassed?" Izzy asked.

Birdie chuckled. "I think she loved every minute of it."

It was much later that night, after a long soaking bath and a mug of Sleepytime tea, that Birdie finally crawled into bed and pulled the puffy down comforter over her still chilly body. But it wasn't the weather chilling her from the inside out. It was the week, one in which an image haunted her when she was alone.

It was Josh Elliott, unmoving on the damp ground, his face looking up blankly at the overcast morning sky. She could still feel his eyes on her, as if he were asking her what happened.

Except that he knew what happened.

And right now it appeared he was the only one who did.

The knitting evening had been wildly successful as far as knitting went. The slouchy hat she was knitting for her grand-daughter, Abby, was nearly ready; Cass's ski cap looked less frightening. Nell's chili and the wine had been perfect for soothing spirits.

But it was the tangled ideas and thoughts and facts that had lingered above them the whole evening, pulled down and talked about, then let go of, only to float away again, that they all had carried home. Names gathered and relationships touched on, but all of it refusing to line up in a neat and orderly way.

Missing were the things that would connect all those names and ideas in some reasonable way. Although *reasonable* wasn't a word readily applicable to murder.

There was always one thing, Birdie thought. A touchstone. The one thing they hadn't talked about, at least in a meaningful way—a way that would bring a murderer to light. It was the man Birdie had knelt down beside on a dreary Sunday morning and wished a peaceful passing.

Without knowing who Josh Elliott was behind his birding gear and quiet ways, they would never be able to connect all those tangled thoughts.

She switched off her bedside lamp, lay back on the pillows, and looked out her bedroom window at the dark autumn night. Slanted moonbeams fell across the white comforter. Birdie traced a silvery white beam with her finger, and then she looked out and whispered into the light of the moon:

"So what have you done, Josh Barlow Elliott, to make someone want to kill you?"

Chapter 23

Nell was on her second cup of coffee, with most texts and emails answered and the *Times* open on the kitchen island, when Ben walked in from the garage.

"Where've you been?" Nell asked as Ben walked across to her seat in the kitchen.

"Sorry." Ben leaned over and kissed the top of her head. "You were in the shower, and I forgot to leave a note. Jerry Thompson asked me to come over to talk about some of Amelia Elliott's family business. Father Northcutt was there, too. Apparently, he had access to Amelia's personal papers."

Nell brows lifted. "Why? What kind of papers?"

"It didn't have anything to do with the murder investigation, at least not directly. The chief did say he thinks they're getting closer, once they can turn some of the circumstantial evidence into facts. Phones were ringing off the hook while I was there. It's grim."

Nell shuddered. "Grim doesn't begin to describe it."

"But this was something else. Larry Northcutt is involved, too. Do you have Jillian Anderson's contact information?"

"The padre?" Nell asked, picking up her phone, her fingers moving. Then she put it down. "I just forwarded it to you. But why do you need Jillian's number?"

"I need to talk to her. It turns out she's in Josh's will."

"His will? That's interesting. I didn't think people his age normally had wills, even though it's probably a good idea. The Elliotts were well off. And if he had the foresight to think ahead, more power to him. But why would Jillian be in it?"

"The whole thing is curious. It isn't your normal, run-of-the-mill will."

"Go on," Nell said, refilling coffee cups.

"Josh's mother talked to me once about financial things. Not that I'm a financial expert, but I know business law, and Father Larry thought I might be able to offer her some guidance with what she wanted to do. I suppose he contacted me because both Amelia and I were involved in similar family businesses and all the things that spin from that. The padre was at the meeting then, too."

"When was this?"

"A few years ago. I remember the meeting but had almost forgotten what it was for."

"Was her husband there?"

"No, and at first, I thought that was unusual. But realized later that it made sense. It was her money, her company. The Barlow fortune, not the Elliott's. And we were just sharing ideas."

"What kind of ideas?"

"Ideas about family companies and wills, trusts, all those things. What you do to make sure everything is in place should you not be around anymore. Amelia was a nice, quiet woman who didn't like thinking about money. But she also didn't want it misused."

"Misused? How could that happen?"

"That wasn't clear. But what *was* clear was her loyalty and affection for her own father and mother and grandparents, who had worked hard building up the company and the family fortune. She was interested in using their legacy to help the community they loved. She said it was the spirit in which her family had lived. Amelia's life seemed to be one of giving."

"Birdie indicated that, too. But she talked more about Amelia's giving of herself. The financial part is a surprise. And generous."

"Right. Amelia didn't broadcast her financial generosity. Like I said, I'd almost forgotten about that talk, but apparently, she acted on what we'd talked about shortly after. But with a twist. And in a way that surprises me, which I just found out about today. Something I wouldn't have thought of. It wouldn't have pertained to the Endicott family company and trust. I suppose that's why."

Ben poured himself a cup of coffee and sat down, then began fiddling with a stray pencil on the island. His long legs straddled the stool.

"You sound mysterious, Ben."

"I don't mean to be. It's just unusual. I'm still getting my arms around it. Amelia wanted to start a foundation that would benefit Sea Harbor's needs. And she pretty much wanted all her money to go into it. Even the company."

"How generous."

"It was. That part isn't that unusual. It's how she chose to manage it and how complete it was that was unusual. Many families establish a foundation, but they don't put their entire fortune in it. And then there's the fact that while she was alive, she wanted to relinquish control."

"It sounds like the end result of all this is that Josh was cut out of his mother's will."

"Actually no. Josh was involved in planning the foundation with his mother. A Boston lawyer Amelia's father employed helped with its formation. But Amelia relied heavily on Josh's ideas, because she wanted him to be in charge. Basically, it would normally have been Josh's inheritance they were putting in this fund. She wanted to pull out a hefty amount for him, but he said he'd be fine without that."

Nell laughed. "My head's spinning."

"Here's how Amelia did it. With Josh's help—and that Boston legal group—they created a foundation, with Josh in control of it. It was all legal, put together perfectly into a trust. This was several years before Amelia died. She did it partially to protect the Barlow family's money."

"Why did it need protection?"

"Apparently, Peter Elliott was misusing funds—and other things, too—for some time before he died. Amelia wanted the money that her parents and grandparents had worked so hard for to help other people, but not to help a man she had lost respect for."

"So Josh inherited this?" Nell looked puzzled.

"Yes. But it wasn't the kind of inheritance we think of. It was a fund, with goals and stipulations and regulations. That's what Josh inherited. Profits from the family's commercial real estate company also go into the foundation. And if it's sold, that money goes into it, too. Josh has been controlling it for several years now. Controlling meaning he could distribute donations to worthy places of his choosing. Like I said, Amelia trusted him completely. The trust itself had a living allowance for her. And one for Josh. When you think about it, Josh was supporting his mother, since he had control of the trust. Legally, she would have had to ask him for money—although, of course, they didn't do it that way."

"This is amazing. So Josh was wealthy?"

"No, actually, he wasn't, but I guess it depends on how you define *wealth*. It was the family foundation that had money. And that money could only be given away, not used by Josh for personal reasons. Father Larry said that Josh himself had wanted it done that way. There's money built in for salaries and expenses."

"So we think Josh has been donating money to who knows where all this time?"

"We *know* he has. And obviously, without fanfare. He lives simply, so he worked under the radar. Which, again, was how he and his mother wanted it managed. Most people have no idea where donations to library development or soup kitchens or education projects or homeless shelters come from when the donor arranges it that way."

"So Josh must have lived mostly on his teacher's salary?"

"Well, no. That's another curious thing about all this. After his first month or two there, he declined to take a salary at the high school."

"Why?"

"Who knows? Didn't you mention that he kind of did his own thing at the school? Maybe forgoing a salary gave him an edge to do that?"

"Do the teachers know about that?"

"The principal would, but probably not the teachers. Salaries and salary discussions are always kind of off limits in schools. Father Larry knew about the salary thing, but only because Josh told him. It was a personal matter. Josh's grandparents founded the company, and I doubt very much if Josh is poor. He probably inherited from them. And maybe that's the reason he didn't take a salary from the school. He simply didn't need it. But he wanted to teach."

Nell thought about that. "Salary aside, I can kind of understand the other teachers not liking him being allowed a certain latitude or freedom that they didn't have," Nell said. "And why did the principal allow him to do whatever he felt like doing? I wonder if there's more to it."

"Maybe. But from what Father Larry has told me about Josh Elliott, he may not have even been aware of any antagonism

among the staff. Public schools are always holding fundraisers
for new 3D printers, computers, that sort of thing. It's possible
that's where Josh's salary went."

Nell chuckled, wishing she had had the chance to know Josh
Elliott better. He was her kind of people. "Izzy heard talk in
the yarn shop that some of the teachers were upset he hadn't
been fired. Principal's pet, they called him."

Ben laughed. "I'm not sure I'd want that moniker if I were a
teacher."

"Did Josh's father have access to any of the family money
before he died?"

"As CFO of the real estate company, he had a salary. An extremely generous one, apparently. He liked big boats and cars
and a rather grand lifestyle, as evidenced by their home. And to
give the guy credit, he worked his payroll so other top employ-
ees got very nice salaries, too, especially Leon Mancini, the man
who took his place when he died."

"Birdie told me Amelia was quiet and shy. But she must have
been a strong woman to have protected her family's money the
way she did."

"Right. Her husband didn't have access to any of it. However, that's another thing that Father Larry talked about. Josh
had begun thinking more about the family company in the
weeks before he died. I'm not sure what he was thinking, but
apparently, running the real estate business wasn't ever in his
life plan, so it must have been something else. But we didn't
have time to get into that. Hopefully, I'll learn more about it
today."

"Leon Mancini seems to be doing a good job in his stead,"
Nell said. "The company has a good reputation."

"True. And is making money. But who knows? He talked to
Father Larry about his ideas for the company, so I'll learn more
when I see him later. Apparently, Father Larry and Amelia
were very close friends, and sometimes Josh would consult

with the priest to be sure his mother would approve of ideas he had for the foundation."

"This is interesting," Nell said. "But it's terribly confusing."

"And that reminds me of what I have to do next." Ben took a drink of coffee, then took out his phone and checked his contacts. "Jillian's contact information came through. Thanks. I need to get in touch with her."

"So we've circled back to Jillian Anderson," Nell said. "This is all quite a story."

"I guess it is. And you're right. It all does come back to Jillian. And no, she's not rich."

"All right, then. What does it mean?"

"It means Jillian Anderson is now in charge of the Barlow family private foundation."

Chapter 24

Rose Anderson parked her bike near Henry Staab's small stone house on the edge of the Hilltop Cemetery.

The morning sun hadn't yet warmed up the ground, and she pulled her jacket close, warding off the ocean chill. She glanced over to the woods in the distance and immediately saw the narrow path that Henry's clunky boots had created. Although she'd made many visits to her mother's grave without even noticing the split between the thick bushes and trees, it now appeared as if it were lit with floodlights. Obvious. An easy sprint to the lookout area, as Henry explained it. His secret path.

Rose shivered and quickly turned away.

She walked in the opposite direction, making her way up the familiar curving path to her mother's grave. She carried a small pot of mums that she'd picked up at Market Basket on her bike ride over. The flowers looked a little worse for wear, having bounced around in the bike basket, but Rose found that weirdly appropriate. She felt worse for wear, too.

Could she have handled anything worse with Tommy Porter? she wondered. Maybe she'd done it on purpose, a kind of payback to her mother, who had laid all of this on her. But mostly, she didn't want to think about it.

She took a few breaths as she reached the top of the gentle slope leading to the place where her mother and father were buried. The cemetery was quiet and empty this morning, just as she had hoped it would be. Her afternoon visits were often shared with widows and widowers, all of whom would see Rose and come over, wanting to make her feel better, trying to engage her in a conversation about the best kind of floral decorations to bring when the weather turned bad.

The morning silence was soothing. She walked down a side, treed, row to her mother's grave, then knelt down on a patch of dried leaves near the headstone. The crackling of the leaves seemed magnified in the quiet air.

She leaned over and brushed the gray stone marker clean of leaves and balanced the pot of mums against it.

A ragged, unexpected sound surrounded her. She realized with a start that it was coming from her. Sadness and anger and love and hate, all crowded together, vying to get out.

"It's all your fault, Mom," she cried, tears rolling down her cheeks. "Every bit of it. I'm miserable. Jillian's miserable. She's grieving, and she won't talk to me. I should have told her the truth right away. I should never have promised to keep secrets, to interfere in my own sister's life. What was I thinking? What were *you* thinking? Secrets are the devil's curse."

She sat back on her legs, wiping her cheeks with her jacket sleeve, and stared at the grave, as if waiting for an answer. An apology. Round circles of sunlight filtered through the branches of the tree and onto the grave, dancing as the branches swayed.

"But guess what, Mom?" she said, finding her voice again, which was suddenly stronger and more robust. "Have you heard the news? He's dead, Mom. *Dead.* The Elliott family—all of it—is gone. Was it all worth it? Can you rest in peace now?"

Henry Staab stood behind the enormous oak tree a short distance away. He hadn't intended to eavesdrop. He had seen Rosie's bike, and he had wanted only to give the poor girl a hug.

But now he wished he hadn't come up at all.

Chapter 25

Jillian Anderson had gone rogue.

"I don't know where she is," Mae told Nell.

Nell had picked up lattes and headed to Izzy's shop, knowing Izzy and Mae would be in early, getting ready for the day.

Izzy had immediately ushered the two other women down to the knitting room to soak in the silence while it lasted, leaving the CLOSED sign on the unlocked door.

"I'm thinking that I'm not a very good aunt," Mae said as she sat down on a chair at the old library table.

Izzy and Nell joined her. "You're a wonderful aunt, Mae," Izzy said. "A little bossy maybe, but at least you don't discriminate in your bossing. You boss me around, too."

Nell was distracted, still trying to get her mind around the whole family foundation idea. Was this a good thing for Jillian? And how would she react? It would be life changing, at the very least. And what if she didn't want the responsibility? What does one do when given someone else's family foundation, which one might not want?

Ben hadn't said enough to clarify much of anything, and when she had left the house, he was still in his den, rereading the Elliott and Barlow legal papers before contacting Jillian. It was all a confusing scenario.

She had hoped fervently that he'd be able to figure it all out.

"So why is Ben looking for Jillian?" Izzy asked, pulling Nell out of her thoughts.

"You know Ben. He seems to get himself put in the middle of things," Nell said, brushing off the question and turning to Mae. "So you haven't talked to her?"

"Nope. Haven't had the chance. Not since that non-memorial service. But at least I know she's breathing," Mae said.

"Who's breathing?" Birdie called out. She was standing in the archway at the top of the three stairs. She walked down quickly, trailed by Purl, who was looking for a lap to sit on. "All of us, I hope."

Nell pulled out a chair for Birdie and moved the extra latte over. "Here," she said. "A sixth sense said you might be dropping in."

"That same sixth sense that kept me awake last night, telling me that we are in a dark place and need to find the sun. Or, at the least, Josh Elliott's killer. But first tell me who's not breathing." Birdie sat down and took a sip of the coffee.

"No, she *is* breathing," Mae explained. "Jillian. But she's like a ghost in the night. I see the lights in the cottage at night, so I know she's there and safe. And a couple times I've seen her heading out, sometimes in hiking gear. Sometimes gear for the Y. Sometimes she takes the Jeep. I'm a bit of a voyeur, but I figure it's my right and duty. She did tell me that she's taking time to pull herself together. And she followed it with a hug. She's a good girl."

"Woman," Izzy corrected.

Birdie made room for Purl on her lap and looked over at Mae. "That's wise of her. Jillian seems so independent, and I think she knows herself well, both physically and spiritually.

Probably being alone right now is comforting for her, and the way she can handle this terrible loss," Birdie said.

Nell listened, her mind still cluttered with Ben's news, and wondered how Jillian, independent or not, would handle another major happening in her still young life.

Mae nodded at Birdie's comment. "That's true. Jillian knows herself far better than I did at that age. But handling grief seems to be something you learn as it happens. When I lost my husband, I was the opposite. I didn't want to be alone. I needed this yarn shop more than anything in the world. I needed all of you, but I needed the customers even more, I think. They were just far enough removed. They were like mirrors, allowing me to see myself in good ways. To bring me back to life so I could help them find exotic yarns or special needles, or show them how to fix a missed stitch. Or just to greet me happily when they walked in, and then tell me I'd made their day when they left. Like a family without the entanglements. It saved me. How's that for a selfish take on all this?"

"And with Cliff?" Birdie asked. "What helped you through losing your brother? The loss of a sibling is a whole other kind of loss. And you and Cliff were so close."

"Cliff? I still haven't gotten over Cliff's death. I'm still grieving. He was way too young. He shouldn't . . . he shouldn't have died. And he wouldn't have, if only . . ." Her voice dropped off, then came back again, more animated. "Cliff was . . . he was simply the most generous, loving person in the world. I was thrilled when he brought his dental practice back here to Sea Harbor so we could stay close." Mae stopped, as if not sure what she would say next.

"I understand that feeling. It's how I felt when Izzy moved here," Nell said.

"Well, it wasn't all heaven," Mae said, as if she hadn't heard Nell speak. "But even when it wasn't, when Cliff was digging himself out of unhappiness, we were still, well, just a few blocks apart. There were days I was aware of too much going on with Cliff. Things about his family life. Elizabeth's way of mothering Rose and Jillian. And then I'd worry."

"But they were a great family," Izzy said. "At least the two members I know are wonderful. Well, make that four. Cliff was wonderful. And Elizabeth came in the shop often. Always cheery and talkative. Mostly about the girls, but I got that."

"Of course. Sure," Mae said quickly. "But all families have their things. And sometimes it was hard because I'd see those times, too, not just the amazing, joyful ones, like the birth of Rose and Jillian, their birthdays and accomplishments. But the way Elizabeth took over their lives. She needed to know every single thing going on with them. And then controlling that. Or trying to. Fortunately, she gave birth to two strong-minded girls who had minds of their own."

"She was a helicopter mom," Izzy said. "That's what people call it."

"A good description. Smothering mother is how I thought about her sometimes. Cliff was a minor bystander once the twins were born. But to give Cliff and Elizabeth both credit, I don't think the kids noticed how it was. Their dad adored them and worked hard to forge a presence in their lives. And I've heard them talking happily about their childhood. When they were older, they were involved in so many activities, they were happy just knowing they were loved. And they were definitely loved."

"Do you know why Cliff was unhappy?" Izzy asked.

"A combination of things. I think he and Elizabeth saw their relationship differently. He was a great dad, but when he committed to the marriage, he wanted a wife, too. Once the kids were born, she didn't need Cliff anymore, or at least that's how I saw it. Elizabeth wanted separate rooms. She'd have liked separate houses, I think, if they could have afforded it. She didn't dislike Cliff. She just didn't need him anymore. She wanted him there as the kids' dad, someone to buy life insurance and establish college funds, but not to be there with her. It wasn't a great situation for someone who is prone to depression, anyway."

The others were silent, not wanting to interrupt. Mae wasn't known for talking about personal things, but somehow they sensed it was what she needed today.

"I remember when they were dating and Cliff asked me how he could be sure he really loved her. They'd been dating for a couple years. And wise old me told him that he would just know when it was right. But if he didn't feel that certainty, he needed to be fair to her and let her know. If he did feel it, he should go all in. She was already in her midthirties, older than Cliff, and she talked about having children constantly. I didn't think it was fair of him to let his uncertainty stretch out through her childbearing years."

"What happened?" Birdie asked.

"He married her. And had children. I truly think the sole reason Elizabeth went after Cliff was to have children. I should be ashamed to say that, but I'm not. Most people in our family were pretty fertile. Several sets of twins. He was a good catch. Our family had a monopoly on fertility and depression." Mae shook head. "Poor Cliff had both."

"Those aren't my memories of Cliff, but except for dental checkups, I only got to know him personally when the girls were teenagers," Izzy said. "He came in the shop sometimes because Jillian and Rose were here so much of their time. And, honestly, in those days, the kids' teen years, he seemed very happy. In fact, more than a lot of people with teenagers."

"That's the side of Cliff that I saw, too," Nell said, thinking back to the likable dentist she and Ben had both been fond of. "Ben and I even talked about it. Happy with his accomplished daughters. Excited about their futures. Happy with life. Ben was having some serious dental work around that time, but he loved going in. Imagine—he loved going to the dentist. He and

Cliff would get so involved in talking about sailing that I almost had to pry him out of the chair."

Mae smiled at their comments. "Sailing, yes. He loved it. He bought that beautiful big Hinckley sailboat about that time. Elizabeth couldn't swim and never once set foot on his boat. Cliff took me and the girls out some. And another good friend or two. He started doing volunteer work when the twins were in high school. Although we weren't Catholic, he and Father Northcutt became good friends. He helped a lot in that soup kitchen." Mae paused, her mind seeming to go somewhere else.

"I remember those days. Cliff and I bonded over dishing up soup," Birdie said. "There was another friend there, and the three of us seemed to end up on the same schedule. We liked each other and had a good time."

Mae watched Birdie as she talked, as if wanting her to say more.

But Birdie just smiled into her own memories.

"You're right. All three of you," Mae said. "I was seeing the glass half full, thinking of the earlier years. Something did change around that time. Yes. He looked better, healthier. For a time there, Cliff truly loved life." Her expression changed as the time line of her thoughts progressed.

"I think it was shortly after the girls went off to college and Elizabeth was spending most of her time in New York, checking on the girls. Cliff was happy. And then suddenly he wasn't. It was like his world fell apart in a day. He wouldn't talk to me when he started to fall apart, when the gray came back. Nor did he talk about those surprising years when he was so happy. But . . ."

"But?" Birdie asked.

"But . . . well, I knew my brother well. And I knew that it wasn't only the sailboat that had changed his life. But then . . . well, then he died. A good man who died too young."

Birdie had been quiet, but she looked up now, as if Mae needed her affirmation, too, that her brother was a good man.

"I knew Cliff nearly his whole life," she said. "And I did see that sadness a few times. We talked about it some. I know what you're saying, Mae. But you need to remember how happy he was before that."

Birdie looked at Mae to see if perhaps they should move on to another topic, but Mae seemed to want to hear more.

"I know what you're saying, Birdie. I know Cliff was truly happy for a while. I didn't pry, but he had found a new life. I don't know if it was his love for sailing and the beautiful new boat he had purchased or something else . . ."

Birdie chuckled. "And does it matter? Maybe it was volunteering at the soup kitchen with me. Whatever it was, it was quite nice. I was very happy for—"

A loud knocking from above interrupted Birdie's sentence, shattering the quiet in the knitting room.

Mae jumped up and looked at the clock as she wiped her eyes. "Oh, dear, I guess I'd better get to work. I don't want the boss to fire me." She managed a laugh as she nodded at Izzy and started moving toward the stairs.

"Mae, just one more thing," Birdie said, holding up one hand.

Mae turned.

"I've been concerned about Rose. I haven't seen much of her. Have the girls spent time together this week?"

"I'm not sure, but Rose checked in with me a night or two ago. She was with Lucky Bianchi—they'd been working on the fashion runway for the show. It seems to be a good diversion for Rose. When she talked about their project, she looked happy. She asked me if I'd seen Jillian, too, so I would guess that means no, she hadn't seen her, or she wouldn't have asked. She asked it so tentatively that it made me sad. Like she thought she had no right to ask about her own sister. She was hurting. I know she was."

Mae paused, then shook her head. "Sea Harbor is a funny

place—when you're trying to avoid people in this town, you run into them on every corner. Not so when you'd love to see someone's smile. Or frown. Or just to give them a hug. That's when they're nowhere to be found."

Then she put a smile on her face, turned away, and was gone, hurrying up the three steps to greet the customer—one of many who knew that CLOSED signs in Sea Harbor didn't always mean what they said.

After Mae left, Birdie, Nell, and Izzy sat quietly for a while, their hands cupped around cold lattes. Finally, they reflected on the unusual conversation they'd just had with Mae.

Izzy looked across the table at Birdie and Nell. "There were things said about Cliff Anderson just now that were not said out loud. What was I missing?"

"My dear Izzy, you never miss a thing," Birdie said. Then she picked up her bag from beneath the table and pushed back her chair. "But here's what's happening right now. Luna will be here any minute—in fact, I think I just heard her voice. She's going to help Mae for the day. Mae said there are no classes scheduled. It will be mostly customers hanging out down here, knitting, and feeling safe and comfortable, and forgetting what's going in the world beyond the shop's door."

"That's definitely a public service you provide, Izzy," Nell said. "A very real need right now."

"I didn't know Luna was coming in," Izzy said. "We usually know she's coming in when we see her. Sometimes I think you know my shop better than I do, Birdie."

"I have my ways," Birdie said, her eyes smiling. "I suggest what we need right now is to get some fresh air and clear our heads." Her coat was already on, and her purse strap over her shoulder.

"Excellent idea," Nell said, pushing back her chair. "Besides, it's almost lunchtime. Cass is meeting us at Harry's deli when she can get away."

Izzy frowned as she got up and collected the empty coffee cups. "Why do I get the feeling you two are clairvoyant? Or seeing things I'm not? Or speaking in ways I can't hear? Cass is meeting us?"

"It isn't only the kids who send texts with their phones out of view," Nell said.

Izzy laughed and tugged on her jacket. She started for the stairs to check in with Mae.

"No," Nell said. "That won't do, Izzy. You will never escape if you go up there."

She hooked her arm through her niece's, and the three women walked toward the alley door stealthily, ignoring the sounds of increased footsteps and voices above, along with Luna Risso's loud, ringing admonitions to a woman to take her needles away from her child immediately. "Or she'll poke her eyes out," she scolded.

Chapter 26

Harry Garozzo's deli had the usual noisy crowd in the front, waiting in line to pick up cheese and bread, dinner, tubs of Italian wedding soup, and sundry other take-out delicacies for the weekend ahead.

Behind the counter, a robust Harry, wearing his usual smudged white apron, waved to them. "Table is ready, ladies," he called out while cutting a hunk of mortadella into thin slices for his mortadella panino.

"Ready?" Izzy said. "Geesh. How did Harry know we were coming?"

"I think he just assumes we'll be by one day or another," Birdie said. She smiled and waved to her longtime friend, mouthing a thank-you.

They walked through the wide opening into the restaurant part of Harry's deli, a room that backed up to the sea, with red-and-white-checked plastic tablecloths on the tables, and chef-shaped salt and pepper shakers that looked a little like Harry and his wife Esther. The wide windows captured million-dollar views of lobster and fishing boats going out to sea, a few sailboats determined to get a couple more weeks in before putting the boats to bed for the winter.

And just as Harry had promised, the table was ready. Tucked into the farthest corner of the room, it was set with glasses, mugs, plates, and utensils, with a small RESERVED sign in its center, smudged with a dab of tomato sauce, which made them think Harry himself had put it there. Their own little boardroom, Harry called it. A place for them to solve the problems of the universe.

They had barely sat down when a familiar voice greeted them.

"So what'll it be, favorite ladies?"

The three women looked up into the smiling face of the young waitress who had become a part of their lives in recent years. As the best friend of Cass and Danny's nanny, Molly, Shannon Platt was privy to all the goings-on in the Seaside Knitters' lives. She'd even learned to knit in the past year.

Nell noticed her glancing at the empty chair. "No worries, Shannon. Cass'll be along. She had the audacity to hand out paychecks to her crew first."

Shannon laughed. "My kind of boss. Paychecks are good."

"What's going on over there?" Birdie asked, pointing across the room to two small tables pushed together to seat six women.

Shannon looked over. "Oh, it's some of the high school teachers. I swear they have more days off. 'Meetings,' they say. Hah. But today they're only off for lunch. Poor them."

"Do you know any of them?" Nell asked.

Shannon looked back to the table. "Sure. All of them. But not well. The only one I really know is sitting at the end of the table. She was in the knitting class Molly and I took."

"I thought she looked familiar," Izzy said. "Natalie something. Simpson, I think. Nice person."

"She is. Molly and I went out with her a couple times. In fact, she introduced me to this new guy I'm seeing. Josh Elliott's death was hard on Natalie. The whole school, but Natalie was a friend of his." She turned back to the table. "But it was hard on all of you, too. On everyone. It's all kind of hard to get your mind around."

They all agreed.

"You probably hear a lot of talk about it in here, Shannon," Izzy said.

"It's pretty much all people talk about. Mostly questions. Who did it? Why? How could this happen? And then people try to come up with answers, but there aren't any. At least as far as we know, anyway. It's frightening when you think there might be someone out there. Or maybe sitting in here. Maybe wanting to hurt someone else." Shannon shivered.

"Hopefully, things will return to normal soon," Birdie said. "The one thing that won't be normal is the loss of Josh Elliott. He'll be terribly missed."

"It must be difficult for the teachers who worked with him," Nell said, although she wasn't at all sure that was true. At least not for a few of them. She looked over at the table again.

Shannon nodded. "Well, I guess not everyone likes everyone. I did hear Josh's and Jillian's names pop up here and there. Like, once or twice—or maybe, like, ten or twenty times."

"Oh?" Izzy looked up.

"You know how it is. A couple teachers would mention hearing that the two of them were spending time together outside of school. Even camping out together, which sometimes was said as if they'd violated some invisible code or something. That sort of thing. The school is just like any workplace, I guess. People talk. People know what's going on in each other's lives, even when they don't really know. You know what I mean?"

Yes, they knew that well.

"I don't see the principal over there. Does she join them?" Nell asked.

"Judith Garvey? No, I don't think she does lunches with the staff. But I think they like her. Sometimes I see her out walking or at the Y. She likes that sort of thing and maybe gets her exercise in at lunchtime."

Nell looked over at the group, trying not to stare at them. She suspected that Judith Garvey probably stood a little apart from her teaching staff, creating a certain boundary maybe. Especially now, when dealing with the tragic death of one of her teachers. It couldn't be an easy task.

"Hey, what have I missed?" Cass said, coming up beside Shannon as she scribbled down an order for three Venetian soups.

"Just everything." Shannon grinned, moving aside to let her sit down. "But what would you like today, Ms. Catherine Halloran Brandley?"

"I'll have what they're having," Cass said with a grin.

"Ah. One of my very favorite old, old movies," Shannon said with a chuckle, then hurried off.

Cass took a drink of water, then looked across at Birdie. "Okay, one thing I know. We're not any closer to knowing who murdered Josh Elliott, at least not from the look on your face, Birdie. You're not sleeping. That's not good."

Birdie smiled with a sigh. "You're right. At least last night I wasn't."

"Too many threads," Izzy said. "It's so difficult to find any order in all this."

"That's what it is. Yes. I keep trying to pull my thoughts together, expecting them to result in a perfectly put together jigsaw puzzle. But nothing fits. I couldn't get Josh off my mind last night. I thought back over conversations the four of us have had or ones we've listened to the past few days. And I finally realized part of the problem."

They all looked at her.

"We don't know enough about Josh Elliott himself," she

said. "We especially don't know what he could have done—or not done—to make someone want to kill him."

They all thought about that for a minute, and then Izzy said, "It's true. We know his good qualities . . . his likability. His teaching ability . . ."

"The police say it wasn't random. So for some reason, someone felt they had to end Josh's life," Nell said.

"Exactly," Birdie said, pouring herself a cup of tea from the pot Shannon had left on the table. "And I know Chief Thompson and Tommy Porter are doing a great job gathering information, probably with a board on the wall that lists all possible suspects. At least that's how they do it on my BBC mysteries. But the police have to follow protocol. Obey investigative rules and such. And we don't have to do that." She finished with a smile.

"Yes," Izzy said, unfolding her paper napkin and pulling out a pencil. "I couldn't sleep last night, either. And it's what you said, Birdie. We're going in so many different directions, and they don't seem connected. Maybe some of them aren't. Like the argument between Rose and Jillian . . ."

"And yet that does connect to Josh in some way," Nell said. "Why was Josh such a thorn in Rose's side?"

"She seems to just brush it off if you ask her," Cass said.

"The one thing we do know is that Rose is under this enormous shadow of guilt, and that's terribly painful," Birdie said. "We need to get rid of it."

"So . . ." Izzy continued, writing Rose's name in caps in the middle of a circle on the napkin.

The smell of soup interrupted the conversation's flow as Shannon appeared with bowls filled with their order. Izzy moved her napkin to the side as the waitress expertly placed them on the table without spilling a drop.

"Wow," Cass said, closing her eyes and breathing in the fragrance of minced vegetables floating in a light herbed broth, with basil, pine nuts, and sweet marjoram swimming among the vegetables. "Those Venetians," she said. "They definitely know how to make soup."

"And so does our Sicilian friend Harry," Birdie said with a smile.

While the others dipped their spoons into the flavorful soup, Izzy took her napkin back, straightened it out, and drew a line out from Rose's name. At the end of it, she wrote: *Worried about Jillian's relationship with Josh.* And another line out from Rose's name ended with *Keys lost at site of crime.* Josh's name then appeared in a circle of its own, with a line connected to Rose's.

She held up the napkin.

"A good start," Birdie said, wiping a tiny piece of carrot from the corner of her mouth.

"I think Rose was more than just worried about Josh and Jillian's relationship," Cass said slowly, thinking as she talked. "She seemed to truly dislike Josh," she added.

"Although she told me she didn't know him well enough to dislike him," Birdie said.

"Well, maybe resented him? Resented the time Jillian spent with him? Or something else that maybe we're missing . . ." Cass said.

"Cass may be on to something," Nell said slowly. "There's more to Rose's reaction to their relationship," she said. "Figuring it out may be important, because right now, the feelings she's expressed in public about him are so terribly damning for her. Surely, a motive writ large on that big police board of suspects."

Izzy put her spoon down and turned to Birdie. "Birdie, you never said much about the night Rose turned up at your house. Could she have said something that night that might shed some light on all this confusing mess?"

Birdie thought back to her surprise dinner guest. She hadn't said anything about it because somehow it seemed private and completely unrelated to Josh's murder. Rose had been upset and had just needed someone to listen to her, someone to make her feel safe. She thought back over the conversation, which in retrospect seemed a bit disjointed. But Rose was in a tough situation now, and maybe even stray pieces of conversation might help.

"It was a meandering conversation about different things," Birdie said. "She talked about Jillian, which you'd expect. She was aware of how utterly terrible Josh's murder was for her sister. I think Rose felt Jillian's sadness almost viscerally. And yet she realized she had given her sister such a hard time about Josh that she was probably the last person Jillian would want to talk to."

"And, unfortunately, she's probably right about that," Nell said.

Birdie nodded. "And she talked about her family—about her dad a little."

"Her dad?" Izzy asked. "That reminds me of something I'd forgotten, because it didn't seem important at the time. That day in the bar when Rose confronted Josh, telling him to get out of Jillian's life, she mentioned her father. Something like, 'What about my dad?' And I think she mentioned her mom, too. Like Josh being in Jillian's life was bad for her whole family, and he should be aware of that."

Birdie sat in silence, thinking back to their earlier conversation with Mae. She knew Cliff Anderson and liked him very much. His depression wasn't something she had noticed. But she had noticed the change in him when he was volunteering and how he enjoyed getting to know others doing the same work. She would see him often. And she watched him come alive. She frowned. "It's strange. Rose didn't connect her parents to Josh Elliott when she talked to me. I can't imagine he even knew them. His parents may have, but not Josh, not unless he was a dental patient. And yet . . ."

". . . Rose was making a connection there," Izzy said, finishing the sentence.

"But it could have been an innocent one," Nell said. "Rose seems to still be having some problems with her mother's death. Maybe she was simply saying she had enough to worry about coping with her parents' deaths without having to worry about Jillian's relationship, too."

But even Nell seemed to be pushing too hard to explain the odd connection.

"It's especially curious since Rose's parents aren't with us anymore," Birdie said. "But she did seem interested in Josh's family when she was talking with me that night. Especially his mother."

"Like if Josh had a nice mother, maybe he'd be right for Jillian?" Cass said. "That doesn't sound like Rose. She is a smart, logical woman. And that reasoning is neither."

"I agree. But there was something there, something in her face," Birdie said. "As if she was pleased that I said he had a nice mother."

"Did she say anything else?" Nell asked. "As disjointed as these things may seem, I do think they're worth thinking about. Maybe together, we can find a reason in them to explain Rose's behavior."

"A reason that will prove she's innocent," Izzy said flatly.

"There was one more thing Rose talked about," Birdie said. "It might have been the real reason she came."

With the soup bowls almost empty, Birdie had everyone's attention.

"She asked me about promises and secrets, and the morality of keeping them."

"What?" Cass said, surprised.

"The questions weren't frivolous. She seemed truly burdened by them. She had made a promise. I suspect it was to her mother. Maybe even a deathbed promise."

Izzy looked down at her napkin, now slightly smudged with Venetian soup. Another spoke came out from Rose's circle. *Promise made*, it read at the end. And two more words followed, with a question mark. *To mother?*

"Sorry to interrupt," Shannon said, appearing at their table with a handful of napkins, several small plates, and a platter of cannoli. She set the plates and the platter on the table and offered the napkins to Izzy. "You can have my order pad, too, if you want real paper."

Izzy laughed and took the napkins.

"Oh, and Harry says the cannoli are a requirement for you today. You look too serious, or so the boss man says." With that, the waitress was gone, making her way expertly around tables, greeting late lunchers, and picking up checks and large tips, which Shannon most often received, along the way.

Izzy looked down at the creamy cannoli. "I'm almost too full for these."

Cass eyed them. "Me too. But orders from Harry can't be ignored. He'll never let us back in. Take away our table. All those things." She passed around the cannoli.

"You know, there's someone else here that we've nearly forgotten about," Birdie said. "Someone connected to the girls, and if not to Josh, at least to the place where he was killed."

"Henry Staab," Nell said. "Yes, you're right, Birdie."

"Not that he could kill a flea," Birdie added quickly. "But he is very fond of Rose. Jillian too."

"That's right. And he said Rose visits her mother's grave more often."

"And argues with her mother?" Cass asked.

"It seems so," Birdie said. "Perhaps like I talk to Sonny, although we don't argue much."

"I haven't seen Henry for a while," Birdie said. She looked at Nell. "Why don't we pay him a visit? Maybe we can pull something out of him that will make the damning things that surround Rose not so damning."

"Excellent idea. We talked only briefly when I saw him the other day."

"I'll take some mums with us. I probably know half the people buried there."

Izzy made a note at the bottom. *Tasks*, it read.

Birdie smiled.

"Well, before Luna fires me, I suppose I should get back to work." Izzy slipped a cannoli into a small box Shannon had provided, and pushed back her chair. She was about to stand when a vigorous wave from halfway across the room stopped her.

Harper Mancini, her long blond hair cascading over one shoulder, was walking quickly toward their table. Izzy waved back, and the others looked up.

"Goodness," Birdie said. "Look who's here."

Harper leaned down and hugged Birdie. It was a warm embrace, as if they had been friends for a very long time. And much to Nell's, Cass's, and Izzy's surprise, Birdie hugged her back.

Harper pulled away and greeted everyone else around the table, sending an air kiss to Izzy.

Birdie took a moment to catch her breath and then introduced Harper to Nell and Cass.

"I feel like I know you both," Harper said, reaching out her hand and greeting them warmly, as if they, too, were now on her good friends' list. "I've seen you in Izzy's most amazing shop, which I dearly love. And I know you are all friends. And gorgeous knitters."

"Is Leon with you, dear?" Birdie asked. "Or would you like to sit and talk to us for a minute or two?"

Izzy set her cannoli box on the table, as if she knew this might take a while.

"Leon? Here? Oh, no, Birdie. Never. This was a ladies'

lunch." She turned back to wave at her companions, who were now heading toward the door. "We just finished. Harry's food is so delicious, especially if you're Italian. Which I am now." She smiled proudly and sat down. "Those are my tennis friends. We lunch after our lessons. They're really nice gals."

Then she turned her attention to Birdie. "I know I'm interrupting, Birdie, and I'm so sorry, but I really need to talk with you. I'm so glad I saw you over here."

Her contagious smile began to dissolve as she started to explain why she needed to talk. The words began in a normal tone, then started to come out faster and faster. Harper pressed her palms onto the tabletop to keep herself still.

"I'm just so terribly, terribly sorry for Leon's unforgivable behavior at Josh Elliott's funeral. Is that what I should call it? Or the service we went to. But he didn't really mean to be disrespectful. He's one of those people who doesn't like funerals. He just doesn't."

Without stopping for a breath, she went on, talking so fast now the women listening were trying hard not to miss words.

"He really didn't want to go to Josh's funeral. He said he would be a hypocrite if he went. But that made no sense. So I begged him. 'Josh is Mr. Elliott's son, for heaven's sake,' I said. Though I didn't know Mr. Elliott, because that was before we married. And then he died. But Leon told me how they were good friends. So how could he not go to Josh Elliott's service? He was his friend's son. It didn't matter if he liked him or not. He really wasn't being himself and especially not that day. He took his tiredness out at the worst possible time. Right there in the church hall."

Birdie put up a hand to let her rest, but Harper went on without a break.

"But I told him that no matter what was going on, one didn't just walk out like that without even thanking the hosts, whether he wanted to be there or not . . . whether he liked the deceased or not. He just shouldn't act like that at a—" Her chest rose and fell, and her cheeks had lost their glow, replaced by moisture on her forehead.

Izzy reached over and rested her hand on top of Harper's. "Hey, it's okay, Harper. Take a breath. Deep . . . That's it. Now let it out. Slowly. That's right."

Harper did exactly as Izzy directed.

"There. Better? You were getting a little light-headed. Not breathing can do that to you."

Harper managed to smile. "I'm so sorry. I just had to get that all out. I love Leon, but I am so sorry that he acted that way in front of Birdie and all the birding group. And at Josh Elliott's funeral. So awful."

Birdie sent a grateful nod over to Izzy for calming her down. Then she looked at Harper, whose eyes were now moist. "Harper, you shouldn't have to apologize for your husband's behavior. Not ever. People should do that for themselves."

Harper leaned over and gave Birdie another hug, her face filled with emotion.

Nell smiled as she watched the warm, grateful embrace. Harper Mancini was a sweet young woman, and certainly proof that opposites attract. Leon Mancini was, as Ben would say, a shrewd businessman. And, apparently, one who didn't like Josh Elliott at all. But he had a sweet young wife who clearly loved him—even though he had walked out on a memorial reception in a church hall.

"Now," Birdie said, "how about a cannoli?" She slid the platter over to Harper.

Harper declined, then picked up a fork and took a taste. "And please understand," she said around a mouthful of pastry, "my Leon is a good man."

"I'm sure he is," Birdie said.

Nell added, "People handle tragedies in different ways. And the funeral is certainly the culmination of this tragedy."

Harper nodded. "Yes, but that was another reason for us to go to the funeral. To be with Polly Farrell and our wonderful birding group. Josh was a part of that group. It would be comforting and a good thing to go. We were like a family."

She looked over at Birdie and smiled. "All the birder people are so nice, even when they're cranky, and being together at such a sad time, after losing one of our own, would help Leon. I just knew it would. He loves watching the birds."

"Bird-watching is probably a good way for your husband to relax," Cass volunteered, still trying to figure out exactly who this friendly woman was. "Everyone with a stressful job needs a way to unwind, a good hobby."

Shannon, noticing that there was a newcomer to the group, leaned in between Cass and Harper and asked if anyone would like more tea or water.

Harper looked up, smiling up at Shannon. "I would love a glass of red wine, please. And your cannoli is absolutely amazing. Thank you so much, Shannon."

Shannon left, a smile on her face.

Harper picked up the conversation. "Yes, Cass, that's it exactly. You understand. He works so hard, and when he's home, always in his den. And so often closing the door behind him." She rolled her eyes. "At least I can be with him when we're out watching the birds. I enjoy being outside. Although it will be sad without Josh."

"You said Leon enjoyed working with Peter Elliott," Nell said. "I wonder if Josh's funeral reminded him of Peter's accident and his funeral. Maybe that's why he didn't want to be there?"

Harper thought about that, her fork in the air, then she took another scoop of cannoli and answered definitively, "No, I don't think that was why, Nell. Leon didn't want to go because he didn't like Josh."

"What?" Cass asked, having a better idea now who Harper was. The nice gal married to the older guy who had managed

Josh's family company since Peter Elliott died. "Josh was a great guy. What was not to like?" she said.

Shannon was back and discreetly placed a glass of red wine at Harper's place. Harper looked up, thanked her profusely, and took an immediate drink. Then she looked back at Cass.

"Yes, he was a great guy, Cass. That's exactly what I said to Leon." Harper's face lit up, as if she'd found a great new ally in Cass. "Why didn't he like this wonderful guy? I don't have a clue."

"Could he have been jealous of him?" Birdie asked. "Remember when Josh rescued you because of your poor ankle?"

"Oh, pooh. I wished that had been true. I would like to have made him be a little jealous. But he wasn't. I think he knows he's the only one for me. Frankly, I just don't get it. Josh was not in Leon's life, really—well, except for the birding things and the business, sort of. Which paid Leon fistfuls of money. So how could he dislike him?"

"What do you mean?" Cass asked. She picked up another fork and began working on the last of the cannoli.

"Well, he told me that Josh Elliott never liked the family business and wanted nothing to do with it. And that was good, Leon said. At least he wouldn't mess up the company, like some rich kids did. He taught kids. He knew nothing about business. His dad and Leon were the businessmen. And on and on."

"So Josh had nothing to do with the company. Interesting," Izzy said.

"After Mr. Elliott died, which was before I was in the picture, like I said, Josh went to the annual meeting sometimes. Just to make sure there was an Elliott on the board or whatever. It'd be held at a fancy hotel. After Leon and I tied the knot, I'd get to go, too. There was plenty of great shopping, an amazing dinner, and swimming pools. I'm pretty sure I saw Josh at my first one a couple years ago. So that was about the extent of his involvement in the company. Mine too," she said with a grin.

"So those occasional meetings and our bird-watching sessions were the only times Josh and Leon were together?" Birdie said.

Harper took a sip of wine, then paused, as if she'd been mistaken. "Well, yes, Birdie. I think so. Except for a couple weeks ago. Josh Elliott called an unplanned company meeting. Not at a fancy hotel. It was right at the company offices over in Beverly. And just for a select few of the higher-ups. It was on a Sunday, I remember, and with no notice. Which Leon didn't like at all. But the message said it was mandatory. Some business thing. Leon didn't want to go that day, either, just like the funeral. He thought Josh didn't have the right to call them in on the spur of the moment, since Josh had nothing to do with the company, anyway. And especially not on a weekend."

"But Leon went?" Izzy asked.

Harper nodded. "Looking like an old grump. Complaining about Josh ruining his Sunday golf game. He said Josh rarely showed up at meetings, and now was calling for one on a Sunday. How dare he. But his language was a little more colorful."

"Well, Harper, I'm afraid I get that," Cass said. "My crew would be mad, too, if I scheduled a meeting on a weekend. I'm afraid I'm with Leon on this one, much as I loved Josh."

Harper toasted Cass with her glass of wine. "Here's to you, Cass. I was mad, too."

"Well, I hope it was worth missing the golf game," Nell said, smiling. She wasn't sure where the conversation was going. Harper was vivacious and sweet, and clearly enjoyed talking, but the restaurant was nearly empty, and she could see the staff waiting to clean up.

"Well, not so you'd notice, Nell," Harper said. "He'd much rather have been out on the course. Leon was even more angry when he got home that afternoon. No, not angry. He was off-the-wall furious. When I asked why, he said some things that weren't very nice about Josh."

"What kinds of things?" Birdie asked, frowning.

"Oh, just calling him names. Some words you wouldn't want to hear me say. I'm not sure I'd even pronounce all of them right. And I'd have to go to confession. This time when Leon went into his den, he didn't just shut the door. He slammed it. Really loud. It wasn't our best Sunday, that much I remember."

"But things have calmed down at home since then, I hope," Birdie said. "People don't stay angry forever."

"Well, Birdie," Harper said, swallowing her last bite of cannoli. The smile was gone again. "You saw him that day at Josh's memorial affair. He left without even saying good-bye. His manners certainly haven't improved."

Chapter 27

Nell drove into the driveway, unusually tired. The lunch had involved more conversation twists and turns than the four women had anticipated. She tried to think back over the conversation with Harper, somehow feeling that tucked inside of it was something they should be paying more attention to. But it had switched directions too quickly to find straight lines to follow.

The relationship between Josh Elliott and Harper's husband was a curious one, considering Leon Mancini's ties to the Elliott family. Harper had made some interesting points. Birdie had agreed. But what was equally curious, Birdie had said, was that their relationship as fellow bird-watchers—and very accomplished ones—wasn't really adversarial. The two men simply didn't have one.

But, both women had agreed, it was probably a good thing that Josh didn't get involved in the company. That kind of rift between the owner and an executive in a real estate firm could have been disastrous. The contentious Sunday meeting that Harper had described spoke to that fact.

Nell spotted an old Jeep parked across the street. Wondered

about it briefly, then walked into the short back hallway of the house. She hung her keys on the hook and walked into the family room, spotting the closed den door.

It was just as she suspected. Ben was exactly where she had left him, sitting behind the old desk, pondering over the complicated Barlow family trust that now rested in the hands of a young high school teacher.

She poured herself a glass of water and settled at the kitchen island, checking emails and texts and the day's mail, glancing occasionally at the closed door.

Just as she finished stacking up the bills to be taken care of later, the den door opened. Jillian Anderson, followed by Ben, walked out.

"Hi, Nell," Jillian said.

Nell looked at her tired eyes and pale face. Multi-streaked curly hair stuck out from a baseball cap, and her jeans looked like she'd been camping out in them for days.

"Oh, Jillian," Nell said softly, walking across the room. She wrapped Jillian in a warm hug.

Jillian's smile had been sad, but when she pulled away, it was Nell who had tears in her eyes. She could feel the raw pain of Jillian's loss as she hugged her.

Ben excused himself for a minute. "I have a call," he said. "But I made some coffee." He motioned toward the coffee corner on the kitchen counter.

Jillian welcomed the coffee mug Nell handed her and sat on one of the tall kitchen stools. "How's Aunt Mae?" she asked. "I know she's probably worried. I'll check in with her. I just needed to be alone for a while."

Nell nodded. "Then that's what you should do," she said. "And your aunt understands. She's suffered loss in her life, too." She handed Jillian a pitcher of cream and sat down beside her.

There was a pause. Then Nell asked, "Have you seen Rose?"

At first, Jillian seemed to be more interested in the color transformation of her coffee as she stirred cream into it than talking about her twin.

"I don't mean to pry," Nell said. "But I think she's suffering, too."

Jillian nodded. "I know. But I just don't have room in me right now to bring us together the way we need to be. Or even for her to bring us together. I know Rosie so well, but this thing she had about Josh, what she was trying to do—it's still too present, too hurtful. Too unexplainable."

Nell wanted to say that she didn't understand it, either. Nor did Birdie or Cass or Izzy. In fact, no one but Rose seemed to know why she had tried so hard to pull her sister away from someone Jillian had truly and honestly fallen in love with.

"But I know she didn't kill Josh," Jillian said, her voice almost a whisper. "I know that. She's my sister, and she loves me—and I love her."

Nell got up to give Jillian some space and fiddled around in the refrigerator, bringing out a round of Brie. She placed it on a cheese board with a bowl of crackers—knowing that neither of them would touch them.

When Nell sat back down, the cheese board and napkins between them, Jillian surprised her by tentatively taking a slice of cheese and spreading it out on a cracker. She took a nibble, then put the cracker down, and brought up the reason she was there in Nell and Ben's home.

"Ben told me that he's talked to you about Josh's plans," Jillian began.

"Yes," Nell said. "Your life has taken many turns these past days. Very difficult ones." She watched Jillian's face but saw no clues as to how she felt about this latest curve.

Jillian nodded. "But I've had help navigating them. Ben is a very wise man." She lifted her mug and sipped her coffee slowly.

Peace, Nell thought. That was what she was reading in Jillian's presence. Somehow there was peace there, buoyed up by a bottomless sea of sadness.

"Josh and I talked about so many things," Jillian was saying, looking up from her coffee. "We trusted each other with our lives, our hearts. But this . . . this isn't exactly what I was thinking about when we talked about things like that." Jillian managed a small smile. "This is new. But each day with Josh was new. And now he's added yet another new day."

"Your trust in each other must have been deep for you to be taking this so calmly."

"Our trust was complete," Jillian said.

"And you trust this new focus will fit into your life," Nell said. She had started to ask a question, but it had ended in a statement. She could see in the young woman's face that when she said they had shared complete trust, there were no exceptions.

"Nell, you must wonder about me. I probably sound naïve or like I'm on something. I get that. But Josh and I were connected in a way that what the other thought of or wished for was accepted by us both with a whole heart. It wasn't dependency. It wasn't that. It's just that we were bigger, larger together than we were separately."

Nell refreshed their coffee, watching the color come back to Jillian's face as she talked about Josh. It was almost as if Jillian had Josh there with her, which made Jillian's somewhat hazy words easier to comprehend.

Jillian continued. "And before you say anything, I know that sounds goofy or otherworldly or made up." She paused, then shrugged. "It's not."

"I wish I had known Josh," Nell said.

"Well, you know me." Jillian smiled.

"Yes," Nell said. Then she affirmed it again, knowing, as the thought settled, what Jillian had meant. It clearly had nothing to do with one person giving up independence. It was, in a way, the opposite.

Ben walked in from the den, putting his cell phone back in his pocket.

"I'm sorry for deserting you two. That call took longer than I expected." He poured himself a cup of coffee and sat down across from the two women.

"So," he said, looking from one woman to the other. "Jillian, I think Nell is feeling what I felt earlier. You are an amazing young woman. I didn't know you well before, but what I know now makes me look forward to the future. I didn't know your mother, but I knew your father, and I know how proud he would be of you this week. And frankly, your ability to absorb all that we've talked about today is nothing short of amazing."

Jillian put her elbows on the counter and looked over at Ben. "That's nice of you to say, and I appreciate it, but I don't need that. I don't aim for amazing. Or for anyone to be proud of me, not even my dad. I really don't. I do owe you thanks, though. You've been a great support to me today."

"Well, I've thrown a lot at you."

"Yes, but in addition to explaining things that could have taken me months to understand, you've been a great listener and a guide. A friend. Both of you."

"Ben is definitely all those things," Nell said. "But even if you don't aim for amazing, you are."

Ben took another drink of coffee, then put on his readers and pulled out some notes he had taken during his phone call. "I have one more thing to add to what we've talked about, Jillian. That call was from the attorney who had been on retainer for the real estate company. He and Josh had been friends outside the company, too, and apparently, Josh had trusted him with his thoughts and dealings. It seems Josh had been giving serious thought to selling the company. In fact, he'd started putting things in motion shortly before he died."

Jillian listened and nodded but showed little reaction.

"Did you know this? Did he talk over any of the details with you?"

"No, but he probably wouldn't have. Josh and I were living a minute-to-minute life together, not because we thought it might ever end, but just because there were so many other things that we wanted to fill each of those minutes with. As selfish as that sounds, it's what we tried to do. Oh, sure, we weren't nutty about it. Real life entered in. But when it was just us, we blocked out things that didn't matter to us. Commercial real estate companies, for example. They were a big no-no."

Ben chuckled. "Well said. But Josh did talk about this idea with Father Northcutt, his mother's good friend. Larry knew Amelia as well as anyone could have. Josh wanted to make sure his mother would approve of him selling it. According to the priest, Amelia had once told him that she kept the company only to keep her husband busy. Once Josh had that confirmed, he started putting things in motion, finding a broker and so on. A family-owned real estate company over in Hamilton was interested. The owner wanted to combine the Barlow company with his own."

Jillian nodded.

"You knew?"

"No. But it's what I think Josh would want to do. From what you told me earlier, the sale money would go into the foundation, making it even stronger, to help more people, more children, more schools, more soup kitchens, and a hundred more *mores*. That would be Josh. He wasn't into real estate."

"Is the company sold, then?" Nell asked.

"To all intents and purposes, it is. There's some filing to do," Ben said. "But it will be completed shortly. The new owner will probably take it apart before putting it back together again.

As soon as the t's are crossed, the sale will go through, and the money will be put into the foundation."

"What happens to the company?" Nell asked.

"It will essentially be gone."

Ben looked at Jillian, who was listening with a half smile, but her thoughts seemed to be worlds away from commercial real estate.

Nell was watching Jillian, too, but her own thoughts were elsewhere.

And troubled.

Chapter 28

"Is it the chrysanthemum color you're running out of?"

Izzy and Birdie walked into the yarn shop after lunch at Harry's.

Birdie nodded and pulled out a piece of paper with the dye lot number on it. "I was one skein short. I think it was because I spilled coffee on one of the balls. I can't have my granddaughter smelling like Peet's Coffee."

Izzy chuckled.

The shop was surprisingly calm, with just a few customers wandering around and the click of needles coming from the fiber room. Mae was standing behind the checkout counter, lifting herself up on her toes, then down again. "Good for my bones," she called out to Izzy and Birdie. "It's so quiet even Luna left. She likes chaos. This calm makes her nervous."

Izzy headed over to the merino wool cubbies to find a matching skein for Birdie's slouchy hat.

The front door opened again, this time with a breeze as Laura Danvers rushed in, her dark hair flying. She gave Birdie a hug, then spotted Izzy across the room and yelled out to Mae at the checkout counter.

"Hey, Mae. May I steal Izzy for an hour?"

Izzy walked over and handed Birdie the yarn. "Hey, Laura. What's up? Steal me for what?"

"There's a short assembly at the high school today. Some of the students wanted to have their own kind of farewell to Josh Elliott. I thought you might like to go over with me."

Izzy looked over at Mae.

"Go," Mae said. "All's quiet on the knitting front. But don't forget that gigantic raise I put in for."

Izzy gave her a thumbs-up and headed toward her coat.

Laura looked over at Birdie, but before she could invite her along, Birdie was slipping her shop bag over her shoulder and smiling brightly at Laura.

"A tribute to Josh," she said. "What a lovely thing for the students to do. I'd like to see where Josh taught and maybe meet his coworkers. I haven't been in high school for a very long time. Shall we go?"

"It smells the same as my high school," Izzy said, following Laura through the wide double doors of the large building.

"I know," Laura laughed. "Smelly locker rooms, cafeteria food, and that heavy, pungent-smelling cleaner they mop the floors with every night. Now, don't go getting nostalgic on me, Iz."

Izzy laughed. "I liked high school. Even the smells."

While Laura signed them in, Izzy stood still, looking down the hallway, seeing the shiny floors and the familiar bulletin boards. She tried to imagine Abby, her curly-haired preschooler, heading for her locker someday, laughing with friends.

"It's quieter than I imagined," Birdie whispered, feeling the need to be quiet in the silent hall.

"Until classes change and a noise bomb explodes," Laura laughed. She pointed at the row of gray steel lockers. "You know what's interesting? Kids don't use their lockers much, at least the freshmen don't. Or at least my freshman doesn't. She and her friends would much rather carry thirty pounds of books on their small shoulders. We are raising kids who will have major back problems."

"That pains me to think about it," Birdie said. "I have trouble with my tote bag some days."

"I loved my locker," Izzy said. "I had it all decorated."

"Of course you did," Laura laughed. "Okay, enough nostalgia. Let's meet the powers that be." She held open the door to the administration offices.

A young woman sitting at a desk in a large open area greeted Laura warmly, then spotted the other two women and jumped out of her chair. She was around her desk and hugging the two women in a heartbeat.

"Good grief, Shannon Platt," Birdie said, laughing. "We just left you at the deli. Since when have you taken up teleporting?"

"I know, it's crazy, isn't it? I don't have any college classes on Friday, and Harry only needs me at the deli until two. A guy I've been dating does some accounting work for the school, and told me about this easy part-time gig, so I took it. I come in once or twice a week for a couple hours to be pleasant and do this and that. So, voilà, here I am."

"The high school sure lucked out," Izzy said. "I'm sure you are great at this and thats, and most definitely at being pleasant."

"You work harder than anyone I know," Birdie said. "Be sure to find time to live, dear Shannon."

Shannon promised, then laughed. "But this is my last semester. And then I will be completely smart and able to conquer the world. Maybe my friend Molly and I will open a restaurant. She'll cook, and I'll be the one directing things. Along with this boyfriend, if he lasts. He's into numbers and spreadsheets. Maybe we'll fit him in, too."

She noticed Laura then, standing patiently behind Izzy.

"Oops. Sorry, Laura. I didn't mean to ignore you. But these two women are like second mamas and grandmas and friends all at once, and this is the last place I'd expect to see them. But I'm guessing they didn't come in to see me."

Laura laughed, then inclined her head toward a closed door, lifting her brows in a questioning way.

"Ms. Garvey. Sure. Go right in." She looked over at Izzy and Birdie. "The principal's door is always open to Laura. She's like a goddess here. The golden link between parents and teachers. And believe me, that takes some doing."

"Goddess, hah!" Laura broke out laughing. "But some days I do feel like I spend more time here than my daughter Daisy." She knocked lightly, then opened the principal's door.

Judith Garvey stood up immediately and walked around her desk. "Welcome. Laura always brings me such nice surprises. It's good to see you again, Birdie."

"And this is my friend Izzy Perry." Laura stepped aside and Judith reached out her hand to Izzy.

"It's wonderful to actually meet you, Izzy. I know your yarn shop all too well. It's a wonderful place, but my pile of unfinished knitting projects is requiring its own room." She motioned for them all to have a seat.

"It's a curse," Izzy said, laughing, as they all took a seat.

Judith returned to her own. "I've enjoyed getting to know Mae Anderson, too. We've played mah-jongg together a few times. Lovely lady."

"Be careful with her," Laura said. "I played bingo with her at an event once. She's brutal and doesn't take kindly to losing."

The principal chuckled and promised to do so.

Birdie sat slightly behind the others, watching the nice dynamic between Laura and the principal. How lucky to have a parent like Laura, she thought. Someone so intelligent, energetic, and giving of her time to support the school programs. Judith Garvey clearly respected her. All good things. She wondered if that was the kind of mutual admiration Josh Elliott and the principal had had.

Judith looked more herself today than she had the day of the funeral, Birdie thought, then smiled at her own thought. She had no idea what "looking like herself" even meant. But she certainly appeared more comfortable today in loose slacks, loafers, and a jacket.

"Laura has probably told you about the small program the students have put together. A very thoughtful thing to do. And you are more than welcome to attend."

Birdie thought about the shift in opinion about what might be helpful to the students. They'd heard from Judith a few days before that the teachers wanted a very short service—one that ended up without much mention of Josh Elliott. It was nice to know the principal also listened to the feelings of the students, which seemed to differ from their teachers.

"How are the students doing?" she asked.

"Remarkably well. The teachers, too. We are a strong family. We will get through this."

"But Josh definitely left a hole," Laura said. "A huge one. We've had long talks with Daisy. I'm sure all the parents have."

"Yes," the principal agreed. "It's difficult to lose a teacher. Especially one as talented as Josh Elliott."

Birdie wondered if there was a slight relief in Judith Garvey's yes. As if, as sad as it was, the principal had been under stress trying to keep everyone happy and Josh had made that difficult sometimes, from what she'd heard.

Birdie frowned, scolding herself. She was overthinking things these days, and she knew why. It was Rose. The young woman's sad face when she had shown up at her home had somehow endeared Rose to her. The poor woman was walking around with a weighty cloud of suspicion on her shoulders, which was so difficult, especially in a small town.

Perhaps her desire to lift that cloud was ruining her judgment. Teachers were people, for heaven's sake. Some liked Josh, and a couple didn't.

His offbeat conduct may have caused the principal stress and the teachers resentment.

But it certainly wouldn't have caused Josh's murder.

She tuned back into a conversation about school programs that was going on around her When there was a lull, Birdie brought the conversation back to why she had wanted to come with Laura and Izzy. What better way to get to know Josh better than in the place where he had spent his days?

"Did Josh Elliott fit in here easily?" she asked.

Izzy looked over at Birdie, always amazed at the way Birdie could ask questions, ones that might sound confrontational coming from someone else. But never from Birdie Favazza.

Judith Garvey didn't answer quickly. Her brow wrinkled in thought. "Josh was a wonderful teacher," she said, "and I think all the teachers respected that. He was brilliant. He knew how to reach even the most disinterested students."

"But what about the faculty? His coworkers? Did he fit in with them? With the school routine? I have heard he was somewhat of a renegade."

"There were a few complaints," Judith admitted. "I suppose some of the teachers considered his teaching techniques a little unusual. But here's the thing about Josh"—she half smiled and shook her head—"He either didn't notice or didn't care."

"And you?" Birdie asked, her voice gentle.

"Me?"

"Did you notice . . . or care?"

Judith's brows lifted in surprise at the question.

Izzy's did, too.

"It must have been difficult for you, balancing that sort of thing," Birdie said.

Finally, Judith said, "Yes, I did notice. The teachers here aren't afraid to speak their minds. And I cared, too. That is my job. But firing Josh Elliott, as some of them requested, would not have been a good idea."

Birdie started to ask why but held back. This was a social visit, after all, not an inquisition into hiring and firing policies. Which, she chided herself, she had no right to ask about, anyway. And from the look on Izzy's face, she would soon be accusing Birdie of watching too many *Vera* reruns.

Sensing a slight note of uncomfortableness in the principal's posture, Laura asked when the assembly was being held. "We don't want to miss it," she said. "And I'd like to take my friends on a quick tour of the school first, if you don't mind."

"That's a wonderful idea." Judith stood and walked them to the door. "Be sure they see the new equipment in the auto mechanics department and the technology room. We are becoming high tech."

Judith paused with her hand on the knob and turned toward the guests.

"It's really been a pleasure having you stop in like this. One thing a principal doesn't have, especially if you didn't grow up here, is friends—and not much time to make them. That takes energy and time."

She looked at Birdie. "Anyway, I do hope I see you again. I'd like to talk some more. And I presume I will see you both at the knitting fashion show that my students are talking about. I know it will be wonderful, Izzy."

For a brief moment, Izzy looked surprised, as if she didn't know what the principal was talking about. As if being in a high school had completely taken her out of her world. She laughed as she appeared to come back to reality and realized what the principal was talking about.

"Oh, yes," she said, chuckling. "And then there's that."

Laura started the short tour: a quick look at the sleek and buzzing technology room and the auto mechanics department.

"Amazing, aren't they?" Laura said. "Everything's up to date at Sea Harbor High."

Through the glass window, the women saw a large open room with a high ceiling and a garage door on the opposite side. An array of tools and gadgets, ones Birdie remembered seeing in Pickard's Auto Repair Shop, filled the space. An actual car sitting on a lift, up for repair.

"Amazing," Birdie said. "And so helpful to many of the kids. My friend Shelby Pickard will hire them all."

Laura led them down a long hallway to the auditorium. "I'm taking you the back way, so we're not trampled by a sea of teens."

At the end of the hall, Laura opened a heavy door and motioned them into a back corner of the auditorium, a place to stand in the shadows and watch the students who were already filing in.

"This is delightful," Birdie said. "The energy of youth. Just look at these amazing young people. They're beautiful. Our hope for the future."

Laura and Izzy looked at Birdie, then at each other. It wasn't exactly what they saw as they watched kids teasing and jostling and madly thumbing their phones as they piled into the auditorium seats.

But as usual, Birdie slowed down their thoughts. She was, no doubt, right.

"Do the students have to come to these assemblies?" Izzy whispered to Laura, although the noise coming from the students ensured that no one could possibly hear their conversation.

Birdie leaned in to hear her answer.

"Yes," Laura said. "It's one of Judith's rules. She told the teachers that it builds community and they are obligated to come with their class."

"Hmm," Izzy said and glanced at Birdie.

Birdie read her friend's thought and filed it away.

Everyone went to the assemblies.

Unless you're Josh Elliott.

An attractive young teacher walked out on the stage, and the crowd grew quiet, as if a giant comforter had fallen down on them, enveloping everything and everyone in the room.

"Oh, look. It's Natalie Simpson," Izzy whispered to Laura. "We saw her a couple hours ago, at lunch."

"She's great. Loves the kids."

"And loves to knit," Izzy added. "A sign of character."

The program, which the students had titled *Life with Mr. Elliott*, was indeed, as the principal had called it, short. But each second and minute of it was a tribute to Josh Elliott.

They had patched together videos taken with their phones and had put them together with a recording of biomusic playing in the background, the sounds of birds and water, waves and wind in the trees.

It was a video that, Birdie said later, should have been at Sundance. There were no words, only the sounds of nature, as cameras captured students sitting in silence beside a vernal pond, watching tiny tadpoles dance about; building glaciers; and doing a half dozen other things, all glimpses into their life with Mr. Elliott, who was always in view, guiding, motioning, watching, kneeling down beside a student, listening. Finally, as the music faded away, the camera captured a circle of students and their teacher lying in silence beneath a magical lunar eclipse.

As the film came to an end, the student videographers came onstage to much applause and whistles, and the screen lit up again with a shot of a giant globe created entirely out of dozens of students' signatures. Above the world, the words *Thanks, Mr. Elliott* seemed to waft slowly across the night sky.

Izzy, Birdie, and Laura slipped out the back door before the students got up and followed Laura down the hall.

"What a beautiful send-off," Birdie said. She wiped a trace of moisture from her eyes.

"I wish Jillian were here," Izzy said. "It was wonderful."

"Jilly will see it. I spotted Shannon over on the side, videotaping the whole thing. Jillian probably isn't ready to face this place yet, but Shannon will see that she gets it."

She pushed open the door with the large TEACHERS' LOUNGE sign on it.

A woman sitting by the window stood up quickly at the sound. Her magazine fell to the floor. She was a large woman, with a severe look on her face.

"Is it over?" she asked Laura.

"It is. You missed a nice tribute to Mr. Elliott. The kids and Natalie Simpson did a great job."

"I'm sure they did," she said indifferently. "Now may that be the end of it. We've been in mourning long enough."

Before Laura had time to respond or introduce her to Izzy and Birdie, the woman walked past them and left the room, her low heels making loud noises on the polished hall floor.

"Well, you have almost met Hazel Wallis. She didn't care much for Josh Elliott, which explains why she was sitting in here instead of in the auditorium."

"I saw her at the church," Izzy said. "She wasn't especially friendly to Jillian, either."

"No, she probably wasn't," Laura said, shaking her head. "I suppose going to that service was one thing she wasn't able to get out of."

"I heard the teachers were in charge of the memorial service," Izzy said.

"Teachers?" Laura said, surprised. "Oh, no, it wasn't the teachers who plan—"

The door opened again, cutting off her sentence, and Natalie Simpson hurried in, her smile wide. "Izzy, I thought you might be in here. I spotted you in the back, and I'm so glad I caught you before you left. And you must be Birdie? I've seen you in the yarn shop and around town, too." She smiled and shook Birdie's hand.

"I hope I was behaving myself," Birdie said.

Natalie laughed.

"You and the students did a lovely job with the video," Birdie said. "It certainly brought me closer to Josh Elliott. Even without hearing voices—or maybe because of it—you could feel his connection to the students. There was a magical vibe."

"Thank you, Birdie. It was a hard-fought fight to be able to do it, but it worked out."

"What do you mean?" Laura said. "It was a wonderful idea. The kids obviously loved it, and the teachers, too. I could tell."

"Well, you know how it is, Laura. There're always a few. And they don't hesitate to knock on Judith Garvey's door. She was actually going to go along with the grumps. But apparently, some parents called."

"I'm surprised," Laura said. "When we spoke with Judith earlier, she seemed to think it was a good idea."

Natalie's brows lifted. Then she shrugged and turned to Izzy and Birdie. "One of the loudest voices just walked out of here. Did you meet her?"

"There wasn't time for introductions," Laura said. "Hazel was in a hurry."

"Of course she was." Natalie chuckled.

Laura shrugged, holding back a smile.

"Laura is too polite about things," Natalie said. "She has to be as PTO president. But I don't have to be. The kids call her Witch Hazel, which is appropriate. Every school has one."

"She can be difficult," Laura said gently.

"How?" Izzy looked at Natalie, not wanting to put Laura on the spot.

"Oh, a thousand reasons. But the one that is timely is the campaign she started to get Josh fired. She has been here a long time and really resented him. Intensely disliked him, I would say."

"That's a shame," Birdie said. "But it sounds like Josh could handle things like that."

"Yes," Natalie agreed. "And I didn't mean to be so harsh. It's just that Josh was a wonderful person. I hated seeing him treated badly."

"What does she teach?" Izzy asked.

"I know what you're guessing, Izzy. Wrestling coach, right?" Natalie said.

Izzy chuckled.

"No, our dear Hazel is head of the auto mechanics department. It's actually a good department. Well equipped and the kids get hands-on experience. She does a decent job. It's the other side of her that is a problem."

"But it sounds like Josh had the school principal on his side," Laura said.

"On his side?" Natalie asked.

"Backing him up in the face of adversity. Or in the face of Hazel Wallis," Laura said. "Look at all those wonderful things the students did in your video. Some of those events were out of the mainstream curriculum, I'd guess."

"That's true," Natalie said. "But it was odd, actually. It wasn't just Hazel who wondered how Josh could go outside the curriculum—and outside the school—the way he did. I think even Josh might have thought it was a little odd, but then, I don't really know."

"What was odd?" Izzy asked.

"That Josh never lost his job. Judith Garvey could be tough when she wanted to be. And she hasn't hesitated to let other teachers go. And for lesser reasons, or so it seemed to some of us. Like missing too many staff meetings, too many absences, just plain being teachers who didn't seem to like their jobs. That sort of thing. But don't get me wrong. Many of us were thrilled he wasn't let go. It's just that he did have some leeway that others didn't seem to have."

"So he asked for some liberties, some special things, and got them, while the others didn't?" Izzy asked. "That does sound like some kind of favoritism. Something that could cause problems."

"I don't think that's how it went. Josh just taught how he wanted to," Natalie said. "I doubt if he asked anyone for permission or even thought about his teaching methods as breaking rules or being outside the mainstream way of doing things."

Laura shifted from one foot to the other, then looked up at a gigantic round clock on the wall.

Birdie watched the expression that passed across her face. The woman should be a diplomat, she thought. Laura was worried the conversation was moving into an area that the three of them probably shouldn't be privy, too, and very soon, Birdie thought, she would move them all away from it.

As if reading Birdie's thoughts, Laura looked at her, then Izzy, and spoke to all three women. "I hate to break this up, but I have to pick up my middle school daughter shortly. Would you two mind if I drove you back to the yarn shop now?"

"And I need to run, too," Natalie said. "My class will be on the ceiling if I don't get back. But I'll see you soon, I hope."

Minutes later Birdie and Izzy were back in Laura's SUV, heading out of the parking lot just as a parade of yellow school buses drove in.

"I'm sorry for all that gossip," Laura said. "Things can get screwed up so easily. I think Natalie was very attracted to Josh and was maybe a little overprotective."

"Attracted in a romantic way?" Izzy asked.

"I don't know. Again, it's gossip. A few of the teachers thought she had a crush on him, if that's what you call it. But it was one-sided entirely. In fact, they said Josh probably didn't even notice."

"And now she and Jillian have become friends, so somehow it got worked out," Izzy said.

Birdie sat quietly in the backseat. She was anxious to get home. Things slipped too easily out of her head these days. She needed a quiet place to sit and to examine some threads of Josh Elliott's life. The things he did or didn't do. Perhaps that was where they would find the answer.

Once they had all those threads lined up, they could throw out the ones they didn't need and begin to knit the rest of them together.

Chapter 29

"Has this ever happened before?" Nell asked. She looked around the room at her nearest and dearest friends. She was still dumbfounded by her failure. She had forgotten Friday night dinner. At her home.

Except it wasn't just Nell's failure.

Izzy had realized what day it was when Laura dropped her off that afternoon and asked what she and Sam were doing that night.

"Tonight?" she'd asked with a jolt. "Friday night?"

Birdie had forgotten, too, until Mae had reminded her.

"It looks to me that Cass and I were the only ones who remembered," Danny Brandley said. "But that's because Cass always plans on Nell's leftovers for our Saturday and Sunday dinners, our amazing nanny's nights off."

Sam walked over to the fireplace end of the room with a tray of drinks. "It seems like a night for martinis," he said.

Danny Brandley picked up one and handed it to Nell, then helped himself. "It's been that kind of week, that's for sure."

Nell agreed.

After Jillian and Ben had finished talking that afternoon, Jillian had mentioned that she was going to the Y for a late afternoon swim. Nourishment for body, spirit, and her brain, she'd said. She would feed them all in equal amounts. Nell had joined her, realizing her own brain was muddled and a long swim was exactly what she needed.

And it was. Until as she was drying off, Izzy called, reminding her it was Friday night. "What can I bring for dinner?" she asked.

What Nell had really needed wasn't a swim, after all. It was to prepare food.

She had also forgotten to send the large group text out that morning, reminding friends that, as usual, there'd be dinner at the Endicotts'. So most of those wouldn't come. But there were always those who never read the text and just came because that was what they did on Friday nights. The regulars. And they would be there, even if she called and suggested that all of them go out for Indian food or pizza.

Ben, she thought, hanging her coat on a hook as she came in from the Y. *Of course.* He'd have remembered and picked up steaks or pork loin or a few pounds of cod. All would be well.

But that hope was dashed when she found him asleep on the small couch in the den, his feet falling off the end and his glasses down on the tip of his nose.

It was Izzy who'd saved the day. "Shepherd's pie," she said happily. "My one specialty. I had a super-big one in my freezer and got it out yesterday to thaw. I didn't realize it was so huge."

It was perfect, Nell thought. Things often turn out just as they should. An evening of drinks and heaping helpings of the aromatic and comforting dish, with a fire to ward off the autumn chill. And dear friends. Because they were the ones who always showed up.

They were all tired. The lazy conversation and the crackling flames suited the evening, and although no one admitted it, it seemed that for that brief time, they'd tacitly agreed to ignore what was troubling them and concentrate on the news that Cass and Danny's Joey had mastered the fine art of testing Magic Markers on the wall behind his crib. Then on to a discussion of the garments for the fashion show, and the runway Willow, Rose, and Lucky were working on twenty-four seven.

When the men agreed to clean up the dishes, hiding without much success that it was an excuse to retreat afterward to Ben's den and watch the rest of the Celtics game, no one objected.

As soon as they were gone, Birdie looked into the fire and addressed the elephant in the room.

"My mind is so cluttered that it hurts. I need some clarity, some way to line up things so at the least we can understand where all this is going. That lunch today was full of so many dangling threads I could knit sweaters for all of Sea Harbor with them. And our visit to the high school . . ." She looked over at Izzy. "I don't know what to think about that, but—"

Cass interrupted. "High school? Who went to the high school? My high school?"

Izzy quickly explained the impromptu trip.

They all agreed that the video sounded wonderful, and that if it had been part of the church memorial service, people would have gone away with a memorable glimpse into who Josh Elliott was and how he lived. But at least the school got to appreciate it, and if Laura had a say in it, parents would, too.

"Laura was a perfect tour guide, and the principal was very gracious, considering we popped in on her without notice," Birdie added.

"Which reminds me, "Izzy said. "That school is really up to date. You should take a tour, Cass. You might want to go back and try again."

"Hah," Cass said.

"So those are the pluses from our trip," Birdie said. "But I sensed some undercurrents, too."

Izzy agreed. "Something wasn't as I expected it to be. It's like something is lurking in those polished hallways. Something's there, but not there. I think our lunch was like that, too."

"Gaps," Cass said. "Huge gaps."

"Yes," Izzy agreed.

Nell had been listening carefully. "There's something else I need to tell you. Something to add to all of this. I don't know where it fits yet, but we'll figure it out. I didn't say anything at lunch because Ben hadn't yet met with Jillian."

"Jillian?" Izzy said, alarmed.

"No, nothing bad," Nell assured her. "Just surprising."

Nell quickly filled them in on the fate of the Barlow family foundation and the unique details surrounding it.

"Josh left Jillian a foundation to manage. That is amazing," Cass said.

"It's a huge responsibility," Izzy said.

"Jillian took it all with calm and grace. She seemed at peace with it, welcoming it as if she were being given a part of Josh. She didn't even register surprise. Later she told me that she'll simply change directions. She'd learn about foundations, become a student for a while instead of a teacher. She wasn't sure teaching was for her, anyway, and had thought there might be something else ahead for her. Josh saw to it that there was."

"She's an interesting young woman," Birdie said.

"But doesn't this present a motive?" Cass said.

"You mean because of money, right? I wondered about that at first, if it would be something the police would have to follow up on. But it really isn't," Nell said. "There's a decent salary built in for a manager, and money for maintenance things, but Jillian wouldn't have access to anything else, not for herself, anyway. The foundation is a family one, and its use is carefully controlled."

The second reason Jillian couldn't be considered a suspect, the one that no one would bring up—but that all adhered to staunchly—was the one that didn't hold up in court. Namely that Jillian Anderson was an amazing and honest woman, and she didn't have a murderous bone in her body. And no, she would never have murdered the man she clearly loved. That was ridiculous.

Emotions and intuition. Secret weapons the Seaside Knitters valued and held dear. Weapons they knew professionals couldn't depend on, but they could—and did. And often with great success.

There were plenty of what-ifs that were thrown into the air as they briefly tried to be objective about the family foundation angle, pretending that they didn't know Jillian Anderson, that she was a stranger, maybe even a coldhearted one. A face without a heart. The approach fair-minded prosecutors would need to adopt.

But the what-ifs were as thin as the coffee Izzy made in the yarn shop, so thin they were eliminated summarily and thrown into the fire.

"Jillian Anderson's young life has endured more twists and turns than most people experience in a lifetime," Birdie said. "But she will deal with this. And do an amazing job. It will certainly change her life. I'm wondering if it will change anyone else's."

"What do you mean?" Nell asked.

Birdie shrugged. She wasn't sure what she meant. But she had put it out there in case someone else did.

"We're thinking too much about the family foundation," Izzy said. "At least until we learn more."

"I agree. Father Larry said something at the memorial that may be relevant. At least something to consider," Cass said. "I remember it, because Lucky once said it about Josh, too. He said Josh was honest to a fault."

"Hmm," Birdie said. "Sometimes I think the good padre says things he wants us to notice. In this case, not to make us honest like Josh, but because his honesty may have worked against him."

They thought about that as Izzy scribbled down notes, drawing lines and circles.

"There's something else about the foundation that we need to consider," Nell said. "The amount of money in it is about to grow."

Izzy stopped writing, and everyone's attention turned toward Nell.

"Apparently, Josh had decided to sell the real estate company. That doesn't have anything to do with honesty, but it could be a reason for someone to resent him."

"Resent him? Why?" Izzy asked.

"It's a valuable company, and the sale was done quietly."

"So other companies might have wanted a chance to bid on it," Cass said. "I get that. If another lobster company—a competitor—went up for sale, I'd at least want the chance to buy it. That may be a bit far-fetched, but if we pick it apart—the whole sale element—maybe we will find something better."

"When was it sold?" Birdie asked.

"Quickly, a few days before he died, though Josh didn't plan it to be so fast. He thought it would take weeks, maybe months. He wanted to give the company time to prepare. But someone approached him before he had a chance to put anything in motion. It seemed to be a perfect deal. The new owner wanted it kept quiet until everything had been filed. The sale was never announced before Josh was killed."

"Who bought it?" Izzy asked.

"Someone from Hamilton who already had a similar company. An acquaintance of Josh's, apparently. The new owner plans to take this one apart and put it back together again."

"Like Humpty Dumpty," Izzy said.

"That one didn't work out so well, did it?" Cass said.

"And it's not great news for the people who work there," Izzy said.

"No," Nell said.

There was a pause as they tried to fit the sale of a company into the murder of a talented teacher.

"If Josh was truly honest to a fault—and a nice guy—I wonder if he'd have told people about his plans ahead of time. People who'd be affected by the sale," Cass said. "Customers, people who depended on the company . . ."

"But only if the sale happened," Izzy interjected.

Birdie pulled her brows together. "There are so many pieces to this. I think we all need time to think about it. Poke holes where we can. If we can."

Nell got up and brought back a pot of coffee and cream. "Decaf," she said.

"How would anyone know that Josh would be up there in that difficult-to-find campsite during the night?" Cass asked. "And on that night."

"That's a good point," Izzy said. "Jillian knew. Rose maybe. Henry Staab might have known."

"The whole bird-watching group could have figured it out, knowing he often camped out before group bird-watching." Birdie spoke reluctantly, realizing she suddenly felt protective of her group. "But it seems a drastic measure for anyone to take. And certainly none of the birders would be so bold as to kill someone and then show up the next morning to look at birds."

The others were silent, trying to get inside a murderer's mind. *Bold* was probably right up there somewhere.

Finally, Izzy said, "Okay, our thoughts are all bouncing off each other." She scribbled on her sheet as she talked.

"Yes," Birdie said. "And that's a good thing. We know we're getting close. But we still need to think more broadly. We need to look further. Deeper. But I'm not sure in what direction."

"Exactly," Nell said. "We're learning more and more about Josh. But not enough. Josh may have talked to other people. People we don't know."

"And don't forget the schoolteachers' lounge," Izzy said. "We heard today that a lot of gossip goes on in there, including what staff members do on weekends, where they party, even where they hike or camp out."

"I almost forgot that," Birdie said. "Interesting. So a disgruntled teacher wouldn't necessarily have trouble figuring out where Josh spent his leisure time."

"Henry Staab knows that area like the back of his hand," Birdie added. "He probably keeps track of people who hike around the old granite woods."

Birdie looked at Nell, her brows lifted in a question. Nell nodded and smiled back.

Cass laughed and shook her head. "You two. You just carried on a conversation without talking."

"It has served us well," Nell said with a smile, knowing that her Saturday morning was now planned.

Izzy, feeling the strain of the day, tried to put things into order. "Why would someone kill this man who was a great teacher, loved nature and *birds*, for heaven's sake? And who didn't seem to be hurting anyone else, other than irritating teachers who didn't seem to get the same freedoms Josh did?"

"Can anyone add to that?" Cass asked.

Birdie thought for a few minutes, and then she remembered

something she'd blocked out of her mind in an attempt to protect her bird-watching group. "Betty Warner," she said. Then realized too late she was targeting her birder friends, something she didn't want to do.

"Who?" Izzy and Cass said in unison.

"A nice woman who's in the Feathered Friends group. That day the bird-watching group met, she warned me not to go into the woods. She also warned me not to walk on the slippery rocks, and since she has consistently told me to hold the bottom of my grocery bag when Ella and I have grocery shopped, I didn't think anything of it. She somehow thinks I need warnings. She's a nice, considerate woman."

"Do you think she knew what you'd find in the woods?" Izzy said, almost to herself. "That's strange."

"Why would she do it?" Cass said. "A checker at Market Basket?"

"That's what makes this so difficult, doesn't it? Do any of us know what a murderer looks like? Thinks like? What they do in the daytime?" Nell said.

"Did this Betty and Josh ever talk?" Nell asked.

"No. Never. She did cast angry looks his way sometimes. But he was so knowledgeable about birds that I assumed she was jealous."

"Do you know anything else about her?" Izzy asked.

"Besides the fact that she works at the grocery store and loves bird-watching, I know that she's a single mom who works hard and has a son who went to Gloucester High, and now he drives one of those huge, noisy collection trucks."

"You mean garbage trucks," said Cass.

"Well, yes. I have always had a soft spot in my heart for people who do that work."

"I imagine his mother felt the same way," Nell said.

"Well, yes," Birdie said. "She told Polly that her sole wish for her son was that he'd go to college, which she herself had never been able to do. It almost broke her heart when he didn't, Polly said."

"So you're tying this to Josh. How?" Cass asked.

"I'm not sure," Birdie said. "Polly said something happened in his environmental science class." Birdie wrinkled her forehead. "Actually, I'm not sure Polly told me the whole story. But I know that I saw Betty sending daggers Josh Elliott's way." She managed a tired smile. "I think I was grasping at straws, and that's not fair to Betty. Let's erase that one."

"It's been a long day," Nell said. "I'm having trouble remembering, too."

Noises from the den announced that Sam, Danny, and Ben were tired, too. Or they'd lost interest in the game.

Just as Izzy started to get up, her phone vibrated, sliding across the coffee table.

She picked it up and looked at the screen, then frowned. "It's Mae," she said, reading her name on the screen. "Mae never calls me at night."

The others were already up, cleaning up cups and glasses. They stopped only when they heard Izzy say, "Oh, no, Mae." And then, "Don't worry. We'll check."

She hung up and looked around at the others.

"Izzy, what's wrong?" Nell asked.

"Everyone's okay," she said quickly. "But Mae's concerned about Jillian. She called Mae, asking for the name of a tow company. She's over at the Y, Mae said. You were there with her earlier, right, Aunt Nell?"

"Yes, but Jillian stayed on. She says sometimes if the pool lanes are open, she can swim for hours." Nell looked up and checked the clock on the bookcase. "If she's still there, then that's what she did."

"It seems she did. But she had a flat tire when she left. She told Mae it was no big deal, but she needed a tow."

"So Mae's worried?" Ben asked, overhearing the conversation.

"She is. Everyone's a little nervous these days. And thinking of her niece alone in a parking lot when things are still so uncertain in this town is a worry. Your mind goes crazy and imagines bad things."

"I can head over there to be sure she's okay," Ben said. "She's a pretty self-sufficient lady, but maybe she'd like company. The rest of you have kids to get home to, and, Nell, you're exhausted."

"That'd be great, Uncle Ben," Izzy said. "Thanks. And I kind of told her you'd check on her."

Ben chuckled and headed for his coat.

"I'm going with you," Birdie said, already in her coat and carrying her bag. "You can drop me off on your way home."

It took just a few minutes to arrive at the almost empty parking lot at the Y. The red Jeep was easy to spot, but what surprised both Ben and Birdie was Tommy Porter, in workout clothes, standing next to it, and an unmarked police car and driver nearby. The tow truck driver stood idly by, looking bored.

Jillian raised one hand and waved when she saw the new arrivals. "Hey, I'm fine," she said. "You didn't need to come all this way."

"We packed a lunch for the ten-minute drive," Birdie said, keeping her voice light, while her heart tightened at the sight of Tommy.

"I'm glad you're here," Tommy said, his face serious. "I was working out in the weight room, and when I left to go home, I found this."

"I'm a 'this' now?" Jillian said, trying to tease the look off his face.

Tommy ignored her. "Someone let the air out of the driver's

side tires," he said. "Probably a couple hours ago, when the lot was full and no one noticed. They're pretty flat."

"Teenagers?" Birdie asked. But she knew that was simply the first thing people thought, and it was a shame, after seeing the thought SHHS teenagers had put into a memorial for a teacher they respected. It wasn't teenagers who had done this. She felt sure of that.

Tommy shrugged. "I don't think so. The tires weren't cut. Someone pulled the pins out of the valves. Not a normal kid way of doing bad, illegal pranks."

"So you think it was intentional, that someone knew this was Jillian's car?" Ben asked.

"Yes. The car is pretty noticeable. I knew it was Mae's old Jeep when I walked out of the building. Everyone does. She's got all those political and knitting stickers and who knows what all over the back of it—and Jillian's faculty parking sticker, too. And there's that big dent that Mae created while backing into a fire hydrant. Anyway, I want to get some photos. See if we can get some prints. Maybe you can take Jillian home?"

"Prints? Jeez. Are you sure you need to do all that?" Jillian asked.

"I'm sure," Tommy said. His voice was unusually stern. "We'll get the tires taken care of and get the car back to you. But this isn't a joke, Jillian."

"Why would anyone do that? Half the people in town don't even know me or remember me."

"Did you see anyone at the Y you knew?"

"Tommy, I was in the pool—"

"Not the whole time. You and I sat in the main hallway, talking for a while. Did you see anyone pass us that you knew?"

"No, I didn't. Did you?"

Jillian's comeback was supposed to be humorous—Tommy Porter knew everyone in Sea Harbor. Of course he saw people he knew. But Tommy let it fall flat.

"Tommy, you're scaring me a little. This doesn't make sense."

Tommy looked at Jillian, hesitated, then said, "No, it doesn't make sense. But I think whoever did this knew that this was your car. Knew you were in the Y. And they did it on purpose. To send some kind of message."

He pulled a plastic sheath out from beneath his jacket.

Birdie and Ben moved closer.

"This was stuck underneath the tire," Tommy said.

Inside the protective plastic was a torn piece of paper with a half dozen words, large and bold, scribbled in black marker. It read:

Due U want to be next? MYOB!

Chapter 30

Izzy stood with Birdie near the merino wool cubbies as Birdie read labels and picked out several more skeins of the fine merino yarn.

"Are you making more slouchy hats?" Izzy asked.

"Yes, and these are perfect colors," Birdie said, reading them off the labels. "Midnight Garden for Rose, and Mosaic for Jillian."

"Mosaic seems appropriate for Jillian," Izzy said. "There are so many pieces in her life right now. If only we could put them all together quickly." She absently picked up one of the skeins from the cubby and touched it gently.

Birdie remained quiet, knowing Izzy had more on her mind than yarn. She did, too.

"Sam and I had a feeling we should wait with Aunt Nell last night until Uncle Ben came home. We were glad we did. This damage to Jillian's car adds a whole awful dimension to everything, a really frightening one. What is going on? I hate all this. And I especially hate this for Jillian. And what does that even mean, to tell Jillian to mind her own business?'" Izzy stopped and looked down, composing herself, then asked, "How was Jillian when you dropped her off?"

"She was far better than the rest of us." Birdie glanced over at Mae, who was standing at the computer, pressing keys with a force they didn't require.

Mae looked up. "I can hear you, you know. I'm not deaf." She gave up taking out her frustration on the computer and joined Birdie and Izzy near the wall of cubbies.

"What did you think, Mae?" Birdie asked.

"I saw her for all of two seconds when the police brought the car back. It was late. We both went out into the driveway. The car's fine, Tommy said. I think he had them put new tires on it. Jilly's an unusual woman. I think she has her dad's ability to somehow calm her soul in the midst of adversity."

"She did seem calm," Birdie said. "She's still processing losing her closest friend, and I think all the rest of this is just noise. The one person she'd want to discuss all this with is gone."

"But that note was a clear threat," Izzy said. "You can't just ignore it."

"It was, yes, but it's odd," Birdie said, her forehead puckering. "A misspelled word. Text abbreviation. Torn paper. Tommy thought it was off a flyer at the Y, maybe pulled out of a trash can."

"So, do they think it was spontaneous, then?" Izzy asked. "Someone saw Jillian there and took the opportunity to frighten her?"

All three of them stopped and thought about what that meant. That the murderer was working out at the Y? Or, worse, swimming in a lane next to Jillian?

"But why threaten Jillian? What has she done?" Mae said. "Nothing. Her relationship with Josh could not have meant anything threatening to anybody."

Birdie took a quick breath. *Except for her sister.* But she swallowed the thought and said slowly, "We still don't know why Josh was killed. It sounds like the person who wrote that note might think Jillian knows something, may know whatever Josh knew, whatever that great unknown is that was great enough to take someone's life for."

Mae looked toward the door. Several customers walked in, smiling and waving at the three women. Mae immediately put on a smile and walked over to greet them, then motioned toward a new display of silk yarns they might want to check out. She waved at Birdie and Izzy and headed back to the checkout counter, more comfortable with customers than with talking about things she had no control over.

Birdie and Izzy retreated to Izzy's office, where Izzy asked more questions about the parking lot incident, trying to get her arms around it.

"I took a picture of the note with my phone," Birdie said. "Tommy made the mistake of putting it down on the hood of the car while he explained to Ben how the tire valves had been manipulated." She pulled out her phone and showed the picture to Izzy.

Izzy looked at it carefully. "Do you think this is real?"

"Real?"

"I mean the misspelling and the text abbreviation. It looks like something a kid might do. Could it be a prank?"

"A kid. Are you thinking a student might have done it?" Birdie said, enlarging the photo and looking at it again.

"Or that someone wanted us to think it was a student."

Birdie took a deep breath and shook her head. "Either way, whoever did this knew Jillian and Josh were close. And if it's real, it might mean Jillian is in danger."

When Izzy was called away to help a customer with questions about the fashion show, Birdie stayed behind and looked at the photo again, then slipped the phone into her pocket and walked through the shop.

She picked up her bag of yarn from Mae, then spotted Izzy

near the knitting room steps with a customer and went over to say good-bye.

Judith Garvey turned around, holding several skeins of Mongolian cashmere yarn. "Birdie, what a wonderful surprise," she said warmly. "Three times in one week. I am feeling blessed."

"It's so nice to see you again." Birdie smiled, then looked at the buttery soft yarn in Judith's hands. "This is beautiful yarn. What fine taste you have."

"Oh, no, it's Izzy here with the amazing taste."

"Well, whatever you make with this will be beautiful. And if you don't knit anything, it will be a gorgeous addition to that yarn room you're building."

Judith laughed, seemingly pleased that Birdie remembered their conversation. "You know, I think it's the feel of the yarn as much as the knitting that I love. It comforts me."

"Of course it does. And we all need that," Birdie said. "Especially these days. I may have to come back later and buy some of that, too."

"Comfort or yarn?" Izzy asked.

"Both, my dear Izzy," Birdie said, giving Izzy a quick hug. She bid Judith a good day and quickly made her way through a growing crowd of Saturday morning customers and out the front door.

Nell was right on time. Waiting at the curb.

"What a wonderful woman," Judith said, watching Birdie walk away.

"Yes, she is. Birdie is . . . Birdie is my beacon of light," Izzy said. Then she stopped, surprised at herself for what she'd said. Somehow it was almost too personal a thing to say to this woman, nice as she was, since she was practically a complete stranger. It almost seemed as if she'd revealed one of those emotions that the four knitting friends held near and dear—and kept private.

Silly, she said to herself. *What's the matter with you today? Next, you'll be telling her that Aunt Nell is your patron saint and guardian angel all wrapped up in one.*

She pulled herself together. "Okay, Judith, tell me what you're planning to knit with this absolutely magnificent yarn?"

"Oh, my dear, that's where I need someone like you, Izzy. I touch and feel the yarn, but I don't have a single idea in my head as to what to do with it."

Izzy looked through the door to the fiber room and spotted an empty sofa. "We haven't quite reached the mayhem stage in here yet. If you'd like, we can sit in that quiet room, and I'll show you some patterns that would look beautiful knit with this yarn."

They had the room to themselves, with the exception of the beautiful animals photographed and captured in watercolors and oils on the walls. Izzy had long ago dedicated the fiber room to those whom she called her founding mothers and fathers—sheep and goats, llamas and alpacas, even camels and rabbits—all captured in beautiful art on the walls.

"I feel well protected in here," Judith said, taking a seat and looking around at the rocking chairs, the built-in bookcase, and the fleece-providing animals around the room.

"We all need that these days," Izzy said, pulling a book of patterns off a bookshelf. She sat down next to Judith.

Judith didn't answer, her attention suddenly focused on the customers milling around in the main room of the shop.

Izzy looked up. "Did you see someone you know? A lot of the kids come in on Saturdays to knit. There's a drop-in class today in our knitting area."

"Oh, I'm sorry. Yes. I thought I saw Jillian Anderson. Does she shop here?"

Izzy looked out but didn't see anyone. "It might have been Jillian. She practically grew up here. Jillian's like family to me.

She's been spending most of her time alone this week, so it'd be nice if she's here today. This has been a very sad time for her."

"Yes, it has." Judith's voice dropped. "I've been thinking of her a lot. I encouraged her to take all the time she needed, but to come in to talk to me if she wanted to. I feel helpless at times like these. We all grieve in different ways. I wanted to respect hers."

Izzy nodded, looking again through the doorway, wondering if Jillian had come to see Mae or maybe was down helping with the class.

Last night had been a shock to all of them, even though Jillian, somehow, had seemed the least disturbed by it. Uncle Ben had said she didn't seem to take the vandalism and threatening not very seriously.

Yet Tommy Porter had said the incident wasn't "nothing." It was deliberate. And most kids, unless they were in some kind of auto mechanics class, wouldn't have known how to pull the needle out of the tire valves. Or whatever it was.

Izzy brought her attention back to Judith, hoping that the news of the tire incident wasn't out. Uncle Ben had said the police would keep it quiet.

"Have you gotten to know Jillian very well?" she asked. "Laura says she's a wonderful teacher, which is no surprise. She used to help people learn to knit here in the shop when she was just a teen."

Judith seemed to brighten up upon hearing the comments about Jillian. "She's done a very good job at the school, yes. Parents have praised the way she interacted with their shy or nervous or self-conscious teens. She seems to have a gift for that."

"And the other teachers?"

"The staff enjoyed working with her, too. With the exception of one or two. We have a teachers' lounge, as you saw, and sometimes those places can breed ill will. People talk. Things get passed around. Even things that have nothing to do with school. Outside things."

Izzy nodded, not sure where the conversation was going. Judith was clearly upset about the gossip.

"It's like any office gossip, I suppose. People know who goes away on weekends, who goes to parties, who goes to what club, that sort of thing. I don't like it, but I can't stop it."

Izzy thought about that, remembering the lounge at her law firm. Judith was right. There was always some gossip going on. "So do you think people talked about Jillian and Josh camping on weekends?"

"Who knows? My weekends were probably discussed, too. In fact, I'm sure they were." Judith shrugged. "It goes with the territory, I guess. But Jillian and Josh's relationship was never displayed in the school. I wasn't really aware of it until these past days."

"Why do you think it would have bothered people?"

"Maybe by association. Some resented Josh's teaching style. And Jillian helped him with some of his more innovative projects, so maybe she was wrapped up in that resentment. But putting all of that aside, Jillian brought a brightness to our hallways." Judith glanced out into the main room again.

The principal looked a little lost, Izzy thought.

"Were you wanting to see Jillian? I can find her if she's here," Izzy said.

"Oh, no. I was just thinking about her. She's a special individual and has the personality for helping these kids. I'm sorry that's she's going in a different direction. It's another loss in this dark week. But I can certainly understand."

"She isn't continuing her practicum?" Izzy asked. But she wasn't really surprised. Why would Jillian go back to a school filled with memories—some she would probably like to forget, and the good ones buried. And she certainly had other things on her mind right now.

"She dropped a letter off at the school and asked Shannon to give it to me. It was gracious, as you'd expect from her. She said she's pursuing new interests. She wants to get involved in things that will honor Josh Elliott and what he believed in . . ."

Judith left the sentence hanging with an unspoken question mark at the end.

Izzy found herself smiling, but she left Judith's question dangling there, keeping her own happy thoughts to herself. What a perfect gift Josh had left to Jillian.

Judith waited another second, then filled in the silence, completing her own sentence. "And she's so smart and capable, I've no doubt that whatever she chooses to do will be wonderful."

Izzy listened and nodded, then picked up the pattern book and turned to a page. "Here's a pattern that would work well with that yarn."

Judith looked at it absently.

"Will Jillian's departure cause a problem in the schedule?" Izzy asked, unable to drop the subject completely.

"No, we'll work around it. These next couple of weeks are going to be unusual, anyway. We'll be bringing in more counselors to help the kids. And our staff is resourceful. Our parents are understanding, especially under these circumstances."

"Speaking of students and teachers," Izzy said, suddenly remembering Birdie's comment the night before. "I don't mean to change the subject so abruptly, but I've been wanting to ask you something."

Judith looked up from the pattern book.

"Do you remember a student at the high school whose last name was Warner? He may have had a problem with one of the teachers. His mother is in Birdie's bird-watching group."

Judith closed the pattern book. "Of course. I remember Sidney Warner—it wasn't that long ago. A handsome boy. Charming too. And I remember Betty, his mother. She works so hard.

Raising a teenager by yourself must be difficult, but she'd do anything for that boy. She adores him."

"Birdie said the same thing. She mentioned that he had problems with a class or two, which worried Betty."

Judith nodded. "It didn't worry her. It devastated her. Every now and then Sid's social life got in the way of studying. He was well liked, fun loving, and sometimes that got in the way of studying. Anyway, Betty was determined that he keep his grades up so he could go to college."

"Was he in Josh's class? I've heard how he refused to let kids fail. Laura said parents loved that about him."

Judith listened carefully. Then she said, "I'm afraid Betty was one parent who didn't think of Josh as a hero. It's true that Josh worked with students who failed a test, reteaching, in some cases, what the child had missed. Then letting them take it again a second—sometimes a third and fourth—time. Parents appreciated it, too."

"And Betty Warner?"

"She liked his way of teaching in principle. But her son objected to retaking a test, absolutely refused. Betty was desperate for him to pass. So Josh tried. He set up study times with him. But Sid wouldn't show up. Betty wanted Josh to give him a break, to somehow make it work so he'd pass the course no matter what."

"A difficult situation for a teacher. And students and parents, too, I'd imagine." Izzy looked at the principal, commiserating. "And principals. You have a difficult job, Judith."

"Thank you for saying that. It is difficult. I tried to calm Betty down. She wanted so badly for Sid to have a better life than she had had, and she knew college could be part of the answer. I talked to Josh about it. Asked him to make an exception and to somehow make it work."

"Did he?" But Izzy knew the answer before she asked the question. She'd learned enough about Josh Elliott to know he wouldn't have given a student a passing grade if he wasn't passing. And the reason he wouldn't do it was for the sake of the student. Not his mother. Not even for the principal.

Judith shook her head, her smile sad. "But that's who he was," she said quietly. "It was both his fame and his folly."

"And Sidney?"

"After his show of disapproval for the whole thing, Sidney threw a desk across the room, quit school, and never came back."

Chapter 31

"You're right on time." Birdie walked out of the yarn shop and pulled herself into the passenger seat of the SUV.

Nell let the engine idle for a minute, looking over at her friend. "Did you sleep okay last night?"

"Better than I expected. The episode at the Y was jarring, even though Jillian handled it all with great calmness, trying to convince everyone that it was a prank. I'm not sure she really believes that, but she definitely didn't seem frightened by it."

"Are you?"

"I don't know. But somehow, Nell, I think we are finally getting close to finding out who killed Josh Elliott."

Nell didn't answer, but Birdie's optimism was always welcome. She checked the traffic, then pulled away from the curb and headed toward the Hilltop Cemetery and an overdue visit with Henry Staab.

At Birdie's suggestion, they stopped at the nursery on their way and packed a dozen pots of mums into the back of Nell's car.

"I never go to a cemetery empty handed," Birdie said with a smile.

It was a sunny day, with an autumn-crisp breeze, the kind of day that keeps spirits up, even when they have every reason to be down.

They drove up the curving road and pulled into the parking lot near Henry's stone house. Ahead, granite monuments and headstones diverted the sunlight, sending wavy beams of light across the well-tended lawns.

"It's a beautiful place up here. So restful," Nell said as they got out of the car.

As if he'd overheard the compliments about his cemetery, Henry appeared in the doorway of his small stone house and limped over to the car, his arms outstretched. "Not one, but two beautiful ladies. How much more can one old heart take?"

"Not much, Henry," Birdie said. She looked down at his ankle, bulky in an Ace bandage.

"Good as new, if it ever was new," Henry said. "Now, why are you here? I want to think it's because of me."

"Of course it is. But let's sit on those benches over there. Harper's not here to help us pick you up." Birdie pointed to a trio of wrought-iron benches beneath a gnarled old oak tree.

"Nope, she's not, far as I know. But Rose Anderson was here not a half hour ago. She's a strong one, too, probably from all that biking she does. She'd help."

"The bench, Henry." Birdie took one of his arms and began leading him over to the seats.

"Rose was here?" Nell asked as they all three faced one another on the cold seats.

"She's a regular," Henry said. "Always on Fridays. But she came today, too. Stayed longer."

"Henry, where is that path you told me about the other day?" Nell asked. "Your secret way through the woods."

"Oh, yeah." His eyes sparkled as he looked at Nell. "Now, it wouldn't be a secret if I told you about it, would it?"

Nell chuckled, shaking her head. "Henry, you already told me about it. And others, too, if I remember."

"Okay, okay. You mean the one to the lookout and camp-site." Henry nodded to a spot across the small parking lot where the woods began. "I made the path myself, you know. But I'm bighearted. Every now and then, I share it with special people. But sometimes a trespasser sneaks in."

"How do other people even know about it? The only thing up this road is the cemetery. It's not exactly on the hiking maps," Nell said.

"No. But people explore, you know. Hikers sometimes think cemeteries are public property, not a resting place for families. Sometimes it's kids tearing through on their bikes or trying to do grave markings."

"Do you see many hikers up here?" Birdie asked. "I know that people hike over near the old quarry."

"You're right. Most hikers start out on the other side of the hill, near the old quarry. People don't even know the woods really start on this side. And that's fine with me."

Henry grinned, enjoying the company and a chance to talk.

"However," he went on, "I'm not saying I never see hikers over here. Some serious hikers who know these hills and woods sometimes end up around here. But I don't let people park here unless they are visiting their loved ones so that discourages people who want to just drive up and hike. But then there are others, people I know. And who end up knowing about my se-cret path to the old lookout and the ocean beyond."

"That's the one you showed to Rose, right?" Birdie asked.

"Yep. Jillian, too, but you probably know all about that." He smiled, as if his comment had triggered a happy memory.

They didn't know. But stayed silent and let Henry go on talking.

"I let her and Josh Elliott park here. They would hike into that little campsite behind the lookout and spend time there. Sometimes a night or two. They'd always bring me some beer and sausages on their way. I liked that Josh—he was a good man. Their rendezvous was our secret. I never talked to anybody about it. They knew their secret was good with me."

Nell and Birdie both tucked the information away. Henry's secret was now theirs.

"Rose was up here often, too, you told me. You hiked together, right?" Nell almost felt guilty for asking. And repeating Rose's version of being near the campsite, wondering if Henry would deny it, seemed unfair, like she was testing how truthful Rose was. But it was already out there.

"Rose? Well, sure." Henry's answer came reluctantly. "She knew Jillian and Josh came up here. Rose is no dummy. So one day when she was here, arguing at her mother's grave, I suggested she take a hike and clear her head. She was upset that day, so I went with her. I showed her my lookout bench, and then we tromped back to the campsite and sat for a while, just talking. About life, I guess. She's a good person with a heavy heart. I don't know why she had this thing about Josh. I told her I liked the guy, and I asked her what her beef was."

"What did she say?" Nell asked.

"She just shook her head and said it was complicated. And that she didn't really know Josh. It wasn't that she didn't like him. But he wasn't right for Jillian. That was as much as she'd say. But she didn't sound convinced of any of it. In fact, she seemed a little resentful of having to get involved in her sister's life that way."

"Henry, I know this is a strange question, but do you remember where you sat at the campsite?" Birdie asked.

"Me and Rose?"

"Yes."

"Sure I do, because Rose fell when she got up and spilled her backpack. We were sitting on the rocky ledge that goes around the firepit. She wasn't hurt, though. We brushed her off and stuffed things back into the pack."

He looked at Nell. "I told you about it, Nell, remember? I

gave it to you that day. Her hat musta fallen off when we were reloading up her backpack, and we didn't see the darn thing."

"Thanks, Henry," Birdie said. "That's really helpful."

"I won't even ask you why."

Birdie smiled. "Good."

"So, Henry, are you thinking no one else knew about that campsite?" Nell asked.

"I'm not saying that. Others could have known about it. I don't know for sure. Our bird-watching people, for example. In fact, I saw that lady from the grocery store exploring up there once. What's her name, Birdie?"

Without waiting for an answer, Henry went on. "But most hikers park at the old quarry and hike in the woods on the opposite side of the quarry. There are real trails over there, and it's all marked. So they go that way, which is just fine with me. I like my road less traveled, I guess."

They sat for a moment, all three of them looking across the parking area to Henry's woods. His own path. A good old man who cared about his cemetery folks and his private trails and helping people who are hurting sometimes.

"I wonder sometimes if I coulda saved Josh," he said, his eyes sad, as the conversation turned to the fatal incident that was floating around in all their minds. "Josh usually told me when he and Jillian were going to be at the campsite, or when he was going up alone, but I didn't think anybody would be out that night. I knew from my weather tracker about the quick storm that'd be coming our way in the middle of the night. It was going to be a downpour. Some lightning, too. No time to be in the woods, though Josh probably didn't know it was coming. He camps in all kinds of weather."

"Did you hear anything that night?" Nell asked.

"I went to bed early that night—well, mostly every night these days—but got up a couple times way before the rain started. I wanted to be sure all the windows were shut. Nor'easters can do damage up here. Even short-lived rainfalls, and it was clear we were going to get one. I did hear noises once, but there wasn't a car or anything around. And hikers don't usually hike that late at night, even the few I know."

"What kind of noises did you hear?" Birdie asked.

"Branches breaking, that kind of thing. I walked over to the woods and could tell there was something in the woods. I have a family of foxes that come out at night sometimes. But then I thought I saw a flash of something a little ways up the path, like a flashlight. I decided it might have been a quick flash of lightning or my eyes were seeing things. I was half asleep. So I went back and gave the other half of sleep a chance."

"Do you think whoever killed Josh got to the campsite along this secret path? Not going past the old quarry?" Nell asked.

"Sure I do. The police thought so, too. It was something about the path—the branches broken intentionally or something—though the downpour had wiped it out things good. It was a muddy mess the next day. But that's why I feel so dog-gone sad that I didn't go find that noise." Henry's face fell as he looked toward the woods, as if his path had had something to do with Josh's death. A death maybe he could have stopped.

He looked away from the woods.

"And if what you heard was a murderer, you just might have been killed, too, Henry Staab," Birdie said. She reached over and touched his hand.

Henry puffed up his chest and quickly changed the topic. He turned toward the cemetery, stretching his arms out, and taking in the graves and the carefully tended grass, the pots of flowers and colorful leaves dotting the graves.

"All these folks," he said, "they're family, you know? The Andersons are here, the Garozzos and Barlows. Hallorans too. And Favazzas. Great Favazzas. So many good people . . ." He turned and smiled at Birdie, then looked out over the curving land, the centuries of Sea Harbor families. "Oh, the stories they could tell."

"And you, too, Henry," Birdie said quietly.

"Do the hikers you mentioned have family buried here?" Nell asked, lightening the conversation.

Henry seemed to appreciate it. "Sure, some. Some don't. Maybe they live here now, but the family is from someplace else, where they have family plots. People used to do that, buy for the whole family. Generations. Even aunts and uncles sometimes. Now they don't do that so much. People move around too much.

"But now and again one of the hikers will wander around the place, and it gets them thinking about preparing for the great beyond and maybe buying a plot here, so I'm pretty friendly. I don't throw anyone out on their ear. I'm not the sales guy for plots here, but I do a pretty good job helping the sales guys out sometimes. Sold one recently to a serious hiker who's hiked all around these woods. Probably knows more trails than I do. Bought a real pricey plot, too. Up on the hill, with a great view of the water. People like that I'd reward with a key to my path." Henry laughed.

"Was it someone we know?" Nell asked.

"Who?"

"The hiker who decided to be buried here."

Henry scratched his head. "I'm not so good on names these days."

Birdie and Nell smiled.

"Well, anyway, we brought some mums," Birdie said. "I thought maybe for Josh's mother. Maybe Jillian and Rose's parents?"

"Sure, let's go. It's a pretty sight up there."

They loaded the mums in Henry's wheelbarrow and headed up the hill.

"They're over there," Henry said, pointing to the small lane that led to the Anderson parents' graves. "Like I said, Rose was here earlier today, but she didn't leave any flowers. Maybe she came to apologize."

"What does that mean, Henry?" Birdie asked, setting down two small pots near Elizabeth Anderson's headstone.

"Sometimes she comes up and talks to her mom, and sometimes they argue."

Nell placed a pot at the twins' father's grave, then took the others and set them on graves that were missing flowers. "She misses her mother, I suppose," Nell said. "Elizabeth was close to her daughters."

"Well, I don't know much about that. Rose had a near collapse here yesterday, poor girl. And maybe she felt she owed her mother an apology. My take was that her mother owed her one, but what do I know? But I do know that somewhere along the way, Elizabeth Anderson laid a heavy load on Rose Anderson's shoulders. It's been a rough road for her."

"Henry, I'm not sure we know what you're talking about," Birdie said.

"Don't you ever talk to Sonny Favazza, Birdie? Sure you do. I'd bet my life on it. Well, Rose talks to her mother often. And it's not always so nice. She just lets it loose."

He stopped talking and looked over at the headstone, as if he'd like to add a few words of his own.

"I'm ashamed to say I accidentally listened in yesterday. I was just coming over because I had seen her arrive, but when I got up here, I heard her yelling at her mother something fierce. She was crying hard and asking her mother if she was finally happy now and could rest in peace."

"Why did she think her mother was finally happy?" Nell asked.

"It wasn't said like that. It was said with anger. It was like, okay, all the Elliotts are dead. Are you satisfied now? That kind of thing. As if her mother had singlehandedly killed each one of them. Rose was distraught. Not making much sense. But it gave me the chills. I wanted to comfort her, but I walked away instead. I knew she wanted to be alone."

Henry himself looked like he needed comfort. Birdie walked to his side and rested a hand on his shoulder. "Are you okay, Henry?"

Henry took a step away and stood as tall as his five-foot body allowed him. He looked directly into Birdie's eyes. "Bernadette, if you want my opinion—and even if you don't—I'm giving it to you. I think Rose Anderson's mother asked for something from her daughter. A promise or something. Maybe she even did it on her deathbed—those are the worst kind. I've seen it happen. And it created a weight on this poor woman that is crushing her. And I think you better help her get rid of whatever it is."

A short while later, Birdie and Nell got back in the car and waved good-bye to Henry as they tried to digest their conversation with the caretaker.

As Nell began to back out of the parking space, Birdie put her hand up and asked her to stop the car. "Henry is waving something at us."

Birdie rolled down the window, and Henry came shuffling over to it, holding out a tablet.

"Here it is—the family name I couldn't remember. The one on the new plot I arranged. Hikers are good customers." He handed the tablet to Birdie. "It's plot 127B. We even took a hike together to the lookout bench. Had a great talk. 'Special people, special care.' That's my motto. Besides, the plot was a really pricey one, the last one at the very top of the hill. A great view."

As Henry talked on, Nell leaned over, and she and Birdie scrolled down until they came to the line in the Excel chart for plot 127B. They read the name. Then stopped and looked at each other. And then they read it again and scanned the whole page, thinking somehow that that might clarify it.

"I'm good at my job," Henry said, interrupting them. "Gotta

go now." He reached through the open window and took the tablet back, then gave another wave and turned away.

The two women sat still, watching Henry shuffle off.

The conversation going down the hill was pulled in two directions: Helping Rose Anderson before she collapsed beneath secrets and promises. And meeting with Izzy and Cass to pull together enough of the growing number of loose yarns to find out who had killed Josh Elliott. They were so close, Nell said, that she could almost feel the murderer's breath on her skin.

Birdie winced. And agreed.

Helping Rose was first on the list.

Nell pulled the car into a gravel parking lot in front of a small, out-of-the-way coffee shop. First, to collect themselves, and second, to try to digest their cemetery visit. The first was done easily. Slow breaths. Open minds.

The second would take longer than they intended to spend in a coffee shop that served even worse coffee than Izzy's. But during the time it took to get through that one cup of coffee, they planned out the rest of their morning—to talk with Mae and to see if Father Northcutt was in a talkative mood.

First things first, they both decided. And Rose Anderson's aunt was first.

Henry Staab was a wise man, indeed.

Chapter 32

Mae sounded surprised and happy at the lunch invitation when Birdie called. Luna would be thrilled to be in charge for a short time. But no matter, she'd meet them at Polly Farrell's tea shop in one hour.

Father Northcutt cooperated also. When Birdie and Nell drove into the rectory driveway, he was outside in the rectory's small yard, wearing baggy jeans and an old Mighty Mac jacket. Beside him, a small dog that looked like a racoon was yelping for the padre to throw the ball he held in his hand.

The two women got out of the car and walked over.

"Who's this?" Nell asked, crouching down and petting the dog, one clearly of questionable lineage.

"This is Eleos. A retirement gift. People in the parish thought I needed a friend. Now, I ask you two, do I look like I need a friend?" He laughed jovially, and the dog immediately rolled over, begging for a belly rub.

Nell crouched down and did the honors while Birdie asked for a moment of the priest's time.

"Well, truth be told, I am off to Eleos's first dog training class shortly. But let's see what kind of damage we can do in a few minutes."

They stepped aside to give Nell more room.

"Eleos?" Birdie asked, looking down at the sweet pup, who seemed to smile beneath Nell's gentle rubbing.

"Ah, Eleos . . ." he said slowly. "Eleos is the personification—dogification?—of mercy and clemency," Father Northcutt said. "Some believe that among the gods, Eleos is the most useful to human life in all its vicissitudes. And I am thinking that it might be one of those vicissitudes that brings you here today. How can I help?"

Birdie smiled and quickly filled him in on what he'd no doubt observed himself—Rose Anderson's painful struggle.

And her thoughts on its origin. "I worked in that soup kitchen, too," she said, with a twinkle in her eye.

He smiled. "And you'd like us to explore thoughts about those dear people we both became very fond of," Father Larry said, rubbing what looked like the beginnings of a retirement beard. "And how to relieve a wonderful young woman of the pain of secrets and promises."

"And we'd like to explore it with you, not in your role as a priest but as a good friend," Birdie said.

He nodded. "And as a good friend, I will do that. We both suspect Rose's suffering was unknowingly imposed on her by her mother. I knew Elizabeth Anderson well. And I liked her. She was complicated and never quite worked out her problems, to the detriment of other good people. But underneath it all, she did love her girls very much. She was in pain herself those last days. And I don't think she would knowingly have thought her wishes would cause her daughter pain or would pull her daughters apart."

And in the few short minutes before Eleos's first lesson in what humans expected of dogs, Birdie, Nell, and Father Northcutt confirmed what the Greek god of compassion and mercy would surely have dictated.

They left the rectory a short while later, with plenty of time to settle into the corner booth in Polly's tea shop before Mae arrived. But Mae was early, too, and appeared in the cozy tea shop two minutes later.

To Birdie's and Nell's surprise, Mae was followed through the door by Rose and Jillian.

"I know you ladies well," Mae said, pulling up an extra chair. "You wouldn't pull me out of the yarn shop on a hectic Saturday because you like my smile. So if we're going to talk about my dear nieces, which I suspect we are, I thought they should be here. There have been enough secrets in this family for ten lifetimes. I'm through with them."

Jillian and Rose were gracious and sat down, but it was clear they were not sure why they were there. Nor did they want to be.

Before anyone had a chance to explain, Polly brought over a pot of tea and a large platter of crusty grilled ciabatta sandwiches. They were layered with heirloom tomatoes, creamy burrata cheese, which dripped down the sides, thin slices of grilled red peppers, and sharp provolone on the bottom. Polly smiled and nodded and disappeared as quickly as she came.

Birdie looked over at Rose, met her eyes, and smiled. And then she thanked Mae.

"You are a woman of many dimensions," she said to her old friend.

Mae took a quick comical bow and then suggested they get down to business. She didn't have all the time in the world, she said.

"It's a difficult conversation to begin," Birdie said, her eyes on Rose. "In some ways you are not unlike Josh Elliott—a man I've come to know and appreciate and admire these past sad days. A man who loved deeply."

She felt Jillian tense at the mention of his name and then relax into her chair. And she gave a smile, one meant for herself.

"And, as Father Northcutt put it, Josh was honest to a fault, a quality that you have, too, one that made you intent on keeping your promise to a dying woman," Birdie went on.

The tea shop was full, but Polly had given them the one quiet table tucked away in a far corner of the cozy restaurant, as if anticipating that it was exactly what they needed.

"I was thinking about your dilemma, but in a vacuum, not knowing enough to think clearly. And then Mae jogged our memories about something that at the time seemed unrelated—that there were a few years in your father's life when he seemed peaceful. And truly happy. It was during the time he volunteered with me in the church basement."

"We were in high school, I think. He loved doing that," Jillian said. She looked off into the air, seeming to retrieve memories of her own. Putting them together.

Nell started to speak, but it was Mae who picked up the conversation, looking at Jillian and pulling her attention back to the matter at hand. "Jilly, your amazing father, my wonderful brother Cliff, fell in love with another woman when you were in high school. Remember those amazing years and how happy he was? Your mother was a good person and loved you girls with her whole heart, just like your father did. But she didn't love your father. And she didn't want a divorce. Just distance."

Mae paused and picked up a sandwich and took a bite, then put it down. "I denied my brother's relationship because I didn't want him to have it. As if denial ever helped anything." She shook her head, as if scolding herself. "I may not be as wise sometimes as Birdie here makes me out to be. But then, finally, I saw how this love filled something in him. He loved you girls 'to the moon and back,' as that little book he read to you said. But this was a different kind, something he'd never had from your mother. He became a deeper, more fulfilled person because of that love. Better for you two. Better for everyone around him. And so much better for himself."

Mae took a drink of water but held up a hand to indicate that she wasn't finished. She looked at Rose and Jillian. "You two were in high school, and if you remember, those years were glorious years for all of us. Your father was so happy." She looked at Birdie. "The volunteer years . . ."

"Yes," Birdie said. "Amelia Elliott and your father fell in love right before my eyes, while working in a soup kitchen beside me. And all I knew was that I loved both of them." She smiled and shook her head. "I just didn't realize they were *in* love with each other."

Jillian took in a quick breath, her face flushed. "Amelia Elliott. Josh told me about his mother. About her falling in love for the first time in her life, and how it fulfilled her. It was like him and me, he said . . ."

"So Josh knew?" Nell asked.

"He didn't know who it was. His mother didn't want him to know. He thought it was because he was teaching at the high school already and knew so many people in town. That it could cause problems. But he said it was the first time in her life that his mother was truly happy. His dad had been a nasty person."

There was silence as memories were dusted off, years calculated. And realizations made.

"Father Northcutt was a good friend to both your father and Amelia," Birdie said. "It wasn't in the role of priest necessarily, but as a wise, good friend who knew that one doesn't go looking for great love. It finds you. Even in places like soup kitchens."

Rose was sitting quietly, taking it all in. Everything she already knew but didn't know at all.

Birdie watched her, seeing her trying to put things in place. "I finally realized what you were going through, Rose. And why. What a horrible burden your mother had unknowingly put on you. Promises that you felt you had to keep. Secrets that were keeping you and your sister apart when you needed each other most—secrets and promises that you shouldn't have had to make. Or keep."

Rose wrapped her arms around herself, shivering.

Jillian was silent, her face unreadable. Finally, she looked at Rose. "You knew all this? About Dad?" Her voice was strained.

"No, Jilly, no. Not until Mom was dying. She called me in often during those days when we were winding things up at NYU, usually with instructions for the rest of our lives. Yours, especially. But one particular day . . . It was after we had told her about the teaching program here in Sea Harbor and my gallery arrangement in Canary Cove . . ."

Rose took a deep breath and plunged in. "I thought she'd be thrilled. Especially with your plan, one she'd consider safe and sensible. But she asked me to come to the hospital later, and alone. She had the nurse put the NO VISITORS sign on the hospital door and then had me sit on the side of her bed, close to her. She had something very important to tell me, she said.

"She began talking about the affair, which she had known about, she said, but she'd been busy with her own life and all our high school activities and, as she put it, 'It kept your father out of my hair.' So she was okay with it—until she wasn't. It was when we were in high school, thinking of going off to college and her life was changing. She wouldn't have us. And she resented our dad terribly, probably because he was so happy. When she moved away from Sea Harbor after Dad died, she took her hatred for the Elliotts with her, blaming them for nearly everything in her life. Even her illness. It was crazy.

"And finding out we were going back to Sea Harbor made her crazy. Maybe it was the medicine, I don't know. But somehow she knew Josh Elliott was still teaching at the high school— probably from friends she had kept in touch with. And you'd be right there, near him. When she said his name, it almost frightened me. My mother wasn't mean. She was egocentric, maybe, but not mean. But that day . . ."

Birdie looked at Jillian, but there was no reaction. She was listening with full attention.

"There was something about our dad loving someone else that filled her with venom. She grabbed my hand so tight, it hurt. 'What I am telling you and giving you are instructions for life,' she told me. And the instructions came out as if she had been practicing them for days. First, I was to promise her that we, Jilly and I, would never have anything to do with the Elliott family, and she called each member of the family by name, even though Amelia Elliott and the dad, too, were no longer alive. Second, I was to protect Jillian with my life from 'that family.'"

She looked over at her sister. "My job was to make sure you and Josh Elliott never connected with each other, ever. There was no room, she said, for that family to ever enter our lives again. And the final thing she asked of me was a promise. A promise that I would never ever tell you any of this, Jilly. Not about our parents. Not about the Elliotts. She made me promise over and over and over again, still clinging to my hand."

Birdie watched a myriad of emotions play across Rose's whole body as she talked. She was sad and angry at once, but freed somehow of a huge lump that had been growing inside her.

Rose caught her breath for a moment, and then she said sadly, "And that was it. She finally let go of my hand and rested back into the pillows. She managed to smile at me, a satisfied, almost happy smile, as if all would be well now. She thanked me for being such a good daughter and for doing this one last special thing for her. Then she closed her eyes. And she died."

There was little left to say. The processing needed to begin, Birdie thought.

And a short while later, Jillian and Rose put their uneaten sandwiches in take-home boxes and gave everyone at the table a hug. They were going over to her cottage behind the gallery, Rose said.

"A place to let things settle," Jillian added.

Rose nodded and offered a half smile.

She walked around to Birdie's side of the table, leaned over, and whispered near Birdie's ear. "Interventions take time," she said. Then she embraced Birdie tightly. "Thank you."

Chapter 33

By late afternoon, Izzy was exhausted. She leaned against the wall near the knitting room archway, checking her phone texts and trying to smile at customers making their way up the stairs and toward the store's front door.

She scrolled down the list of texts, then stopped at a curious one from Cass.

It was an invitation—from Cass—to dinner the next day at Nell's. **For food and work. No men.**

Which was a moot point, anyway, since Izzy knew that Sam and Danny were taking the train into TD Garden for a game and that Ben had left early that day for a weekend meeting in Boston.

She wondered briefly if Nell knew about the invitation to her own house. Then let it go. Knowing Cass, Nell quite possibly didn't know.

She put her cell phone away and glanced down into the knitting room and was relieved that it was almost empty, with just a few stragglers bundling up their half-finished creations.

"Sit down or fall down?" a voice asked in her ear.

Izzy jerked her head up and looked into Shannon Platt's smiling face.

Her own tired face turned into a smile. "I don't see you for months, and then every time I turn around, there you are."

Shannon laughed her full laugh, which was always a little too loud but was contagious and made everyone around her smile, too, even if they had no idea why. "Well, don't get tired of me, because I am turning into a top-notch knitter and may be hanging around a lot."

It wasn't until Izzy stepped up a step that she noticed someone was standing behind Shannon. A good-looking guy she didn't recognize, taller than five-foot-eight Shannon, a Red Sox hat planted on a full head of dark hair and one palm spread out on Shannon's back.

Hmm, she thought.

"I just dropped in to introduce you to my friend," Shannon said. She stepped aside and held out one hand. "Ta-da."

Izzy laughed. "Well, Tada, it's nice to meet you."

The man grinned, a dimple showing in one cheek.

Izzy liked him already.

"In real life we call him Cole," Shannon said. "Cole Pisano. I told you about him, Iz. Cole does some accounting work for the school."

"Oh, sure," Izzy said, shaking his hand. "And you helped this multitalented woman here get a job over there. I think if Shannon ever left town, half the businesses in Sea Harbor would be scrambling for help, because she works at most of them."

"She's amazing, right? And she went back to college, too," Cole said proudly, as if he'd somehow been involved. "She ruins the grading curve for all those young college kids."

"Oh, pshaw," Shannon said, laughing. Then she looked at them both, her brows lifted. "But go on, please. I didn't mean to interrupt this interesting conversation."

Izzy just shook her head, chuckling. "Are you here for yarn?"

"Nope. I just wanted you to meet Cole. We're headed to Lucky's Place, and I saw that the lights were still on in here."

Izzy looked down the short staircase and noticed that now the knitting room truly was empty. Upstairs, Mae was busy helping the last customer before closing down the computer and heading home.

"Can you sit for a minute?" Izzy asked. She turned toward the knitting room and could sense the nods or headshakes passing between Shannon and Cole behind her back as they silently asked the other what they wanted to do. *New romance*, she thought to herself, feeling suddenly ancient.

Soon a "sure" echoed from each of them, and they followed her down the stairs. She motioned toward the chairs and couch near the fireplace. "No fire, though. It's almost closing time." Izzy walked over to the small miniature refrigerator near the stairs and looked inside. "Wine or beer?"

"Wow. You're even set up to entertain," Cole said, taking the beers and handing one to Shannon. "And in a yarn shop. Terrific. I think I'm missing my calling. I like this setup."

Izzy laughed. "But give me an Excel chart or algorithm—or essentially any numbers above ten—and you lose me. Tell me about yourself, Cole. You're a number cruncher, I hear."

"I'm called a lot of things, but for right now, yes. That's one of them. Sort of. My dad is an accountant in a large Boston firm. I think that's what convinced Ms. Garvey to hire me."

"She hired you for your dad's credentials?"

He laughed. "Who knows? Maybe. I sure didn't have much experience. The job I actually applied for was the assistant coach for the freshmen basketball team."

"Oh," Izzy said, surprised.

"I do know enough about accounting. But I love basketball, hence the application. Anyway, I did realize that I live in a real world, and the job she offered seemed a better way to ease into it. And it made my dad happy, I suppose."

Izzy held back a smile. Sometimes she thought it would be nice to be ten years younger. "So what is it that you do, then? Payroll, that sort of thing?"

"Yes. It really is number crunching, I guess. No basketballs involved. It's fairly cut and dried. Accounts payable, receivable. I haven't been on board long. Since Sea Harbor is small and doesn't have the big machinery behind them like some schools do, it's all low key. Staff members decide how they want to receive their checks—mail or direct deposit, which is what most do these days. Some still don't trust it, though, and those paychecks go right to the school and are distributed. There aren't too many left who do it that way. Josh Elliott was one of them, which I always found surprising, because he was such a cool guy."

Izzy nodded.

"I was in high school Josh's first year of teaching. He had innovative ways of teaching even then, but I hear the last couple years he became a real master at tapping into the way kids learn," Cole added.

"Kids loved it, but teachers sometimes grumbled," Shannon said. "It never made sense to me. He was such a good teacher."

"It's good that Judith Garvey realized his teaching talent," Izzy said.

"True," Shannon said. "But one Friday I actually thought it was happening. That he was going to be fired."

"What? When?"

"Well, it was the end of the day, shortly before Josh died, and I was still in the office, shuffling some papers around. He walked in, looking very serious. He said hi, but without any small talk, and then walked into Ms. Garvey's office. He didn't have an appointment, so I figured she had called him on the phone. He just walked on in, a little like Laura Danvers does."

Izzy laughed.

"Anyway, he was in there for a long time. Now, Josh Elliott wasn't known for that sort of thing—long meetings. He wasn't a long talker, you could say. So I thought it must be something serious. I thought maybe Hazel Wallis had gotten her way. I'd seen her and Ms. Garvey talking recently. But then when he came out, he didn't look like someone who had just been fired, although I'm not sure what that looks like, never having been fired. At least not yet. He just looked kind of sad. But serious."

"Was Judith sad when she came out?"

Shannon thought back. "Actually, she didn't come out. At least not while I was there. But I did see Josh as I was leaving. He was carrying some new equipment into his classroom. He told me he was going to do this great experiment with the kids the next week and was bringing in some special sound equipment. He was going to teach them how to listen to birds talking to each other, to distinguish one conversation from another. It sounded so fascinating that I asked if I could come. I'd pretend I was a bird, and he laughed and said sure, I could come," she said, her face sad at the irony of it, that the kids would never get that amazing class session. "But, anyway, that told me he hadn't been fired."

"You'd make a good detective, Shannon."

"Inspector Shannon Clouseau, that's me." Shannon finished her beer and set the empty bottle on the table. "But actually, I should have known that Josh wasn't going to be fired. It isn't Ms. Garvey's modus operandi."

Izzy laughed. "Okay, enough with the fancy words. So what is her modus operandi?"

"According to the scuttlebutt, she always fires people over margaritas," Shannon said, grinning. "They go to that little restaurant near the museum, just off Harbor Road. La Contenta. Great name for it, right? I can't decide if I think that's a nice way to fire people or cruel."

Beside her, Cole grimaced and said, with feigned disapproval, "It's cruel. Margaritas? Oh, jeez. An extra-dry martini maybe, but margaritas?"

"You don't like margaritas?" Shannon asked in a false stunned voice. She looked over at Izzy. "Our relationship is in the 'learning all about each other' stage. He just lost a point."

"I'd say you're a good match for one another."

They both scowled at Izzy. Then laughed.

Shannon stood, then turned and looked at Cole, who was still sitting on the couch. "Okay, you. As amazing as Izzy and her store are, they don't serve Lucky's truffle fries."

"It's the truth," Izzy said, standing. "Lucky owns the rights."

Cole pulled himself out of the deep cushions, then walked over to Izzy and surprised her with a quick hug, a thank-you, and a "Hope to see you again."

Izzy hoped so, too.

"Speaking of Lucky," Shannon said, picking up her bag, "Molly Flanigan and I were at Lucky's a couple days ago when the happy trio came in. And from the looks of their clothes, they had just painted something enormous, like the Empire State Building, maybe. But they seemed to be having fun."

"What happy trio?"

"Lucky and his ladies, which the bartender called out when they walked in. And which the 'ladies' in the scenario immediately scolded the guy for, setting him straight on ownership rights. The ladies were Willow and Rose."

"Oh, those three," Izzy said. "My catwalk crew."

"So they're all working on that runway for you?"

"They are. And for some reason, they are telling me very little. It's a lesson in trust, Lucky tells me."

Shannon laughed. "He's right. But that's assuming you trust Lucky."

Izzy smiled. "I know whatever Willow and Rose create for it will be great, but I'm keeping my fingers crossed that we end up with a runway that's walkable."

"Lucky'll come through. He always does." Shannon had an amused look on her face.

"What's that smile for?" Izzy asked.

"I was just thinking about Lucky. I watched the three of them from my spot at the bar that night. And although I don't have any actual confirmation of this, you understand—no one *told* me—I have this feeling that Willow Adams is playing matchmaker. It will break hearts all over the Atlantic seaboard if she achieves her goal."

"What?" Izzy said, holding two empty beer bottles midair. Her eyes widened. "You think—"

But Shannon was already flying up the steps, her laughter softer now, as nice Cole Pisano whispered something sweet in her ear.

The air was crisp, the sky darkening, when Izzy finally locked the shop doors and called it a day. Saturday movie night was just ahead with her two favorite people in the whole world—the only ones who could make her forget the sad and tragic days they were all wading through. The only ones she could cuddle with in front of the TV, eating popcorn and laughing and crying together, watching whatever movie her almost five-year-old Abby had carefully chosen.

"You picked a movie about rats?" Izzy asked when Abby and Sam had FaceTimed her earlier that day with a movie night report. Abby had giggled and explained that they were making dinner, too, and it would be like the movie. "It's a *theme* night," she'd said slowly, as if her mother might have trouble understanding the word *theme*. "Radda-ta-two," Abby had sung gleefully over the phone.

Izzy had smiled, trying to image Sam and Abby making rata-touille. She had wondered, smiling to herself, if either of them remembered they disliked squash *and* eggplant. But Abby did like tomatoes. That was good, but it was usually when it was on pizza or spaghetti.

She stood on the shop's steps for a minute, breathing in the earthy smells of the season, the musky-sweet smell of the leaves that had collected around the curb.

It was quiet for a Saturday, the usual bustling crowd hurrying home from shopping absent, as were the early birds heading to Jake's tavern or the Ocean's Edge restaurant for an early meal. Even voices seemed lower and more subdued. The somber effects of a murderer in their midst.

Izzy got in her car, buckled up, and headed down Harbor Road, her heart full as she thought of the quiet evening ahead.

As she neared the museum, she slowed down. Then, on an impulse, she made a sharp left turn.

The large red LA CONTENTA sign was lit up a few doors down from the museum. She slowed down, opening the passenger window, and breathed in the fresh, pungent smell of cilantro and cumin that floated out the door. It made Izzy's stomach growl. She made a mental note to visit the restaurant soon. Abby loved tacos.

She slowed down to a crawl, looking through the windows into the well-lit restaurant. It was nearly empty, with only a few families eating at the early hour. Squinting, she looked again, then pulled over to the curb, stopped completely, and stared.

Sitting at a small table near the far window, Judith Garvey was holding a double walled glass of the restaurant's acclaimed margaritas. She lifted it high, then tapped it against one held by her companion.

Izzy thought she could almost hear the clink of Hazel Wallis's equally large glass.

"Oh, my," she said to her windshield, then pulled back onto the street and made a hasty exit home—to a movie about rats.

Chapter 34

Nell stood alone on the deck, watching the sun as it sank below the sea in a show of brilliant gold and crimson and orange waves. It was almost blinding. Her family back in Kansas was tired of her saying it, but the light on Cape Ann at sunrise and sunset was truly unique. And breathtaking. Almost enough to sustain one during rough times.

She pulled her heavy hooded sweater close as the ocean breeze ruffled her hair. An "Izzy original," knit from a laundry basket full of leftover yarn. A scrap sweater, Izzy had called it. But that description didn't fit at all. It had come together as a sunset masterpiece, one with all the spectacular colors she was right now viewing from her deck. A soft, bulky, warm sweater that made her feel comforted and safe.

But even feeling that she was wrapped in Izzy's love and the beautiful sunset couldn't help the sensation she had that something was about to burst, that if only she could distance herself from earth for a minute and then look back on it, things would make sense. Maybe Ben being gone this weekend had thrown her into this mood? They'd both regretted that his meeting had fallen on a weekend, when staying home seemed to be a much better option.

But there wouldn't be a good weekend or a good day or a good week, not until Josh Elliott's killer was found.

She shuddered at the frustration she felt, wondering if she should head to the Y and work it out of her system. It was still early enough.

She walked back inside, thinking of Henry Staab and the surprising pieces of information that had been scattered in their conversation. *And important*, she thought. They added more lines that begged to be connected to Josh Elliott on Izzy's napkin.

Her phone pinged, interrupting her thoughts, and she looked down, hoping the text was from Ben, telling her he was coming home early. It wasn't. She read the brief text.

How absolutely ungracious of me. Forgot to invite you, Nell. We're meeting at your house tomorrow to work and eat. Hope you can make it.

Nell laughed. Well, at least Cass had given her something to pull her out of her tangled thoughts.

The Y was calling to her, and now that she'd been invited to a meal at her own house, Market Basket was calling, too.

The checkout line at the market was longer than Nell thought it'd be at this time of day. But finally, she made it to the head of the line and pulled her fresh dill, pasta, and vegetables out of her basket and placed them onto the conveyer belt. She straightened up and looked at the checker, smiling, as her items inched forward. The woman wasn't looking at her, intent on running the groceries through her scanner. Carefully and judiciously. *An introvert*, Nell thought, wondering if that made the job easier or more difficult. Nell glanced at the name tag pinned to her jacket: BETTY, 22 YEARS AT MARKET BASKET.

Nell's eyes widened. She always liked the tags and being able to thank the person by using her or his name. But she was used to the tags indicating one year or two or even ten years of working in the store. Twenty-two years was certainly a long time to be standing on your feet, dealing with customers' groceries and idiosyncrasies. As she watched the woman rotate the tension out of her broad shoulders, she thought she looked familiar, but anyone who had been working at the supermarket for that long was probably familiar to half of Sea Harbor.

As Betty handed Nell her receipt, she called out to another person that she was taking her break. Then she mumbled at Nell that she should support her bag on the bottom and hurried off, leaving Nell still standing at the counter.

Betty Warner. Of course. She was Birdie's Betty from the bird-watching group. She'd seen her from a distance at the memorial service—and probably dozens of times right there in the store.

As Nell walked out the exit door, she spotted the woman again, sitting on a bench at the corner of the store, eating a sandwich. And looking sad. Or mad. Nell couldn't be sure. She had that kind of face, one not unfamiliar with life's adversities.

Nell walked over to the woman. "Hello, Betty," she said. "We meet again."

The woman looked up. "What? Did I forget your receipt?"

"Oh, no. I just wanted to say hello. I'm a good friend of Birdie Favazza. She has said nice things about you."

Betty frowned, as if to say that wasn't possible. "Birdie's a good lady," she finally said.

"She says the same about you. You're a hard worker and a good mother. Not to mention an excellent birder."

The woman looked down at her sandwich, then put it back into the bag. "I don't know why she told you that."

Nell wasn't sure which element she was referring to, her bird-watching or her mothering ability. She tried another topic. "The loss of one of your bird-watching members must be so difficult for all of you. I'm so sorry—"

Betty cut her off. "Don't be sorry," she snapped, shaking her head. Then she looked up at Nell, her face pulled together in anger or sadness, Nell couldn't be sure. But it was a painful expression either way.

"I hated him," she said. "I hated Josh Elliott. For a while, anyway."

She was weeping now, and Nell was at a loss of what to do. "I'm sorry. I didn't mean to upset you like this," she said.

Nell was silent then, as Betty Warner seemed to be reliving a painful moment in her life.

"My smart, wonderful son couldn't pass his science test. He was going to fail and refused to take it again. It wasn't like my boy. I hated Josh Elliott for not figuring it out, for not finding a way for him to pass. I wanted to kill him. That night Sid confessed to me that he had taken something that morning, some drug a kid talked him into taking to keep him awake for finals. But it didn't. It made him act crazy. They were playing a joke on him. So I went back to the school and tracked down Josh Elliott. I told him about Sid. About the pill. The teacher listened to me. Believed me. He thought Sid was a good kid. He'd talk to him, he said. They would figure it out. He'd have to pass the test, he said, but he would, Mr. Elliott felt sure. And then it all went to hell."

Nell sat down beside Betty. She watched the woman's face redden as she stared at the cement beneath her feet, breathing hard. Her head shaking. A few gray hairs were visible beneath the brown.

Nell waited silently. Not at all sure where the great anger and despair she saw in Betty Warner's face were coming from. She looked defeated.

Finally, Betty straightened up and took a long deep breath. She let it out slowly, her eyes still on the cement, while tears streamed down her cheeks. "I wanted to tell Birdie Favazza about this to get rid of the pain. She always looked like she wouldn't mind, but I just couldn't do it. So now you can listen and tell Birdie Favazza. And maybe the pain will go away."

Nell steeled herself, completely unsure of where Betty was going with her story. And uncomfortable about entering into a stranger's private life, something Betty Warner might regret later. She thought about calling Birdie but knew that Betty Warner would probably be long gone before Birdie could arrive.

Before Nell could do anything, Betty started in, telling a perfect stranger how her life had all fallen apart.

Nell listened as carefully as she could to the distraught woman and her open sharing of one awful day in her life, which she still seemed to be living.

After what could have been ten minutes or thirty, Betty stood up and mumbled that her break was over. She wiped her eyes with her sleeve, tossed her uneaten sandwich into the trash, and walked back into Market Basket.

Nell stood and watched the woman walk away from her. She wanted to go after her and wrap her arms around her, but she knew instinctively it wouldn't be welcome. Maybe being able to unburden herself had been help enough.

She sat in her car for a few minutes, trying to process the painful day in Betty Warner's life. She reconsidered her decision to go to the Y. It was getting late. But she also needed to put some distance between herself and Betty's emotional story before she'd be able to see it clearly.

The after-work crowd had taken over many of the machines when Nell arrived at the Y, but she was finally able to find a free treadmill at the end of a row. She put in her earbuds and found a playlist on Pandora to keep her going. In no time she was almost up to her usual pace, her heart beating faster and her body already beginning to replace stress with movement. Slowly, her mind let go of disturbing thoughts, and the sounds of easy jazz seeped in, replacing the emotional day.

Eventually, she slowed the belt, her face damp and her spirit more intact than it had been, and brought the machine to a cool-down mode.

At first, she thought the voice she was hearing was coming from her earbuds, but when she heard it again and made out her own name, she paused the treadmill completely, pulled out her earbuds, and looked around.

Merry Jackson stood a few feet away, wiping perspiration off her face with a towel.

"Hi, Nell. I didn't want to scare you by getting too close. And I smell. I just got out of a crazy hard spin class. I promise not to hug you, but I didn't want to leave without saying hi."

"Merry, this is great. A wonderful Saturday night surprise." Nell grabbed her towel and, wrapping in around her neck, stepped off the machine.

"Are you headed out, too?" Merry asked.

Nell nodded. "I just needed a quick pick-me-up. Something to clean out the cobwebs."

"I'm heading out, too. Want to grab some juice on the way?"

In a few minutes the two were settled in the small café off the open lobby, drinking pomegranate juice and picking at two brownies Merry had insisted were healthy and nutritious.

"I love this place, don't you? It's pretty much my social life," Merry said. "I see everyone I know here. And if I don't want to talk to anyone, I just duck into a class. Or put earbuds in, like you were doing when I completely broke into your peace and quiet."

"It was good timing. I was winding down from a crazy day. So fill me in on what's going on in your life."

"Well, business at the Artist's Palate has slowed down a lit-tle, even though we've started turning the giant heaters on some nights. People just don't like sitting out on the deck with a murderer around."

"It seems to be true on Harbor Road, too. You're also at the high school, right? What's it like there?"

Merry nodded. "Subdued. I've been directing the choir for a while now. The Anderson twins were in my choir the first year I helped out. I love those kids."

"And now Jillian's there doing some teaching herself. Do you see her?"

"Once in a while, but we don't have much time to talk. I can't imagine what she's going through right now. She didn't advertise her relationship with Josh Elliott at all—both of them were very discreet—but it was clear to me that they were extremely close. Not with hands all over each other or things like that, but they were, I don't know, connected somehow in a really beautiful way."

Merry smiled as she thought about Jillian, then seemed to remember something. "Oh, there was only one time that they even acted like they knew each other. The school had a staff picnic before the semester started, up at the old granite woods. Jillian was hanging out with another teacher—not Josh. But as people were cleaning up to leave, I saw them slip off into the woods."

"The woods?" Nell said, then switched subjects. "Do you know many of the teachers?"

"Some, mostly because I've been there for a while. But the music department is in its own little corner. There are some good teachers there, though. And a couple of dodos."

Nell smiled. "I guess that happens."

"The principal, Judith Garvey, is nice," Merry said. "She was in the spinning class I just took. She put me to shame."

"She has a handful to deal with right now. How's she doing?" Nell asked.

"Okay, I think. She's handled a couple of difficult times before. Not a teacher being killed, but things with the students. Like a young guy—he was in my mixed choir—being arrested in front of the school on some drug charge. It was pretty awful."

Nell frowned. "That's a toughie. What happened?"

"Apparently, some students called the police, as a joke

maybe. There was also a rumor that a teacher called the student in. But whatever, the police showed up just as school was letting out and found drugs on him. I remember Josh Elliott being upset. He liked the kid. Judith was upset, too."

Nell sat perfectly still, trying to put the pieces of Betty Warner's sad story into the same framework as Merry's, but before she had a chance, Merry went on talking.

"You know, Sea Harbor High has improved a lot, replacing outdated equipment, things like that. The school sure needed it. And some of the departments are getting attention—and the principal, too—for creating some state-of-the-art setups. Not so much for the music department, though. We still limp along."

Merry looked over at a group of people milling about in the athletic center's lobby, chatting and laughing.

She lowered her voice and nodded toward the group at the desk. "There's one of the lucky department heads over there. The one with the black hair tied in a knot."

Nell looked over. It was the teacher she'd seen at the memorial service, without her pearls today. The woman who had turned to stare at Jillian, as if she had no right to be at Josh Elliott's funeral. Or maybe no right to be anywhere.

"Hazel Wallis," Merry said. "She benefited hugely from some of the improvements. She also had a real problem with Josh Elliott. Hazel wants everything for herself and her department. She resented Josh's way of teaching and that he sometimes seemed favored."

"I've heard something about that," Nell said.

"So you probably know Hazel wanted him fired. But to Judith Garvey's credit, she didn't. Hazel has always been like that, though, as long as I've known her. You do one thing she doesn't like, for whatever reason, and she refuses to let go of it. She bad-mouths people. It's like a character defect. It's no wonder her own grown kids have all moved to California."

"What does she teach?"

"Auto mechanics. And she's good at it. In fact, she and the students have fixed many a faculty member's car. It's a great perk."

Nell wondered silently if she also knew how to damage cars. Or tires, at least.

"Her department is actually pretty amazing," Merry said. "It gets attention in the press, too."

Nell watched the teacher's movements as she chatted with the group of women. She seemed self-assured and happy with herself.

And happy that Josh Elliott was finally gone? Nell wondered. "Did you say that Judith Garvey is here tonight?"

Merry nodded. "I think those two came in together."

By the time Nell got home, she felt like the single day was at least fifty hours old, hours taken out of her normal life. A long bath and soft fleecy pajamas helped bring her back to the real Saturday night, as did a warm house and a cup of tea before bed.

She checked her text messages to find out that Jillian would be dropping something off early in the morning. Something Ben had said he'd look at. She couldn't stay. A morning hike with Rose was on her schedule.

With Rose. Well, that was good. She knew it might take the sisters time to figure out things between them. And around them. But they would. She'd worried about Rose for weeks, but she could see that her self-assurance was coming back. The fashion show project was good for her. Even Mae had noticed that in spite of the tension between the sisters, Rose was slowly coming back to her old, confident self. It amazed both her and Ben that although Rose had to be aware that the police hadn't eliminated her completely as a suspect in Josh Elliott's murder, she seemed to be rising above it. She looked happy.

When the phone rang, Nell knew it was Ben, calling to say good night.

After sharing their days, Ben said, "Jillian's dropping something off for you tomorrow."

"What is it?"

"Some of the files regarding Josh's will. Some scribbled notes from Josh. She wants to understand the whole thing more thoroughly. She said she's finding things that don't make sense to her. Things Josh highlighted, like maybe he thought they needed attention, too."

"She's amazing. It sounds like she is ready to make a go of all this. Izzy texted me that she's resigned from the program at the school."

"That's probably wise. I think she will bring fresh eyes to all this foundation business. You might be able to bring a new perspective to whatever she's bringing by, too. That's if you feel like reading it, Nell. You help out many nonprofits."

Nell grimaced at the thought of being faced with lots of numbers and legalese. She would politely refrain, she told Ben sweetly.

The long bath and the call from Ben had performed magic, and within minutes of crawling into her wide bed, Nell was sound asleep, and for the first time since Josh Elliott's death, she didn't fall into confusing dreams of tangled skeins of yarn and disrupted skeins of birds.

Chapter 35

Cass picked up Birdie Sunday afternoon and a short while later pulled into the Endicott driveway. Izzy appeared at the same time, jogging up Sandswept Road and waving at her friends. Her hair was pulled back in a ponytail and bounced between the straps of her backpack.

"Show-off," Cass yelled from the driveway. She climbed out of the car with a bag over her shoulder.

Birdie got out on the passenger side and removed a covered plate from the backseat. "Ella made carrot cake. She said it's brain food."

"Of course it is," Izzy said, her words coming out in huffs as she leaned forward, her hands on her knees, catching her breath.

The scent of dill and wine drifted out as Nell opened the front door and urged them all inside.

"This is where we need to be today. I think you're omniscient, Cass," Izzy said, heading toward the open kitchen at the other end of the room.

"I don't doubt that Cass is a marvel," Birdie said. "But what makes you say that?"

"I feel full of little pieces of things. I think we all do." Izzy walked to the sink and poured a glass of water. "We need to spread them out on the table and find straight lines. Or at least curved ones. But not tangles. I'm not into tangles."

"I agree," Nell said. "Hopefully, between the four of us, we can make sense of it all. We're all on the same wavelength. And I think that's why you invited us all to this party."

"You're right," Cass said. "I don't sleep well with messes in my head. All we need is that little thing called proof. Or sufficient evidence. Let's find it."

"I feel that way, too," Izzy said. "Rearranging our thoughts may help. Combining and subtracting."

Nell glanced over at the old pine table, which had been in Ben's family since his parents had built their dream vacation home in Sea Harbor when Ben was a baby. After many renovations, it was now a large roomy house that Ben and Nell called home. In the process of making it their own, they'd saved all the keepsakes they could. "There's room to spread out over there," she said, pointing at one of them.

"The subtracting is the most important thing of all," Birdie said.

Nell nodded. She knew they were skirting around the murderer. Knew they were close. But they could reach the person who had killed Josh Elliott only by getting the other suspects out of the way.

Izzy took seltzer and soft drinks out of the fridge, and Cass helped by adding a giant basket of chips to the middle of the pine table. "These are vegetable chips," Cass said. "More brain food."

Nell brought over a bowl of M&M's, an old Endicott staple when there was work to do and decisions to be made.

Izzy rubbed her fingertips across the thick pine table. "Aunt Nell, do we get to carve something into this table? I think the whole Endicott history is revealed in these little grooves."

Nell laughed. "Your Abby has already left her mark in several places. No carvings yet, but the permanent markers have made some beautiful circles."

"Circles?" Cass said. "Perfect. Izzy can do another Venn diagram. Or we can use this." Cass pulled a large dry-erase board from her bag. "Danny claims he's caught many bad guys in his mysteries using this." She put it on the table.

"That's a good tool," Birdie said. "It will help keep us on track. We're procrastinating about this." She looked at each of them as they pulled out chairs and sat down. "Procrastinating is tempting because a part of us dreads the ending. It will mean someone we know has done something truly horrible. Taking someone's life."

Birdie sat down, her words circling the table.

The others grew quiet, sobered by the truth in Birdie's words. Someone they knew. Someone who quite possibly was a good person underneath it all. A good person who did a terrible thing.

"Okay, so let's start." Izzy picked up a marker and wrote *Rose* at the top of the board.

Birdie looked at the name and shook her head. "What an awful burden Rose's mother left her with. But you're right, Izzy. Although one burden has finally been lifted, this other one will be there until the murderer is caught."

"And that can't be soon enough," Izzy said.

"But at least she's down near the bottom of the list now," Nell added. "Especially with Henry's confirmation that the two of them were together at the campfire when she lost her key chain."

"True," Birdie said. "And dear Henry has never considered the concept of lying a useful thing, even for someone he's become fond of. I have no doubt that his version of that day is accurate."

Nell moved the conversation along. "Birdie, I had an interesting talk with your friend Betty Warner yesterday. She told me that she hated Josh. And that she wanted to kill him."

Eyes opened wide around the table.

"But she didn't kill him, or at least I feel sure she didn't," Nell said. "She hated him briefly, her mother's love blocking out reality." She looked over at Izzy. "But there are versions of that story. And then there are other versions."

"I thought I heard her son quit school?" Cass asked, turning to Izzy.

"I thought so, too," Izzy said.

"That's not exactly what happened," Nell said. And then she repeated the real reason Betty Warner's life fell apart.

The others listened intently, imagining a boy's life ripped out beneath him. And his mother's along with it.

"Oh, that poor boy," Birdie said when Nell had finished the story.

"She wanted you to know what happened, Birdie. She trusts you, but it was easier to talk to a stranger. And I'm convinced that if she'd wanted to kill anyone, it wouldn't have been Josh Elliott."

Izzy scribbled a few notes next to Betty's name as all of them felt a mother's pain. But they felt other things as well.

"While we're on the topic of high school, there is a woman on the faculty who seemed to hate Josh Elliott—and for longer than a few hours, like Betty."

"Hazel Wallis," Izzy said, reading Birdie's mind. She added the name to the board. "Hazel Wallis, who may or may not have been fired yesterday." Izzy gave them all a quick recap of Shannon's visit and her interesting comment about how Judith Garvey fired people.

"Jeez," Cass said. "Is that being nice? Or mean?"

"Shannon's question exactly," Izzy said. "I'm not sure. But on my way home, I passed the restaurant, and there in the window were Judith and Hazel . . . holding up huge margaritas."

"Interesting. Although Hazel could have been celebrating the demise of someone she considered a major thorn in her side," Cass said.

That was a sobering thought.

"Or contributing to a young student's problems . . ." Cass said.

"While Shannon is on our radar, there's something I wanted to throw out there. Her boyfriend does paychecks for the school, and he was kidding about Josh getting a paycheck the 'old-fashioned way,' as he called it," Izzy said.

"What's that?" Birdie asked.

"By check, instead of electronically . . . direct deposit."

"Half my fishermen get it by check, too. I'm trying to educate them," Cass said.

"But Josh took himself off the payroll a few years ago," Birdie said. "He didn't want a salary."

"Exactly. But he got one, anyway," Izzy said.

Birdie repeated the conundrum, listed it on the board, and moved on.

Nell repeated her conversation with Merry Jackson. "She confirmed how much this Hazel disliked Josh. But she didn't look like someone who had lost a job she loved. Her department has been updated and has received some good press."

"What department is she in?" Birdie asked.

"She's head of the auto mechanics department. The kids learn a lot, according to Merry."

"Cars?" Birdie asked.

"Jillian's Jeep," Cass said.

Izzy scribbled a note next to Hazel's name.

"Where did you see Hazel?" Cass asked.

"At the Y. Merry sees her there often."

"Hmm," Birdie said.

They all nodded, reading Birdie's mind.

"I have another tidbit about firing people," Izzy said. "Again from Shannon."

"Shannon is becoming our very own spy," Birdie said.

Izzy repeated Shannon's observation of Josh's trip to the principal's office. " 'To be fired,' was Shannon's first thought."

They thought about that quietly. The people Josh had touched, for better or for worse.

The lines were still ragged. They had a way to go. Izzy added another name to the dry-erase board.

Leon Mancini.

"Leon Mancini had a good reason to kill Josh," Cass said. "Money."

"And maybe to give Harper the life she wanted and probably deserved for loving a man like him the way she did," Izzy said. "All Leon knew was that Josh planned on selling the company sometime in the future. But if the sale didn't happen, Leon's life wouldn't change. His oversized salary would remain, and he and Harper could live happily ever after."

"Harper seems very bright beneath her chattiness," Birdie said. "I wonder how much she knew . . ."

Nell was quiet, listening. Finally, she said, "I think Leon thinks more about Leon than about Harper. He is fortunate Harper doesn't realize that. And I doubt he killed Josh. He would know he'd be a perfect suspect once the facts were out there."

It was an unusually impatient comment from Nell, and they all realized she wanted to get down to what they were all thinking, why they were all there. And it had nothing to do with Harper. Her attention was focused on how in heaven's name they would be able to pull it together.

"Maybe we need a break," Nell said. She got up and went over to the stove and put the salmon casserole into the oven to warm.

As she turned back, a sudden thought made her detour into Ben's den. She returned to the table a minute later with a thick leather notebook. "Jillian left this here early this morning. It's a collection of papers and notes about the foundation that she wanted Ben to take a look at when he gets back. Josh had been going over it in the days before he died. It might be a long shot, but maybe Josh can help us with what we're missing."

Izzy opened the file and leafed through the papers in it, then handed a few to Cass. "Numbers, Cass. It's right up your alley." She looked up at Nell. "What did Ben say about this?"

"Not much. Just that I could look through it if I wanted to. There are records of donations that were made from the fund Josh's mother had started. I think, from what Ben has told me, that Josh's interest was finding groups that he believed in and that needed support. I don't know the details of it, but apparently, the donations were made in a way that not even the recipient would know from whom they were coming. Only why the organization was receiving them. Fortunately, the family had a tax attorney who kept things on the straight and narrow."

"So if a donation came into our library?" Birdie asked.

"The library director might not know where it came from, but would certainly be very happy." Nell began pulling papers out of the file folder.

"From the dates scribbled on these pieces of paper, Josh probably started straightening these all out because he was planning on selling the company, which was a part of all this," Cass said. She frowned at the amount of paper on the table. "I get the feeling Josh didn't care much about computers."

"I think he liked the outdoors more. Reception is probably not great around campfires," Izzy said.

Cass laughed. "Campfires do have a greater allure. But he probably printed these off so he could scribble on them." She opened the metal binder apparatus and removed a large stack of pages from the thick notebook. "Not great for the trees, but better for us, since we can spread them out."

"Oh, my," Birdie said, scanning down one of the pages. "The Barlow family was very generous." She read off a number of local organizations that had benefited from their generosity. "And not just once, but several times. Remember when the soup kitchen was turned into a comfortable dining room, table-cloths and all?" She looked up at the ceiling and smiled. "Thank you, dear Barlows."

Nell picked up one of the sheets of paper, and her eyes widened. "Look at this."

It was a list of donations to institutions all over the county, but the one Nell pointed to was closer to home. Attached were designations of how the grant money was intended to be used. "No wonder some of the departments are as wonderful as they are. Sea Harbor High received such generous grants to improve old equipment and make the program top-notch."

"And no wonder the principal loved Josh Elliott," Izzy said.

"That would definitely have been a good reason. But she must have had another one for liking him," Nell said. "They were anonymous grants."

Birdie put on her glasses and looked over the statements. "There are notations directing the donations in some cases. Like this one." She pointed to the music program. "Goodness. The Barlows must have loved music. You could buy many grand pianos with this."

Nell looked over at the printout. "That's interesting . . ." She thought about Merry Jackson and wondered if she knew about the money that was coming. If it was coming . . . She repeated her short conversation with Merry.

Izzy and Cass were running their fingers down more of the sheets, checking out the grants, the designations. Cass passed them around, along with a stack of Post-it notes. And they all got to work.

Birdie picked up a ledger sheet that indicated the profits from the real estate company that fed into the foundation. There was a red line around the title and notes in the margins, indicating a decrease in donations from other years. Clearly, a difference that Josh intended to check.

Each of them took a sheet and scrolled through it, making note of the handwritten notations, circled figures, and arrows and lines, seemingly an attempt to balance things out. Question marks when numbers didn't seem to match up. Grants that seemed to have slipped through the cracks or ended up in the wrong place. Or didn't seem to end up anywhere, unaccounted for.

Two hours later they sat back, exhausted. Their faces drawn. Outside, the sun had disappeared.

Nell got up and turned on the lights, then stared down at the old pine table, now holding a straight line of yellow Post-it notes.

They all looked down at the tabletop—at the tale of a murder spelled out in yellow squares.

Ben arrived an hour or so after the women returned from a meeting with Chief Thompson and Tommy Porter, where they'd handed over the Barlow family foundation papers, complete with notes and lines finally connected and leading to the textbook motive for murder: power and money.

Sam and Danny appeared at the Endicotts' shortly after that, home from the game and remembering that Nell was making salmon casserole. But they were greeted with much more.

The story poured out between forkfuls of salmon and refreshing, much-welcomed glasses of wine.

So many threads had finally been untangled—even short strands that couldn't stand alone but fit in perfectly in the big picture, like the hiker who had purchased an expensive plot in Henry's cemetery. And then had been rewarded with directions to Henry's shortcut to a great private campsite, should the hiker ever be interested.

Tommy Porter stopped by the house later that night, in time for the last piece of Ella's carrot cake. He brought with him a full report on the evening's events.

"You guys deserve it," he said gratefully. "We took your mountain of information, added it to ours, and headed out to Judith Garvey's new home north of town. It's a great place, with an ocean view. She was home entertaining her good friend Hazel Wallis."

"Of course," Izzy said. "Probably having celebratory margaritas."

Tommy chuckled. "Ms. Garvey acted as if she had almost been expecting us. She acknowledged that she had suspected things were happening that were beyond her control. She is very bright," he told us.

"But her good friend Hazel Wallis," Tommy said, "was surprised and practically in tears, almost whimpering. Ms. Wallis was anxious to remove herself as far as possible from Judith Garvey. And in doing so, she blurted out things we weren't even that concerned about. That she had given the tire tool to Garvey, but she didn't know what it was for. And then she went on to bigger things, like how much Judith disliked Josh Elliott, but she couldn't fire him, because she wanted to continue using his teacher's salary.

"Also, something you surmised, Nell. Judith was behind Betty Warner's poor kid getting arrested for drugs. She knew the kids had planted drugs on him, but she looked the other way, then called the police. She thought it would get her good PR about being hard on drugs. Also, Hazel knew Judith went out to the woods that night, but she didn't know why, of course. And she went on and on, without us asking her a single question," Tommy said.

"How did Judith respond to all that?" Nell asked.

"Well, she had some choice words for her friend. Some even I hadn't heard before. And then, rather than deny anything at all, she seemed inordinately proud of what she'd done. She'd turned her school into a remarkable place to educate kids, she said. She was an amazing principal. And there was plenty of grant money to go around, so if she took a little of it for herself, what did it matter? The school didn't need all of it. Spending money on her few personal needs should have been barely an issue of concern."

"So it seems the only flaw in her plan," Ben said, "was that Josh Elliott was behind most of those wonderful grants."

Tommy nodded, getting up to leave. "That and the pile full of things that these four amazing women here pulled together."

He tipped his Red Sox hat to Nell, Birdie, Cass, and Izzy, along with a grateful smile, and headed out into the night.

He was barely out the door when Cass exploded. "Proud? Proud of what! Not one of the things that woman has done is anything to be proud of. Skimming money off grants? Rerouting grant money to do favors for friends? Ruining a student's life? What kind of person does those things?" She held out her wineglass for a refill.

But they knew what kind of person. Judith Garvey had hidden that person effectively for years with lies and power and knowing when to smile.

Nell looked over at the empty box Jillian had dropped off earlier that day. She looked over at the three men sitting at the table. "Apparently, Josh Elliott had finally gone over the records and figures, probably because he was going to put the company on the market and needed to know the particulars."

"Josh was bright," Ben said. "It probably didn't take him long to figure out what she was doing."

"And being the gentleman he was, Josh made a late afternoon visit to her office, not to be fired, as Shannon thought at first, but to let her know that he was going to tell the school board what she had done," Birdie filled in. "He would give her a couple days to do it herself, if that would be preferred."

"Honest to a fault," Cass said. "He lived up to it, for sure."

"And it cost him his life," Nell said.

They thought back to their brief meetings with Judith Garvey, how everything had seemed just a bit off-kilter.

"One of the hardest things for me to stomach is how she ruined a seventeen-year-old kid's life," Cass said. "Miserable woman."

"And Sid's mother's," Izzy said, shaking her head. "Judith lied so expertly about all that. I almost bought it."

Judith had lied easily about nearly everything, it seemed, as the four women revisited the suspicions that had been building daily. Little things, like how she had blamed the teachers for the non-memorial service she had insisted be held. The better to get rid of Josh Elliott's memory fast, to move on.

"Why the slashed tires?" Danny asked.

"It was as we suspected," Birdie said. "Once Judith knew the grants had come from Josh, she thought he might have shared something with Jillian. Or she might know something or find something that would incriminate Judith. A good scare might keep her quiet."

"She wasn't very tuned in to her own staff, was she?" Nell said. "As if Jillian could ever be shushed up about something like that."

"I don't think Judith Garvey is capable of thinking about other people's feelings," Birdie said. "It's very sad. She's clever and learned proper responses to get her where she wanted to be, and to get what she wanted to have."

"There's one thing that still seems to be hanging. Why didn't she fire Josh, like the teachers wanted her to?" Sam asked. "You said she didn't know Josh was connected to the grant money."

Izzy chuckled. "Plenty of people wondered about that.

That's when supersleuth Shannon and her nice boyfriend, Cole, came in. We knew Josh told Judith to take him off the payroll shortly after he started working there. Father Northcutt even kidded him about it. But it turns out Judith never did take him off. Cole confirmed that. And it was clear to us in looking through the files, too. So every other Friday his paycheck came to the school, and Judith took it, then transferred it to an account that she'd set up. For herself."

"What's especially sad about all that," Nell said, "is that from everything I've learned about Josh Elliott these past days, he would have been happy to give her his paycheck. All she had to do was ask."

Chapter 36

In the end, the runway show was a whole town affair and, for some of them, a whole family affair.

As often happens in small towns, there was some discussion beforehand about whether a fashion show should be held in a bar. The editor of *Knitting In Style* magazine called Izzy immediately when she heard.

But Izzy quickly assured her that Lucky's Place was, well, yes, a bar. But not just a bar. And it would all be fine, she promised, smiling into her cell phone and using her most convincing voice.

And then she collapsed into the small chair in her office and wondered if anyone would miss her if she didn't show up.

The day finally came, with the sun shining down on Sea Harbor, as if celebrating the town's first runway extravaganza—sure to be a YouTube sensation.

Izzy had wanted to go over to Lucky's Place as early as he'd unlock the doors for her, but her nerves were so tightly wound that Sam had insisted he drive her. "A car crash wouldn't be the best way to get this show on the road. It might take away the headline you're going to get in the NYT."

Izzy had laughed. And then agreed.

She stood now in front of the main entrance, where a full-blown sign with beautiful knitted lettering announced the show. Casual cutout photos of knitters, young and old, knitting and modeling, laughing and serious, invited the audience to a show filled with personality.

Izzy stood there for a minute, taking in the sign, breathing deeply, and welcoming the joy she felt at that moment as it worked to replace the past weeks of stress and sadness and drama. And thankful resolution.

A nearby sound took her attention away from the sign and toward the now open front door of the bar. Lucky Bianchi stood there, filling the space, arms outstretched.

"Hey, beautiful. Welcome to my humble bar," he said, smiling.

Izzy returned the smile, then took a deep, calming breath, walked over to him, and took his arm.

Not to be dramatic, she assured Lucky, but so she wouldn't fall over.

And she didn't, but just barely. Lucky's arm became a true help as they walked inside, past the magazine's video cameras, past the chairs that wrapped around the runway.

And stood in front of Lucky and Willow and Rose's runway.

It wasn't the narrow carpeted catwalk Izzy had expected. Not a nicely sanded and painted narrow stage for the models to promenade from the beginning to the end and then back again. She had seen enough TV runway shows to have a runway pictured in her mind. Nicely and tastefully done. And safe. That had been Izzy's hope.

But she had never seen one like this, not even in the Paris fashion shows she'd seen.

Lucky had built the runway in parts, which fit together like Abby's toy railroad tracks. The parts, slotted together, curved into a U shape that began near the granite fireplace in the bar's largest room and looped around on the other side of the fireplace. A flat sea-blue carpet lined the entire walkway, and a large stage curtain, made of thick wool strands in all the colors of the sea, hung from a curtain track.

"Just like in Paris," Lucky told her. "Our beautiful models have a private place from which to make their entrances."

Two of Laura Danvers's girls stood on either side, ready to part the yarn curtain as the models moved in and out.

But what nearly stopped Izzy's heart was the sides of the runway. Wrapped around them from beginning to end were thousands of strands of hand-dyed yarn that had been strung together and fastened to the stage. The yarn's colors, carefully chosen, created a panoramic scene of the ocean, from high tide to low tide, sunrise to sunset, ending with the evening sea. From a distance, the panorama appeared to be a painting, but as Izzy moved closer, the painting came to life, moving with the slight breeze made by bodies, like the sea itself.

"It's just magnificent," Izzy said to herself, her voice hushed by the wonder of it all.

She felt an arm wrapping around her shoulder.

"Do you like it, boss lady?" a voice whispered.

Izzy turned and looked into Rose's beautiful, happy face.

Izzy teared up and wrapped Rose in a hug. "It's perfect," she whispered, her voice shaky. "Just perfect."

A short while later, Izzy walked onto the stage and urged everyone to find their seats—a difficult task, as people were walking slowly around the curving runway, following the sea's journey on the amazing yarn panorama.

After a short introduction and the appropriate thank-yous to *Knitting in Style* magazine, Izzy invited the packed crowd to enjoy the show and walked off the stage.

The music began, and Sea Harbor's first runway show got

underway, turning Lucky's Place into a festival of fun and beauty and life.

The two youngest models began the show—two-year-old Joey Halloran, clutching the hand of his older best friend, Abigail Perry, both wearing soft cotton knit sweaters created by Luna Risso. Joey's featured a smiling bright red lobster, and Abby's reflected her joyous spirit with a magnificent rainbow design, complete with a pot of gold at the end.

Izzy and Cass stood in the back, their hearts bursting with pride as the audience waved and cheered their children around the entire loop.

A stream of teens from the high school came out in short knit dresses in every wild color that they could find in Izzy's shop, with strands of their hair dyed to match. All wore tall white boots with strands of yarn fastened to the sides and waving in the breeze as they walked.

Midway through the show, Luna Risso appeared in all her glory, wearing her own design, a loose, flowing jumpsuit that covered her ample body, its wide legs flapping as she walked, with brightly colored yarn fringes all along the sleeves and ankle cuffs. It was amazing and unique and so like Luna that the audience cheered and stomped their feet.

Luna beamed and bowed several times along the way.

And after a parade of unique dresses, all elaborately described by Merry Jackson, the volunteer MC, she announced the last in the show.

After a short trumpet sound, Jillian Anderson walked out, smiling in a long, shimmering dress, sleeveless on one side, with an elegant arm covering on the other. Tiny gold beads dotted the sleeve cuff; and on the front, a wave design moved down the entire fitted dress in golds and blues and greens. It was Rose's creation. Her talented sister's design. Simple and breathtaking at once. And knit by Jillian with love. She'd found the pattern in a notebook of designs Rose had showed her. And it proved the perfect sketch to help Jillian complete her runway garment.

Flashes of light lit up the room as the dress—and model—were captured on cell phones and cameras and videos. Following Jillian, the entire cast of models paraded out until the runway was filled from end to end. A spotlight circled the living loop of knit fashions, the models bowed, and finally, they strode back through the parted stage curtain in a gloriously happy line.

Celeste Stanley, the editor of *Knitting in Style* magazine, which had sponsored the project, walked out onto the magnificent runway, a portable mic in her hands. She looked around at an audience that was still beaming from the show they'd just watched. She was distinguished looking, dressed in a watery-blue knit suit that, the program noted, she had knit herself.

The audience clapped in approval and appreciation as she introduced herself. She briefly explained how the show had come to be, how they had combed the North Shore to find the perfect yarn shop to partner with. And how Izzy Perry's Studio Yarn Shop and its crew had not only been their top pick but had also surpassed all expectations.

This time the audience exploded in applause.

Celeste smiled broadly. "I agree one hundred percent. This show goes beyond my imagination. And I get paid for imagining. It was magnificent."

And then she waved for Izzy, Mae, and Luna to come onstage, which they did, and to enormous applause.

"We have three more heroes to acknowledge," Celeste said when the clapping subsided. "Without them this show wouldn't have happened. Willow Adams, Lucky Bianchi, and Rose Anderson," she read from her program, then looked out at the crowd. "Would you three please come take a bow for creating the most incredible catwalk in history. It is truly a work of art."

The crowd began clapping even before Willow appeared and climbed the steps from her seat in the audience. She looked around for Lucky and Rose, shielding her eyes against the lights as she scanned the crowd. There was no sign of them. She glanced at Celeste with a slight shrug of her shoulder.

Celeste smiled brightly, then called the names again.

Finally, as the applause grew to a thunderous sound, Willow looked over at the curtained entrance to the stage. She frowned, then walked over to the yarn curtain, pulling it apart.

Appearing in full view and oblivious to the open curtain, Rose and Lucky stood together, embraced in a kiss worthy of the final scene of a perfect, award-winning show.

Feeling the sudden breeze, they pulled apart quickly.

Rose gasped.

They dropped their arms and stared out at the crowd.

The audience laughed and clapped and cheered and stomped their feet.

"What do we do now?" Lucky whispered to Rose, his face red.

For a minute Rose was unable to move or breathe. Finally she managed both, leaning in toward Lucky and whispering through a frozen smile. "Pretend we're in a movie."

"Movie?" Lucky frowned.

"You know, *Love Actually?*"

"Love who?" Lucky mumbled, the redness on his face deepening with every clap and whistle coming from the crowd.

Rose reached for his hand and squeezed it, a perfect calmness suddenly flowing through her body. She looked toward the back of the audience where Jillian stood, her whole being smiling over at her sister.

Rose smiled back, the single look between the sisters saying more than words.

She squeezed Lucky's hand harder, and said, "Just smile, Bianchi. Just smile."

All's well.

BELUGAH SLOUCH HAT AND BEANIE
By Kelly McClure

From the Designer
I use just one skein of "Maxima" by Manos del Uruguay for the slouch hat. The merino is lovely and smooshy and makes a wonderful drapey slouch hat. This pattern is also written for a beanie-style hat.

Skill Level
Rookie, Apprentice, Virtuoso, Genius

Size
Adult small (size 21–22" head) and large (size 23–24")

Finished Measurements
Slouch hat: 11 inches tall (not including pom) and 9 to 10 inches wide, lying flat
Beanie: 6.5 inches tall

Gauge
20 sts = 4" in stockinette st (St st) on 5 mm needles
18 sts and 36 rows = 4" in patt st on 6 mm

Yarn
100 grams, 218 yards (199 m) worsted weight merino wool
Suggested brand: 1 skein "Maxima" by Manos del Uruguay

Needles
4 mm 16" circ, 6 mm 16" circ, 6 mm dpns

Notions
Tapestry needle or teeny crochet hook
Stitch markers

Instructions
With smaller needles and long-tail method, CO 80 sts for small size and 88 sts for large size.
Join in the round, being careful not to twist sts. Pm for beg of round. Sl m throughout.
Round 1–12: K2, P2 to end.
For large size *only*, pick up 2 extra sts on Round 12. 90 sts.
Brim should measure approximately 1.75" from CO (or work until desired length).

Change to larger needles.
Begin pattern stitch (see instructions below). Work in patt st until hat measures approximately 5.5" from CO for beanie and 10" from CO for slouch (or to desired length), ending with a Round 2. Begin decreases.

Pattern Stitch:
Round 1: *P4, K1*, rep from * to * to end of round.
Round 2: Knit.

Decreases:
Change to dpns when sts become too tight on circulars.
Maintain patt st unless otherwise stated.
Round 1: *P1, P2tog, P1, K1*, rep from * to * to end of round. 16/18 sts decreased. 64/72 sts.
Rounds 2–4: Work even in patt.
Round 5: *P2tog, P1, K1*, rep from * to * to end of round. 16/18 sts decreased. 48/54 sts.

For Beanie Only
Round 6: Knit.
Round 7: *P2tog, K1*, rep from * to * to end of round. 16/18 sts decreased. 32/36 sts.
Rounds 8–9: P1, K1 around.
Round 10: K2tog around. 16/18 sts decreased. 16/18 sts.

Round 11: Knit.
Round 12: K2tog around. 8/9 sts decreased. 8/9 sts.

For Slouch Only
Rounds 6–8: Work even in patt.
Round 9: *P2tog, K1*, rep from * to * to end of round.
16/18 sts decreased. 32/36 sts.
Round 10: Knit.
Round 11: P1, K1 around.
Round 12: K2tog around. 16/18 sts decreased. 16/18 sts.
Round 13: Knit.
Round 14: K2tog around. 8/9 sts decreased. 8/9 sts.
Cut yarn and tie off. Weave in ends.
Enjoy!

I am grateful to the talented designer Kelly McClure, who has given me permission to pass along her Slouchy Hat pattern to all of you.

Kelly designs knitting patterns from a country homestead in Prince Edward County, Ontario (Canada). She also dyes yarn and has taught knitting in Nepal. She created Bohoknits in a camper van while traveling across Canada on a three-month journey. Without access to patterns, she began creating her own. Her wonderful designs have since appeared in stores all across North America.

And as a Canadian, Kelly says, "I have knit my way from the east coast to the west coast of Canada, and if living in the chilliest parts of the country has taught me anything, it's how to stay warm! When I'm not thinking about yarn, I'm drinking tea, treasure hunting, or walking in the woods with my dog, Lois, and little boy, Cameron."

Contact information for Kelly McClure:
Email kelly@bohoknits.com or PM her on Ravelry with questions.
You can also find @Bohoknits on Instagram and Facebook.

Chicken Chili

Nell loves to make this chili as the temperature begins to drop, the leaves fall, and a hickory-scented fire warms the air. She also cooks by taste, frequently adding and subtracting the spices. So do what suits your taste buds best (and feel free to choose what's available on your spice rack). Enjoy.

Servings: 8
Prep time: 15–20 minutes
Cook time: 35 minutes

INGREDIENTS
1 Tbsp olive oil (more if needed)
1 cup diced sweet onion
2 cloves garlic, peeled and minced
3 (14.5-ounce) cans chicken broth
2 (4-ounce) cans mild green chilies
$1\frac{1}{2}$ tsp ground cumin
$\frac{1}{2}$ tsp paprika
$\frac{1}{2}$ tsp dried oregano
$\frac{1}{2}$ tsp ground coriander
$\frac{1}{4}$ tsp cayenne pepper (optional)
salt, to taste
freshly ground black pepper, to taste
2 (15-ounce) cans cannellini beans, great northern beans, or equivalent, rinsed and drained well
$\frac{1}{2}$ cup half-and-half (more if needed)
1 (8-ounce) package light cream cheese, cut into $\frac{1}{2}$-inch cubes
$1\frac{1}{4}$ cup frozen or fresh corn
$2\frac{1}{2}$ cups shredded cooked chicken (rotisserie cooked chicken from the market works fine)
2–3 Tbsp fresh lime juice
2 Tbsp minced fresh cilantro, plus more for garnishing
2 medium avocados, peeled, pitted, and sliced (optional)

Garnish options (any or all, arranged in small bowls): tortilla chips, shredded Monterey Jack cheese, sour cream, diced tomatoes, sliced black olives, minced cilantro.

Heat olive oil in a large pot over medium-high heat. Add onion and sauté 4 minutes. Lower heat, add garlic, and sauté 1 minute longer.

Add chicken broth, green chilies, cumin, paprika, oregano, coriander, and cayenne pepper (if used). Season with salt and black pepper to taste. Bring mixture just to a boil, and then reduce heat and simmer 15 minutes.

Measure out 1 cup of the beans and transfer to a food processor along with $1/2$ cup of the cooked chicken broth. Puree until nearly smooth and set aside (This step is optional, but it will make the soup very creamy).

Add cream cheese to the chicken broth, along with corn, whole beans, and the reserved pureed beans. Stir well and simmer for another 10 minutes. Stir in chicken, lime juice, and cilantro.

Ladle the chili into bowls and arrange avocado slices on top of each if desired. Serve at once with the garnishes of your choice.

Don't miss the next Seaside Knitters Society mystery from
Sally Goldenbaum . . .

THE HERRINGBONE HARBOR MYSTERY

It's beginning to feel a lot like summer in Sea Harbor,
Massachusetts, and beachside shopkeepers are getting ready
for the annual wave of tourists. But even before the season
starts, the heat is on to find a killer . . .

The Yarn Studio's Seaside Knitters have their hands full
designing new classes for vacationers, as well as testing each
other's originality by creating a single blanket together.
Birdie's teenage granddaughter is also visiting for the summer,
and soon has plans with her friend Daisy to start a dog-
walking business. Meanwhile, the Lazy Lobster and Soup
Café's local fare is gaining newfound attention with the addition of a well-known Boston chef. It's sure to be another
beautiful, busy time in their tight-knit town . . .

Until Birdie spots a huge blaze from her balcony one evening,
frighteningly close to knitter Cass's lobster business. But the
morning brings news that it was a house in small Fisherman's
Cove, and a familiar fisherman is found dead inside. Not only
did the young women walk his beloved sheepdog, Squid, they
may have been the last people to see him alive.

When questions surface about the actual timing of the man's
death, it turns out something is more than fishy. As suspicion
rocks usually placid Sea Harbor, knitters Izzy, Birdie, Cass,
and Nell must pick apart tangled secrets and wrap up false
accusations—before the killer hooks another victim . . .

Available from Kensington Publishing Corp.
wherever books are sold.

Visit our website at
KensingtonBooks.com
to sign up for our newsletters, read
more from your favorite authors, see
books by series, view reading group
guides, and more!

Become a Part of Our
Between the Chapters Book Club
Community and Join the Conversation

Betweenthechapters.net

Submit your book review for a chance to win exclusive
Between the Chapters swag you can't get anywhere else!
https://www.kensingtonbooks.com/pages/review/